What the Owl Saw

What the Owl Saw

Second in the Buenaventura Series

Gerald W. McFarland

SUNSTONE
PRESS

SANTA FE

Sunstone books may be purchased for educational, business, or sales promotional use.
For information please write: Special Markets Department, Sunstone Press,
P.O. Box 2321, Santa Fe, New Mexico 87504-2321.

Cover painting "Adobe in the Rockies" by L. Jack Dunn
Book and Cover design › Vicki Ahl
Body typeface › Book Antiqua
Printed on acid-free paper ∞
eBook 978-1-61139-268-5

Library of Congress Cataloging-in-Publication Data

McFarland, Gerald W., 1938-
 What the owl saw / by Gerald W. McFarland.
   pages cm. -- (Second in the Buenaventura series)
 ISBN 978-1-63293-008-8 (softcover : alk. paper)
 1. Warlocks--Fiction. 2. New Mexico--History--To 1848--Fiction. I. Title.
 PS3613.C4393W47 2014
 813'.6--dc23

                               2014016481

WWW.SUNSTONEPRESS.COM
SUNSTONE PRESS / POST OFFICE BOX 2321 / SANTA FE, NM 87504-2321 /USA
(505) 988-4418 / ORDERS ONLY (800) 243-5644 / FAX (505) 988-1025

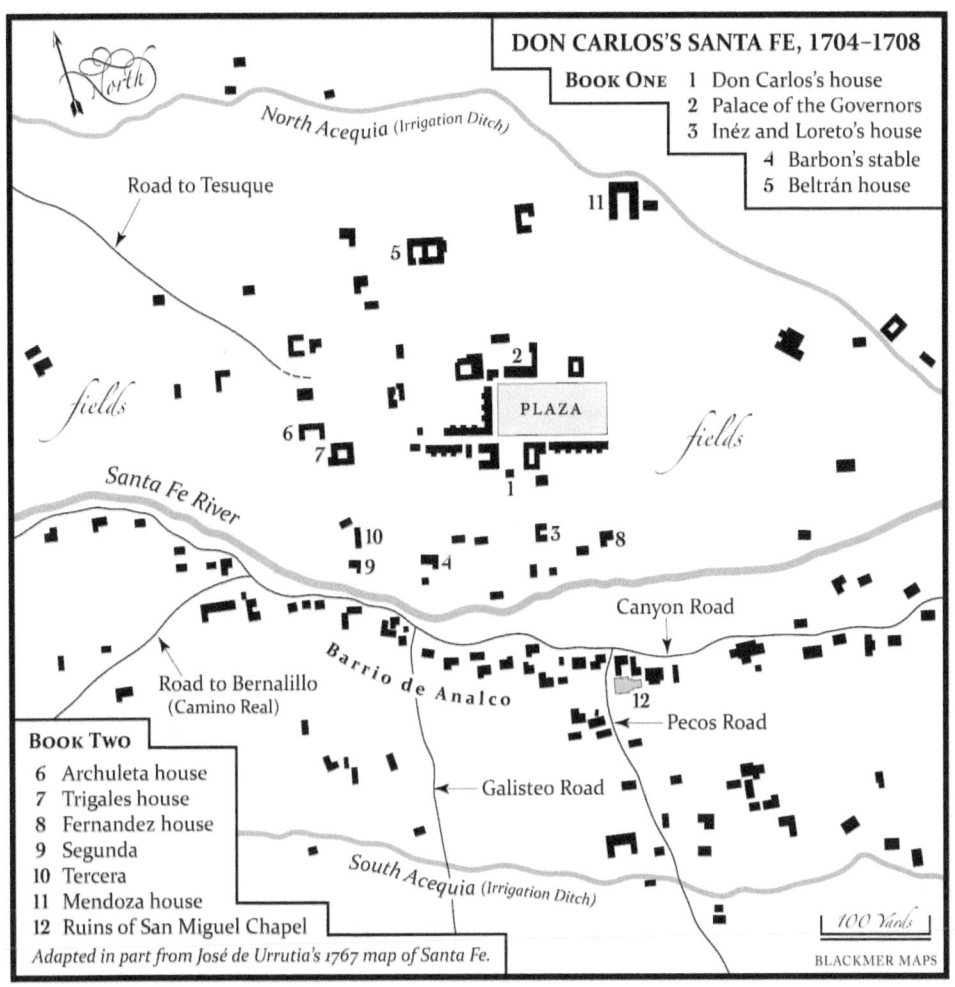

DON CARLOS'S SANTA FE, 1704–1708

BOOK ONE
1 Don Carlos's house
2 Palace of the Governors
3 Inéz and Loreto's house
4 Barbon's stable
5 Beltrán house

North Acequia (Irrigation Ditch)

Road to Tesuque

fields

Santa Fe River

PLAZA

fields

Road to Bernalillo
(Camino Real)

Barrio de Analco

Canyon Road

Pecos Road

Galisteo Road

BOOK TWO

6 Archuleta house
7 Trigales house
8 Fernandez house
9 Segunda
10 Tercera
11 Mendoza house
12 Ruins of San Miguel Chapel

Adapted in part from José de Urrutia's 1767 map of Santa Fe.

South Acequia (Irrigation Ditch)

100 Yards

BLACKMER MAPS

Map by Kate Blackmer

Preface

$\mathcal{T}$he events described in *What the Owl Saw* occur during the two-month period of January and February 1706. Most of the action takes place in Santa Fe, New Mexico, the home of Don Carlos Buenaventura, the novel's central character. Readers familiar with modern-day Santa Fe need to set aside their image of a state capital with a population of nearly 70,000, many handsome residences, and a bustling commercial and tourist life. Don Carlos's Santa Fe was a geographically isolated Spanish colonial town, a small agricultural settlement with perhaps twelve hundred residents, most of whom lived in one-story, three- or four-room houses adjacent to garden plots and fields that were scattered throughout the town.

Don Carlos Buenaventura is the protagonist's secret name, known at the start of the novel to only two close friends, who are also privy to the fact that he is a powerful brujo in his sixth life. The rest of his acquaintances know him as Don Alfonso Cabeza de Vaca, a well-educated man in his early twenties and the son of a wealthy Mexico City aristocrat. By virtue of his birth and his position as private secretary to the governor of New Mexico, he qualifies as a member of the small circle of less than a dozen families that constitute Santa Fe's upper class.

Early eighteenth-century Santa Fe Society was hierarchical, its levels determined by both caste and class divisions. In its simplest form, the caste system separated Santa Fe residents into three broad groups: Spanish townspeople at the top, mestizos (the mixed-race offspring or descendents of Spaniards who married Indians) in the middle, and, at the very bottom, Indians. There were further distinctions within each caste. Spaniards born in Spain had higher status than those born in New Spain; light-skinned mestizos were viewed as superior to dark-skinned mestizos; and Indians who had adopted Spanish names and become baptized Catholics were regarded as a step above tribal peoples who had not acculturated. Class distinctions based on family, wealth, and occupation separated townspeople within each caste. Spaniards who were wealthy enough not to have to do common labor had a much higher rank than the town's Spanish soldiers, farmers, and servants, and among the latter, a rich woman's personal maid had a far higher status than a scullery maid.

Within this structure of caste and class, it is apparent that Don Alfonso, despite his privileged birth and education and his position as a government official, is something of an anomaly. He chooses to live in a house with only four rooms, a dwelling more typical of the homes of ordinary townspeople than of aristocrats. And by the time *What the Owl Saw* opens, he has also renounced his claim to inheriting his father's title and estate. Before long he is engaged in activities that no other man of his class would have considered appropriate, such as taking off his coat and doing physical labor beside his servants and hired laborers. Although nothing in the text indicates that he has considered the origins of his motivation for these seemingly aberrant behaviors, we know from *The Brujo's Way*, the first book in the Buenaventura Series, that in each of his previous lives he had always chosen to be born into mestizo or Indian families of modest or even low status, and we can infer that he felt at home with such people, among whom brujo powers were recognized and even valued.

These elements of caste and class in early eighteenth-century Santa Fe society provide a realistic backdrop to the story of Don Carlos Buenaventura, a brujo who is skilled in transformations and sustained by the energies of the wild landscapes into which he frequently escapes, and who also has to function, as Don Alfonso Cabeza de Vaca, in a social world that is significantly more complex than the simpler worlds he knew in previous lives.

I don't believe anyone writes a book unassisted. I know I never have. In the course of the various stages of this book's preparation, I received crucial assistance from generous people. Julie Collier and Jim Parks, two Leverett, Massachusetts-based raptor rehabilitators who founded Wingmasters, introduced me to several owls, injured birds of prey, with which they have worked. Kate Blackmer of Blackmer Maps skillfully steered me through the process of creating a map of Don Carlos's Santa Fe. Richard M. Dell'Orfano, Dennis Shapson, and Wilhelmina Van Ness made helpful contributions to the refinement of the text. Helen M. Wise read the full manuscript with great care and thoughtfulness, and James Clois Smith Jr. and Carl Condit of Sunstone Press of Santa Fe responded to my many questions with unfailing efficiency.

In addition to help from these individuals, I benefited from research in the writings of many historians and from the work of an early twentieth-century folklorist, Aurelio M. Espinosa, whose "Spanish Folk-Lore in New

Mexico," *New Mexican Historical Review* (April 1926), is the source of the four-line traditional Spanish *versos* that I quoted in the story.

Special mention must be made of the contribution of my incomparable editorial advisor and wife, Dorothy J. McFarland, who brought her skills as a student of literature, an author of several books, a poet, and a professional editor to bear on improving the quality of the writing and the conceptual scheme of *What the Owl Saw* at every step along the way.

1

Nightmare

Someone was shaking him and saying, "Alfonso! Alfonso! Wake up!" When he didn't respond immediately, the voice came again more loudly, "Wake up!"

He opened his eyes to find Pedro Gallegos, his manservant and friend, leaning over him with a concerned look on his face. "What's the matter?" Pedro asked. "You were shouting, 'Go away! Leave me alone!' What set that off?"

Still half-caught in the dream and half-muffled in sleep, he croaked, "A dream, a terrifying dream."

"Alfonso, in all the time I've known you, you've reported many vivid dreams and never one that frightened you. What was so terrifying?"

"Wait a minute. I have to sit up." He struggled to sit upright amid the tangle of bedclothes and restore his mind to his normal consciousness. He took a deep breath. "It started pleasantly enough," he began. "I was in my mother's womb. She was five months pregnant. I was enjoying myself. Warmth, plenty of food, and relative quiet, except for my mother's heart beating nearby. I was humming to myself and revisiting pleasant moments from previous lives when suddenly everything turned dark."

"Alfonso. Of course it was dark; you were in your mother's womb. No light was getting in there."

"Not dark as an absence of light, but dark as in some lurking menace."

Pedro was grumpy about having been awakened from a sound sleep, and he was becoming impatient. "It's the middle of the night. You're safe in your own bed in your own house, not in your mother's womb being threatened by some unknown menace."

"That's just it. This wasn't some unknown menace. It was the presence of Don Malvolio, my enemy through several lifetimes, who killed me in my last lifetime, aided by a treacherous woman named Violeta. He almost succeeded in using his sorcerer's powers to destroy me, body and soul, forever. Only by drawing on my innermost resources as a brujo was I able to escape with my soul and consciousness intact. But he's closing in on me again. It was his presence I felt, I'm sure of it, and I was shouting at him to go away."

"Alfonso, Alfonso. It was a dream about something that happened more than twenty years ago, and in a place far from here. Today the sun will rise on the last day of 1705. You're in Santa Fe in New Spain's New Mexico province. You're a well-respected government official who has served ably as the governor's personal secretary. There's no evidence that Malvolio is anywhere nearby. You're confusing the imagined with the real."

"Easy for you to say; you didn't have that dream. Something bad is about to happen."

"That's possible," Pedro agreed. "We know there are rumors that Governor Villela is going to resign and that his replacement, who supposedly will arrive in Santa Fe in the near future, may want to appoint someone besides you to be his personal secretary. But that's all rumor, and if it happens, you'll land on your feet as you always do. Quit worrying. Especially, quit worrying about Don Malvolio. Lie down and go back to sleep. If I don't get back in bed with my wife soon, María is going to come looking for me, and we'd be forced to tell her that a dream has you shaking in your boots."

Don Carlos—Carlos being the name he'd always used as a brujo, though Alfonso Cabeza de Vaca was the name by which he was known in Santa Fe— eased himself back down in the bed, pulled up the tousled covers, turned over and muttered, "I'm not wearing boots." He quickly drifted off to sleep.

He soon started dreaming again and found himself on a trail in a desert region of northern New Spain. No one else was visible, but his sense that an invisible menace was lurking nearby returned stronger than ever. When he looked around in the dreamscape, as great brujos are able to do, no threatening animal or person came into view. No Don Malvolio; no Violeta; no one who might mean him harm, not even a future governor who would deprive him of his job. Nevertheless, he was filled with dread that grew in intensity until it woke him up.

When he awoke his heart was pounding and he was bathed in sweat. He breathed deeply until his body returned to normal and the feeling of dread dissipated. He closed his eyes and dozed off again, and this time there were no bad dreams, and in a little while he was awakened by soft kisses on his cheek and ear. Still half-asleep, he imagined that his beloved Inéz de Recalde had sneaked into his bedroom and was delivering sensual licks to his face.

Licks! He opened his eyes, and by the light of the moon that was streaming in one window he saw Gordo, the household's guard dog and source of all-around comic relief, gazing at him with adoring eyes. Carlos burst out laughing.

Sensing that it was nearly four o'clock, the hour that he usually got out of bed, he arose and dressed. He loved the quiet of the early hours when his housemates—Pedro and María and Diego, the Pueblo Indian who cared for their horses—were still asleep. Often he used the time before breakfast to read in several manuscripts that his Jesuit tutor and spiritual mentor, Father Stefano Urbina, had given him. One manuscript contained excerpts from the writings of the Desert Fathers, early Christian monks who had sought solitude in the Sinai desert. Another was a selection of sayings by Hindu mystics, practitioners of Tantric meditation, a subject to which his recently deceased friend, Zoila Herrera, had introduced him. Regardless of whether or not he read anything, every morning without fail he sat silently for at least an hour and practiced the Tantric-style meditation that Zoila had taught him, focusing his attention on the seven energy centers she called chakras that were found along his spine from its base to the crown of his head.

Those were his usual before-breakfast activities. Today, however, he felt restless, as though he had unfinished business to do. With an effort he settled himself, tried to focus his mind, and practiced his chakra meditation. When he finished, his mind was clearer but his body was still restless. He put on warm winter clothing—the room was chilly, and he knew it was very cold outside—and started for the bedroom door that connected to the kitchen. Gordo, all white except for a black spot around one eye, hopped off the bed and danced excitedly around the room—danced, that is, as best he could with his lame left rear leg.

"Come along," Carlos called to Gordo as he left the bedroom, walked through the kitchen, and out the back door of his compact four-room house. He turned left, heading toward the town's main plaza a hundred feet away. Gordo jogged along at his side, eager to see what adventure his master had in mind at this strange hour for an outing.

The air was still and cold, the temperature well below freezing. A gibbous moon in a clear, star-filled sky illuminated the landscape.

When they reached the plaza Gordo let out a whine, turned tail, and ran home. The sight that greeted Don Carlos's eyes spooked even him. The Santa Fe of December 31, 1705, with its many buildings, was gone. Except for the Palace of the Governors across the plaza, everything lay in ruins, and even the Palace of the Governors showed signs of having been partly wrecked. But the plaza was full of hundreds of human figures, grayish and insubstantial in the moonlight, but recognizable as a crowd of Spanish and Pueblo men, women, and children.

The scene was silent, although it was obvious from the open mouths of many of the spectral figures that shouts, cries, and moans were being uttered. Directly ahead, in front of the Palace of the Governors, was a line of Spanish soldiers in full battle dress. Between the soldiers and Carlos's position on the south side of the plaza stood dozens of Pueblo men, their wrists and ankles bound. Off to the right were other Indians, similarly bound, their faces stricken. As Carlos watched, a Spanish officer commanded the soldiers to aim their harquebuses and fire a soundless volley at the captives, who fell grievously wounded or dead. Others were prodded forward to meet their fate as the soldiers went through the awkward process of reloading their weapons to fire them again.

Don Carlos recognized the formidable Spanish officer who had raised his arm in the command to fire, and he realized at that moment that what he was seeing was an event from an earlier time. The Spanish officer in the scene was his stepfather, General Rodrigo Alvarez, the commander of the soldiers who had accompanied Governor Diego de Vargas's 1693 expedition to reestablish Spanish control of New Mexico after the Pueblo Revolt of 1680 had driven the Spanish out. Carlos had killed enemies in battle, but executing captives in punitive cold blood was abhorrent to him. As he watched his stepfather's face he saw no sign of regret at what the man was commanding his soldiers to do. Indeed, from what Carlos personally knew of General Alvarez, Carlos believed his stepfather took satisfaction from showing the Pueblo rebels that defiance of Spanish authority would be crushed in the harshest way possible.

Don Carlos watched, repelled and horrified, remembering the events that had led up to this moment. The Pueblo rebels, having fortified themselves in the Palace of the Governors, had defied Vargas's demands that they surrender and submit to Spanish rule. Vargas's soldiers had besieged the Palace of the Governors, cut off the defenders' water supply, and forced their surrender. The Spanish victory and the subsequent execution of seventy Pueblo rebels had taken place almost to the day twelve years ago, on December 30, 1693. Don Carlos's brujo awareness had enabled him to see the torrents of negative energies that still swirled around the town and its plaza. It was possible, he assumed, that other Santa Fe residents also felt these dark reverberations but dismissed them as products of the icy winter weather and long, black nights.

Don Carlos turned away from the scene on the plaza and thoughtfully walked back to his house. Gordo was waiting for him at the back door with an anxious expression on his face. "It's okay, my little friend," Carlos said to him. "Everything's going to be all right." Then he tried to persuade himself that this was true. What he had seen at the plaza seemed to account for his bad dreams. The dreams had nothing, he told himself, to do with the prospect of losing his job, or with the threat of Don Malvolio being in pursuit of him. And yet he wasn't entirely convinced. He had a nagging feeling that his dreams of dark portents had other sources than the horrors that had accompanied the Spanish reconquest of Santa Fe in 1693.

The following Sunday, as had been his custom for several months, Carlos escorted Inéz to Sunday Mass. He had declared his love to her, and she and Pedro were the only people in Santa Fe who knew his secret identity as a brujo. This morning he called for her at the home of Nicolas and Lucila Archuleta, friends with whom she'd been staying, and he and Inéz, the Archuletas, and their son Gerardo walked to the small chapel in the southeast corner of the Palace of the Governors.

Carlos was not a pious Catholic, as Inéz was well aware, having probed the issue some time earlier. "Why," she had asked him, "do you attend Mass every Sunday when you don't believe a word of the creeds or Catholic doctrine? Is it just out of habit that stems from the education you received from your Jesuit tutors?"

"Nothing of the sort," he had replied. "I like being seen with you in public, and even if it weren't for that, I enjoy being with you, any time, any place."

"Don't be evasive. There's more to it than that."

Echoing her, as though he didn't know what she meant, he had said, "It?"

"Yes, 'it.' Why do you attend Mass, really?"

"By virtue of being the governor's private secretary, I have a high social rank. Since Catholicism is the glue that holds Santa Fe society together, it would be cause for comment if a man of my status didn't show up for Mass regularly. Our friends and neighbors among the town's leaders would see it as not conforming to the behavior they expect from a member of their social circle. My attending Mass, therefore, isn't simply expected, it's an essential part of my social role as Don Alfonso Cabeza de Vaca. You wouldn't want there to be any hint, would you, that I am not a conventional *hidalgo* but a brujo named Carlos Buenaventura?"

"That goes without saying! Your true identity must remain a secret.

However, social reasons don't explain why you seem to enjoy Mass—and even look forward to it."

Don Carlos had paused before answering. "The best efforts of my Jesuit tutors, including Father Stefano, of whom I was fond, didn't manage to reduce my skepticism about Catholic creeds and dogmas. But on occasion I am deeply moved by the Mass itself—the total effect of the incense, the Latin chants, the choreography, if I may call it that, and, most of all, the moment when the priest elevates the Host, which to all appearances is a simple piece of bread—yet to me it's much more."

Inéz had been surprised. "You believe the Church's teaching that the bread becomes the body of Christ?"

"No, not in a literal way," Carlos had admitted. "That's too narrow a description, and I'm a heretic—at least by the Church's standards. When, as sometimes happens, I'm swept up by the solemnity, the beauty, and the drama of the Mass, at the moment that the priest raises the Host above his head, I feel the Church has managed, quite unknowingly, to point to something profound, a deep spiritual mystery."

"Is this an expression of the mystical path to which Zoila introduced you?"

"Yes," he had said, and they had left it at that.

At the beginning of Mass, Carlos's mind wasn't on anything so elevated as the mysteries of the Divine. His thoughts kept drifting back to the anxiety-inducing dreams he'd had three nights earlier and other oppressive dreams he'd had subsequently. Ill at ease, Carlos kept shifting his weight in an unsuccessful effort to evade discomforting thoughts.

Inéz leaned over to him and whispered, "My! You're twitchy this morning. What's the matter? I've never known you to be so restless. I hope it's not something I said or did."

Carlos vigorously denied that possibility. "Not so! You're perfection itself."

"Are you still pining for your lost love Camila, even though it's months now since she married Rafael and they moved to El Paso del Norte?"

"No, this has nothing to do with Camila and Rafael." People were looking crossly at Carlos and Inéz for having a conversation during Mass. "I'll tell you more later," he whispered, and in so saying he had a sudden realization that there was more to tell, more than dreams or a vision of terrible events that had taken place in the plaza a dozen years earlier.

Since the vision, he'd talked with a member of Santa Fe's army garrison who'd been present the day the seventy Pueblo rebels had been executed, and this veteran soldier had told him that during the twelve years the Pueblo rebels had occupied the Palace of the Governors, they had converted the old military chapel, the very room in which Carlos and Inéz were attending Mass, from a Catholic place of worship into a Native sacred site. They'd removed or defaced all the Christian symbols, including the crucifix on the wall, and had built a kiva, an underground ceremonial site, beneath the floor of the former Spanish chapel. After the Spanish recaptured the Palace, Governor Vargas had the kiva destroyed, the pagan spirits who'd occupied the place exorcised, and the Catholic chapel restored. What Carlos had just realized was that he and Inéz were standing directly over the location of the kiva and that he was feeling the suffering of both Spanish and Indian victims of the Pueblo Revolt.

The feeling persisted during the Mass, so much so that the presences in the kiva of the past coexisted for him with the ritual being enacted at the altar. He found the mixture deeply disturbing. He wanted to tell Inéz about it, and at the conclusion of the Mass he followed her out of the dimness of the chapel into the pale winter sunlight with the intention of unburdening himself immediately. Putting his hand on her arm, he asked if she would go for a walk with him before she returned to the Archuletas'.

Inéz, however, also had things on her mind. She turned to him and said impatiently, "Don't you remember that the Archuletas are having a dinner tonight for the Beltráns in honor of their daughter Elena's eighteenth birthday? You should — you were invited! I've agreed to cook the whole meal. Lucila's regular cook, Nina, will help, but I need every available minute to prepare the menu I've planned."

"I didn't know you were responsible for the cooking," Carlos replied, taken aback. "Is that really necessary?"

Inéz sighed. "As I've repeatedly told you, since that horrible man whose name I will not speak spent all my money and left me without a peso, I have to find a way to earn my living. I've been cooking on occasion for the Archuletas as a way of thanking them for their hospitality in giving me a roof over my head these past months. Tonight's dinner is different, something of an audition."

"Audition?" Carlos asked. "Audition for what?"

"For a paid position as cook for the Beltráns."

It should not have been a surprise to Carlos to hear that Inéz, like himself, had anxieties about earning a living. Or that what for him was only the possibility that he would have to find a new source of livelihood was, for her, a pressing necessity. She had said as much before, and frequently. But Carlos had fallen into thinking that she had become comfortable as a member of the Archuletas' household and that that situation could go on indefinitely.

"Oh," he said, rather inadequately. "I thought..."

"Yes," she replied. "You didn't think my need for a job was serious. Well, it is, and I hope this dinner will get one for me. Now, if you'll excuse me—. Oh, I see Joaquin is signaling to you. You'd better go and see what he wants."

With that, Inéz turned and hurried off by herself, leaving the Archuletas to converse with other leading members of Santa Fe society, as was the post-Mass custom. After watching Inéz's departing back for a moment, Carlos went to see what Joaquin had to say.

2

Shocks

Joaquin was, indeed, gesturing to Don Carlos to come over. Carlos and his stepbrother had become friends during the two years since they'd arrived in Santa Fe in January 1704. Carlos had also become fond of his stepsister-in-law, Francie, and more than fond of her pretty ladies' maid Camila Lobo, whom he'd asked to marry him. But Camila had chosen instead to marry Governor Villela's son Rafael. Carlos had told Inéz the truth when he said that the loss of Camila no longer distressed him. In the six months since Camila had chosen Rafael over him, Inéz had more than taken her place.

As Carlos approached he could see from Joaquin's face and his unusually stiff bearing that something was very wrong. "Alfonso," Joaquin said without any preliminaries, "a courier arrived late yesterday with advance information from the large immigrant caravan that's on its way to Santa Fe. One letter he carried was addressed to me, and it confirmed what I feared; I'm ordered to return to Mexico City to answer charges of dereliction of duty in my handling of that alleged horse-stealing incident involving two brothers from Jemez Pueblo. I was told to be ready to leave with the traders' caravan as soon as it starts its return trip.

Carlos was shocked. "Damnation!" he exclaimed. "I never thought it would come to that. Your investigation of the incident was thorough, and your resolution of it was fair and humane. Of course, your father would have dealt with the accused brothers harshly."

"Let's leave it at that," Joaquin said, his face set, clearly not wanting to pursue the topic.

Without a word they began walking in the direction of Joaquin's residence at the Presidio. "There was also a letter addressed to Governor Villela," Joaquin went on in a controlled tone. "Its exact contents are unknown to me, but the courier, Amado Murillo, is an old friend, and his father is a highly placed Crown official in Mexico City. Consequently, he's heard rumors about the contents of the letters he delivered to the governor."

"And these rumors are...?" Carlos asked.

"They're pretty much the same as those that first reached us several months ago. It seems that Governor Villela's request to retire has been granted, and he'll be allowed to return to Mexico City to be near his wife's sisters and elderly mother."

Carlos's eyebrows went up. "We knew that was a possibility, although the governor has never said as much to me, even though I'm his private secretary."

"Yes," Joaquin agreed, "but he's very old-style military. I expect he didn't feel free to speak to you until his orders were official. What is surprising," Joaquin went on, "is the identity of the new governor. According to Amado, Vice Governor Ignacio Peralta will be promoted to the post."

"But Peralta isn't a military man," Carlos protested, "and a military background is invaluable for the governor of a province in which Native raiders are a persistent threat."

They had reached Joaquin's residence. Joaquin invited Carlos in and steered him into the *sala* (the main room). Ignoring the possible consequences of New Mexico's governor lacking military experience, he merely said, "Peralta will be given an honorary title of colonel."

"Hmmm," Carlos observed noncommittally. "Do you know who's to be the new vice governor?"

"He's arriving with the trade caravan. His name is Salvador Cabrera, and he's coming with his wife Regina and a son your age named Marco."

"I knew a Marco Cabrera in Mexico City," Carlos said. "We used to fence at my old master's salon. But I don't think Marco's mother was named Regina."

"This Regina is a second wife, much younger than the first. In fact, she's about the same age as her stepson." Joaquin sat down and indicated to Carlos that he should do the same. Then he looked at Carlos directly. "I haven't yet told you the truly bad news. Amado says that the packet he delivered contains a document relieving you immediately of your duties as the governor's secretary. Apparently, a condition Señor Cabrera placed on taking the post of vice governor was that his son would be appointed secretary to the new governor."

Well, Carlos thought, there goes my job. "Do you think," he asked cautiously, "that your father, my stepfather, has worked behind the scenes to bring this about, and perhaps your recall too?"

"I don't know," Joaquin replied, "but he has a great deal of influence in high government circles, especially with anything concerning affairs in Santa Fe, because of his role in crushing Native resistance after the Pueblo Revolt. And you earned his enmity when you defied him after your mother's death, and by becoming your friend I'm tarred by the same brush. Please don't misunderstand. I don't regret in the least our friendship, and I don't blame you for what you did. You had just cause to defy him, but such actions have consequences, and it seems you've lost your post as a result."

Despite his dismay, Carlos had a curiously positive reaction to the news of his dismissal. If that—and that alone—had been the source of the dark cloud hanging over him the last three days, then things were less dire than he had feared. He began to see the brighter side of the situation. The current vice governor and he had never developed a close relationship. In fact, he had his doubts about how well Ignacio Peralta would do in the top post in the province. Carlos concluded that he might well be better off leaving the Crown's service altogether, even though he had no idea how he would now earn his living.

Carlos stood up and was preparing to leave when a thought came to mind. "One more thing," he said. "Who's to replace you as commandant of the Presidio garrison?"

"I'm told," Joaquin replied, "that the captain in charge of the contingent of soldiers who accompanied the caravan northward will replace me. His name is Tito Posada. I know nothing about him, except another bit of bad news. Apparently, he and his wife—I don't know her first name—are bringing a full complement of servants with them."

"I see," Carlos said, immediately grasping the import of this fact. "So

Pedro's María will be out of a job too. No more part-time work for her at the commandant's residence."

"That's true," Joaquin replied, "but she's a capable worker, and I expect she'll soon find a place in another household. Amado says there are several upper-class families in the approaching caravan, and surely at least one of them will need more servants. I know that Francie and I will recommend her strongly as a loyal and skilled employee."

"That ought to help," Carlos agreed solemnly. He took his leave of Joaquin and hurried across the plaza to his small house.

He found his manservant, Pedro, in the kitchen making lunch. They sat down together, and Pedro listened in silence to Carlos's account of Joaquin being recalled to Mexico City, Governor Villela's retirement, and Carlos's loss of his job. "I'm most worried," he told Pedro, "about María. It seems that the new commandant and his wife are bringing servants with them, which suggests that they won't need María's services."

Pedro didn't seem particularly troubled. "She'll find work soon enough. But," he added, "you'll be unemployed too and looking for a new source of income." For some reason that Don Carlos would have been at a loss to explain to anyone else, Pedro's statement sent them into a fit of laughter. "Things will work out," Pedro declared at last when their laughter subsided.

"I'm sure we'll come up with something," Carlos agreed.

Pedro changed the topic. "Did Inéz tell you that she's cooking the entire meal tonight and that she's serving a menu of traditional Basque dishes in memory of her mother?"

"She told me she's cooking tonight but didn't mention the Basque menu. She seemed rather short-tempered, more so than she's been for months now."

"Wouldn't you be?" was Pedro's retort. "This is a major audition for her."

"So I gather. She used that very word, audition—for a position as the Beltráns' cook, evidently."

Pedro gave Carlos a look that Carlos could not quite read. "Inéz," he said, "has been staying with the Archuletas for months now. Señora Archuleta has been very welcoming, but María tells me Inéz feels she has been there too long. She needs to find a job in some household, and the Beltráns' cook has just quit. So Señora Archuleta has invited the Beltráns, the Peraltas, and the governor and his wife to dinner to show off Inéz's talents as both a cook and a hostess."

That evening, when he knocked on the Archuletas' door, Don Carlos was dressed in his best outfit, brought with him from Mexico City two years before. As befitted his social standing, his attire was in excellent taste without being ostentatious: black stockings with dark-brown breeches, a mahogany-colored coat with a modest cascade of cambric and lace at the cuffs, and a white silk cravat. The door was opened by a manservant to whom Carlos gave his hat and his cloak, after which he sat down on a nearby stool to remove his boots and change into evening pumps.

At that moment the Archuletas' son, Gerardo, appeared to guide him into the *sala*. That's a first, Don Carlos thought. Gerardo was shy and bookish and normally avoided social encounters. As if acknowledging Carlos's surprise, Gerardo explained, "Señora Recalde told me to greet people."

As they entered the *sala*, Don Carlos saw that he was the last to arrive. Many of the leading members of Santa Fe society were present. Governor Villela and his wife Isabel were seated. New Mexico's vice governor, Ignacio Peralta, his wife Pilar, and their pretty twin daughters, Juliana and Victoria, were standing to one side with Lucila Archuleta and her husband Nicolas, the provincial government's attorney general, while Lucila showed off some Pueblo pottery that she had recently bought. Inéz hovered nearby, chatting with Javier and Cristina Beltrán and their daughter, Elena.

Though the party had been planned to honor Elena on her birthday, the arrival the day before of the courier bearing official confirmation of the governor's retirement—news of which had quickly spread—made Governor Villela the guest on whom everyone's attention focused. Whether in honor of Elena or out of a sense of the dignity of his own position, the governor had chosen to wear his finest and most eye-catching attire. His knee-length open coat was of brown satin, with padded and billowing white silk sleeves gathered at the wrists. The coat had a scarlet lining that matched the crimson of his silk stockings, and the shirt under his coat was also of silk, and gold in color. His hair, worn in the fashion of men of his class, fell to his shoulders, its darkness showing streaks of gray.

Inéz may have spent all day in the kitchen, but in social status she was a friend of Lucila Archuleta's and acted as her co-hostess. Like the other women present, she wore a full-skirted dress with a very tight bodice that dipped to a deep V just below its narrow waistline. Carlos, who was familiar with such dresses from his days in Mexico City, was always astonished that women could breathe in them. But, he had to admit, they caused great admiration in the viewer. Inéz's dark-red dress had a square neckline bordered with a strip of black braid that emphasized the whiteness of her skin, and her black hair was pulled back from her face and anchored with combs. Her color was high, and she moved with assurance and grace.

After a signal from Lucila, Inéz rang a small bell, smiled, and addressed the assembled guests. "I've planned a dinner that features various dishes from the Spanish Basque region, the land of my childhood. The first of these, the soup, will be familiar to you, having already made its way into Spanish cooking, but it is Basque in origin. The main dish and the side dish will be, I hope, something new to you and a little unusual. And now, since we are all assembled, let's move to the dinner table."

Inéz led the way over to a long table that was set for fourteen and lit by candles. She indicated the seating—Governor Villela and his wife on either side of Nicolas Archuleta at the head of the table, and next to them the Peraltas; the Beltráns were at Lucila's end, and Carlos, Inéz, and the young people in the middle. Inéz left the room and soon returned with two maids who helped her distribute bowls of soup. "Were it mid-summer," she announced, "the soup course would have featured *porrusalda*, a leek soup typical of the Navarre region where I grew up. But since it's mid-winter I've chosen to serve *sopa de garbanzo y chorizo*." Compliments were soon coming from every direction to the effect that the soup was delicious.

While the soup bowls were being cleared, conversation turned to the news that a large party of new colonists would soon arrive in Santa Fe. "Yes, it's true," the governor declared. "The courier who arrived yesterday told me that the winter supply caravan is less than a week's travel from Santa Fe."

"Anyone of note in the group?" Nicolas Archuleta ventured to ask.

The question appeared to make the governor uncomfortable, and he didn't seem ready to provide a detailed report. After a moment's hesitation, he replied. "You may have heard that Joaquin is being called back to Mexico City to answer questions about his two years of service here. I have no doubt that he will provide satisfactory answers, and I intend to speak forcefully and highly of his contribution to the province's peace and well-being. Nevertheless, he is being replaced, and the approaching caravan includes a contingent of soldiers, one of whom is Captain Tito Posada, who will assume command of the Presidio garrison. I'm told that he is accompanied by his wife, Margarita, and a number of servants. Also, Cristina Beltrán's sister, Bianca, and her husband Raul Trigales are among the newcomers. Another member of the party is a doctor, Fabio Velarde. As for others of interest, perhaps news of them should wait a bit, since I see that the main course is about to be served."

Inéz and two maids appeared with a tray of small dishes, which they began to distribute. "This Basque side dish," Inéz announced, "consists of *patataks*, potatoes, boiled until they are tender but not mushy. The sauce contains bacon, onions, paprika, and eggs. The main dish is leg of lamb with mushrooms"—a manservant came in bearing a steaming platter of lamb slices that smelled delicious—"prepared Basque style in wine sauce. I will not burden you with too large a dose of Basque language, but the name of this dish in Basque is *Bildotz Istera Anoa Zaltzan Oneduekin*. What a mouthful, yes?"

Inéz's brief switch from Spanish to Basque had an odd effect on Don Carlos. He was startled by what to his ear was the extreme foreignness of her words. Also in pronouncing these few Basque words her voice had a throaty tone distinctly different from her normal speaking voice. Inéz had never before tonight said even a single Basque word in his presence, and hearing her do so for the first time made him realize that her fluency in Spanish had led him to think of her as a Spanish woman. Here was a side of her—her Basque origins—about which he knew next to nothing.

The Basque potatoes and leg of lamb were consumed to universal acclaim. The vice governor's wife, Pilar, asked Inéz for the recipes to pass on to the Peraltas' cook, and Lucila Archuleta chimed in to say, "We have been so fortunate to have had Inéz with us these past months. She has treated us to many delicious meals, both Spanish and Basque."

"Thank you," Inéz replied, "for your kind words. Let me take this opportunity to say how eternally grateful I am to Nicolas and Lucila for giving me a refuge in my time of need. Such generosity is extraordinary. I propose a toast of gratitude from the bottom of my heart."

That toast complete, Governor Villela stood up. "I also wish to offer a toast," he declared. The governor paused before continuing. "With my son Rafael and his bride Camila's departure for El Paso del Norte, Isabel and I have less to tie us to Santa Fe. In earlier communications with Crown administrators in Mexico City" (not a letter dictated to me, Don Carlos observed), "I indicated a readiness to leave my post as governor. We have been here for eight years, eight very good years, but Isabel would like to return to Mexico City, and I agree with her that the time is ripe for a change. My toast, therefore, is one of gratitude to all of you who have made our time here so pleasant and memorable."

Once everyone had taken a sip of wine, the governor continued. "Bear with me through a second toast. I congratulate my long-time colleague,

Ignacio Peralta, who has served New Mexico ably as its vice governor for six years and who now, having received an honorary commission as a colonel, will succeed me as governor." An outburst of warm congratulations to the Peraltas — Ignacio and Pilar and their daughters, Juliana and Victoria — prevented further discussion until Nicolas Archuleta finally managed to ask, "Is it yet known who will assume the post of vice governor?" Don Carlos thought Señor Archuleta had had some ambitions in that regard, and he was sorry that he was to be disappointed.

"Yes," Governor Villela replied, "among the large party of colonists soon to arrive are Salvador Cabrera, the new vice governor, his wife Regina, and a son — a bachelor, all the unmarried young women of our circle will be glad to hear" (a comment that provoked general laughter and caused both Juliana and Victoria Peralta to blush) — "whose name is Marco."

These announcements set off another period of general conversation around the table, giving Don Carlos a chance to quietly appraise how well everyone was taking the news Governor Villela had just divulged. The governor looked more relaxed, as did his wife Isabel, pleased that their immediate future was settled. Vice Governor Peralta, about to become Colonel Peralta and governor of New Mexico, showed every sign of being elated at his promotion.

Vice Governor Peralta stood up and proposed another toast. "I know that everyone," he said, "will join me in expressing our gratitude on behalf of all New Mexicans to Governor Villela for his many years of wise leadership through exceedingly difficult times."

Cries of "Hear! Hear!" resounded through the room, wine glasses were lifted, and everyone drank to Governor Villela.

Nicolas Archuleta rose and lifted his wine glass. "Allow me to add a toast to Elena Beltrán on her eighteenth birthday, wishing her great happiness, now and in future years." Elena, a brown-haired young woman with a soft face and a plump figure, blushed and looked pleased. Across the table from her the vivacious Peralta twins smiled at each other, as if sharing a secret joke. Carlos, always observant, suspected that the Peralta twins disliked Elena. Gerardo Archuleta, sitting across from Elena, showed little interest in her or, for that matter, the Peralta twins.

Rather shyly, Elena took the floor. "My thanks go to everyone for the lovely gifts you sent to me earlier today. Those gifts, together with this dinner and Señor Archuleta's toast, have touched my heart. You have my deepest appreciation." With this, she sat down again. General conversation resumed.

Cristina Beltrán, seated to Carlos's right, recognized that the governor's announcements might also affect Carlos. She leaned over and whispered, "Do you expect to continue as secretary to the governor, Alfonso?"

"Please keep this to yourself, Cristina," he replied. "Apparently, I'm to be relieved of my duties and someone else appointed in my place."

"That's shocking," she said, genuinely upset on his behalf.

"Shhh!" he whispered back. "Let's have no more on that topic tonight. We can discuss my situation another day." But he noticed that Inéz, who was behind him serving dessert, had overheard what he'd said. He glanced at her and saw a look of concern flash across her face. It was immediately suppressed, although her eyes momentarily met his and he could tell that she was upset at the news of his dismissal.

Dessert was an almond tart with a rich custard sauce that was new to Carlos. "This dessert," Inéz announced, "*tarta de almendras con natillas*, is also Basque in origin. I have made it in honor of my *amatxu*, the Basque word for mother. During my childhood, she made this tart as a Sunday treat for our family. I confess that I loved to lick the bowl in which my mother made the custard, which contains eggs, cream, and sugar and is flavored with cinnamon sticks and vanilla. The first portions are quite small, so I hope everyone will feel free to ask for a second slice."

Most of the guests took up Inéz's offer of a second helping and Gerardo surprised Don Carlos, who'd never seen the young man display enthusiasm for anything except books, by asking for a third slice of the tart. Carlos also noticed that Gerardo had been following Inéz's every move with an adoring gaze.

Once dessert had been finished and the guests had risen from the table, Carlos had a chance to approach Governor Villela and ask how big the soon-to-arrive party of colonists was. "Large," the governor replied. "Very large; almost two hundred members."

"In your opinion, Excellency, will it be hard for the town to absorb so many newcomers at once?" Carlos inquired. "Where will they all live?"

"I don't see that as an insurmountable problem," the governor replied. "Many have relatives in Santa Fe, and they can stay with them, and I'm confident that other townspeople will show hospitality to the newcomers until they find permanent residences as servants in households or workers on farms in the vicinity. Others may accept land grants from the provincial government to establish a new town or towns in the valley."

The need of the colonists for places to live made Carlos think that he might earn his living in real estate after his present appointment ended. Stimulated by this idea, he decided to talk it over with Pedro, and to tell Inéz at the first opportunity. Though the day had started badly, now everything seemed to be going well; his apprehensions had faded and his bad dreams began to seem unreal. He caught Inéz's eye and gave her a confident smile, and for a few moments, as the governor continued to talk about the caravan, he stopped listening.

Suddenly his attention was arrested. "Amado," the governor was saying, "the courier who delivered the packet of official documents yesterday, told me that he'd passed a second party, a much smaller one, that was also headed north and was now a day or two ahead of our new colonists, although they'd traveled together through the dangerous Jornada del Muerto part of the Camino Real. This second party," he continued, "is composed of three entertainers. Amado described them as two very attractive women, said to be excellent dancers, and a handsome man who is a magician. I expect their performances will be a welcome diversion in the midst of a Santa Fe winter."

The word "magician" chilled Carlos to the core. Was it possible that this magician was a sorcerer in disguise, possibly even Don Malvolio or an apprentice of his? The very thought reawakened Carlos's apprehensions that dark forces might be bearing down on him. He remained so distracted by this possibility that he scarcely noticed when the other guests began to leave. Finally becoming aware that the party was winding down, he paid his respects to the Archuletas, who were bidding their guests farewell. Then he stopped to say good night to Inéz. Attempting an untroubled and complimentary tone, he said, "You carried off both your roles—as cook and co-hostess—perfectly. The food was delicious."

Inéz wasn't going to be put off so easily. She grasped his arm and asked, "What's the matter? You were smiling at me as if everything was fine, and then something was said that upset you—and don't deny it; I could tell."

"Yes," Carlos admitted. "The governor said that a man calling himself a magician is on his way to Santa Fe. I think it might be my old enemy Don Malvolio, or an apprentice of his."

Not without admiration, Inéz replied, "Your fertile imagination never ceases to amaze me. I'm sure this person will turn out to be just an ordinary sleight-of-hand magician."

"I suppose you're right," Carlos agreed, clearly not believing her.

"You're a very bad liar," she replied. Obliged to continue her duties as the party's co-hostess, Inéz didn't pursue the topic. She contented herself with brushing his cheek with hers in a formal way and seeing him out the door.

As Don Carlos crossed the plaza on his way home, he stopped for a moment to study the horizon to the south, the direction from which the two parties of newcomers, the one composed of colonists, the other of three entertainers, were approaching. It was just as he'd expected. Despite light from the waning moon, the sky to the south of Santa Fe was abnormally dark. He did not believe his perceptions were the products of an overactive imagination.

3

Changes

Carlos arrived home from the Archuletas' dinner party to find Pedro in their kitchen, having a glass of wine. He looked up and said, "María's still at Joaquin and Francesca's, helping with the baby, who is colicky. Diego decided not to wait up for you and has gone to bed."

"That's fine," Carlos replied. "You're the one I need to talk to."

"Before you do that," Pedro said, "tell me how Inéz's dinner went."

"She outdid herself, and as I was leaving, I overheard Cristina Beltrán tell her husband that she's going to ask Inéz to start as their cook as early as tomorrow evening."

"Good," was Pedro's only comment. A patient person and a man of few words, he waited for Carlos to report further.

Carlos continued, "As for the rest of the evening, several statements Governor Villela made during dinner confirmed details of the changes that are in the works. The new commander of the Presidio garrison and his wife are indeed bringing servants with them, which means that María will soon be out of a job."

"I told you I'm not worried," Pedro replied. "She'll find something, maybe with the Beltráns or another family. What about you? You'll soon be unemployed too."

"I have some ideas on that topic, Pedro. Remember the two vacant houses west of here on our side of the river? Only a few weeks ago you and

I talked about possibly buying the one that's slightly nearer the plaza and repairing it as a home for you and María once you begin a family, which, if I'm not mistaken, will be soon."

Pedro looked astonished, and it wasn't easy to astonish him. "How the devil did you know that? She told me only yesterday. Were you eavesdropping?"

"Nothing of the sort," Carlos replied with a chuckle. "My brujo vision is such that yesterday morning I noticed that a new life is beginning in your wife's womb."

Pedro grunted. "Sometimes I forget that you're a brujo, you make such a good show of being a government bureaucrat."

"That's a good thing, as it turns out," Carlos said. "I've told you about Don Malvolio, the sorcerer who almost finished me off in my most recent previous life. He's still after me. I never got around to telling you that when I visited Manuel Tapia last spring on my return trip from Mexico City, he reported that Don Malvolio had stopped in Nombre de Dios to ask what had become of his apprentice, Mateo Pizarro, the sorcerer I fought and killed. Manuel didn't tell Malvolio about my role in Pizarro's demise, but from what Malvolio said to him, Manuel believes my old nemesis has picked up my trail, having somehow traced me at least as far as Nombre de Dios."

"So?" a very skeptical Pedro replied. "Nombre de Dios is a long way from here. Surely you're not still worried about the lurking menace that was on your mind after that dream you had."

"Yes, I am. Tonight the governor reported that a three-person party headed in this direction is led by a magician. Calling himself a magician is precisely what a sorcerer who wanted to disguise himself would do, and I think this magician is Malvolio or one of his apprentices."

Pedro looked dubious. "You're seeing sorcerers under every bush. He's probably just an ordinary magician."

"That's what Inéz said, too. You're probably right," Don Carlos conceded, inwardly feeling annoyed because neither Pedro nor Inéz was granting any credence to his intuitions.

"Wait and see," Pedro advised. "What was your earlier point about those properties?"

"Governor Villela says the party of colonists that's coming is large— almost two hundred men, women, and children. They'll need places to stay. If we can buy one or both of those properties and renovate them, we could turn a good profit by selling or renting them to some of the newcomers. Can you ask around tomorrow morning and find out if they're available?" Becoming aware of the expression on Pedro's face, Carlos stopped in mid-thought. "Why the frown, Pedro?" he asked. "Do you have a bad feeling about my proposal?"

"Not about purchasing the house we've already talked about. But buying the one next door, the one closer to the river, might be a mistake."

"How so?" Carlos asked, genuinely puzzled. "It's almost the same size and in no worse condition than its neighbor."

"They call it Casa de Dolores."

"House of Sorrows? I'll certainly need to rename it."

"That's not the real problem. María told Ana Lugo that you might buy its neighbor for us, and Ana warned her that the House of Sorrows has a bad reputation. When the Pueblo Revolt happened, a young couple lived there. The man was the sexton for the Chapel of San Miguel, the mission church for the Indians. It was the first place the Pueblo rebels attacked and set on fire. Juan Ortiz, the sexton, saw flames rising from the chapel's roof and rushed over to save the sacred objects. But the rebels were still in the church wrecking the place, and they seized him and cut his throat. Juan's wife, Ramona, had followed him. She saw what happened and ran back to their house. Some rebels chased after her, but when she got to her kitchen, she grabbed a knife and killed herself."

"Ah!" Carlos agreed. "A terrible story."

"That's not the end of it," Pedro continued. "After the Reconquest a family moved into the house intending to fix up it up, but they didn't stay for even a week. They said that they were kept up at night by the sounds of a woman weeping."

"Are you suggesting that the house is haunted?" Carlos would have scoffed had he not himself so recently encountered ghostly spirits of past tragedies.

"Maybe so," Pedro replied. "Perhaps you ought to spend a night there to see if Ramona's ghost is still around."

Pedro's remark came across as a dare, so Carlos told him he would do just that.

María arrived home a moment later, and Carlos gave her a broad smile. "Congratulations!" he said.

She blushed and looked at Pedro. "Did you tell Don Alfonso?"

"No," Pedro replied. "He somehow figured it out on his own. You know he's an expert on women."

María couldn't let that pass without teasing Carlos. "If he's an expert, how can it be that the women he loves always get away?"

"I hope not always," Carlos said, thinking of Inéz.

Soon Pedro and María excused themselves to go to bed. Carlos stayed up and gathered some items—a heavy cloak and a thick wool blanket—he would need if he were going to spend part or all of the night at the House of Sorrows.

Once he was ready, he quietly let himself out the back door of his place and walked the short distance to the House of Sorrows. He entered it and settled down in the former *sala*, which was in bad condition. A slightly charred, rough-hewn beam lay on the floor, having fallen from the roof. He sat on the beam, crossed his legs, and fell silent.

The first sound he heard was the babble of water in the nearby Santa Fe River. Initially, it was a soothing sound and he listened intently. Soon, however, he seemed to hear voices that were murmuring words he couldn't make out. Gradually, one sound became more prominent than the rest, a bubbling noise that became ever more insistent. Carlos could understand how someone in the house would interpret the sound as a woman sobbing, weeping for her lost husband.

Carlos was congratulating himself on having solved the mystery of Ramona, the weeping woman of the House of Sorrows, when a shadow in the far corner of the room caught his eye. The more he studied the shadow, the more it appeared to be a figure, a woman who was holding her face in her hands. There was now no doubt in his mind that the sound he heard was her sobbing.

What to do? He was no priest who could exorcise this ghost, and her tears came from a sorrow he could scarcely imagine. He spoke directly to her in gentle tones. "Ramona, Ramona," he said, and he was surprised when she looked up.

"Ramona, Ramona," he repeated. "You have suffered a very great loss and have wept for Juan and yourself for twenty-five years. Surely, it is time to let this house be occupied by people who deserve to live in peace, hope, and happiness. I intend to buy it, restore it, and find a family that needs a good place to make a home. Is there anything I can do to help put your soul at rest? Perhaps"—here he made an intuitive leap—"I could locate your bones and see that they get a proper burial."

Ramona's ghost sat motionless for an hour, and Carlos waited. Finally, he decided to prompt her. "Yes, I know the priests won't bury someone who died by her own hand, but I am not bound by the same conventions. If you'll show me where to find your bones, I will gather them and take them to a sacred site" — he was thinking of the place that he and Inéz called their Sacred Pool — "and see that they are buried with prayers and sacred songs."

He waited and waited. He began to think that he'd been talking to himself and that nothing would come of it. But gradually the sadness of Ramona's story and of the tragic events of the Pueblo Revolt and the Reconquest began to overwhelm him. Tears ran down his cheeks. He put his face in his hands and wept.

Then he felt a presence next to him. He looked up and thought he saw a wispy cloud, rather like fog, waft out the open door of the house. Admitting to himself that all of this was probably the product of his imagination run wild, he picked up his blanket and followed. The spectral glow moved down the slope from the house to the bank of the river and paused, hovering above a crevice in the riverbank. Carlos knelt down and used a flat stone to dig in the dirt and pebbles that filled the crevice. After several minutes of digging he found a human jawbone. More digging and he turned up a few ribs and part of a pelvis. These, he was sure, were Ramona's bones. Either she'd dragged herself there or someone else had tossed her body into the crevice. He wrapped the bones in his blanket and stood up. Speaking to the emptiness around him — no spectral shade was visible — he promised, "I will come back during the day when the light is better to look for more bones."

Don Carlos returned to the House of Sorrows and spent three more hours sitting in it without hearing any sound except the natural murmur of the river. Finally he stood, gathered up the blanket and its contents, went home, and slept until dawn.

Monday morning came, and not long after sunrise Don Carlos heard Pedro stirring about in the kitchen and joined him for breakfast. Once perfunctory greetings had been exchanged, Carlos sketched for Pedro how he had spent his vigil at the House of Sorrows.

Pedro took it all in and asked, "Do you believe it was a ghost?"

Carlos shrugged. "Honestly, I couldn't tell you anything for certain. This experience didn't draw on any brujo training I've had, unless it was the refinement of close attention. I thought at first that the sound of the river was the source of the voices people heard. As for the rest — the cold, the long silence, and knowledge of Ramona's story may simply have put me in an intensely focused mental state that enabled me to intuit the matter of the bones. All the same, I believe something deeper and more mysterious happened."

Pedro grunted and nodded his head, apparently not feeling more needed to be said.

Carlos had made his decision about buying the house. "Based on the silence in the house once I'd collected Ramona's bones," he said, "I'm confident that we can buy it. If possible, do it today, and negotiate with the owner of the other house. While you're at it, inquire about the vacant lot that's next door to see if we can afford it too."

Pedro asked how much to offer for the properties. They kicked the topic back forth, eventually settling on prices that seemed right to them. Next they turned their attention to household chores, and once those were completed, they set out to implement their plans for the day. Pedro headed off to make inquiries about the houses and the vacant lot, and Carlos walked to his job at the Palace of the Governors. The sun had been up now for two hours, there was no wind, and the day promised to be bright with relatively mild temperatures for the time of year. Feeling invigorated, he entered the building and was surprised to find that the governor was in his office earlier than usual. Poking his head in the door, Carlos said, "Good morning, Excellency. That was an enjoyable occasion last night, wasn't it? My congratulations to you on your retirement."

The governor smiled. "You're most generous." He dropped his eyes to his desk where an envelope lay unopened.

To save his boss any embarrassment, Carlos said, "Rumor has it that I'm to be replaced in this position as soon as the new vice governor and his son arrive. No matter what, I want you to know that it's been a pleasure to serve you these two years. I can't imagine a better working situation than the one you've created for me."

The governor looked slightly taken aback by Carlos's forthrightness. He picked up the envelope from his desk and replied, "I very much regret to say the rumor is true. This letter is addressed to you, but I know from a communiqué sent to me that you're to be relieved of your duties. I hasten to add that this news was a total surprise to me, and I'm dismayed. If we were closer to Mexico City, I would fight this to the fullest extent."

"I'm grateful for your expression of support," Carlos said, "but what's done is done. It's certainly not the end of the world. Indeed, on hearing the news I concluded that perhaps it's time for me to try my hand at a new occupation."

"You're taking this very well," the governor observed. "What else do you have in mind?"

"May I speak confidentially?" Carlos asked.

"Of course."

"I strongly suspect that my stepfather, whose enmity I've incurred, had a hand in this decision. What he doesn't know is that it won't harm me greatly because I have money I received in return for a favor I did for a friend while on my trip last year to Mexico City. I intend to invest some or all of this money in Santa Fe real estate, in hopes of turning those properties into a source of income."

The governor smiled broadly. "I have no doubt that you'll succeed. What's more, your plan gives me an idea. Until now my best idea for rewarding you for your faithful and effective service to me was to advance you two months' pay, one for each full year you've worked in this position. But now that I know your plans I want to offer you a piece of property to help launch your new career. I refer to the small house I own near the river southeast of the plaza. It's known as the Fernandez place. I originally received it from your stepfather. I believe he'd acquired it as payment for a debt owed him. The place was a wreck, and he never made any improvements on it. When he was about to leave for Mexico City, he deeded it to me, saying that since it had no significant market value at the time, he couldn't think of any better way to dispose of it.

"I've had it renovated to the point that I've been able to rent it for two years now, and have gotten all the money back that I'd spent toward its repair. I didn't sell it because I thought Rafael might want a place of his own that wasn't under his parents' roof. Now that my son has left for El Paso del Norte, I'd like to sign the deed over to you. My hope would be that your benefitting from something your stepfather gave me will make some small amends for his having spent your inheritance — yes, I know about that — for the benefit of his two younger sons rather than you, as he should have done. If my offer is acceptable to you, I'll have our attorney make out the deed to you later today." Carlos gratefully agreed to the governor's offer, feeling at once astonished and overwhelmed.

"With regard to business," the governor said, redirecting the conversation to other matters, "you've completed nearly all the reports and letters that are presently required. I don't expect to have anything more for you to do, and I'm sure you would like to have these final weeks in office to start your new enterprise. Also, Isabel and I are busy preparing to leave Santa Fe as soon as the caravan begins its return trip to Mexico City. What I suggest is that you stop by my office every morning from now until my last day as governor. I'll be here early. If anything has come up that needs your attention, I'll hand it over to you then. Do whatever is required, and the rest of the day is yours to use as you see fit."

Carlos managed to get a "thank you" out before the governor could stop him. He then excused himself and set out on his next piece of business, which was to stop by the Archuletas' to see Inéz.

A maid answered his knock and showed him to the *sala*. There he found Lucila Archuleta and Inéz talking with Ana Lugo about some items Ana, a servant in Carlos's stepbrother's house, had brought by.

Before Inéz could say a word, Lucila, with a look of great concern on her face, said, "I gather from what was said last night that you may be about to lose your position as the governor's secretary. What will you do?"

"The good news," he replied, "is that the governor is deeding a small house to me—the four-room pink adobe place south of the plaza near the river—and I intend to start a new career in real estate, renting or selling houses."

Lucila nodded. "That's the Fernandez place. I heard that Governor Villela had it fixed up, but perhaps you can ask for a higher rent if you make a few more improvements before a tenant moves in. I suppose you'll need help with those renovations, if you hope to have them complete by the time the party of colonists arrives."

"Pedro's very handy as a carpenter, and Diego and I will pitch in."

Ana Lugo spoke up. "All my relatives," she declared, "both here in Santa Fe and Tesuque Pueblo are indebted to you for saving my brother José from being hanged. I'll send a message to my two cousins, Rubén and Lázaro, who helped you renovate your present house. I'm sure they'll be on your doorstep Wednesday at the latest, ready to help."

"That would be very generous of them," Carlos replied. "I can certainly use their help, though I hope they'll let me pay them this time. Last time they insisted on working for free."

"If they insist on working for free, you'll just have to accept the gift." Ana made this statement gently but firmly, and it ended any possible debate.

Carlos turned to address Inéz. "After last night's dinner, it didn't surprise me to overhear Cristina Beltrán say that she was going to invite you to be their new cook."

"Yes," she replied, looking happy. "I'm to start with dinner tonight."

"Excellent!" Carlos declared. "I'll stop by later to hear the details, but right now I need to get home and discuss real estate deals with Pedro."

Inéz said, "I have something I want to tell you. Must you rush off?"

"Yes," he replied, hastening to add, "I promise to return in an hour or two." Inéz looked disappointed, but she didn't object otherwise.

When he reached his house, he found Pedro waiting. "I checked," Pedro began, "on the House of Sorrows, the other abandoned house, and the vacant lot. You're in luck. All three are for sale. The houses are available at low prices because the owners can't afford to make them habitable. I went out on a limb and offered to buy both houses, going over the limit you'd set for me by fifteen pesos. I figured we'll have to wait a while on the vacant lot."

"Excellent!" Carlos replied. "A few extra pesos aren't a problem, but you're right that I don't have enough cash on hand now to purchase the empty lot too. And in any case I'll soon own a third house that the governor is deeding to me. Lucila Archuleta says it's called the Fernandez place and that it's been occupied until recently. Although it's in good shape, we might want to make a few additional improvements. And another bit of good news is that Ana says her cousins, Rubén and Lázaro Lugo, will help us renovate these places."

Pedro nodded. "I'll visit the owners of those two houses right away, get a formal agreement to buy them, and make a list of materials we'll need for renovations."

"The cost of materials," Carlos said, "will put me a little on the debit side, but I think we can handle it, especially if we rent the Fernandez place immediately to immigrants in the caravan. If everything works out the way I think it will, we'll be in good shape. Now if you'll excuse me, I promised Inéz that I'd be right back to talk with her."

Carlos arrived at the Archuletas' to find Inéz packing her belongings with help from Pedro's wife María. Lucila Archuleta was hovering to assist, if needed. María spoke first. "I came over to tell Inéz that Señora Beltrán has invited me to work for her temporarily, and that she intends to get me a position in her sister's very large household as soon as the caravan arrives."

Lucila broke in to say, "I'm truly sorry to have you leave, Inéz. You've been like the daughter I've always wanted. And your presence has finally awakened my son's interest in women! He is so shy and always has his head buried in a book. When I suggested that he take one of the Peralta girls to the fiesta last fall, he replied that neither of them was smart enough for him. As for Elena Beltrán, he said he thought she was too fat. She's plump, not fat. The trouble is that he just wasn't interested. He's too much like his father, whom I love dearly, but who at Gerardo's age was so scholarly and inward-gazing that I thought I would never get his attention."

Everyone laughed at this description of the male members of the Archuleta family.

Inéz interrupted the laughter to say, "Lucila, I'm so glad to hear what you said about Gerardo. Perhaps Don Alfonso should take him in hand and teach him how to court women, a subject on which Alfonso is an expert." This was said without an edge, as far as Carlos could tell, and the women responded by sharing another round of happy laughter.

Rallying as best he could to being teased, Carlos said, "Elena would be a good project for you ladies. She's intelligent and would be very attractive if she lost a little weight."

"I think," Lucila observed, "she eats too much out of loneliness. The other girls in our circle have never warmed up to her — 'too smart for her own good,' they say." Ever the optimist, Lucila added, "Perhaps one of the young bachelors among the new colonists will have a particular liking for plump women," a statement that occasioned more laughter.

"Everyone, I'm glad to see," Carlos commented, "is in good spirits. If it's all right with the two of you" — nodding to Lucila and María — "I would like a few moments to speak alone with Inéz." The two women were quick to comply. Lucila said she would find the family's coachman and have him load Inéz's belongings for delivery to the Beltrán house, and María excused herself to go home to have lunch with Pedro.

Turning to Inéz, Don Carlos said, "Do you have time before lunch to take a walk to the plaza?" Inéz nodded. She went to the hallway to get her winter cloak before going outside.

Carlos and Inéz walked the short distance from the Archuletas' to the plaza and began to stroll around its perimeter. The sun was almost at its zenith and its mild warmth, reflecting off the surface of the plaza, felt beneficent.

Inéz broke the silence. "Is there anything more you'd like to tell me about this still-unseen threat that's been worrying you? I apologize for dismissing your concerns so abruptly last night. I want you to know that I take them seriously."

"Thank you," Carlos said. "I've been bothered by many things I haven't had an opportunity to talk to you about." As briefly as possible, he recounted the dream that left him with a sense of dread, his vision or hallucination of the execution of the Pueblo rebels on the plaza, his awareness of the still-powerful presence of the kiva underneath the chapel, and his chill of apprehension on hearing that a magician was making his way toward Santa Fe. "There's a dark presence coming from the south, I'm sure of it," he insisted.

They stopped walking, and after a brief pause, Carlos said, "When I heard that a magician was on his way here, I was immediately struck with fear that this magician is my old enemy Don Malvolio, or an ally of his, and that he has picked up my trail. If this is so, and I believe it is, I need to strengthen my brujo powers. They weaken when I live in a town, and I've been spending too much time in Santa Fe. I need to get out in the countryside as soon and as often as possible."

"By day or at night?" Inéz asked.

"Both, and whenever I can get away."

"It's very cold at night this time of year," Inéz objected.

"Don't worry. I'll dress appropriately. I need to prepare myself."

"What is it between you and this Don Malvolio?"

Don Carlos sighed deeply. "It's an old and complicated story, and I only know pieces of it. As I told you last autumn at our Sacred Pool, I belong to a small group of brujos known as the Sun Moiety, whose motto is 'Do no harm.' Don Malvolio is aligned with, and is perhaps the leading figure in, a loose alliance of sorcerers known as the Moon Moiety, who are committed to the opposite. I have personally encountered Don Malvolio only twice, both times in mortal combat. The first time I prevented him from stealing a rare jewel that would have given him enormous power. The second time he killed me, although I preserved my consciousness and was reborn in my present life."

Inéz interrupted. "This sense of dread, this dark presence you feel approaching—clearly it spooks you. I don't understand brujo powers, but your reaction to Malvolio makes him seem like something…supernatural. Do you think he serves the Devil?"

Don Carlos was taken aback. The idea had never occurred to him. "No," he said quickly. "That's not it." Then, suddenly, he saw an image of himself bound and hanging upside down from a chandelier as Don Malvolio's knife sliced through his throat. A shudder went through him. "The body remembers," he said half-audibly.

"What?" Inéz asked, not catching his words.

"The fear. The fear is natural. The last thing I remember from my previous life is him slitting my throat. I seem to have a body memory of it, and the body is afraid."

"Yes," Inéz murmured, as they resumed their walk. After a few moments she went on. "I have another question. Last autumn you said that most brujos and witches were malicious and thus were aligned with the Moon Moiety. Is that right, or might there be some who occupy a middle ground, not trained as you were but not malicious either? People with unusual abilities but otherwise just like ordinary people acting with mixed motives and toward mixed ends, both good and bad?"

Don Carlos thought of Xochi, an Indian woman he'd met on his travels who was feared as a bruja but who used her powers only to protect herself. "Yes, I suppose it's possible," he replied, not quite sure where Inéz was going with her question.

"I ask," she began, "because—and this is what I wanted to talk to you about—since I did that Basque dinner and thought about my mother and my childhood, memories keep coming back, stories I completely forgot about after my mother died when I was twelve. These were family stories she told me that had been handed down by my grandmothers through five generations. My mother told me these stories over and over again from the time I was a very small child. But I put all that, my whole childhood, behind me after her death.

"What she told me," Inéz continued, "was that a hundred years ago, even though all our neighbors in the Navarre region were Catholics, many still practiced the old Basque religion. The countryside was full of sacred sites, often caves, where people believed the gods lived. They were storm gods and fertility gods who controlled the weather and the fruitfulness of crops and animals and humans, and many people felt they were very important to their everyday lives. Two of the most important gods were Mari and Aker, and I suppose people didn't see much difference between praying to the Virgin Mary who lived in heaven or to the goddess Mari who lived in a sacred cave. Her consort, the god Aker, often took the form of a he-goat, and the meadows in front of the caves where people gathered for ritual celebrations were known as *akelarres*, because *akelarre* means 'the field of Aker.'"

Don Carlos looked troubled. "In Spanish," he said, "*aquelarre* means Witches' Sabbath, the ceremony witches hold to worship the Devil."

Inéz sighed. "Yes. Well, you see where this is going. My mother said that when her grandmother's grandmother was a young woman, someone had a dream, and this person dreamed she was flying, and she flew to a meadow in which the rites of the Old Religion, which she called witchcraft, were being practiced. She told the village priest, and he called for everyone who had been to the *akelarre* to go to confession, which they did, and that was the end of it for a while.

"But something terrible had been stirred up, because soon the abbot of a nearby monastery called in the Holy Inquisition. All sorts of people were rounded up, even children, even some priests, and summoned before the Inquisition. My mother said that a sister of her grandmother's grandmother—this sister's name was Graciana—was arrested. She was about twenty-five—a little older than I am. She had a very strong soul, my mother used to say. Yes, Graciana said to the Inquisitors, she had been to the *akelarres*, but no, she was not a witch. The Inquisitors were adamant that Aker—the he-goat—was the Devil, and that anyone who participated in the *akelarres* was a witch. This she would not confess to, even under torture. The Inquisitors found her stubborn and unrepentant and condemned her to be burned."

Inéz took another deep breath. "This is a long story, I know, but I don't believe that my aunt Graciana or any of those other followers of the Old Religion were evil or worshipped the Devil, but we call what they were doing *brujería*, witchcraft. Do you really believe that only Sun Moiety brujos use their powers for good and that all other brujos and brujas are aligned with the Moon Moiety and pursue evil ends?"

Inéz stopped and turned to him. Her face was white and her voice was shaking. Don Carlos took both of her hands—cold, he noticed—in his and said soothingly, "It's all right, sweetheart."

Her breath caught in sobs, and she turned her face away. "I'm sorry," she said. "I didn't know talking about it would make me so upset." She inhaled deeply and began walking again. "All sorts of women in my childhood, and in my mother's family, were herbalists and healers, but they didn't worship the Devil. Even that horrible man whose name I try not to speak and who was vicious and cruel and mean—I don't believe even he worshipped the Devil!"

"Sh, sh," Carlos said, his concern for her temporarily wiping out his dread of Malvolio and his dark powers. "You've raised a lot of questions about things I've never thought about. But right now I'd say that human passions like greed and envy and resentment and revenge are what make people want to do harm, and not a pact with the Devil. And unusual abilities like healing or seeing auras or talking to animals can, with training, be developed. But I certainly don't believe, now that I've thought about it, that most people with those abilities are also, or necessarily, malicious or evil."

Inéz wiped her eyes surreptitiously, lifted her head, and began to walk with a more determined stride. "Sorry," she said again. "I would like to talk about this more, but right now let me change the topic and ask you to explain the news that came out this morning at Lucila's that you're investing in Santa Fe real estate, changing from bureaucrat to businessman."

"That's the general idea," Carlos said, recovering his usual equanimity. "At least I'm going to give it a try."

"Lucila says the house the governor has given you is in good repair but lacks furniture. Perhaps you can rent it furnished if you use the things you removed from the house I shared with that horrible man—with Loreto," she said, making an effort to name him. "You put them in storage in case I would ever want them, but I absolutely do not ever want to touch them again. As I recall, there are two beds, two chests, kitchen and dining tables, several benches, and various kitchen utensils. You ought to get a better rent if you furnish the house with those things. Take them as a thank-you gift for helping to free me from that monster."

Don Carlos started to express his gratitude for her generosity, but she cut him off. "I'm not being generous at all. I want to rid myself of everything directly connected with those seven years of degradation at that man's hands. Use them or burn them."

Carlos was about to put his arm around Inéz to comfort her, but she moved away slightly and said, "Gestures of affection aren't appropriate for us in a public place like this." Carlos looked reproved, and she hastened to explain. "Oh! Don't get me wrong. It's very important to me to have secured a cook's position in the Beltráns' household and to prove that I can provide for myself independently. And Cristina Beltrán told me that a condition of my employment is that you and I exercise great restraint in our relationship. Javier Beltrán is a prominent local businessman, and his household must not be a source of scandal. I sense that he and Cristina are quite easy-going, but they have a public reputation to maintain, which means that you and I must be exceedingly discrete in our conduct." She stopped, then added. "I don't mean to be so abrupt. But it's odd. Not long ago I told you that I wanted to go very slowly where intimacies were concerned. However, it's one thing to choose restraint freely and another to have it imposed by conditions of my employment.

"Also," she continued before he could comment, "I can see now that I won't have time for long rides in the country or for fencing with you, even if we want to resume our bouts, as I had hoped. And you were going to instruct me in the Brujo's Way! Just when and how can that happen?"

Don Carlos said, "Let me give you a lesson in the Brujo's Way starting right here and now."

Inéz looked skeptical. "Here and now, in a public place?" she asked.

"Definitely," Carlos replied. "I'd already been thinking that the way to start would be by studying what I call the sorcerer's vision. You experienced sorcerer's vision during our picnic when you saw that every plant and animal had an aura of light around it."

"But," Inéz protested, "we had chewed peyote cactus buds, and I'm not going to try that here in the plaza, even if you have some in your pocket."

"We don't need to ingest peyote to see auras," Don Carlos assured her.

"I don't understand," she said. "How can we practice the sorcerer's vision here while walking around the plaza in the middle of Santa Fe?"

"First of all, I suggest we sit down on that bench." When they had done so, he said, "Start by looking at the three old people leaning against the wall of the building across from us. What do you see?"

After a moment Inéz, a bit puzzled, said, "Three old people standing in the sun, leaning against a white wall."

"Can you see their auras?"

"All I see is two women and one man. Otherwise they're ordinary Pueblo people in typical Indian garb. I don't see anything resembling the auras we saw on our picnic."

"Fair enough," Don Carlos replied. "Now follow these instructions. Soften your vision. There are many techniques for doing so, but my favorite approach would be to avoid looking directly at those three Natives. Try closing your eyelids half way and gazing at the scene with your peripheral vision. Relax and be patient, even if nothing seems to be happening."

They sat in silence for ten minutes before Inéz spoke. "I can't say that I see any pulsing, colorful auras as we did on our picnic, but I am getting a different impression of the three Indians than I did at first. My sense of the woman on the right is that she's very sick. The woman on the left isn't sick but she lacks vigor. Although the man has had a violent past, he's no threat any longer — and what on earth leads me to spout such nonsense is beyond me."

"Those are excellent intuitions. Keep looking as I tell you what I see," Don Carlos said. "The woman on the right has a dim aura that's barely visible even to my practiced eye, indicating that she's very sick. The woman on the left has a dull gray aura, which means that she has little life energy. The man's aura is the easiest to see. Concentrate on him, especially the right side of his upper body. Continue to use your peripheral vision. Tell me if you can discern anything at all."

Another long silence followed. "I see, or think I do, a dark spot in his hand."

"What color?"

"I'm not sure, but it's dark and seems to be pulsing."

"You're picking this up very fast, Inéz. The dark color is red."

"Yes!" she exclaimed. "I can see it now. He has killed more than one person, although that's nothing more than a wild guess."

"Wild guesses can represent accurate intuitions, and intuitions, when a skilled brujo has them, can result in accurate insights—visions of true conditions."

"I suppose," Inéz observed, "that brings us back to your intuition that dark forces may be threatening you. I can only hope your worst fears won't be realized. As for myself," she added with a beguiling laugh, "I'm not sure I'm seeing anything other than whatever my friendly local brujo suggests I should. And right now this brujo's student had better get back to work or she'll lose her new job almost before she's started it."

"I know you'll do well," he told her. "In fact, I'm wondering whether one of your specialties as a bruja in a past life wasn't preparing curative potions, a type of folk magic with a rich history. Healing seems to be part of your Basque family heritage."

"You're really serious in making a suggestion like that, aren't you?" Inéz asked.

"My deepest identity is as a brujo. I hope you'll learn to love Don Carlos Buenaventura the brujo at least as much as you love Don Alfonso Cabeza de Vaca, fencer, rider, picnicker, and real estate investor."

"You needn't worry," she said with a smile. "I'm fond of both of you. Let's get together tomorrow around two o'clock—after lunch and before I have to start dinner, and we can practice more sorcery or whatever it is we're doing. Now please walk me to my new home."

4

Owls

After walking Inéz to the Beltráns', Carlos went directly to his place just south of the plaza. No one was in the house, but he found Diego mucking out stalls in the attached stable on the side of the house away from the plaza. "Diego," he said, "how would you like to join me for a moonlight ride tonight?"

Diego, sensing an adventure in the offing and always eager for new experiences, grinned and said, "Oh, yes! Is there any chance that José Lugo could come too? He's working so hard as a blacksmith's apprentice that he scarcely has time for fun any more—this will be fun, won't it?"

"I trust we'll have a good time," Carlos replied. "Why don't you go to the blacksmith shop and invite José to join us here at eight o'clock for dinner, after which we'll take our ride."

"Pedro's not coming?" Diego asked.

"I haven't talked with him, but I'm pretty sure he'd rather get a good night's sleep in his own bed. I need him to be well rested for the renovation work we're going to be doing tomorrow on the houses I've recently acquired."

"Aren't I supposed to help with the renovations?"

"Of course, Diego, but you're young and can go without much sleep. Besides, we're not going to ride all night."

Having settled these details with Diego, Carlos grabbed a bite to eat and went looking for Pedro. He found him at the Fernandez house that Carlos had acquired from the governor. Pedro reported that it would take a crew of men no more than a day or two to make the improvements he and Carlos had discussed.

"I'm pleased to hear that," Carlos said. "And I have a piece of good news too. Inéz wants to give us the things we rescued from Loreto's house. Renting the place furnished will bring in more pesos."

Diego outdid himself as cook that evening. "This combination of potatoes, beef and bacon bits, and goat cheese is delicious," Carlos told Diego. "Did you come up with this recipe on your own?"

"No," Diego replied. "Inéz told me the recipe."

After they'd cleared and washed the dishes, Don Carlos turned to his two young friends. "The moon has come up. Let's get started. Bring blankets, because when we get where we're going, you'll be waiting around in the cold for a while. I'll ride Eagle; José, Pedro says you can take Pepper; and Diego, we need you to ride Alegría, who will be getting almost no exercise now that Inéz is a full-time cook."

Don Carlos led the way to the road that went north from Santa Fe toward Taos Pueblo. The purpose of the trip, as he'd told Inéz, was to reinvigorate his brujo powers. His life as a town-dwelling Spanish bureaucrat always caused his powers to weaken. To restore them and practice his brujo techniques he needed to go into the deserts and high mountain wilderness of New Mexico, landscapes that served to put him strongly in contact with his brujo identity.

As he and his two young companions rode along, the countryside around them palely illuminated by the moon in its last quarter, Don Carlos observed that they asked no questions about their destination. They had accepted him as their leader, and although he was their elder by no more than two or three years, their upbringing in Pueblo families led them to respect his choice to tell them more only when he was ready. That would not be long, given the purpose of his trip.

The three riders soon reached a trail that turned off from the road to Taos and proceeded eastward toward the mountains. A short distance from their destination, Carlos signaled Diego and José to dismount. At last he explained his intentions. "We'll stop here. Just beyond this little meadow, at the base of a cliff, is a pool. You can see the glimmer of the moonlight on the water. We don't want to frighten off creatures that come there at night to drink. Your job is to stay here while our mounts graze in this grassy area. You can take turns—one keeping an eye on the horses, the other dozing—but you may also find it interesting to watch the pool to observe which animals show up.

"I'm going to go off by myself. First I'll climb partway up the cliff and later I'll spend some time in the underbrush on the floor of the narrow canyon ahead. The task I've assigned myself is learning to imitate the screech owl's call. There's one right now. The screech owl has a distinctive, sorrowful-sounding voice, like a wail that starts at a high pitch and then descends. I'll be moving around trying to duplicate their calls. You can amuse yourselves by seeing whether you can tell the difference between the resident owls and Don Alfonso's imitations. Keep track of which direction the true and the imitation screech owl calls come from. A couple of hours ought to be plenty of time for me to complete this exercise."

What Don Carlos told his friends was a cover for his real intentions. Over many lifetimes, he had become highly skilled at the sorcerer's technique of transformations. Tonight he intended to transform himself into a screech owl and move about the nearby cliffs and the brushy part of the canyon, exploring the screech owl's nature and strengthening his own powers in the process.

Once safely out of sight of his companions he effected his transformation into a screech owl, a small but highly intelligent night creature. He undressed so that his movements would not be impeded by his clothes falling around him when he changed into an owl. Then he stood beneath a tree and visualized an owl's form. This was aided by a screech owl voice that came from a short distance away, its mournful wail piercing his human consciousness and grasping his inner being as surely as an owl's talons hold their prey. He felt the fingers of his hands extending into feathers, and, lifting his arms (which were now wings), he flew upward to a branch a dozen feet above where he'd been standing. Fully embodied now as a screech owl, Don Carlos felt the elation and empowerment that always accompanied his best transformations. For the next half hour he practiced flying until he could move from tree branches to cliff ledges and back without any awkwardness.

Having succeeded at flying, he began to practice his screech owl calls. His initial attempts, he felt, were more hysterical than mournful, and too short in their movement from high to low pitch. But an hour later, after listening to many vocalizations by the area's resident screech owls, of which there were four that he could distinctly identify, he was satisfied with his performance. He flew to a tree only twenty yards from where he'd left Diego, José, and the horses. At that point he could hear two screech owls fairly close at hand—one to the south of his companions and another on the cliffs to the east. He answered each call made by the other two owls, one of which seemed to become more insistent—as though angry—as time passed. Don Carlos was about to quit his performance when he heard a whooshing sound and realized that he was about to be attacked by one of the owls. At the last moment before impact, he made a big jump to his left on the tree limb. The owl missed him and landed on a nearby branch.

"This is my territory," the owl declared, glaring at Don Carlos. "Get out!"

"I'm not trying to steal your territory," Don Carlos replied calmly, "and if you would look closely, you would see that I'm not an owl but a man who has taken an owl form."

The owl peered intently at Don Carlos. After a long time, she declared, "I'm astonished, and what surprises me even more is that you're a Spaniard. I've heard that a few Native shamans can manifest themselves as owls, but I never imagined that a Spaniard could do so. You're a brujo, I suppose."

"Yes," Don Carlos admitted. "And I'm sorry to have upset you, but I've always enjoyed flying and I wanted to practice screech owl calls."

"Your first attempts were terrible," the owl said. "I thought it might be some Native kid playing around. But your recent calls fooled me. I thought another owl was moving into my territory and not leaving, despite my best efforts to warn him off. What's your purpose other than entertaining yourself?"

Don Carlos gave the owl, whose name was Jimena, an edited version of his problem with the approach of dark forces. "My situation isn't so different from yours, except in mine an evil sorcerer may be coming into my territory in hopes of killing me. One of my skills as a brujo is the ability to change myself into nearly any animal, and I wanted to practice my transformation technique in case I need it in a battle with this enemy."

"I can understand that," Jimena replied. "If that's what you're up to, I guess I'll go back to my business, unless there's something else you have to say."

"There is. I'm wondering whether you've ever met Elvira, a skunk who lives near here. She told a woman friend of mine something personal. I'm wondering," Carlos continued, "whether Elvira gives reliable advice."

"That old skunk!" Jimena said with a chuckle, if that odd sound was, indeed, a chuckle. It's not easy to tell with screech owls. "Yes, she's usually reliable, especially where matters of love are involved. But if you want my opinion about advice from creatures who live around here, I'll say this. Don't listen to anything Cousin Coyote says; he's an inveterate liar. Grandmother Spider is very helpful if you need to find someone, and Sister Porcupine is full of excellent advice about self-defense. Now I really have to get going." And Jimena flew off.

Don Carlos decided he'd done enough for one night. He returned to a tree above the spot where he'd left his clothes, dropped to the ground, returned to human form, and got dressed. He walked the short distance to where José and Diego were waiting and found them wide awake and eager to talk. "We heard lots of owls," José declared. "One of them sounded very odd. Was that you trying to imitate a screech owl?"

"Probably so," Don Carlos admitted. "I wasn't very good at it at first."

"I guess you got better," Diego said. "After a while we couldn't tell one owl's call from another's. We believe we heard five owls in all, three close by and two farther off. Do you agree?"

"That's my count too," Carlos replied. "Good job. Let's head home and talk later. Tomorrow night would be a good time to talk, if you'd like to join me for another trip then." They both indicated they would.

Don Carlos managed to get four hours of sleep—all he'd ever needed for most of this life and all his previous lives too—before Pedro called him to share a hearty breakfast of *huevos revueltos*, bacon, toast, and coffee. They had just begun to eat when there was a knock at the kitchen door. It turned out to be their Tesuque Pueblo Indian friends, Rubén and Lázaro. Carlos greeted them in their Tewa language, *"Woa'ah tamu,"* and the two carpenters replied in kind.

"I appreciate being greeted in my own language," Rubén said. "Not many white men even try."

"Don't get your expectations too high," Carlos replied. "I can't do much more than count to five, name the sun and moon, and call that fat four-legged over there—pointing to Gordo—a *Tséh.*" (The latter comment amused everyone, just the effect Carlos had sought.) "I very much appreciate," he added, "your offering to help us. Please sit down and have some breakfast."

Pedro, Carlos, and their Tesuque friends had started to eat when Diego, whose bunk was in the hayloft over Don Carlos's stable, and José, who'd spent the night with him, stumbled in blurry-eyed for breakfast. Six men around the table made for a crowd, but the food was good and the atmosphere was friendly.

Don Carlos had wanted to ask José something for a long time and thought the moment was right to do so. "José, I understand that your uncle was one of the medicine men who led the Pueblo Revolt and later was executed for his part in the rebellion. Is that so?"

"Yes," José said calmly. "General Alvarez had my uncle and sixty-nine other Pueblo people executed in the plaza in a single day."

"Are you aware," Carlos asked gently, "that General Alvarez is my stepfather?" He paused and José nodded. "Why then," Carlos asked, "are you willing to have anything at all to do with me?"

"You are different!" José said with great feeling. "I didn't know that at first, but you went to a lot of trouble to save me, a Pueblo boy, from hanging for a murder I hadn't committed. I knew then that you are different. And my sister Ana told me that your stepfather has treated you badly—that he cheated you out of your inheritance and has gotten you fired from your job."

Lázaro spoke up. "You have always treated Rubén and me fairly and as equals, not as if we were inferior people. You're our friend, but even if you weren't a friend in that way, as an enemy of our enemy—General Alvarez—you would be our friend."

"Your words," Carlos replied, "touch me deeply. In addition, you're helping me a great deal. So let's get to work. José, I know you'd like to help, but you need to keep on with your training as a blacksmith's apprentice. As for the rest of us, Pedro suggests that we concentrate today on the Fernandez house. With all five of us working at it, we should be able to quickly do what we've planned. Repairs need to be done on the roof. Lázaro and Rubén can handle those. Pedro can fix the window frame and the back door, both of which are off kilter. Diego and I will give the front of the house a new coat of paint, after which we'll do general interior cleanup with help from the rest of you as you finish your repair jobs. If all goes well, we ought to be able to move furniture into the house late this afternoon or early tomorrow."

With those goals in mind, everyone went to work. It was another mild day. More than half their tasks were done by early afternoon, when they took a two-hour break for lunch and a brief siesta. Carlos used the time to call on Inéz. She greeted him at the Beltrán house's kitchen door and broke out laughing. "You have pink paint on your cheek. Have you been playing children's games or working?"

"Things are moving along well at the Fernandez house," he replied. "Diego and I were giving the front of the house a fresh paint job. You can guess the color. Shall we walk to the plaza?"

During the short walk to the plaza, Inéz asked, "Is it true that you took José and Diego to our picnic spot last night?"

"Yes, I need to reinvigorate my brujo skills and that's a good location for doing so. Last night I transformed myself into a screech owl, and with a little practice I produced a call good enough to fool a female owl named Jimena into thinking I was the real thing."

"Why does it not surprise me that your screech owl encounter was with a female?" Inéz said. "Did you mate with her?" she asked with a slight edge to the question.

"Nothing of the sort!" Carlos protested. "However, in the course of talking with her I gathered some information about your skunk friend, Elvira. Jimena said that Elvira is trustworthy and wise—and I'm quoting Jimena now—'where matters of love are involved.' I took that as positive news, since she told you we could marry some day."

"I'm glad Elvira comes with good recommendations," Inéz declared, "but I hope you're not nudging me to decide about marriage. I don't want to think about that topic at present, so please don't ask me to. Let's return to our lessons in the Brujo's Way. There's not a lot of time before I need to be back at work."

"We made good progress yesterday on seeing auras. You can practice that on your own, if you ever have a spare moment. I propose we try something different today. The best place for this exercise will be in the chapel. It will be quiet and unoccupied at this hour."

Inéz laughed. "For someone whose Catholicism seems to be mostly of the keeping-up-appearances variety, you certainly take every chance you can to get me into churches."

"Don't be so suspicious," he said with a smile. "You know that my motives are always as pure as newly fallen snow. All right, perhaps not always. But the chapel's interior is a perfect place to practice one form of the sorcerer's vision, and by going inside we'll also appear to anyone who's watching us—and someone's always watching—to be two pious Catholics going to the chapel to pray."

Don Carlos led Inéz to a place inside the chapel next to a small window through which light was streaming. He then explained what to do. "Let's stand here for ten minutes, or more if you have the time. Look into the stream of light, gazing into it with your peripheral vision the way we did yesterday. Take deep, slow breaths and see what you see."

They fell silent. Don Carlos was impressed with how quickly Inéz became quiet—not just silent but very still and drawn inward. The minutes passed with the timelessness that time has when one isn't counting the minutes. Don Carlos quickly saw what he was hoping Inéz might see, although, who knows, he said to himself, she may well see something entirely different. He couldn't tell whether she was seeing anything unusual until a tear ran down her cheek and she whispered, "Beautiful! A whole universe in a tiny place."

"Can you say anything more?" he asked.

"What I'm seeing—it's more a feeling than a sight—is the tumbling transit of dust motes through the light. They arise, seemingly out of nowhere, tumble along, and then drift out of the light and disappear. Each is like a tiny universe, and perhaps—to some giant entity looking at our world from afar—we don't look much different. All the stuff of life, our worries, our joys, are small from the giant's perspective. Also, the stuff of our lives is, like the dust motes, transitory—it arises, has a glorious moment in the sun, and then disappears."

"I couldn't have said it better," Don Carlos murmured.

"This isn't anything like what I thought sorcery is about," Inéz declared. "No spells, incantations, no flashy tricks."

"That's true," Don Carlos replied. "Most of what passes for magic and wizardry is little more than cheap tricks intended to impress simple-minded people, though the casting of spells is sometimes intended to call forth otherworldly beings to help the magician achieve certain results, sometimes good, more often not. But I agree that what we've seen—or, more properly, brought into awareness—is magical, magic of a deeper sort that reveals, as you said, truths about the whole universe in a small place."

Inéz had to go cook dinner, and Don Carlos needed to get back to help his friends renovate the houses he'd bought. By nightfall, his crew had spruced up the four-room Fernandez house and moved in the furniture Inéz had given him. For all intents and purposes the house was ready to be occupied.

After dinner, Don Carlos, José, and Diego saddled their horses and again rode to the spot where they'd spent much of the previous evening. Carlos asked his friends what, if anything, they'd seen at the pool. They reported that many animals had come for a drink of water, but the one that excited them most was a large mountain lion. Fortunately, the wind was blowing from the pool toward them, so the mountain lion didn't catch their scent. But the horses had smelled the cougar and had been restless.

"Did you see a skunk?" Don Carlos asked.

"Yes, a big one," Diego replied. "I couldn't tell whether it was a male or a female."

"If it's the same skunk Inéz saw," Carlos said, "it's a female named Elvira." José and Diego looked surprised that the skunk had a name but didn't ask any questions.

"José," Carlos then asked, "are there any medicine men living at Tesuque Pueblo?"

"Yes, an old man who's a highly respected shaman."

Don Carlos told José that he was going to hike into the canyon again, and that while he was away, José should draw a map of Tesuque Pueblo in the dirt, making a small circle for the house where the medicine man lived. He said he would explain more when he returned from his vigil.

Don Carlos walked half a mile up the canyon. Tiring of having to push his way through thick brush, he transformed himself into a screech owl and flew off in the direction of Tesuque Pueblo. It was a short flight, so short that he flew in circles to prolong what for him was an exhilarating sensation.

Once he was above the pueblo, he had a clear view of the many houses that spread out in every direction from the village kiva, the underground chamber where Tesuque men conducted their most sacred ceremonies. Although most of the pueblo's residents were inside and impossible to see, four were visible outdoors. Their auras varied in intensity. Two had strong auras, indicating healthy individuals. One person's aura was very dim, a sign of sickness or the infirmities of old age. The aura of the fourth person, seated outside a small house on the edge of the village, was particularly bright. Don Carlos concluded that it belonged to the pueblo's medicine man.

Having seen what he'd been looking for, Don Carlos flew back to the brushy canyon bottom not far from Elvira's pool. He'd dropped to the ground and was about to return to his human form when he saw a large mountain lion approaching. Curious as to what the cougar might have to say, he transformed himself into a porcupine. There was some danger in doing so, but he didn't think the mountain lion would attack a porcupine.

"Good evening," Don Carlos said politely.

The cougar stopped and looked closely at Don Carlos. "You're new around here," the cougar observed. "What's your name?"

Thinking quickly, Don Carlos replied, "Norberto. What's yours?"

Ignoring the question, the cougar asked whether Norberto planned to stay around or was only passing through.

"Just passing through," Don Carlos replied. "However, I wonder if there's anything you can tell me about the old Tesuque shaman who lives near here. Is he wise and reliable? If so, I would like to consult him about a problem I'm having with a Spanish sorcerer."

"The Tesuque medicine man knows a lot about exposing and driving off witches. I learned that from my grandfather, who used to talk with him. Now, if you'll move out of my way, I'd like to take a drink."

After the cougar left, Don Carlos changed into owl form and flew to the place he'd left his clothes, returned to human form, got dressed, and walked out of the shadows of the pine trees to where his friends were waiting for him. Once back at their temporary camp, he studied the map of Tesuque Pueblo that José had drawn. "Please point out for me where the pueblo's shaman lives." José did so. The location was precisely where Don

Carlos expected it to be from what he'd seen on his flight over the pueblo.

A quick ride back to Santa Fe, a good night's sleep, and Carlos awoke to a beautiful Wednesday morning. Today he and his friends shifted their attention to Segunda, as he'd renamed the former House of Sorrows, the second place he'd acquired. It had a sizeable loft for storage and four rooms, only two of which were in good condition. The other two needed a new roof and many repairs. Carlos's friends went right to work, with Pedro, Rubén, and Lázaro undertaking the most challenging carpentry jobs, and Carlos and Diego doing general cleanup and painting chores.

After lunch, Carlos was about to head to the Beltráns' for his daily rendezvous with Inéz when his stepbrother Joaquin showed up with four soldiers whom he'd asked to help Carlos with house renovations. Carlos noticed that his Pueblo Indian friends grew tense at the arrival of the soldiers, not surprising given Spanish soldiers' reputations for being unfriendly to Native peoples. Carlos immediately took measures to create a positive atmosphere. He proposed that Pedro serve coffee all around while he told stories about his friends, both Spanish and Native. A gifted story-teller and skilled at making his audiences laugh, he soon sensed that the tension that had hung in the air had dissipated. He then initiated a brief discussion of the day's tasks. It was decided that Diego, Lázaro, and Rubén would work on Segunda, while Pedro would organize the soldiers in starting to renovate Tercera, the third house that Carlos had acquired.

Carlos walked his stepbrother back to his residence at the Presidio. As they parted, Carlos thanked Joaquin profusely for the help the soldiers were giving him. He then continued on to the Beltráns' mansion, where Inéz was waiting for him to come by.

Inéz seemed happy. "You're in good spirits," Carlos observed.

"I've been enjoying," she said, "our lessons in sorcery, although most of what you've shown me doesn't seem as exotic or mysterious as the word sorcery would suggest. Simple close observation could achieve much the same results. What do you have in store for me today?"

"More of what you quite accurately describe as close observation. What I propose today is that we walk to the far end of the plaza, where the parish church stood before it was destroyed during the Pueblo Revolt." They put on their coats and let themselves out the door. Taking her arm, he steered her to a bench under an old piñon tree that had somehow survived all the fire and devastation of the upheaval that accompanied the revolt. "Let's sit here," he proposed, "and study this old tree. Look at it with your peripheral vision, paying particular attention to your out-breaths. If you get deeply into this exercise you may become aware of the pine breathing in as you breathe out."

"What an odd idea," Inéz remarked. "But I'll give it a try."

A long silence followed, broken when Inéz exclaimed, "I see what you mean! After a while the tree's aura became visible, and I noticed that it pulsed, expanding and contracting in a rhythm identical to my breathing — my drawing a breath as its aura seemed to exhale, and my out-breath coming as its aura seemed to inhale."

Don Carlos had been so deeply involved in observing the same phenomenon that it took him a moment to return to ordinary reality. "You're quick to grasp these lessons," he said, "another indication, as I've suggested previously, that you were a bruja in a previous life. What you witnessed was a central truth of the Brujo's Way — that all creation, animate and inanimate, is intimately connected. Even in times when we feel horribly alone, the source of our life, our breath, connects us with the world outside our bodies. Properly understood, then, there is no such thing as an isolated self."

"So," Inéz spoke thoughtfully, "if we saw our lives from the perspective of what you might call the Great Self rather than the isolated self, everything would appear very different."

"Precisely," Don Carlos agreed. "Let's stay with that awareness a little while longer." They sat, and after a quiet interval turned toward each other and decided to move on. "What are you cooking tonight?" Carlos asked as they began walking.

"You'll find out," she replied with a laugh. "I've been giving Diego recipes for you and your housemates. And by the way, Diego told me that he often bumps into José's sister Ana while shopping on market days. I got the distinct impression that he's noticed what a pretty young woman she is."

"Ana's two years older than Diego, isn't she?" Don Carlos asked.

"Yes," Inéz said, "but I didn't notice that Alfonso Cabeza de Vaca thought it was unseemly to have a friendship with me, even when he thought, inaccurately, that I was four or five years his senior."

"Touché," he declared, with a small bow.

Dinner turned out to be a delicious bean and pork stew with a touch of chili peppers to spice it up. Carlos refrained from teasing Diego about the origin of the recipes or about Diego's growing attraction to Ana. José showed up in time to grab a bowl of the stew before he, Diego, and Don Carlos set out on their next quest.

As they were saddling their horses, Carlos told his young friends that they had a different destination tonight from their previous two outings. "We'll ride south toward La Ciénega until we come to that big cluster of pine trees on the west side of the road. You can wait for me while I explore the area. If all goes well, I have a hunch that something special may happen."

Before long they reached the pine grove Carlos had chosen as his starting point. He left his companions behind and walked to the far edge of the grove. His plan was simple. Tonight he again transformed himself into an owl, this time into a barn owl, a variety much larger than the screech owl and well known for its oval face and white underbody and the ghostly appearance it had when seen at night. He took off and flew south above the Camino Real. At a *paraje* (rest stop) near Bernalillo, he came upon the camp of the supply caravan. Dozens of wagons, a big herd of horses, and the perhaps two hundred people in camp were spread out across a large site. The embers of fifty or sixty campfires glowed red in the night, creating a field dotted by their light that seemed to echo the much more numerous white stars in the clear night sky above.

Don Carlos estimated that the caravan would need at least three more days of travel before arriving in Santa Fe, assuming that no storm came along to impede their movement. That was useful information in regard to his plans to have his houses ready to be occupied by arriving colonists, but gathering information wasn't his main purpose tonight. He simply wanted to explore the night sky and landscape in owl form, so he continued his flight, turning west to reach the nearby Rio Grande, its surface reflecting the moonlight like a giant silver snake winding its way through the valley. His owl-self's wordless sense of being an inseparable part of everything he saw made Don Carlos's inner brujo energy grow stronger. He circled repeatedly above the river, feeling great joy, before turning north to rejoin José and Diego.

He flew back to the pine grove where he'd left his young friends and landed abruptly between José, who was standing watch, and Diego, who had been curled up in his blanket until Don Carlos's arrival in owl form startled him awake.

Using the brujo's technique of projecting his words into the minds of humans with whom he wished to speak—the sounds of which were inaudible—the owl Carlos said in perfect Spanish, "Excuse me for interrupting your vigil. I hope you don't mind. Do you, perhaps, have a question for me?"

Diego seemed completely tongue-tied, but José, who had some knowledge of what to do when one encountered a spirit animal, overcame his surprise and said, "We are honored that you've chosen to speak with us.

Would you be so kind as to give us a message to report to our friend, Don Alfonso Cabeza de Vaca, when he returns?"

"I will answer you first in my language," the owl Carlos replied, and then produced a quite creditable barn owl call, a strange rasping sound: "Kssschk. Do you follow my meaning?"

"I'm sorry to say I can't," José admitted. "Could you repeat the message in Spanish?"

"All right," the owl agreed, "if you'll first tell me your name."

"José Lugo."

Not above having a little fun in an otherwise serious moment, Don Carlos in owl form replied, "I noticed this Don Alfonso fellow snooping around, but I prefer to speak with young Pueblo men. My message is for you, José, though you're welcome to share it with your Spanish friend. The message is this. You have the capacity to become a medicine man, if you wish. Where do you live?"

"Santa Fe."

"I'm sure you have your reasons for living there," the owl-Carlos said. "The trouble is that it's difficult to pursue the Shaman's Way while living in a town. Deserts and wilderness areas are the environments where a shaman develops his powers. Visit those areas often. Now I'm going back to my hunt."

When Don Carlos returned to his friends' camp, their excitement was so great that they had a difficult time giving a coherent account of the barn owl's visit. Don Carlos assured them that he shared their excitement. "Didn't I tell you that something special might happen tonight? Call it a lucky guess, if you wish, but the owl's visit and his willingness to answer José's question is wonderful. Be careful. You shouldn't tell anyone else about your experience unless it's the elderly medicine man of Tesuque Pueblo."

"Are you a shaman, Don Alfonso?" José asked timidly.

Having anticipated the question, Don Carlos had prepared an answer that evaded it. "Have you ever met a Spanish shaman? Who ever heard of such a thing? It's your good fortune to be Tewa-speaking Pueblo Indians. The Shaman's Way is part of your heritage. But if you wish to pursue your heritage, you should keep in mind that many Spanish people—I'm obviously not among them—are hostile to Pueblo religion. My suggestion is that you be good Catholics by day and respectful of Pueblo traditions at night."

Don Carlos hoped he hadn't gone too far or said too much, but he sensed that José had the potential to be a medicine man. He wanted to point the way and let José decide for himself whether to pursue a spiritual path.

5

The Trio

A storm front arrived — cold, sleet, and slushy snow — early Thursday morning. Carlos heard the sleet pinging on his bedroom window when he woke.

A few hours later Pedro had to cook breakfast because Diego slept in.

"You've been keeping those kids up until all hours," Pedro grumbled. "How do you expect them to work the next day?"

Carlos looked up from his bowl of cornmeal mush and replied, "They're young; they can stand it. Besides, there's not all that much work left for us to do. From what I saw last night the supply caravan won't arrive until Saturday at the earliest, and with the weather the way it is this morning, it may take them a day or two longer."

"Yes," Pedro agreed, "today's weather is lousy. But I have another question. Something big happened for José last night, didn't it?"

"Big?" Carlos replied. "Possibly so, though how big depends more on what comes of it than on what happened. I'm probably not supposed to tell you that he had a conversation with an owl."

Pedro, who had long known about Carlos's skill at transformations, grunted and observed, "I don't suppose this owl's name was Carlos."

"I don't believe he introduced himself," Carlos said, and they both broke out into laughter, subsiding just as Diego showed up for breakfast.

"So," Pedro continued, as if this had been their subject all along, "when do you want me to ride south to line up prospects to buy or rent your properties?"

"Saturday morning ought to be soon enough. Today and tomorrow we can finish any remaining interior renovations on Segunda and Tercera. This morning I'm going to visit Inéz after a quick stop at my stepbrother's residence to tell him that the caravan is still a three days' journey from Santa Fe."

Pedro, a little surprised that Carlos would broach that topic with Joaquin, asked, "And how did you get this news?"

"I met a vaquero on the road last night who'd passed the caravan's camp not long ago."

Diego, who hadn't seen anyone one the road the previous night, shot a questioning look at Don Carlos, but said nothing. Addressing him directly, Carlos asked, "Diego, would you like to come along and see what Inéz has in mind for you to cook for dinner tonight?"

Diego agreed happily, and he and Don Carlos got up and put on their winter hats and cloaks. When, after a short walk, they reached Joaquin's residence on the Presidio grounds, Ana Lugo, Carlos's sister-in-law's personal maid, met them at the door and was clearly pleased to see Diego. The mutual attraction was obvious. They conversed shyly while Carlos talked with Joaquin who, as it turned out, was already aware of the supply caravan's probable arrival date.

Carlos and Diego then walked the short distance to the Beltráns' and knocked on the kitchen door. Inéz opened it with the words, "What dreadful weather! Come in. I have a recipe for you, Diego, a green chili dish that ought to get your blood moving after this icy day." She carefully went over the recipe, first telling him the ingredients and then describing the necessary steps in preparing the dish. Diego couldn't read or write, so nothing was written down, but since he came from an oral culture, he would remember every word of Inéz's instructions.

Turning to Carlos, Inéz said, "I don't have a lot of time today and the weather is miserable. What do you suggest?"

"Bundle up, and we'll go to the chapel. At least we'll be inside."

Inéz took a heavy cloak from a hook near the door and pulled its hood over her head. She, Carlos, and Diego walked back to the northwest corner of the plaza. The slushy footing was slippery and the pelting sleet unpleasant on their faces. When they reached the chapel door, Diego went on his way while Carlos and Inéz ducked inside.

They stood at the back of the chapel to let their eyes adjust to the dim light. It was only the second time Carlos had been in the chapel when it was empty of people and no liturgy was being celebrated. His vision, now a memory, of the execution of the Pueblo rebels following the Spanish reconquest of Santa Fe came back strongly, and his brujo senses became fully alert. "Are we going to stand here in the back?" Inéz asked.

"No," he replied. "Let's go up to the front."

"Do you have another lesson in sorcery for me today?" Inéz whispered as they walked forward. "Should I do anything in particular?"

"Let's be silent," he suggested. "A lot can be learned from a practice I call Watching, simply waiting to see what comes up."

He had practiced Watching for many years and knew that there was no knowing in advance what would surface in the silence. He stood still and waited, putting himself into a meditative state by following his breath until it softened in a way that reminded him of a gate swinging gently in the wind—open and shut, back and forth.

He soon became aware of sounds, exceedingly faint at first, as though they were coming from a distant place. He listened intently as the sounds grew stronger, and he recognized the steady beat of a drum accompanied by male voices in a droning chant. He knew immediately what he was hearing and turned to Inéz to ask, "Do you hear anything?"

"Other than my teeth chattering?" she replied.

"Sorry about the cold. We won't stay long, but this is a good opportunity to practice deep awareness. Listen."

After a brief pause, she spoke. "It's so quiet I can hear my heart beating."

"I hear both our hearts beating, but there's another, similar sound too."

"I hear it!" she exclaimed. "It's the beat of a drum. I didn't recognize it at first because I can't imagine where it could be coming from."

"Directly under us," Don Carlos declared.

"How's that possible?" Inéz asked. "There's nothing under us but the dirt floor."

"There once was," Don Carlos told her. "I believe we are standing directly above the spot where the Pueblo rebels built a kiva in which they gathered for their most sacred ceremonies. Governor Vargas had the kiva filled up and the whole chapel exorcised after the Reconquest."

Inéz fell silent again. After a short interval he heard her crying. "It's so sad!" she burst out and buried her face on his shoulder. "So much suffering! First the Spanish are driven away and those who don't escape—hundreds of them—are killed. Then the Spanish return, kill many Indians, and destroy every vestige of the Pueblo people's sacred site."

"Yes, it's a sad story—the treatment of the Natives before the revolt, the revolt itself, and its aftermath. It's very sad."

Inéz looked up, gazed for a moment at the altar area, and gave a muffled gasp. "Look," she said. "Even Our Lady is crying."

Don Carlos turned his attention to the three-foot-tall wooden statue known as La Conquistadora that a Franciscan, Fray Alonso de Benavides, had brought to Santa Fe in the 1620s. When the Spanish colonists had been driven out by the Pueblo rebels in 1680, they had taken her with them. They had brought her back when they reconquered the province. Now, dressed in a richly embroidered gown and cape, Our Lady looked out into the sanctuary. Don Carlos wasn't sure he could see tears running down her cheeks. He thought perhaps it was an illusion resulting from the flickering light of the oil lamps on either side of the statue. But he wasn't going to challenge Inéz's perception. Whatever the physical facts of the situation, her emotional reading of it was true. Sorcery, at least the type of sorcery he practiced, included reading the deep truths beneath superficial appearances.

"That's enough sorcery for me today," Inéz said quietly. Carlos gently took her hand, feeling that her own experience of sorrows opened her to the underlying sadness in Santa Fe's history. "Why," she asked, "is there so much suffering?"

"I often ask myself the same question," he replied, and together they walked out the door of the chapel.

The plaza was deserted. Only crazy people are out in this, he thought, feeling the needles of sleet pricking his face under the brim of his hat. Inéz kept her face down and shivered beside him.

As they turned to the right outside the chapel, Carlos looked out across the plaza and saw what appeared to be several ghostly shapes advancing through the obscuring veil of sleet. He put his hand on Inéz's arm and they stopped and faced the apparitions, which steadily drew closer, finally revealing themselves to be three dark figures on horseback. The three rode straight to Carlos and Inéz and halted.

They were a striking sight. One man and two women, all riding black horses; all bundled up in black outfits, and all of them wearing black scarves wound like turbans around their heads and over their mouths. Only their eyes were visible. Two packhorses following behind them were heavily laden.

"It is a terrible day to be traveling," Don Carlos called out to them.

The three stopped, the man a bit ahead of the two women. The man moved his horse closer to Don Carlos, unwrapped the scarf from his mouth, and said, "Allow me to introduce myself. My name is Leandro de Luna, otherwise known as Leandro the Magician."

In response, Carlos replied, "My name is Alfonso Cabeza de Vaca, at present, though not for much longer, secretary to the governor of New Mexico Province. My companion is Señora Inéz de Recalde. How may we be of service to you?"

"I need directions to a stable for our horses and an inn for ourselves; however, first permit me to introduce my companions, Selena Torrez and

Mara Mata. We are entertainers. I perform magic and Selena and Mara dance. We are sometimes called the Trio."

"You could not have come at a more propitious time," Carlos told them. "You probably passed the annual supply caravan and the many colonists in it who intend to settle in Santa Fe. I'm sure once they reach here there will be a fiesta to welcome them."

The woman who'd been introduced as Selena now uncovered her face and addressed Carlos. "We know about the caravan. We joined them for the trip through the Jornada del Muerto, and in gratitude for the protection they provided, Leandro entertained them with a magic show. But we have saved the best of his offerings and our dances for here and look forward to performing for Santa Fe's citizens."

"I'm sure," Carlos declared, "your magic and dances will be very pleasant diversions from the hardships of life on New Spain's northernmost outpost."

"Do you and Señora Recalde have a household for which we might be invited to perform?"

"Regrettably not," Carlos replied. "As our names indicate, we are not married. Perhaps another year. Who knows?"

Inéz lifted her head, smiling, but with a warning note in her voice, "What Don Alfonso means is perhaps in another two, or three, or more years."

Leandro's eyes flitted between the two of them, and then he asked, "Where is everyone? The town seems to be deserted."

"This weather is scarcely such as to encourage people to be outdoors, wouldn't you agree?" Carlos replied.

"Then the fact that you're out makes you either very brave or very foolish," Leandro observed.

"We're probably a little of both," Carlos said. "We have happy memories of once being caught in a storm, but this sleet is too miserable, and I was about to walk Señora Recalde back to her residence."

"I apologize for delaying you," Leandro commented, "even though I'm sure I would find the full story of that storm of interest."

Carlos wondered whether Leandro's magic enabled him to see his and Inéz's auras. He hoped not. For his part he had been studying the trio of entertainers. He was surprised at how benign Leandro's aura appeared to be—at least at this moment. Its brightness fluctuated in intensity, shifting back and forth between light and dark shades and swirling about like clouds driven by wind. Mara's was also unlike any Carlos had ever seen, a luminous blue-violet, the farthest edge of a rainbow's shades. Selena's aura was the deep coral color of a sunset.

To return to safer topics, Carlos said, "You asked about a stable and an inn. They are not one and the same, though they are owned by two brothers. The stable is the large building you'll see ahead after you leave the plaza by the path on your left. It is owned by Arturo Barbon. He usually has at least three stalls available, though there will soon be intense competition for those places from colonists arriving in the caravan. If Arturo can't accommodate all five of your horses, I'm sure he can recommend someone else who might be able to help. Arturo can also direct you to the inn owned by his brother, Roberto. Whether rooms are available, I can't say."

"We can settle for one room, if need be," Leandro replied. "With apologies for keeping you standing here, I'd like to ask one more question."

"At your service, I'll be glad to try," Carlos said politely, though he had become impatient to get Inéz out of the sleet.

"Are there any skillful fencers in Santa Fe? I've not had a chance to practice for much too long a time."

A dangerous question, Carlos thought. "I wish I could help," he said. "In the past I enjoyed fencing a great deal, but the opportunity to do so hasn't presented itself of late; consequently, I'm both out of practice and overwhelmed with chores related to a new business I've started. I would not take any pleasure from performing poorly. Perhaps there's a worthy opponent for you among the large group of colonists that will arrive a few days from now."

"I hope so. We heard that one fellow, Marco Cabrera, is quite skilled."

Deciding that Leandro would eventually learn that he already knew Marco, Carlos remarked, "He's an old friend of mine. We fenced many years ago in Mexico City."

Mara Mata moved her horse closer to Carlos and Inéz. Her scarf covered all of her face except her eyes, which were startling—a vivid dark violet that stood out against the pallor of the narrow strip of her skin that was visible around them. Don Carlos flinched at the memory of his violet-eyed mistress, Violeta, that Mara's eyes brought to mind. Pulling her scarf down enough to be able to speak, Mara began, "I, too, hope you will attend our performances. One of the dances that Selena and I do is called *Duende*. It is done without any accompaniment by musical instruments except the beating of a pole on the ground. Many audiences find that our performances produce a mood of *duende*—a kind of spell, like an enchantment—in the onlookers. We will hope to evoke that mood in you when we dance for you and your friends."

Though Don Carlos maintained his polite manner, he made it plain that the interview had come to an end. "You can be sure that Señora Recalde and I will take a great interest in your performances and wish you every success, but you must excuse us. The Señora is shivering from the cold."

As the trio of entertainers moved off and Carlos and Inéz made their way to the Beltráns', Inéz whispered, "I was trying so hard to shield my face against the sleet I could barely look at them. What did you think?"

"I'm not sure," Carlos replied. "Their auras were unusual—Leandro's moved about like clouds on a windy day, Selena's was the coral color of a sunset just as the sun sinks, and Mara's was violet like the darkest color in a rainbow. Nothing about their auras suggested anything threatening. They didn't seem to connect with the dark omens I've been sensing. Nevertheless," he went on, "their names are somewhat troubling. Malvolio belongs to a group of sorcerers called the Moon Moiety, and two of the entertainers had moon elements in their names. Leandro's last name, de Luna, is obvious. Selena is a name sometimes used for a moon goddess, and Mara Mata—think of it; a *mata* is a bush, and since it's a name, that's what you hear. But the word also means 'kills.' Mara Kills."

"Was that what made you flinch when she spoke?"

"No," Carlos said, "it was a memory of that treacherous mistress of mine, Violeta, who betrayed me to Don Malvolio. You'll recall what I told you about her. Mara's eyes—their resemblance to Violeta's—startled me."

Inéz murmured something noncommittal about the possibility of two women both having violet eyes. "But," she went on with more animation, "what did you make of Mara's reference to *duende*? Isn't *duende* a word for a ghost or goblin?"

"Yes, and even the common meaning of 'ghost' identifies it with dark forces, but it has another meaning. *Duende*, as Mara Mata described it, is a state of enchantment created by the performer's magnetism. It's also said that to fully enter the state of *duende* one must come to the edge of death."

"Who says that?" Inéz asked.

"I heard it first from Gypsies when I was in Spain in the 1630s during my fourth life."

"Yes, but what does it mean? Is it a matter of speaking, or is it a reality, actually exposing oneself to the risk of death? Can one go too far into a state of enchantment and not come back?"

"Or," Carlos interrupted her, "does one go to the edge of death to gain power? To bring power back from the Unknown?" Something leaped in his mind, and he made a connection. "The Moon Moiety!" he exclaimed. "That might be the source of their power. They draw power from coming close to Death, and they use it to do harm!"

Carlos stopped in his tracks. The sleet, he irrelevantly noticed, was no longer falling and the heavy gray clouds were lightening. "If the magician or dancers go to the edge of death to gain their powers, that's Moon Moiety sorcery!"

Inéz only looked at him, but she felt the force of what he'd said.

"I have no direct experience of *duende*," he went on, "but I had always assumed that the death spoken of in relation to *duende* was a positive state — the death of the ordinary self that I experienced in Tantric meditation with Zoila, an awareness of the oneness of all things."

"You are such an optimist," Inéz commented drily.

They'd reached the Beltrán residence, and Carlos delivered Inéz to her kitchen door. "I won't come in," he said. "You need to get to work, and my housemates will be expecting me home for dinner. I hope you won't feel any ill effects from being out in this nasty weather."

"I'll be fine once I get inside. Please let me know of anything more you learn about the Trio." Smiling, her cheeks flushed from the cold, she opened the kitchen door and disappeared into the house.

6

Recognitions

As Don Carlos walked home he reviewed his first impressions of Leandro the Magician and the two women dancers. Except for the jolt he'd experienced on seeing Mara's eyes, he had been comfortable with, even attracted to, the three entertainers. Feeling rather pleased with himself, once he reached his little house he settled back and enjoyed the savory evening meal Diego had cooked for him and Pedro and María. After dinner he and his three friends did the dishes together and then sat by the hearth fire. Finally, observing that the next day would be busy, he excused himself, called Gordo to follow him, and went to bed. As was typical of him, Carlos dropped off to sleep almost as soon as his head hit his pillow.

Instead of sleeping deeply, he surfaced into wakefulness every hour or so. Shadowy faces and figures flickered through his half-awake consciousness until finally, when he was fully asleep, he dreamed of the first time he had come face to face with Don Malvolio. His body responded as it had at the actual scene in a previous life: his heart pounded and he feared for his life as he fought with Malvolio and saw him die at the hands of an enraged, knife-wielding woman. The violence of the dream brought Carlos, writhing and shuddering, back to consciousness. He lay in bed, a whimpering Gordo trying to comfort him, while he waited for his heart to stop pounding. The woman in the dream was an old woman, not a young woman with violet eyes and the strange name Mara Kills. But it must have been Mara and her violet eyes, Carlos thought, that had triggered the nightmare.

At breakfast, Pedro made one of his typically laconic statements, "Lots of work to do."

Deciding he could be just as taciturn, Carlos replied, "Yup."

"How did we get into this?" Pedro asked.

"I'm about to lose my job, and I needed another source of income. You're helping me keep a roof over our heads, mine, yours, María's, and Diego's. Don't worry. Once we finish these repairs, we'll become men of leisure, sitting back and collecting rent."

"I'll bet," Pedro replied, his skepticism obvious. They walked through still-slushy streets to Tercera and settled down to completing the final repairs on the house. The weather had improved significantly, and by midday the New Mexico sun poured into the protected alcove where they were working, warming them to the point that they were able to take off their coats. They took a short break for lunch and siesta and returned to work.

Fifteen minutes after they'd resumed work Leandro de Luna showed up. "Sorry to interrupt, Don Alfonso," he said, "but I am in need of some advice."

"We are at your service," Carlos replied, "but before we hear more let me introduce you to my friend and right-hand man, Pedro Gallegos."

As Leandro and Pedro shook hands, Carlos studied the magician closely. He was impressed by what a tall, broad-shouldered, and handsome man Leandro was. He looked positively striking in a broad-brimmed hat, a short cape, and a shirt with full bright-red sleeves—an outfit that struck Carlos as rather elaborate for the daytime streets of Santa Fe, but perhaps his intention was to advertise himself as Leandro the Magician. He had a way of looking directly into the eyes of the person with whom he was speaking, his eyes seemingly seeking information that was not superficially accessible. His stance had an alertness to it, as though he was prepared to move quickly if needed. These observations left Carlos with more conflicted feelings than he'd had after their first meeting. He still found Leandro's personality attractive, but he felt wary of the man nevertheless. "What can we do for you?" Carlos asked.

"Here's my problem, actually two problems." Leandro began. "Arturo Barbon was able to put up all five of our horses last night, but he's promised two of the stalls we used to other people for tonight and Saturday too. He said that you've recently bought property not far from his place and that one of the houses has five stalls in back of it. Is there any chance that I could put my pack horses in those stalls for two nights? I would pay you well, of course."

Don Carlos was reluctant to have his affairs and Leandro's become intertwined, but he could think of no reason why he shouldn't accommodate the man's request. He therefore gave his cordial assent. "You can certainly use those stalls until the future owner arrives with the annual caravan a few days from now. If it arrives tomorrow, we'll try to work something out regarding your horses. As for the price, whatever Arturo Barbon is charging you will be fine with me also. Either I or one of the friends who lives with me will bring some hay from our hayloft."

"That's very good of you," Leandro said. "Can we walk to the place together so I'll know where to bring my horses?"

"Of course," Carlos replied, and they began to walk in an easterly direction toward the Fernandez house. "Didn't you say you had a second problem?"

"Yes. As you suggested," Leandro began, "my two friends and I found rooms at the inn run by Arturo Barbon's brother Roberto. But did you hear about the fire at the inn this morning?"

Carlos shook his head and was about to ask for more details when he saw Inéz coming toward them down the lane from the plaza. They stopped and waited for her. "Ah!" Leandro declared gallantly. "Here comes that beautiful friend of yours to brighten our day." Inéz smiled, accepted the compliment gracefully, and fell in step with them as they began walking again.

"Leandro was just going to tell me about a fire at the inn," Carlos said to her.

"Oh," she said to Leandro. "I hadn't heard. What happened? I hope you and your friends are all right."

"The three of us had just finished breakfast and were about to leave the dining room when we saw smoke pouring out of the kitchen. The fire was soon put out, but Barbon told us that he won't be able to serve meals again until tomorrow morning at the earliest."

"Ah!" Carlos said. "So you must be wondering where you can eat tonight."

"Yes. Barbon says there's no other public meal service in Santa Fe."

Carlos exchanged a glance with Inéz, seeing no way out of offering hospitality. "I guess it's either your place or mine," Carlos suggested.

"I can't offer the Beltráns' hospitality," Inéz said. "They're having guests tonight, your stepbrother and his wife, along with some of Joaquin's junior officers, a sort of farewell dinner. That's why I came looking for you to tell you that I'll be too busy cooking to join you for our usual afternoon walk. I'll give Diego a recipe for some large but simple dish he can prepare."

"That sounds good," Carlos agreed, and then added, "Leandro, please take that as your invitation to my place at eight, not the most fashionable hour, but we rise early to start our workday."

Leandro hesitated. "I feel we're imposing on your good graces. I didn't intend to do that."

Carlos took refuge in politeness to cover whatever his real feelings might have been. "Think nothing of it. Diego will be pleased to cook for guests, and everything will be quite simple. You are most welcome."

Inéz turned to go, and Leandro again expressed his gratitude. "You have gone beyond anything we could expect. I hope you'll let us give a free performance for you and your friends soon."

Inéz nodded and headed back toward the Beltráns' at a brisk walk. Carlos watched her figure retreat along the lane for a moment and then told Leandro, "I should warn you that I don't have a formal dining room in my small house. The four of us—myself, Pedro and his wife María, and our young groom, Diego, who also does quite a bit of the cooking—crowd around a kitchen table for our meals. That's well short of an elegant setting for an evening meal in Santa Fe."

"I'm embarrassed that we're imposing on your hospitality. Your generosity is much appreciated. And I've kept you from your work here long enough. If you can quickly show me where to stable our horses, I won't take any more of your time until dinner."

Carlos and Leandro continued walking east along the Santa Fe River from Tercera toward the Fernandez place. When they passed the lane that led north toward the plaza, he pointed out his small house near the plaza's south side. Across from them on their left was a larger house that Inéz had once occupied with Dr. Loreto Tiburcio, who had passed himself off as her father. "That's known as the Tiburcio place," he told Leandro. "You might inquire about renting the house, which has been vacant since Tiburcio fled town in disgrace. It's recently been purchased by a friend of mine and Inéz's named Lucila Archuleta. Up ahead you can see the house we call the Fernandez place. In addition to the five stalls in back of the house it has adequate turnout."

Don Carlos sensed that something else was on Leandro's mind, but he waited to see if the magician would say anything and finally he did. "Your having spoken of this Dr. Tiburcio," Leandro said, "opens the way for me to make a confession of sorts. I didn't mention it yesterday, but I had heard your name before. Indeed, it was a surprise that of all the people we would meet on arriving in Santa Fe, the first we encountered were you and Señora Recalde, the only two of whom we had prior knowledge."

"Oh?" Carlos said with what he hoped indicated nothing more than polite interest. "How did you happen to hear of us?"

"Selena, Mara, and I traveled to Nombre de Dios recently at the invitation of a local rancher who wanted us to perform at his daughter's wedding. While there, we met a strange bald-headed man. It seemed he had arrived in town not long before us and had set up practice as an herbalist. He introduced himself as Dr. Loreto Tiburcio, and he had nothing good to say about Santa Fe. He told us that he had lived in Santa Fe with his daughter, an attractive young widow, and had a thriving medical practice until an arrogant aristocrat with powerful political connections—and he named you—had sought to seduce his beautiful daughter—whose name was Inéz de Recalde. He claimed, quite angrily, that you had spread lies about his medical practice, and that he had had to flee town to avoid arrest and certain imprisonment, even though he was innocent of any crime."

They had reached the Fernandez house and had stopped in front of it.

"Talk about spreading lies!" Don Carlos exclaimed indignantly. "The facts are that Inéz is not his daughter and that the local authorities sought to question Dr. Tiburcio because he had knowingly been prescribing a dangerous substance that made his patients dependent and in some cases much sicker. These facts are well known in Santa Fe. You don't need to take my word for it."

Leandro seemed to accept this. "I'm glad to know the true story. He struck the three of us as a rather unpleasant fellow."

"Yes," Don Carlos replied. "He was a thoroughly bad man. I hope we've cleared that up. But let me ask you a question in return. I'm puzzled why you and your companions have traveled all the way to this remote outpost of New Spain, a backwater by any definition. Surely, there are many larger towns and cities where you could earn a better living as entertainers."

"We are itinerant entertainers and don't necessarily go to places with large populations. Being on the move from town to town, large and small, is normal for us. But it's true we had special reasons for coming to Santa Fe — no, that's not quite right; more accurately, for traveling northward. As I told you, our original destination was Nombre de Dios to perform at a wedding. We were also interested in the town because we had heard that a man named Don Mateo Pizarro, said to be an unusually skillful magician, lived nearby. I thought it might be useful for me to study with him, and we were going to look him up once we reached the town. But upon our arrival we learned that he had died — been killed, evidently — under mysterious circumstances. We asked around and met an Indian, Felipe Gómez, who told us that Don Mateo was an evil man who had enslaved the Indians of a nearby village. Felipe also said that he had told this story to a Spaniard who was passing through Nombre de Dios, and that the man had said he would try to do something about the Indians' situation. Shortly after that Don Mateo was found dead.

"We were curious," Leandro went on, "about what had happened to Don Mateo, and we thought the Spaniard might have the answer. Although this Felipe didn't know the traveler's name, he was able to tell us that the man had passed through Nombre de Dios twice, first while traveling south, the second time northward, apparently headed home, and that he'd left his horse at a local stable where Felipe worked. We located Manuel Tapia, the stable's owner, and asked whether he knew the traveler's name. He seemed uncertain which traveler we had in mind — 'There are so many,' he said — but eventually told us it might be a traveler who introduced himself as Ricardo de Silva." (This was the alias Manuel and Carlos had agreed upon to disguise his role in two incidents known only to them.)

"Based on this information," Leandro continued, "we decided to continue northward, earning our living as we went along and inquiring whether anyone had heard about Don Mateo's death or this Ricardo de Silva. We've now visited every town on the Camino Real from Nombre de Dios to Santa Fe, the last settlement on Spain's northern frontier, without learning any more."

Don Carlos knew he was the man in question, and he decided that the best defense against discovery would be to boldly admit to that fact. With a laugh, he declared, "That stranger who Felipe described as passing through Nombre de Dios twice last year may well have been me, although there seems to be some confusion about names. I have no idea who this Ricardo de Silva might be."

Leandro looked astonished at Carlos's admission. "I remember," Carlos continued, "meeting Felipe. Poor man! He was desperate, he said, to help a relative he believed was being threatened by Don Mateo, and he pleaded with me to do something. I felt sorry for him and I told him I would investigate the matter. My inquiries, such as they were, turned up nothing but unbelievable rumors. And even if they were true, what could I do? I grew up in an aristocratic family in Mexico City, educated by Jesuit tutors. I've led a pampered life, pursuing women and—until now, as you see, when I have to work at something other than a desk job—enjoying various leisure activities. I certainly wasn't about to risk my neck by confronting a magician who was reputed to have powers beyond those of an ordinary man."

"You strike me, on first meeting, as being very capable," Leandro observed.

"Thank you," Carlos said. "I won't deny that I'm resourceful. But it made no sense to involve myself in a situation that was possibly dangerous and, in any case, the business of local authorities."

"Of course you are right," Leandro replied.

To change the subject, Carlos gestured toward the Fernandez house. "Here's the house I spoke of. The stalls are ready to be occupied. I'll send Diego over with hay for your horses if you'll take care of feeding them on the schedule you usually follow. Now I must excuse myself. I've found our conversation of great interest. I look forward to seeing you and your two friends at dinner tonight."

As he walked the short distance to his home, Don Carlos thought he'd handled Leandro's questions as well as possible. He'd admitted a lot without acknowledging anything except coincidences. Still, the fact that the three entertainers had some sort of knowledge of Don Mateo was disquieting. Did that indicate a connection with the latter's mentor, Don Malvolio, or did Leandro's interest in Don Mateo simply arise from a desire, as he had said, to learn more about the magician's craft?

7

Guests

As Carlos helped María set the kitchen table for dinner, he was overcome by an unfamiliar emotion, embarrassment. During his years in Santa Fe, he had never acquired the material goods needed to give a proper dinner party. "Nothing matches," he observed. "There are only four plates that match; the rest are strays."

"You've always lived like a bachelor, and below your class and station," María said.

"Are you reproaching me?"

"No, just stating the obvious. You grew up in Mexico City as the son of a marquis and heir to his fortune, and you must have enjoyed a lavish style of living. At the very least, I'm sure that the dinnerware was of high quality and that everything matched."

"True enough. If anything, my father's preference was for living above our means. He owned a large mansion in an upper-class district and had all the servants required to maintain it. Here in Santa Fe I've never felt the need to surround myself with a rich man's material goods. Besides, after my quarrel with my stepfather, I foreswore any claim to inheriting a title or a fortune, even if any funds were left after he used my inheritance to set up my stepbrothers in society."

"Surely you would change your style of living if you married," María said.

"There's no prospect of that happening in the foreseeable future."

"Hmmm," María said.

"Inéz says she won't consider marriage as of now, possibly ever."

"Do you believe everything a woman tells you?" María murmured.

"I believe Inéz. She's straightforward and honest."

"That's so," María agreed. "She's told you how she feels now. But it's the man's role to woo his beloved, and you aren't devoting much effort to getting her to change her mind. That's what courtship is all about."

Before Carlos could offer a defense of himself, Pedro entered the kitchen from the adjoining two rooms that he and María occupied. He was carrying a bench. "We don't have eight chairs in the house," he said to no one in particular. "María and I can sit on this bench."

"Eight chairs?" Carlos replied, partly out of embarrassment that none of the six chairs they'd collected matched, and partly out of puzzlement. "Why eight? There are only seven for dinner, the four of us and the three entertainers."

"And Inéz makes eight," María declared.

"Inéz told me that she had to cook for a dinner party at the Beltráns'."

María shook her head. "She said she was negotiating with Ana Lugo to serve the Beltráns' guests and that Lucila Archuleta's cook, Nina, had agreed to supervise the final stage of the cooking. She ought to be here any minute."

The sound of footsteps crunching through the remains of the snow outside confirmed María's words, and Inéz entered the kitchen. She was carrying a basket with a wool coverlet over its contents. "María," she said, "please take these rosquillas from me while I get out of my cloak and boots."

Carlos moved forward to help her shrug off her heavy cloak. "Your being able to join us is a pleasant surprise."

She'd seated herself to take off her boots and replace them with indoor shoes. "You didn't really think I was going to leave you alone with those two gorgeous dancers, did you?"

"I wouldn't have been alone with them," he observed in a reasonable tone of voice.

"Dear Alfonso," she said, standing up and brushing his cheek with her still-chilly cheek, "I just want to be sure that you behave yourself, not that I can claim any right to ask you to."

"I have eyes only for you."

"I won't hold you to promises you can't keep," she declared with a laugh, moving immediately to the kitchen hearth. "Everything looks good, Diego," she said. "You've become a first-rate cook." He grinned happily at her compliment.

A knock at the front door of the house indicated the arrival of their guests. A bit flustered by events so far, Carlos exclaimed, "They've shown up at the front door!"

"Most guests assume they should arrive by way of a front door," Pedro observed drily.

"Grab a candlestick, Pedro, so we can guide them through the hallway." He also picked up a candlestick and they made their way into the hall from the kitchen and down the otherwise dark hallway to the house's seldom-used front door. The three entertainers were standing on the veranda, waiting to be let in. "Welcome!" Carlos declared, standing to one side as they entered.

Pedro led the way down the hall. More embarrassment! Small wooden boxes filled with crystals and semi-precious stones lined the sides of the hallway, slightly impeding movement. "Watch your step," Carlos called to his guests. "We seldom use this hallway, so I store my collection of crystals and gemstones in here."

Everyone made it through the obstacle course safely, and the hosts stepped forward to help their guests with their cloaks, Pedro aiding Leandro, Carlos Mara, and Inéz Selena. As the cloaks were being hung up in the hallway, Gordo, fat and friendly as always, made his appearance, wagging his tail in welcome.

"And who's this?" Leandro asked, bending to stroke the little dog's head.

"Gordo is the name we gave him," Diego replied. "Although when we first adopted him, he was anything but *gordo*."

Ushering them all into the kitchen, Carlos did a proper round of introductions. It was the first time he had seen Mara and Selena since the day they had arrived in the plaza on horseback and muffled in black cloaks and scarves against the sleet. He was surprised to find that Mara was quite small in stature, with a heavy head of hair and a heart-shaped face that appeared to belong to a bigger person. Selena, taller, darker, and more animated, seemed the older and more dominant of the two. Both women were wearing everyday dresses, made festive for the occasion with bright scarves tucked around the edges of their bodices. Their hair was tied back with colorful ribbons and their hands and wrists flashed with rings and bracelets of amethyst and rose quartz. Leandro was wearing the same outfit that he'd worn earlier in the day, the most dramatic element being the puffy red sleeves of his shirt. It was the first time Carlos had seen him without a hat, and he was struck by Leandro's curly dark-blond hair and brown-flecked green eyes: another Basque, he wondered?

Before Carlos could give seating directions, Inéz took over. "I suggest that Alfonso sit at the far end of the table and Leandro at the other end. I'll sit on Alfonso's left with Diego beside me, the seats nearest the hearth, from which we'll serve. María can sit on Alfonso's right and Pedro next to her. Selena and Mara, please take the chairs on either side of Leandro. I'm sure everyone's hungry, so Diego and I will serve Diego's split-pea soup, while Alfonso pours everyone wine."

Carlos proceeded to pour. Of course, the wine glasses didn't all match. He finished pouring at almost the same moment that Diego and Inéz finished distributing the soup. Carlos then proposed a toast. "Welcome to Santa Fe!" was his simple salutation.

"Thank you so very much for taking in three homeless wanderers," Leandro replied, and Mara and Selena each offered a "thank you" too.

Carlos noticed that Inéz's seating arrangement had placed the two women guests as far as possible from him. But if her intention had been to prevent flirtation between them and Carlos, the distance presented no obstacle to Selena's flashing and flirtatious dark eyes. Carlos could not but respond whenever she turned her face in his direction—it would hardly have been polite to look away! But he was not the only object of her attention; she praised the soup extravagantly and complimented Diego, calling him "the chef" and giving him a radiant smile, which caused him to blush and duck his head.

"Don Alfonso," she went on, "tell me about your crystal collection. As you can see from my jewelry"—she extended her right hand, with its two rings, toward him—"I love precious and semi-precious stones."

"There's not a lot to tell about the stones," he replied. "For several years now I have been Governor Villela's private secretary. After five days each week of being desk-bound by my bureaucratic chores, I feel like a caged bird with an urgent need to fly free outdoors. Nearly every weekend, I take a long ride in the countryside. I watch for places where crystals or non-crystalline gemstones are found."

"Crystals and gemstones," Selena observed solemnly, "all have special qualities."

"I've heard that," Carlos replied.

"But surely you must know that the presence of those stones in your hallway has a benign effect on you and everyone who lives here."

"I wear lots of amethyst," Mara chimed in, speaking for the first time, "because it's known as the protective stone, and I like to feel protected."

"Selena and I will always protect you," Leandro said, gently placing his left hand on the back of her hand. Mara gave him a grateful look. Carlos wondered what else, if anything, was in back of that exchange.

Selena slipped a ring with a pink stone off her right hand. "Let me give Inéz something as a gift to both her and Alfonso. Inéz and I are almost the same size," she said, turning toward Inéz. "I believe this ring will fit her." She handed the ring to Diego and he passed it to Inéz, who tried it on. It was a perfect fit.

"You're too kind," Inéz murmured. "What is this stone's name and special quality?"

"It's rose quartz and it's called a love stone. Reading people's emotional states comes naturally to me, and I could see from the moment we met yesterday that you have a great capacity for love."

"Did Alfonso put you up to this?" Inéz asked, glancing questioningly at Carlos.

"Not at all!" Selena exclaimed. "But I can also see that he loves you."

"Yes," Mara added, "but don't expect Selena not to flirt with him, or with Diego for that matter. Not to do so would be out of character."

Selena laughed, not taking offense.

"She's a hot-blooded Seville girl with some Moorish ancestry," Mara went on, as though that explained everything. "And Inéz and Alfonso make a very handsome couple."

"All of us agree," María commented, nodding at Pedro, who nodded also.

Inéz immediately steered the conversation to a new topic by asking the three entertainers about their travels. "You described yourselves as itinerant performers, and in traveling to Santa Fe you've certainly come to a remote town. Do you always seek out such faraway places?"

Leandro laughed. "We enjoy visiting new places and always have. Selena and I met years ago in Spain while I was studying with a master magician in Seville. He saw her dance and concluded that I would be more successful if I offered public performances that mixed magic and dance, not that the two are separate, at least in the form that we pursue. He also recommended that we come to New Spain, where he felt our performances would be appreciated, and that's what we've found. Generally, we seek out wealthy patrons who hire us to perform at their homes for special occasions. Our most recent presentation was at Señora Emilia Ceballos's hacienda in Bernalillo. She's a widow and close to seventy, but still full of gusto and vitality."

"We all left hoping that we'd have half as much life in us when we're her age," Selena added.

"How did Mara come to join you?" Carlos asked.

"Mara," Leandro said, "is the New World's gift to us. My teacher had been to New Spain many times over the years. On one such visit he met Mara while she was still very young, and he was captivated by her astonishing violet eyes. He concluded that she would make a perfect third member of our little troupe. Three, after all, is a more stable number than two."

"And your teacher's name is what?" Carlos inquired.

"He has a public career, a quite distinguished career, I might add. But magic for him is a deeply private matter, so he insists that when we refer to him as a magician, we simply call him 'Master' and not reveal his actual name. He has no desire to display his skills in public. His pursuit of magic is more akin to a religious endeavor, a quest to make the unknown knowable, to discover the links between heaven and earth. It was his very high-minded approach to knowledge that first drew me to him."

"That's fascinating," Carlos said, genuinely interested. "Can you say more? Has he discovered principles that organize reality that you can apply in your performances?"

Leandro looked at him sharply. "I see you are informed about these matters."

"Only in the most general way," Carlos replied, retreating quickly and hoping to cover his tracks.

"Leandro," Selena interrupted. "Perhaps you've already said too much." And then she added, almost apologetically, "We performers must have our secrets, since an air of mystery enhances, indeed inspires, *duende* in the performers and the audience."

"There's that word again," Inéz observed. "I'd like to understand it better."

"The best means to that end," Leandro replied, "would be to attend one of our performances. Can you suggest some individuals or families who might enjoy an evening that mixed a demonstration of magic with magical dancing?"

After a few moments of silence, Inéz spoke up. "Let me mention it to my employers, the Beltráns. Señora Beltrán's sister, brother-in-law, and their four children will be arriving soon with the supply caravan. Cristina, that is, Señora Beltrán, has been wondering what sort of festive welcome we could give the Trigales family. A performance by your troupe might be perfect for that purpose."

"Ah!" Selena murmured. "The Trigales family. A pleasant couple with lovely children. We met them during the part of the trip when the three of us temporarily joined the caravan for protection from Apache war parties. I believe that they would receive our offerings enthusiastically."

"Not everyone does—receive your performances well?" Inéz asked.

Selena laughed. "No, some conservative, very straight-laced people find the Gypsy elements in our dances too sensual."

"The dance of life *is* sensual," Leandro declared. "But I hope you'll soon have an opportunity to judge for yourselves. When is the caravan arriving?"

"Tomorrow afternoon," Pedro replied.

"Then perhaps," Leandro said, "we can give a welcoming performance for the Trigales family as early as tomorrow night."

"I'll ask," Inéz told him.

"To change the subject somewhat," Carlos said, "I'm wondering what else you'd care to say about your adventures throughout your travels."

"This might strike you as an odd response," Leandro declared, "but one of the things I enjoy is collecting stories, some of which I use in my performances. Have you heard, perhaps, of Pedro de Urdemalas?"

"Yes," Carlos replied. "He's mentioned by one of my favorite authors, Miguel de Cervantes. Pedro is a *pícaro*, a cunning rogue, a trickster who delights in his ability to outwit his bosses and masters and profit from his schemes."

"What fascinates me about him," Leandro said, "is his popularity as a folk hero; there are endless accounts of his escapades. Why is this? He's certainly not a good man, or a hero. He's out for his own interests."

"That's exactly it!" Carlos broke in. "He's unashamedly, even joyfully, looking out for his own interests, and for ways to get the better of the rich and powerful. That's why he's a hero of folk tales—he's a scamp who turns the tables on the bosses and gets away with it! Tales like that gratify the hearts of people who are mistreated or generally looked down upon by those who are higher up on the social ladder."

"Give us an example," Pedro said. "I want to know about this fellow who shares my name."

Addressing Leandro, Carlos asked, "Would you mind letting me tell my favorite Pedro de Urdemalas story?"

"Not at all. If it's one I've not heard before, I'll be in your debt for adding a new story to my collection."

"A good name for this story," Carlos began, "might well be 'A Tale of Pigs' Tails.' It seems that our scamp, Pedro, is working for a rich farmer who owns a large herd of pigs. This is hard, smelly, poorly paid work. Pedro is not happy, but he needs to eat. What else can he do? Then it begins to rain. It rains and rains. Pedro is up to his knees in mud in the pig pen. What is worse, when the rain finally stops, the mud only gets deeper and thicker from the pigs wallowing in it. Suddenly, like lightning, an idea strikes Pedro! He goes to town, seeks out the butcher, and offers to sell him forty pigs at a very reasonable price. 'And at that price,' he says to the butcher, 'I'm sure you won't object if the pigs have no tails.' The butcher, who is a phlegmatic man, doesn't care if the pigs have tails or not, and asks no questions.

"Pedro goes back to his boss's place, rounds up forty pigs, and cuts off their tails. He delivers the pigs to the butcher, who pays him the agreed-upon price.

"Pedro returns to the farm and tells his boss that forty-one of his pigs have foundered and died in the deep mud of the pig pen. The farmer rushes to the pen and sees dozens of pig tails sticking up out of the mud. He and Pedro carefully inch toward the closest one and, after tugging mightily, they manage to pull the pig out. It is dead, of course, Pedro having killed it and buried it in the mud. The farmer, seeing all the other tails protruding from the mud, assumes that each tail is also connected to a dead pig. Pedro's boss tells Pedro that he is out of a job. But Pedro goes off whistling because he has made a big profit from his scheme."

"Does Pedro ever change his ways?" Inéz asked.

"Not in this story," Carlos replied. "But I think he may reform and become a good man in the end of other stories."

"I don't think that's believable," Mara declared. "A leopard can't change its spots. People don't change."

"Mara! What a pessimist you are!" Selena exclaimed.

"I'm not a pessimist," Mara asserted. "I just prefer the more realistic version of his legend, in which he never reforms. He remains a scoundrel even after he dies."

"How does that story go?" Inéz asked.

"Eventually Pedro dies," Mara replied. "He's sent to Limbo, but he makes himself so obnoxious there that he's thrown out and ends up in Purgatory. Once again he makes such a nuisance of himself that he's kicked out and goes to Hell, from which he's also expelled for being annoying."

"What gets him thrown out of all these places?" Inéz asked.

"In the first version I heard," Mara replied, "every time he's sent to a new place, he gets thrown out because he cheats at cards, even fooling the Devil himself."

"My favorite variation," Selena said, "has him getting thrown out because he's an inveterate seducer, even cuckolding the Devil, which is why Satan has horns."

"Mara and Selena know that I have the best version of all to tell," Leandro declared.

"I don't think it's particularly suitable for polite company," Mara protested.

Leandro looked around questioningly. "Go ahead," Carlos said. "I think we've drunk so much wine" — they had downed three bottles and were starting a fourth — "that we've passed the point of caring too much about proprieties."

"Well," Leandro said with a devilish grin, "in my version, Pedro is thrown out of each place — Limbo, Purgatory, and Hell — in quick succession because he has the smelliest, biggest farts of any man, dog, or elephant. Even Hell's brimstone odor can't suppress the stink of Pedro's farts."

Leandro's version generated a round of hearty laughter. When it had subsided, Mara said in a serious voice. "My favorite story is *La Vida de Lazarillo de Tormes*. Lázaro, as he is called in the story, is born to a family so poor that stealing is a necessity. They are good people, they work hard, but they still don't have enough to eat. Lázaro's father works for fifteen years in a mill, until he is caught stealing grain. He confesses, is punished, sent into exile, and dies honorably in a foreign land. Lázaro's mother then marries a black man who works in a stable; to feed his family he steals from the horses, their bran, their brushes, their towels, their blankets, and even their shoes. He, too, is caught and punished.

"Lázaro's mother takes him and his younger brother and goes to work in a tavern. A blind man comes to stay at the inn and asks the mother to give him the ten-year-old Lázaro as a servant to guide him. She asks the blind man to treat Lázaro well, and the blind man replies that he will treat him not as a servant but as a son."

Mara had warmed to her story in the telling of it, and her eyes now flashed with indignation. "That blind man was not only a liar," she said, "but he was abusive and miserly and played cruel tricks on Lázaro and gave him so little to eat that Lázaro had to steal from him or starve. So, in order to survive, Lázaro learns to be as cunning and crafty and thieving as the blind man. He finally escapes from his blind master and becomes the servant of a priest, who is even stingier with food than the blind man was, and Lázaro is forced to develop even more ingenious ways of stealing from him in order to live.

"Well, the story goes on and Lázaro has several more masters, and learns from each about the hypocrisy and duplicity of the world. But Lázaro wants to better himself, and finally he finds a respectable job as a town crier. He rejoices in his good fortune and overlooks what is bad, and lives in peace with all. So Lázaro is my hero," Mara concluded, "because he overcame so much, and his good nature wasn't ruined by all his misfortunes."

Selena sighed, "Oh, Mara," she said, reaching across the table to stroke Mara's arm.

Later, after the three entertainers had left, Carlos walked Inéz back to the Beltráns'. "What do you think?" he asked.

"About the three? I enjoyed the evening with them. They're unconventional and a bit wild compared with us, but they're fun, and they seem to have a warm relationship with each other. I'm eager to see their performance."

"Nothing untoward about them?"

"Nothing significant. Although the effect of the rose quartz ring—its warmth, which it still retains—is a little spooky."

"I keep coming back," Carlos said, "to the story about their master who won't let them speak his name. The man lives a double life, a public one unknown to us, and a secret one in which he has magical powers that weren't described in any detail."

"A man with a double identity and magical powers," Inéz replied, nudging him gently in the ribs. "I agree that's highly suspicious. Could such a man be trustworthy?"

He laughed. "I don't know about this man they call Master, but if you're wondering whether a man who leads a double life can be trusted, you can always call my example to mind. And rest assured that both Don Alfonso and Don Carlos love you."

"Does that mean that I'm being wooed by two men?" she asked. But before he could reply, she added, "And don't give me your answer now. Your explanation might take too long and I'm a working girl who has to get up early tomorrow."

8

Newcomers

Saturday, the day after the dinner party for the three entertainers, was sunny. The temperature rose into the mid-forties, and the remaining snow and slush on the streets vanished. In the mid-morning Carlos stopped by the Beltrán residence, but found that Inéz was too busy to spend any time talking further about the night before. He walked to the house he called

Tercera and helped Pedro and Diego complete a few final repairs there. After lunch Carlos had nothing in particular to do, and he spent the rest of the day relaxing. He read in the materials on mysticism that Father Stefano had given him and took Eagle out for a short ride. Leandro came by mid-afternoon to say that the dining room at Barbon's inn was back in business; consequently, he and his women friends didn't need to find another place to eat.

Sunday morning was also pleasant. As usual, Carlos escorted Inéz to Mass. She rushed off afterward, explaining that her employer, Cristina Beltrán, was eagerly awaiting the arrival of her sister, Bianca Trigales, her husband, and their children. Everyone who worked for the Beltráns, men and women alike, was scrambling to get the large house the Trigales family would occupy into the best possible shape. Carlos walked home, changed out of his Sunday suit, and set to work on a long-contemplated project to beautify his small house.

As he began work on his project, the midday sun was striking the western face of his house, warming him sufficiently that he took off his coat. Gordo was lying contentedly in the sun on the house's front porch as Carlos dug in the ground on one side of the veranda. He intended to make a small bed of desert plants along that side of his house. Pausing in his digging and looking up for a moment, he saw the lead wagons of the annual supply caravan entering the plaza less than a block to his left. "Come on, Gordo," he said to his little dog. "Let's go see who's arriving."

Wagon after wagon rolled into the plaza, filling it with a crowd of horses, mules, oxen, and newly arrived colonists, including a small contingent of soldiers. Residents of Santa Fe came in great numbers too, seeking out people they knew or simply watching excitedly the arrival of so many newcomers.

Carlos was on the lookout for several parties that Pedro had located when he'd ridden out to the caravan's final camp to see if he could recruit immigrants who might wish to buy or rent Carlos's three properties. The heads of two family groups, the Ortegas and the Díazes, had expressed a strong interest in two of the houses, Segunda and Tercera, that Carlos had recently purchased. The plan for today had been for Pedro and Diego to meet the two families before they reached the plaza and take them directly to the houses in question. The places were close together and only a short distance south of the plaza, near the banks of the Santa Fe River. Since Carlos didn't spot Pedro and Diego among the arriving immigrants, he assumed they had been able to fulfill their part of the day's plan.

His job was to find another newcomer, Dr. Fabio Velarde, a physician who'd expressed an interest in renting Carlos's third property, the Fernandez place, which Carlos had partly furnished with items Inéz had given him.

Before he could ask about Dr. Velarde's whereabouts, he saw Inéz waving to him at the edge of the crowd. He hurried over to her and said, "This must be my lucky day, bumping into you so unexpectedly."

"I'm glad to see you too," she replied. "I have to rush off. I just wanted you to know that Cristina has enthusiastically endorsed the idea of having our three itinerant entertainers perform for us tonight in honor of the Trigales family's arrival in Santa Fe. The plan is for the Beltrán and Trigales families to have an early dinner, followed around eight by the entertainment. Of course, you're invited. Can you make it?"

"With pleasure."

"Then I'll leave you to your business. I've asked one of the Beltráns' grooms to find Leandro and his women friends to tell them about our arrangement. I'll see you tonight."

Carlos immediately returned to the business at hand and began to push his way through the crowd that was jamming the plaza. Gordo, who was exited about all the activity, followed closely on his heels. He heard someone calling his name from off to one side, "Alfonso! Alfonso! Over here!" This proved to be his former fencing partner from Mexico City, Marco Cabrera, the son of New Mexico's new vice governor and the man who was to replace Carlos as personal secretary to the governor.

Marco wove his way through the crowd. Upon reaching Carlos, he gave his old friend a warm embrace. "I'm so glad to meet you right away. You look great, Alfonso. I only hope I feel as good as you seem to after a couple of years in Santa Fe."

"I trust the climate will agree with you, Marco, as it does with me, even these chilly winter months."

Marco dismissed the subject of the climate with a wave of his hand. "Before anything else," he began, "I want to say that I had no idea when I agreed to take the position of secretary to the province's governor that I was pushing you out of a job. I don't know what to do about it now, since I gather you've already pretty much wrapped up your business as secretary. Is there no turning back—perhaps to some other appointment?"

"No, Marco. That wouldn't interest me. I've recently launched a new career as a real estate investor, and if all goes well today, by sunset I'll have sold one house and rented two."

"I'm very glad to hear that, Alfonso. The situation with the secretary's post has been bothering me. Come meet my parents, and while we're on the way over to their carriage, tell me about that very attractive woman you were talking to a moment ago. Is she a love interest of yours?"

"Yes, although for complicated reasons at the moment, I'm not courting her so much as being her friend."

Marco replied with a smile, "That seems a drastic change for you, Alfonso. I well recall how energetically you wooed the young women in our circle in Mexico City."

"The less said about my past amorous adventures to Inéz—her name's Inéz de Recalde—the better," Carlos cautioned his friend, "though in fact she knows all about my previous affairs. She's a young widow and the chief cook in the household of one of Santa Fe's richest merchants, Javier Beltrán. Javier's wife's Cristina is the sister of Bianca Trigales, whom you doubtless met during your trek here."

"Yes, Bianca, Raul, and their children are a lovely family. But come meet my parents. They're only a few steps away."

Formal introductions were quickly accomplished, with Marco describing Carlos as "my old fencing partner, Don Alfonso Cabeza de Vaca." Carlos was quick to offer his sincere congratulations to Salvador Cabrera on his appointment as vice governor of New Mexico. He was also immediately struck by the great difference in age between Salvador, who must have been in his fifties and who didn't appear to be in good health, and his wife. Regina Cabrera could not have been much older than her stepson, who, like Carlos, was in his early twenties. In contrast to her husband, Regina Cabrera exuded life energy, displaying a golden aura that fairly sparkled in the midday sun.

Carlos was about to excuse himself to look for Dr. Velarde when the latter showed up. He warmly greeted the Cabreras, and Carlos saw sparks of interest pass between the doctor and Regina Cabrera that he knew meant trouble. He immediately separated the two of them by inviting Dr. Velarde, whom he was soon calling Fabio, to follow him to the Fernandez place to see if it suited his needs.

Fabio collected his three horses, a riding horse and two packhorses, and followed Carlos to the Fernandez house. They found Leandro distributing hay to the two horses that Carlos had told him he could stable there. Introductions followed, and Fabio and Leandro immediately seemed to like each other. Fabio told Leandro that since the stable in back of the house had room for five horses, Leandro could use two for his horses, and Fabio's three horses would occupy the remaining stalls.

"Has everything been arranged for you and your two friends to perform tonight at the Beltráns'?" Carlos asked Leandro.

"Yes, we're looking forward to it," Leandro replied, and then, indicating the doctor, he went on. "It occurs to me that Dr. Velarde may not want to dine alone his first night in Santa Fe. Would you," Leandro asked, turning to the doctor, "like to join me and my two companions for dinner at the inn tonight? Perhaps you can even attend our first performance, if Don Alfonso will ask the Beltráns and their Trigales relatives on your behalf."

Dr. Velarde and Carlos agreed, and the evening's program was set.

The rest of Carlos's afternoon was devoted to his real estate business. He went first to Segunda, where Diego had already shown the Díazes around. The Díaz family consisted of an older couple, Atilio and Caterina, who were a tailor and a seamstress, and four grandchildren, two girls and two boys, orphans between the ages of ten and eighteen. The elder Díazes struck Carlos as pleasant, responsible people.

Tercera was next door, separated from Segunda by about thirty feet. Elías and Ernesto Ortega, both furniture makers, were brothers who wanted to buy the house and had the wherewithal to do so immediately. They also were likely to do well, since many of the recently arrived colonists would need furniture. The Ortegas had two male apprentices, who in a neighborly way were helping the older Díazes unload the wagon containing their goods.

After an early dinner, Carlos put on his second-best suit and walked to the Beltrán residence. Everyone else, including Fabio Velarde, had already arrived. Cristina Beltrán, after greeting Carlos warmly with the remark that as Inéz's friend he was practically part of the family, introduced him to her sister Bianca and Bianca's husband, Raul Trigales. Raul, Cristina went on, was in partnership with her husband Javier, planning to start a large-scale horse-breeding business that would sell horses to new ranches being established in the Rio Grande valley. Carlos, who immediately liked Raul, expressed both interest and concern, and fell into an animated conversation with him about the number of new ranches that were likely to be established and whether or not the ongoing Apache raids on the outer regions of the valley might deter settlement.

Inéz came over to them with the four Trigales children in tow and asked to introduce them to Carlos. They were charming youngsters. All four were lively, polite, and happy. The eldest was a boy, Cristofer; there were two girls, Carmela and Constanza, identical twins that Carlos found it difficult to tell apart. Anton, the youngest boy, had a particularly winning smile. Carlos, having had little experience with children, was not a good judge of such matters, but he estimated that Anton was about five and Cristofer no more than twelve.

Inéz announced that the entertainment was about to begin and asked everyone to sit, the adults in a row of chairs, the children in front of them on the floor.

Carlos had no sooner settled in a chair than the guests' attention was arrested by a staccato beating of drumsticks on wood, and Leandro made a spectacular entrance from a side door in a series of cartwheels that carried him across the room. He was wearing leggings of contrasting colors—his left leg in yellow, his right in blue—and had a yellow sash around his waist. His torso was loosely covered by a long-sleeved white shirt. He pulled up short at the far side of the room, reached for and donned a red-lined black cape, and with all the gusto of a skilled showman announced, "Ladies and gentlemen! Boys and girls! Let us entertain you with the mysteries of magic and the magic of dance! I guarantee you won't be disappointed!

"I need," he began, "two young assistants for my demonstration of magic. Do I have any volunteers?"

Anton bounded forward before Cristofer could stand up. Carmela—Carlos thought it was Carmela, anyway—was almost as quick to respond. "What are your names?" Leandro asked, leaning forward so they could whisper their names in his ear. "Anton! Constanza!" he announced. Oh well, Carlos thought to himself, I had the wrong twin.

"You are well-mannered, tidily dressed children," Leandro told them, "but it's still my duty to remove objects that you have slyly hidden in your hair, doubtless with the intention of playing tricks on this poor old fellow, Leandro the Magician." With that, he commenced a series of lightning-fast movements, pulling object after object out of the children's hair and ears: a two-reales coin, a poker chip, a tiny handkerchief, two marbles, and a small amethyst crystal. He then stepped back and looked approvingly at the youngsters. "Ah! That's better! I apologize for catching you out, but we have to start our pursuit of magic without any hidden objects.

"Now, to begin." Stepping to a small wooden table that had been placed in the center of the room, he gestured toward three upside-down walnut shells set on it. "Please point to the shell that has a marble under it," he told Anton.

"I have no idea," Anton said.

"An excellent answer," Leandro replied, "because it's an honest answer.

Now let me show you," and he picked up a shell to reveal that it had a marble under it. "Next," he announced, "I'm going to shuffle the shells around. Keep your eye on the one with the marble under it, and when I stop, tell me where the marble is."

It was difficult to keep track of the shells as Leandro moved them rapidly here and there. Nevertheless, once Leandro stepped back, Anton pointed to a shell on the right. Leandro picked up the shell and put on a very disappointed face. "Too bad. No marble. But there are only two left, so you have a better chance to guess right now. Try again."

Anton pointed to the shell in the middle. Everyone groaned when Leandro picked up the shell and no marble was there. "All right," Leandro said, "let's give someone else a chance. How about this pretty girl, Constanza — your sister? — who's standing next to you. Tell me young lady, which shell is the marble under?"

"That's easy," she replied. "There's only one possible choice left."

"Then pick that shell up." No marble was under the shell. "What a disappointment," Leandro observed, "but then you must realize that I'm not called Leandro the Magician for nothing. I admit that I've tricked you. I made the marble disappear. If you doubt me, Constanza, pick up each of the shells. Perhaps that sneaky marble changed shells."

Constanza did as she'd been instructed. No marble showed up. She looked puzzled and a bit frustrated.

"I don't like to disappoint anyone, so let me find the marble for you." Leandro began moving the shells around very fast, pausing now and then to lift one, and shaking his head when no marble showed up. "Perhaps we're looking in all the wrong places," he said. "Constanza, please allow me to check your ear again. The marble may have hidden itself there."

"Aha!" he exclaimed, reaching under her hair to her ear and pulling out a two-reales coin. Placing the coin in her hand he said, "Good discovery, but we're looking for a marble. Wait a moment!" And he reached over to her ear again, seemingly tugging something that had been hidden there. "Maybe I've got it," he announced triumphantly, only to shake his head in disappointment when the object turned out to be a ring. He put the ring in Constanza's hand. "Let's give it one more try," he declared. "Perhaps the marble is in your other ear." Sure enough, he discovered a marble — the same one, as far as anyone could tell — in her other ear. "At last," he announced, with a sigh of relief. "I thought we'd never catch up with that marble." A round of warm applause broke out.

"For my next demonstration—I don't call them tricks, as ordinary magicians do—I am going to mystify you quite thoroughly." Leandro waved his hand and Selena brought in a narrow box with a handle on one end and finger-sized holes across from each other on each side. She placed it on the table, and Leandro announced, "The handle of this box is attached to a sharp blade that can chop carrots and any other object placed in one hole and out the other. Let me demonstrate."

He inserted a carrot in one side of the box and out the hole on the other side. With a dramatic cry of "Hack!" he pushed down the handle, and the exposed end of the carrot, apparently cut by the blade, fell to the ground.

Smiling in a beguiling way at his audience, he asked, "Who would be willing to put his or her finger into the box? A silver peso"—one materialized between his thumb and forefinger, a large coin that gleamed like the face of the moon—"to any takers!" There were no volunteers. "What's a finger lost for one of these beautiful coins?" he said in a coaxing manner. "I assure you that it's completely safe. Don't let your eyes deceive you. I, Leandro the Magician, will protect you." Still there were no takers.

"All right," he continued, "I will demonstrate, though once I've shown you that there's no danger, it will be too late to volunteer in order to collect the peso." He put his forefinger in one hole and out the other side of the box. Lifting the lever on the end of the box so that the sharp blade gleamed in the candlelight, he started to lower the lever. A gasp went up from the onlookers. The Trigales twins turned away, not wanting to see.

Leandro, playing the crowd deftly—he was a superb showman, Carlos thought—hesitated. "Do you think I should go ahead? Perhaps I should test the box with another carrot. This he proceeded to do, and the end of the carrot on the far side of the box once again fell to the ground, a clean cut. "Hmm," he muttered, quite audibly. "Maybe this is more dangerous than I thought. What do you say, should I go ahead?"

Cries of "No! No, don't do it!" were heard all around.

"But if I am the great magician I say I am, then I must prove myself, no matter what the risk. Here goes," he said, inserting his finger in the box. "I will lower the blade, come what may, at the count of three: One! Two! Three!" Whereupon he lowered the lever forcefully. "Ouch!" he shouted, but then laughed and withdrew his finger, still in one piece, from the box. "Magic triumphs again," he declared. Applause and laughter, the latter, it seemed to Carlos, mixed with relief, broke out.

Don Carlos had watched Leandro's performance closely in order to determine if any of Leandro's magic depended on sorcery. Though skillfully executed, the tricks, Carlos concluded, were the products of sleight of hand and required nothing truly magical. Don Carlos felt a grudging admiration for Leandro's approach. Even if he were a sorcerer, Carlos thought, he is too clever to use a sorcerer's techniques in a public setting.

Leandro again addressed the crowd. "Thank you so much," he said, bowing and smiling. "The best is yet to come, a dance performed by my two beautiful assistants. The name of the dance is *Duende,* and it is done in a style known as *seco* or 'dry', that is, without any musical accompaniment."

With Cristofer helping him, Leandro moved the table against the far wall of the room, and Mara and Selena then made their entrance. Both dancers had extended the line of their eyes outward with kohl and wore their hair pulled back from their faces. Their dresses — Mara's was indigo and Selena's emerald green — had wide, elbow-length sleeves and full, soft skirts that stopped two inches above their ankles. On their feet they wore black shoes with solid, slightly curved heels.

The two dancers positioned themselves at the center of the semi-circle of onlookers and stood erect and very still, hands on their hips, gazing above the heads of the audience.

A hush fell in the room, a quiet so complete that Don Carlos, whose hearing was very keen, could hear the sound of Inéz's in-breaths next to him. Only when the stillness seemed to deepen even further did Leandro, who had picked up a five-foot-long staff, strike it on the floor. He then commenced striking the floor repeatedly at a slow pace. On the third strike of the staff, Mara and Selena hit their left heels in unison on the floor, reinforcing the jolt Leandro delivered each time he pounded his staff.

From that point, Leandro continued to strike the floor again and again, and the two dancers echoed his strikes, but not every one. Nor did the women stamp their feet every third beat. The pattern of Leandro's strikes in relation to the dancers' heavy steps was uneven, and it took numerous repetitions — each round done at a slightly accelerating pace — for Don Carlos to realize that the pattern entailed a twelve-beat sequence, with the third, sixth, eighth, tenth, and twelfth being the beats the dancers echoed.

The steady rhythm of staff and heels beating had a powerful effect. The loud, percussive sound reverberated through the onlookers, drawing them into the dance not just as onlookers but also as instruments vibrating with the pounding beat. Never, as the pace of the beat accelerated, did the expressions on the dancers' faces change, remaining somber and strangely impassive. After a time Mara and Selena began to lift their hands until their arms were raised straight up above their heads. Then they began to turn in place counterclockwise, at first slowly and then more rapidly, never losing the count or the beat.

With their arms still above their heads the two women began to sing, a song composed of cries and sustained high notes rather than words. Now, turning so fast that they seemed to be whirling in place, they opened their mouths wide and made a loud, high-pitched trilling that sent shivers down Don Carlos's spine. Eerie, chilling, haunting, otherworldly, he couldn't think of one word that described the sound — it was all of those and more.

At that moment Don Carlos's sorcerer's vision took over, and he saw the auras of the dancers. Selena's sunset-colored aura had spread outward to and into the audience, engulfing the onlookers in a cloud of luminescent red. Mara's violet aura spread upward. Though Don Carlos knew Mara was at the core of the aura, what he saw was not the shape of a body but a column of violet light that rose to the ceiling of the room. The column was not static. Like a flame, it throbbed and pulsed to the *seco* beat of Leandro's accompaniment.

With the twelfth beat of a final sequence, the dance ended as suddenly as it had begun. If the silence that preceded the dance had seemed profound, the silence that followed it was more silent yet — not just a hush of expectation but the absence of sound as though, for a moment, sound itself no longer existed. The effect was dizzying, stunning, hypnotic. That's *duende*, Carlos realized.

It took a few minutes for the audience's mood to return to normal sufficiently for them to break into applause. "Thank you very much," Leandro said, as he and the two dancers bowed. "I know this has been a long and possibly fatiguing day after, for many of you, a very long and tiring trip to Santa Fe. Therefore, Mara, Selena, and I propose that we do only one more dance tonight and save others for what we hope will be future times when we entertain you. This second dance is quite simple to learn and we hope that after a quick demonstration everyone will join in. We call it Spinning. Allow Selena and me to demonstrate as Mara accompanies us with the *seco* beat."

Mara picked up the *seco* pole as Leandro and Selena faced each other, arms outstretched, hands on each others' waists. "What we'll do," Leandro announced, "is turn together, first clockwise, and then after eight *seco* beats — one, two, three, four; one, two, three, four — reversing direction for eight beats or eight steps in a counterclockwise direction. We'll start slowly so that everyone can see precisely how the dance goes."

Turning in place at a slow, almost stately pace didn't look too difficult to Carlos. Leandro and Selena went through the complete pattern, clockwise and counterclockwise, three times, maintaining eye contact throughout. "The only danger here is that one or both partners may become dizzy," Leandro announced. "If that happens, simply move more slowly or stop altogether.

"Now," he continued, "let's divide into pairs. Anton and your magician partner Constanza can be one couple. Cristofer and Carmela another. Husbands and wives—Bianca and Raul, Cristina and Javier—are natural partners. The young couple seated next to each other to my left "— this happened to be Fabio and Elena—"should become a pair. Selena and I will start the dance by pairing with our friends Alfonso and Inéz, Alfonso partnering with Selena and Inéz and me forming another pair. The four of us—one partner in each pair familiar with the dance—will lead off. After two or three circles and reversals, the pattern of the dance should be even clearer and everyone else can join in."

Carlos delivered Inéz to Leandro and turned to Selena, who put her hands on his waist. Following suit, he did likewise. "The only firm rule," Selena said loudly enough for everyone to hear, "is that you must maintain deep eye contact with your partner."

Initially, Mara beat the *seco* pole to a very slow rhythm. Gradually the pace of the beat accelerated, and as it did so the centrifugal force of the movement began to be noticeable. Selena tightened her hold on Carlos's waist, pulling his lower body closer to hers while their upper bodies arched slightly backward. Her eyes were fixed on his in complete concentration. As they spun at an increasingly faster pace, Carlos returned Selena's concentrated gaze until he found himself falling deeper and deeper into her eyes.

Deeper and deeper he plunged until the mood of the night suddenly changed again. Anton and Constanza fell, having become too dizzy to stand up, Cristofer and Carmela followed suit almost immediately, plopping down to the floor on their backsides and dissolving in giggles. Their Aunt Cristina called out, "I can't keep it up," and moved to a chair to steady herself. The room filled with laughter from adults and children alike.

Selena's face broke into a smile and she stopped moving. Carlos was surprised to find that he wasn't at all dizzy. His strongest response was that he found it difficult to take his eyes away from hers. Their outstretched hands were still resting on each others' waists. Finally, Selena pulled away from him, laughed, and said, "If you're not going to kiss me, you may look now to see how your friend Inéz is doing."

He followed her gaze and saw that Inéz was resting her head on Leandro's chest. Then, with a smile, Inéz withdrew from him and said, "Thank you for holding me up; a moment longer and I would have been down on the floor with the children."

Thank yous and farewells followed in quick succession. Leandro and the dancers left first, inviting Carlos to join them in walking to the plaza and on to their respective homes for the night. Carlos demurred, saying that he wanted to linger briefly to speak with Inéz. Fabio, who was about to spend his first night in the Fernandez place, left with the three entertainers. Watching the foursome from a front window of the Beltrán house, Carlos and Inéz saw that Mara, Selena, Fabio, and Leandro were walking four abreast and arm in arm. The four of them broke into a series of skipping steps. Listening closely through the closed window, he could hear that the skipping was accompanied by singing, "Tra-la, tra-la, tra-la."

"They make a lively quartet," Inéz murmured, "playing together like children. I suppose that's another expression of *duende*."

"Yes," Carlos agreed, in a somewhat bemused voice. "*Duende*. Do you like it?"

Inéz lifted her eyes and gave him a sideways glance. "Yes," she said.

The *duende* mood was still on them, encircling them but strangely keeping them apart from one another. With an effort, Carlos broke it. "I thought Leandro's magic was skillfully done," he began, "but it was fairly standard the-hand-is-quicker-than-the-eye trickery. I didn't see any sign that he used sorcery. On the other hand, the *Duende* dance was extraordinary. Did you notice the dancers' auras?"

"Yes," Inéz replied, matching his tone as the mood of *duende* dissipated. "I saw them clearly. Selena's aura spread outward and engulfed the whole room, while Mara's was like a blue flame that reached the ceiling."

"Yes, it was astonishing. And how did watching the *Duende* dance affect you?"

"I was drawn into it," she said. "But I didn't feel that being drawn into a *duende* mood was in any way threatening. So don't worry...." She trailed off, turning her eyes aside again. Then she came back to him. "I'd like to talk longer, especially to discuss what happens in *duende*, but that will have to wait for another time. I have my usual problem of needing to get to bed in order to rise before dawn to start my cooking chores."

"With great reluctance, I'll let you do what you must," Carlos told her. Cristina Beltrán and Bianca Trigales still being visible in an adjacent room, he discreetly brushed his cheek to Inéz's in a formal farewell.

9

Mentors

Monday morning, as he had almost every day for nearly a year, Don Carlos got up before dawn to meditate for at least an hour. His mood was somber. Only yesterday he had learned from Marco Cabrera that their Jesuit tutor, Father Stefano, Carlos's mentor in Christian mystical literature, had died just before the winter caravan had left Mexico City. His other most trusted mentor in his quest to live wisely, Zoila Herrera, the woman who had introduced him to Tantric meditation, had also died, lost at sea, in the preceding year. He was beset by a sense of loss.

Although Don Carlos had never heard of the practice of the student sitting in meditation following the death of a beloved master, he intuitively was drawn to honor Father Stefano in that way. So, with a feeling of reverent affection, he began to sit. He settled into an upright, cross-legged posture, quieting his mind by focusing on his in- and out-breaths. Before long, he fell into a deeper stillness as an inner phenomenon he called his 'body pulse' took hold — an awareness of his blood coursing outward to every extremity of his body and then, like a wave, pulling back — that he never failed to find engrossing and quieting.

What emerged from this stillness was startling, something entirely new to his experience while meditating. He began to feel slightly seasick, as if he were on a rocking boat, or as if the earth were swaying under him. Carlos sat with it, waiting to see if it would continue, change, or simply go away. It eventually became an attack of vertigo so severe that he was forced to open his eyes and focus them on a spot on the wall across from him. The thought crossed his mind that the sensations he was feeling somehow arose from the *duende* state he'd been drawn into the previous night, but his practice was to avoid discursive thought while meditating, and he let it pass. Gradually, the vertigo receded, though when he tentatively stood up, he still felt out of balance. Calling to Gordo, he put on a coat and went out for a walk. The early dawn sky and the sight of his dog cavorting happily cleared his head. The shadows lifted.

When he returned home, even though it was still early for breakfast, Carlos found the other members of his household — in truth he regarded them as his family — sitting down to eat. María hadn't yet left for work, and Diego reported that he'd already fed the horses and turned them out into their corral. Pedro looked up from his bowl of cornmeal mush and asked, "How was the performance last night at the Beltráns'?"

Carlos briefly described Leandro's tricks and reported that he was an adept showman. "The dancing," he said, "was quite" — he paused, searching for the right word — "impressive." But he paused again, finding himself reluctant to call up the images of the dances. Finally, he forged ahead with a general description. "There was a lot of spinning in place, both when Mara and Selena danced and in another dance when the rest of us joined in. The children got dizzy and fell down, and everyone laughed."

Carlos was saved from having to say more by a knock on the kitchen door. He got up, opened it, and found José standing there. He refused to come inside, indicating that he wanted to talk about a private matter. Don Carlos stepped outside, closing the door, and José got right to the point. "I hope," he said, "you can ride with me to Tesuque today and speak with Old Man Xenome. I visited him yesterday and told him about meeting Uncle Owl. Based on what Uncle Owl told me, I asked Grandfather Xenome whether he would help me study to become a shaman. He replied that he's too old and crippled to do everything that's necessary and suggested that you might be able to help. But he wants to meet you before anything's settled."

"Good!" Don Carlos exclaimed. "Let's go this afternoon."

Carlos went back inside, finished his breakfast, and went to call on Inéz. She wasn't in the kitchen, so he walked around the house to the front door and knocked. To his surprise, Elena rather than a servant answered the door. "Inéz is in the dining room, showing the new maid how she wants the table set for lunch."

Elena gestured toward the dining room and started to leave him to find his way. He sensed that she was feeling that he couldn't possibly be interested in her. "Wait, Elena," he said. "I wanted to ask you about last night's performance. Did you enjoy it?"

"Not everything," she replied, "although the magician's performance was good and the dancing was special. The trilling sound the two women made sent chills up and down my spine, and even when they stopped, I felt as though my head was still spinning."

Inéz had come into the room, and having heard what Elena had said, she asked, "What was it that you didn't enjoy about the evening?"

Elena shrugged. "Mostly I felt left out of things. I had to dance with a man I barely knew, and then he left without even saying good night to me." Elena paused and looked at Inéz appraisingly. "I hope you don't mind me speaking frankly, Señora, but I was jealous of you being picked to dance with the magician. I should have gone over after the dance and spoken to him. That way he might have noticed me, and possibly even learned my name."

"There will be other performances, Elena," Inéz suggested as gently as possible.

"No. I missed my chance," she said rather sullenly.

Inéz was not one to give up easily. "Leandro is said to be an avid fencer. Perhaps you could ask him to give you lessons. I'm sure he would be glad to earn a few pesos doing so."

"I've never fenced or done anything physical."

"No problem." Inéz's persistence was, Carlos felt, admirable. "Why don't I give you some introductory lessons in fencing? I'll bet you'll pick it up faster than you expect. This house has a fine fencing strip in the patio. That's a perfect place for a practice session. We could start today after lunch when everyone else is enjoying their siestas."

"I couldn't," Elena protested.

"Yes, you can. This is your chance to learn, and you don't want to pass on two such opportunities in less than twenty-four hours."

Elena, with obvious reluctance, allowed herself to be persuaded. "What should I wear?"

"Wear a top that permits freedom of movement. Pantaloons will be fine for bottoms for the exercises I have in mind. Eat as little lunch as you can, nothing if possible. You won't want to fence on a full stomach. If you get hungry, drink a lot of water. Our fencing session can begin around two."

As Elena went off down a hallway, Carlos turned to Inéz. "It seems that we both have plans that will interfere with our usual two o'clock rendezvous. José has asked me to go to Tesuque this afternoon, and now you've made a date to tutor Elena in fencing. It also seems that both you and I are taking on mentoring roles—you with Elena, me with José."

"Mentoring him in what?"

"Becoming a medicine man. I believe he has talent, and it's part of his heritage too."

"Are you sure that's wise? You're trying to keep your brujo identity a secret. Doesn't helping José study to be a medicine man risk exposing your brujo self?"

"I suppose there's some risk, but I'm willing to try to help him; unless, that is, you say I shouldn't."

"No, I think you should. Just be ..."

"Careful," he said before she could finish the phrase.

"Two minds with one thought," she said with a smile and turned to leave.

Crossing the plaza in the direction of his home, Carlos saw Leandro coming toward him. Carlos waved hello and went over to speak with the magician. "That was an excellent performance last night," he said. "My compliments on a very entertaining show."

"We enjoyed ourselves too," Leandro replied. "The Trigales and Beltrán families are very nice, and afterward Raul Trigales asked us to perform for them as soon as they can get their house in order. As you probably know, it's that big place west of the Presidio." He paused for a moment. "I hope you weren't annoyed by my arranging the partners last night so that I danced with your friend Inéz and you with Selena."

"Of course not," Carlos said in as offhand a manner as he could muster. "We both enjoyed ourselves." He turned immediately to another topic. "I wanted to ask you whether you've contacted my friend Lucila Archuleta about the possibility of renting the Tiburcio place from her."

"As a matter of fact, we settled that piece of business this morning. My friends and I don't expect to become permanent residents of Santa Fe, but Señora Archuleta is willing to rent us the house for a month or two. She's already had a few renovations made and plans to undertake more extensive improvements soon so that she can get a higher rent or a better sale price for it."

"I have mixed feelings about that place. I might have tried to buy it myself except that I didn't want anything to do with a house that has such painful memories for Inéz."

"Didn't you used to visit her there?"

Carlos laughed. "There are no secrets in this small town, and you're learning them swiftly. Yes, I often visited her there and did so quite openly. You'll find the house has an excellent fencing strip in the patio. We used to practice our swordsmanship there, though I'm sure common opinion among the town's gossips was that we were up to something else."

It was Leandro's turn to burst out with a hearty laugh. "I can tell you that if I were alone with a woman that beautiful—those gray eyes of hers are captivating—I would certainly be up to something else."

Carlos said rather coldly, "Our activities there were limited to fencing."

Leandro immediately backed off. "Of course," Leandro replied. "But now," he added, "I'm confused. When we first met, you told me that you're out of practice, but you just said the two of you met to fence."

"I am out of practice. All my bouts with Inéz took place at Dr. Tiburcio's house while she still lived there, which is more than six months ago. We haven't fenced since."

"Is she a challenging opponent?"

"Very, at least when she's in practice."

"Everything you say only increases my curiosity about your friend. Would you object if I invited her to fence with me?"

"No," Carlos replied, although he didn't like the idea at all. "But I hope you'll wait to ask her until I've first had a chance to resume fencing with her. After that you're welcome to invite her to fence; just don't expect her to come to her former house to do so. She won't go there."

"Given my wish to fence with her," Leandro said, "I hope the two of you will resume your bouts soon. And I completely understand her reluctance to visit a place that evokes bad memories. But we're not without alternatives. In talking with Señora Beltrán last night, I learned that there's a fencing strip at her house. Perhaps Inéz and I could fence there."

The man is well informed for someone so new to town, Carlos observed to himself after they'd parted.

Opening the front door of his house a few minutes later, Carlos heard giggles coming from the kitchen. One of the voices was Diego's, but he didn't recognize the other. He went to the kitchen door and looked in to find Ana Lugo helping Diego chop some vegetables. He wasn't pleased and his displeasure showed in his voice. "What's going on?" he said sternly.

"Ana is helping me chop vegetables for tonight's dinner," Diego replied sheepishly.

"This isn't good. The two of you shouldn't be alone in the house."

"You used to visit Inéz and the two of you were alone at her house."

"Allow me to observe," Carlos replied, "that the difference between my visits to Inéz's place and you and Ana being alone in this house ought to be obvious. Señora Recalde is a widow, and though town gossips wrongly assumed that we met for an intimate liaison, such relationships between a single man and a widowed woman are taken fairly lightly—not approved, but regarded as natural rather than scandalous. Consequently, the reputation of neither party is injured.

"Ana, however, is an unmarried woman whose good reputation is her most valued possession, and it must be protected so that her virtue and respectability are beyond question. Rather than alluding to my relationship with Inéz, you might remember my friendship with Camila. You'll recall that we were careful never to have Camila into our house. We socialized here, but always on the front veranda. All I'm asking is that you follow that example. Be practical. Put on your winter coats and take the vegetables out to the front porch. Use the little table near the front door for a chopping block. Visit for as long as you want, but do so in plain sight where all anyone can say is an approving 'It's sweet that Ana and Diego are friends.' And that is how I feel about your friendship. I wouldn't want anything to harm it."

"You're right," Diego said, a bit grudgingly, "though you didn't have to take so long to make your point."

"Fair enough," Carlos said, with a laugh to show he wasn't offended. "Now let's collect the vegetables and take them to the front porch. I'm looking forward to seeing what's for dinner."

Carlos had just finished his lunch when José showed up, and half an hour later Don Carlos on Eagle and José on Inéz's horse Alegría left town on the road to Tesuque Pueblo, some ten miles north of Santa Fe. The two men rode side by side at an easy walk, enjoying the movement of their mounts as they covered the miles.

Finally, Don Carlos broke the silence. "How well do you know Old Man Xenome?"

"Not well. I was born at Tesuque a few years after the Pueblo Revolt. My father died when I was a little boy, and my mother took my sister Ana and me to live in Santa Fe."

"What happened when the Spanish returned?"

"My mother was one of the captured Indians put into service to a soldier. He was a kind man, but after five years he left."

"What then?" Carlos asked.

"My mother found a job cooking for a Spanish family. Bernadino de Sena, the blacksmith I work for now, lived with the same family."

"So you were living in Santa Fe when you came of age to learn the secrets of the kiva and to go on a vision quest?"

"That's right. I had no one to teach me those secrets."

"I've heard," Carlos ventured carefully, "that some Pueblo people shun Indians who choose to live in Santa Fe and other Spanish towns, but that doesn't seem to have led Old Man Xenome to refuse your request that he train you to be a medicine man. If you don't mind my asking, I'm wondering why he was receptive to your request."

"He is my great-uncle by marriage. His wife, who died long ago, was my grandmother's sister. He is also the great-uncle of my cousins Rubén and Lázaro. Those family ties count for a lot. He also feels a debt to my uncle on my father's side, a Pueblo medicine man who was executed when the Spanish returned." Using a term of respect reserved for Pueblo elders, José added, "Grandfather Xenome said that by teaching me the Old Ways, he will honor the memory of my uncle, who was his friend."

"How old is Xenome?"

"At least sixty, though he looks older. He's had a hard life."

"Was he in favor of the Pueblo Revolt?"

"Yes. He hated the brutal way the Franciscans tried to destroy the Pueblo religion. He was proud that several men from Tesuque were messengers for the Pueblo rebels."

"Did he see no good whatsoever in the Spanish?"

"He thought they had brought many good things with them, especially horses, sheep, cattle, and pigs."

"I've heard that Popé, the medicine man who led the Revolt, became almost as autocratic as the Spanish that he and his supporters had driven out of New Mexico."

"That's true, and Grandfather Xenome had a falling out with Popé."

"Why was that?"

"Popé demanded that Pueblo people who had taken Spanish names stop using them. He also said that Pueblo couples married by Catholic priests didn't have valid marriages and they should separate. Grandfather disagreed, and Popé's followers accused him of being a traitor. He feared for his life, so he left Tesuque and hid in the mountains. He stayed in a secret hiding place for several years, until things calmed down."

"Do you know where his hiding place was?"

"I don't think anyone knows. He's kept it a secret."

Don Carlos and José arrived at Tesuque and were greeted warmly by José's cousin Rubén, who had been helping Carlos renovate his houses. After a brief exchange with him, the two visitors rode to the edge of the settlement where Old Man Xenome's small house was located. Don Carlos greeted Xenome with a traditional Tewa salutation, "*Bepuwaveh,*" to which Xenome replied in kind.

Don Carlos had brought the old medicine man gifts: a small pouch of high-quality tobacco he'd obtained from his next-door neighbor Gilberto Barrera, a sharp steel knife that he hoped Xenome would find useful, and three deep green crystals he'd collected near Nombre de Dios. Old Man Xenome declared himself very pleased with the gifts. He thanked his visitors and then asked José to step out in order to allow him to have a private conversation with Don Carlos.

After José left the room, Xenome began without preamble, "Although Pueblo people do not always regard a visit from an owl as a positive omen, I feel that the owl who spoke to José should be listened to. José has asked to learn the Shaman's Way, and I am willing to pass on to him the knowledge I have that can be spoken and practiced in this house. But as you can see, I am too crippled to travel with José to the sacred places where he must go to meet the spirits. For that, another guide is needed."

Xenome paused and looked slightly to one side of Carlos. "You are a Spaniard, and ordinarily a Spaniard would not accompany a young Tewa seeker on his quest; yet the owl who spoke to José said that he could share his message with you. It seems that you may have a role to play in José's quest—otherwise, why would Uncle Owl have included you in his message?"

Xenome paused again, even longer than the first time. He picked up one of the green crystals Don Carlos had given him and said, "Tell me where you found these crystals."

"They're from near Nombre de Dios, and very rare in that area. I was told they grew in only one place, a small cave near the entrance to a canyon."

"You were told?" Xenome's eyes had narrowed, and he was giving Don Carlos a piercing look. The old man still had power when he needed to summon it, Carlos thought.

Don Carlos knew he was being tested, and answered truthfully. "A female cougar came to drink at a mountain spring where I was sitting. I asked her if she knew where crystals of this type were found, and she led me to the cave."

"Have you often spoken with animals or had them speak to you?"

"A few times."

"Which animals?"

"Once with a screech owl, and twice to cougars, the one near Nombre de Dios and a second near here who claimed his grandfather had spoken with you long ago."

Xenome smiled. "I remember that old cougar. In our youth we were close friends. Cougars are, in fact, my totem animals. Did this screech owl live close to a clear spring-fed pool near here?"

"Yes, just a short way to the east of the main road."

"Did you find crystals nearby?"

"Yes. High on the cliffs above the pool. I could tell it was a sacred spot, visited often over a long time, perhaps hundreds of years, by shamans and vision seekers."

"And how did you find the Spirit Ledge?"

"I had ridden to the pool one day and happened to look up at the cliffs. At the place you call the Spirit Ledge I could see a luminosity that I've found is associated with dense concentrations of crystals. I climbed up and confirmed my intuition."

Xenome fell silent for some time. Finally, he spoke. "You have skills — speaking with animals and locating crystals — that I associate with a shaman's powers. Would you consider yourself a shaman?"

"I have no direct knowledge of the Shaman's Way and therefore wouldn't call myself a shaman. My mentor trained me in the realm of transformations, and I became skilled at changing myself into birds, especially raptors. But when I talked with the mountain lion at the Spirit Ledge, I took the form of a porcupine, gambling that he wouldn't attack me."

Xenome seemed amused and gave a gruff laugh. "But you still haven't," he pointed out, "said what you would call yourself."

"I'm going to take a chance here because words can easily be misunderstood. I am a brujo. I'm aware that that word is usually associated with witches and sorcerers who do evil things. But I belong to a small group of brujos, all trained by one master, and our guiding principle is 'Do no harm.' I cannot teach José the Old Ways as you can, but I can promise to accompany him on trips to sacred places and to share with him wisdom that is beneficial to all creatures."

After a brief pause, Xenome spoke. "You can help José with trips into the high country that I can no longer make. I will give him the other teachings here. Shall we call him back?"

"In a moment. I would like to ask your opinion on something. About a week ago I had a feeling that darkness, an ominous and malicious force or energy, was approaching. I saw the ghosts of tragic times wandering the plaza at Santa Fe and I was weighed down with what felt like impending danger. One possible source of this danger is a sorcerer named Don Malvolio. Long ago I prevented him from gaining possession of a jewel, an emerald, which had great power. In obstructing his ambition, I earned his enmity, and he has pursued me ever since with the intention of killing me. Perhaps he is on my trail again. Or perhaps I'm imagining the whole thing."

"Every night," Old Man Xenome began, "I sit outside at dusk. That transition time from light to darkness is the period of the day when all nonmaterial entities, good and evil, are most active. For the past week or ten days, I have noticed that the sky to the south—toward Santa Fe—has been darker than at any time since the Spanish returned and slaughtered so many of my people. I can't tell you what it means or what its source is, but yes—they are dark energies."

"Ah!" Carlos said, strangely relieved to have his apprehensions confirmed.

"Whatever manifests itself," Xenome declared, "I am confident that your warrior spirit will rise to meet it. I believe you have a mountain lion for your totem. Let me give you something that will help you ward off evil. Open that small bag on the shelf where the incense cup sits."

Don Carlos did so and found a copper bracelet consisting of nine square links, eight with a geometric design, the ninth bearing the image of a mountain lion growling defiantly, its paw raised, claws extended, poised to strike a blow. "Go ahead," Xenome told him. "Try it on."

The bracelet fit perfectly. Don Carlos struggled to find words to express his gratitude for such a gift. Finally, he said, "It's beautiful. I've never seen anything like it."

"Yes," Xenome replied. "It's unique. Let me tell you about it. As a young man I made a long journey, walking for many days across the mountains toward the setting sun. Eventually I came to a broad, shallow canyon in which there were ancient ruins. I found the bracelet there, in a ceremonial site our ancestors, the Old People, had abandoned long ago. I knew then that the mountain lion was my totem animal."

"Surely you should keep something that's obviously so precious to you."

"No," Xenome said. "I want someone to wear it whose youthful energy will rejuvenate its powers in these difficult times. Now please call José back."

When José returned, Xenome addressed him. "We've decided to divide your training into two parts. Once a week you will spend a day with me, and I will tell you stories that embody the wisdom of the Old Ways. This I promise to do until I die.

"Don Alfonso will take responsibility for accompanying you into the deserts and mountains where powerful spirits reside—some dangerous, others benign. You must learn to deal with both. I have three quests in mind.

"The first will be the easiest. Make a vigil at the place we call the Spirit Ledge. Attune yourself to the energies of the place and the echoes of the many seekers who've visited it in the past.

"Next, I want you to identify your totem animal. Don Alfonso has some experience with this type of quest, and he will help you find a place where your totem animal will reveal itself to you.

"Finally, I want you to visit the sacred site where I hid for many years when my enemies sought to harm me. It is an ancient village site on top of a mesa. Despite the passage of many centuries, it is still a place of power, and one of its two kivas is in fairly good condition. Sleep every night in that kiva. It will have a profound effect on your dreams. Return there often until a personal vision of your purpose in life comes to you. On your next visit here I will describe in detail how to find this sacred place. Now I must ask you to go. Although I'm tired, this has been a happy day for me. Thank you for your gifts."

Don Carlos and José mounted and rode back to Santa Fe in silence. Words weren't necessary.

10

Provocations

Tuesday morning, the day after his trip with José to Tesuque, Don Carlos got up feeling invigorated by the afterglow of his conversation with Xenome. He settled into his meditation and before long reached a quiet state, albeit not the profound silence he always hoped to attain. That didn't particularly bother him. The depth of his meditations wasn't something he controlled. It was more accurate to say that profound silence came to the waiting meditator, rather than the meditator achieving deep silence through force of will alone.

When his period of meditation had ended, he got up with a feeling of contentment and went into the kitchen to make himself breakfast. Diego soon came in from the stable and reported that he'd fed the horses and turned them out into the corral. Don Carlos poured out a bowl of hot cornmeal mush he'd made for himself and cut a slice of bread for Diego to dip in his mug of coffee. They sat in silence until Pedro let himself in. The first glimmers of light were showing in the winter sky.

Pedro helped himself to a mug of coffee and immediately launched into the topic that was foremost in his mind. He reported that the Ortega brothers were ready to pay the full asking price Carlos had set for Tercera and wanted to buy it without further delay. "Dr. Velarde, on the other hand," Pedro added, "only wants to rent the Fernandez place until he finds a larger house. What if you bought the vacant lot next to Tercera and offered to build Velarde a house he can use as both a home and an office?"

"An excellent idea, Pedro. I'll talk to Dr. Velarde about it."

"So I should negotiate to buy the vacant lot?"

"Yes, and assuming Dr. Velarde agrees, we can pay for it later this week. By then we should have the Ortegas's money in hand. Now if you'll excuse us, Diego and I are going to get a recipe from Inéz."

As they crossed the plaza on their way to the Beltrán residence, Diego tentatively raised a subject that was clearly difficult for him. "José says you're helping Old Man Xenome train him to be a medicine man," he began.

"Yes," Don Carlos replied, and waited for Diego to continue.

Finally Diego said, "I don't think I can become a shaman, but I would like to learn what to do to protect myself and people I love from evil spirits."

"Ah," Carlos said, sensing some deep loss beneath Diego's words. "Don't you have," he asked, "any fetishes from your boyhood, sacred objects with properties that can protect you?"

Diego shook his head and replied, "Nothing at all. I was orphaned as a little boy, and the distant relatives I lived with didn't pay any attention to teaching me the spirit ways."

"You didn't inherit anything from your father? He must have had a medicine pouch with his personal fetishes in it."

Diego's face became inexpressive. "No. An uncle, my father's older brother, took all those objects, claiming they were his by right."

"Ah," said Carlos again.

Diego took a deep breath. "You're helping José," he said. "Can you help me, too?"

"Of course, Diego," Carlos replied. "You and I can take trips into the countryside, and you can search for power objects to put in your medicine pouch." Diego looked relieved and murmured his thanks.

As they reached the Beltrán residence, Diego said, "We should go to the rear of the house and use the kitchen door. Señora Beltrán doesn't want me, an Indian, coming in the front door."

"Shhh," Don Carlos replied, putting his finger to his lips. "I want to surprise Inéz by arriving unannounced." He peered in a kitchen window and saw Inéz at the hearth, stirring a large hanging pot. "Wait here," he whispered to Diego.

He opened the door quietly—silently, he thought—but as he slipped into the room Inéz spoke. "Don't think you can sneak up on me, Alfonso Cabeza de Vaca. I have exceedingly sharp hearing—a girl, as my first fencing master put it, who can hear a gnat shrugging its shoulders in the next room."

Inéz did not turn around, continuing to stir something that smelled very good. She had tied her black hair back with a red ribbon, but a few stray strands, damp from the steam from the pot, were stuck to her neck, where it was exposed by her collarless blouse. Carlos went up behind her and kissed the nape of her neck.

"Watch it," Inéz warned him. "Messing with the cook could get you in a lot of trouble."

"Well worth the risk," he whispered.

"Good old Don Alfonso, the risk taker. Really, you shouldn't be doing this" — but she didn't move away. "What if someone came in the kitchen right now? That wouldn't be a good thing."

"All right," he said, moving away from her reluctantly. "I came by because helping to get the occupants of my three houses settled is taking more time than I expected. Pedro, Diego, and I are probably going to be too busy today to allow you and me to have our usual two o'clock rendezvous. That being the case, perhaps I can use this moment to bring you up to date."

"I have things to report too," Inéz told him, "especially about the fencing lesson I gave Elena. Let's talk after I give Diego the recipe I have for him. I heard you whispering to him outside. Please invite him in."

Carlos went to the door and called to Diego to come in. He watched as Inéz gave Diego careful verbal instructions—first about the ingredients and then the steps in preparing the dish. Once again, Carlos was impressed with how Diego remembered everything after only one time through. When Inéz was done, he excused himself and went on his way.

Turning to face Carlos, she said, "We both have things to report. Why don't you begin? How did your trip with José go?"

"Very well. I've agreed to work with Old Man Xenome. Xenome will instruct José in stories about the Old Ways. I'll accompany him on a vision quest and other trips into the countryside that Xenome is no longer able to do physically. What about you and Elena?"

"It was good, and I enjoyed the chance to get back to fencing. She was timid at first, but before long, she really got into it. I started with simple exercises — how to hold one's sword; what the main moves are called and how they're done. Then we began practicing lunges. We worked hard and she was sweating and panting. As something different I proposed that we go over to a bag of sand that workmen had left in one corner of the patio.

"I suggested that Elena lunge and thrust her sword at the bag. That would, I thought, give her a sense of what touché felt like. She made a few good moves; then she seemed to go at it with even more force, as if she were mentally saying, 'Take that, and that!' I didn't interfere. Her face got very flushed and her expression was — well, not pretty. I let her go on lunging at the sandbag for a while and finally suggested that she stop.

"Afterward I praised all her efforts, but she acted as if she felt she'd done something wrong, and she was quiet and rather sullen. I didn't comment on it, but I tried by my behavior to let her know that she could be whatever she felt like being around me. I suspect that her ingrained polite behavior covers up a great deal. But," Inéz concluded, "she wants more fencing lessons, and that will keep you and me from getting together afternoons this week. I simply have too many things to do while the Trigales tribe is eating with us. Hopefully, they'll find a cook of their own soon."

Carlos agreed. "It looks as though we're both too busy this week. So let me tell you right now about a conversation I had with Leandro. It seems that he'd heard of us from Dr. Tiburcio, who has set up a medical practice in Nombre de Dios. Tiburcio gave him his version of how, falsely accused and innocent, he was driven from Santa Fe, and how I was his chief persecutor."

Inéz's face darkened. "That devil! I never want to hear his name again."

Carlos took her gently by the shoulders and turned her toward him. "I completely understand, but there is one other thing. Leandro said that when they were in Nombre de Dios, they tried to find a magician they had heard of named Mateo Pizarro, with whom Leandro had hoped to study. They learned from an Indian that Pizarro had died under mysterious circumstances about the same time that an aristocratic stranger visited the town. Yes, that fellow was me. They decided to keep traveling north in hopes of catching up with this hidalgo and asking what he knew about Pizarro's demise. I took what I hope was the wise course and admitted that I had spoken with this Indian, but

I insisted, quite convincingly, I believe, that I know nothing about Pizarro's death and that it was a total coincidence that Pizarro died about the time I passed through Nombre de Dios on my way to Santa Fe."

Inéz had blanched at this news. "Oh, Carlos!" she whispered, daring to use his secret name. "Could they possibly suspect who you really are? Please promise me that you'll be exceedingly cautious in your dealings with them." He nodded his assent.

Reluctantly noting that it was time for him to leave, he leaned forward to brush Inéz's cheek with his, only to be stopped by her hand on his chest. "No more kisses today. That's another thing we have to be careful about, given the conditions of my employment."

Carlos smiled and stepped away from her. "Don't worry," he said. "I'm on my way," but at the door, as he was letting himself out, he turned and added, "I assure you, I won't do anything to jeopardize your job."

The rest of the week went as he'd expected. He was extremely busy every day. However, by Saturday market day his schedule was finally becoming less crowded. All his tenants were settled in their respective houses, and he and Pedro were beginning to draw up plans for Dr. Velarde's house on the vacant lot Carlos had just purchased. He'd seen Inéz only once that week because she was also very busy, but the Trigales's housewarming party featuring Leandro the Magician, Mara, and Selena was planned for Sunday evening, and he knew he'd see her there. She was part of the extended Beltrán-Trigales household, and he was included by both wings of the family as her friend.

Don Carlos went to the plaza, which was crowded with merchants, prospective customers, and gawkers, and was pleased to bump into Cristina Beltrán, who was out shopping with a maid. "We can't thank you enough," she told him, "for giving up your daily rendezvous with Inéz to allow her to tutor Elena in fencing. They were just finishing a lesson as I left the house, and I can scarcely believe the changes taking place in my daughter. She is much more energetic and, dare I say it, happier. She told me that Inéz is the best thing to come into her life for years." Cristina's face grew more serious. "I'm ashamed to admit that I didn't realize she had been so unhappy. I can see how important Inéz's friendship is to her. And Inéz is such a good model of maturity and deportment."

As he made his farewells to Cristina, Carlos noticed Selena, Mara, and Leandro circulating through the crowd, and heard them inviting everyone to a special public performance they were going to give at noon Sunday on the plaza. "Astonishing examples of magic and entrancing dances like you've never seen before," Leandro was broadcasting to everyone in earshot.

Carlos's route across the plaza took him in a direction that nearly intersected the Trio's course through the crowd. When he was less than three yards from them, the performers spotted him and greeted him warmly. Leandro called out, "*Hola*! Alfonso! Don't miss our performances tomorrow! Perhaps we can do a special dance in your honor." Selena smiled at him, puckered her lips, and blew kisses in his direction. Mara, who was nearest, broke off from the others, closed the gap with him, and touched him on the arm. "I should warn you," she declared, "that Selena thinks you owe her a kiss from the dance you did together."

"I rather got that idea," he replied drily. "I thought the pleasure of the dance was sufficient."

"Well," she said, "don't expect Selena to give up." She dropped her eyes. "I shouldn't tell you this, but she said that she knew, from our first meeting, that you had a weakness for women, and that she intended to take advantage of it. I didn't know what she meant by that, except—well, I don't know what she meant. She is always flirtatious, and she likes to make conquests. But then she tosses them away, they don't mean anything." Mara lifted her lovely violet eyes to his. "I probably shouldn't have told you that," she said in a beseeching tone.

The conversation had become suddenly intimate. Carlos dismissed the momentary unease he had felt at learning that Selena had seen his weakness, and something in Mara's voice aroused in him a desire to learn more about *duende*. Forgetting the throng of people around him, he asked, as if they were alone, "Can you tell me how you experience the *duende* state when you enter it?"

Mara, too, seemed forgetful of the crowd. "It's a deep experience," she replied. "I go somewhere."

Her answer evoked an echo of the feeling of *duende* in Carlos. "Somewhere?"

"Sometimes I lose myself altogether and enter a kind of trance. When I go that deeply, I faint, or go somewhere and I'm not always sure I want to come back."

Carlos thought about her statement. "If you didn't come back," he said hesitantly, "what would happen to you? Would you die?"

She looked at him more intently than ever and grasped his arm firmly. He realized that she was trembling a little. "Oh!" she exclaimed softly. "This is much too serious talk for such a nice day. Please excuse me. I have to catch up with my companions. We're working, you know." And with this she released his arm and smiled in a way that seemed more than merely friendly, but full of promise and some sadness too. She hurried off.

He turned around to find Inéz standing behind him, obviously having picked up on Carlos's and Mara's obliviousness to their surroundings, if not the actual words they had exchanged.

"Well," she said, "That was interesting. One of them publicly blows kisses to you, and with the other you engage in intimate conversation. Also in public."

Carlos, still confused and somewhat overwhelmed by his encounter with Mara, felt unfairly accused by Inéz. "We were just—" he began.

"Yes. You were just talking." Her tone was calm but he knew she was angry.

"Look, Inéz," he said, becoming somewhat exasperated. "Mara was just warning me that Selena is an aggressive flirt. She said the same thing at our dinner party. She also said that Selena likes to make conquests, but that they don't mean anything to her. Well, give me some credit for resisting her advances. I didn't, for instance, give her the kiss she expected at the end of the Spinning Dance last Sunday, which you wouldn't have noticed because you had your head pressed against Leandro's chest."

Inéz's eyes flashed. "I put my head against his chest because I was dizzy and I was afraid I'd fall down! That was all! And it has nothing to do with…" she broke off. "It has nothing to do with my being jealous because of the way you were talking to Mara. You're probably not even aware of how you can seem to wrap a woman in tenderness when you're talking with her." She turned her head slightly away from him. "Anyway, I have no right to ask you not to look at other women."

Somewhat mollified, Carlos made a gesture with his arm, indicating that they should walk. She took his arm and they fell into step, strolling toward the west end of the plaza.

Feeling it was time for a change of topic, Carlos asked, "How have your recent sessions with Elena gone? I saw her mother just before you came along, and she told me how pleased she is that you're giving Elena fencing lessons. She described you as 'a model of maturity and deportment'—those were her exact words, with which I thoroughly agreed."

Inéz's response was subdued and neutral. "Elena's doing well," she said. "She continues to pick up the basics quickly, and she's obviously having a good time."

"She is fortunate to have such a good teacher," Carlos replied, trying to inject something positive into what he felt was Inéz's unhappy mood.

"You always want clouds to go away immediately, don't you?" she observed. "Well, they don't. I'll get over it, I'm sure, but let's not pretend it didn't happen."

Carlos almost replied, "What happened"—he having let the recent clash of emotions almost instantly dissipate. Making an effort to recall what had passed between them, he said, "I shouldn't have brought up that business with Leandro. I apologize. I was jealous too," he added.

"Thank you for saying that," she replied.

He started to speak, but she interrupted him. "No. Please don't say anything more. It would come out like a platitude, and when I'm in this mood it would only irritate me more." She removed her hand from his arm. They had reached the west end of the plaza, where, unless he were escorting her back to the Beltráns', they would go their separate ways. "I've taken too long a break from work," she said. "I need to get back."

He reached his hand out to her, but she moved away. "I'll be all right," she said. "You have a good afternoon."

"You too," he responded, and watched her walk away.

The whole exchange had been unsettling and left him literally uncertain what to do with himself. The noon ringing of the church bells and a vague feeling of hunger reminded him that it was time for lunch, so he walked home and went to the kitchen and warmed up some refried beans.

Inéz was right, of course, he admitted to himself; he liked everything to be positive and pleasant. All his brujo lives had followed that pattern—and they had all, he reminded himself, been essentially solitary, his many liaisons with women notwithstanding. Having Inéz in his life complicated things, and the advent of Leandro, Mara, and Selena seemed to have complicated things even more, both with Inéz and in regard to his own uncertainty about whom Leandro might be in league with.

But Carlos was reluctant to pursue these thoughts and, having finished his beans, he decided to spend the afternoon visiting his various properties. After quick visits with the Ortega brothers at Tercera and the Díaz family at Segunda, he found a bit of maintenance that needed doing at the Fernandez place and devoted several hours to making final repairs on the corral fence there.

It was late afternoon by the time he got home. The January early dusk was gathering and, despite the growing chill, he felt like staying outside. Taking a blanket, he wrapped himself in it and sat on the house's veranda. Gordo joined him and jumped up on his lap to be petted.

Carlos's mind went back to the puzzle that Leandro, Mara, and Selena posed for him. All three of them were seductive, each in his or her own way, but he hadn't detected anything sinister in them. They just seemed to be, as was often true of entertainers, sensual and uninhibited. Camila's father, the blue-eyed Basque actor who'd left town after seducing her mother, a young innocent, was a good example of the same type. They took pleasure where they found it and expected others to join them in the same carefree way. He'd been such a man himself once.

But what bothered him most about the three entertainers was that he was still uncertain if they had any connection with the strange happenings he had been encountering—the ghosts and tormented spirits he'd seen in the plaza, and the dark horizons looming in the south. They all must mean something, but what, if anything, the entertainers had to do with them, he didn't know.

Just at that point he heard a loud bird cry. He looked up at the building across the lane and saw thirteen turkey vultures sitting on the roof line. Their hunched black shoulders and fierce eyes conveyed ominous intent. He'd never seen more than two or three turkey vultures at any one time in the Santa Fe town limits; even then they'd simply circled overhead, never landing on the roofs of buildings. He was immediately certain that they were spirit creatures rather than flesh and blood. Marshalling his inner forces, he shouted at them, "Go away!" They didn't move.

A few moments passed before one of the vultures launched from its rooftop perch and dropped down to the street, tracing a course like a huge black handkerchief floating to the ground. It walked back and forth not three yards from where Don Carlos was sitting, fixing him with a red-rimmed eye. Gordo, still on his lap, showed no sign of being inclined to chase the big black bird. The vulture stopped in front of Carlos as if it had something to say to him. The message apparently delivered, it took off, launching upward with a great deal of heavy beating of its wings, and rejoined its companions on the roof.

Don Carlos, suddenly energized, dumped Gordo unceremoniously off his lap, shed the blanket, stood up, and flapped his arms. "Go away! Shoo! Clear off!" The vultures didn't move. They began to vocalize, producing a sound akin to raucous laughter. Angry now, Carlos picked up a stone from beside the porch and hurled it at the vulture that had been taunting him most vociferously. It narrowly missed the bird without evoking any response.

Don Carlos picked up another stone and pulled back the sleeve of his coat to expose the mountain lion bracelet. He held the stone carefully next to the bracelet, which became noticeably warmer as he touched the stone to it. The stone too seemed to be acquiring warmth.

The moment the bracelet was exposed to their sight, the vultures began shifting on their perches in a nervous way. Don Carlos stepped into the street, aimed carefully, and hurled the stone toward the line of vultures. With a great rush of wings beating the air, they took off before the stone could reach its target.

"What's going on?" Pedro called, coming toward him from just down the lane.

Carlos gestured toward the roof of the building opposite his house and explained, "I was chasing off some turkey vultures that were annoying me."

"Turkey vultures? What turkey vultures? Can't you be left alone without getting drunk?"

Carlos responded to Pedro's remark with uncharacteristic irritation. "First Inéz accuses me of flirting with the women entertainers, and now you accuse me of being a drunk. What's wrong with everybody?"

Pedro looked him over appraisingly. "Do you want to tell me about it?"

"Not really," Carlos replied, and he turned to go inside. At that moment, Diego came around the corner carrying a kettle containing a stew that Inéz had made for them. The mood of the moment shifted, at least on the surface.

Eyeing the kettle, Pedro called out, "Hey, Diego! What's for dinner?"

Smiling, Diego called back, "We'll find out soon enough." The three men went indoors and busied themselves with chores until María got home and they settled down for a savory dinner, courtesy of Inéz by way of Diego.

As he prepared to go to bed, Don Carlos reflected briefly on the events of the day. Nothing had been resolved. He and Inéz had patched things up, but only partly. The three entertainers were still largely a mystery to him. Then there was the strange confrontation with the turkey vultures. Wasn't it odd that Pedro hadn't seen them while he, Carlos, had? Didn't that prove that they were spirit beings, but of what kind? Who, if anyone, might have sent them to harass him? What was going on?

11

Complications

Very early Sunday morning, Don Carlos had just finished a long meditation when Gordo burst into the room from the kitchen. He was whimpering in fright and ran directly to Don Carlos, jumped into his lap, and moaned and trembled.

Don Carlos was astonished. "What's the matter, old friend?" he asked, stroking Gordo and trying to calm him. "I've never seen you so frightened. What set this off? I'd better investigate."

Had Gordo not looked at him imploringly, Carlos would have gotten up immediately; instead, he spent a few minutes holding the little dog and trying to comfort him.

Finally placing Gordo on the bed with a "There, there, I'll fix things up," Carlos rose, pulled on his pants, shirt, and boots, and headed for the kitchen. As he went through the kitchen he grabbed his coat off a hook near the back door and put it on. Opening the door slowly, he cautiously leaned out. The first glow of light was showing in the east. Dusk, he recalled Old Man Xenome saying, was a liminal time during which spirits, both good and evil, were active. He supposed the same would hold true for dawn.

Looking first to his left toward the plaza, Don Carlos saw nothing but an empty lane with no sign of either human or spirit activity. But to his right, toward the south side of his house where his horses were stabled, he saw the shape of a four-legged animal standing in the lane. It was difficult in the half-light to make out exactly what the creature was, but Carlos felt the hairs on the back of his neck stand up and knew it was a dangerous beast. He could hear the household's horses moving restlessly in their stalls, sensing danger nearby.

As the sky gradually lightened, the two-legged and the four-legged watched each other in silence, neither moving. Finally Don Carlos started walking slowly toward the creature. From a closer vantage he was at last able to see that it was a large wolf, standing broadside in the lane but with its head and pricked ears pointing toward him. The wolf's yellow eyes, visible now, stared at him steadily.

Don Carlos stopped. He held the wolf's gaze until he began to feel as if he and the wolf were both spinning in the middle of some dark vortex. He forced himself to break his gaze, abruptly turning his head away. As he did so, a violent gust of wind came from behind him and, seized by dizziness, he had to spread his legs to keep from being blown off balance. The wind, he was sure, was part of the malicious spirit activity that was manifesting itself.

The wind was tugging at a tarpaulin that was loosely tied over a haystack in one corner of the stable. It pulled free and snapped in the wind like a whip. Ignoring the wolf, Don Carlos took six quick steps to the corner of the stable and reached up with his left hand to secure the tarpaulin. This move pulled the sleeve of his coat back to reveal the copper mountain lion bracelet Xenome had given him. Carlos noticed that the bracelet had become very warm, as though its protective power had gained strength.

When Don Carlos had secured the corner of the tarp, he turned and looked back at the wolf. The eyes that stared at him now were empty. Light was filling the sky and the sun was rising. He walked into the alley to secure the other end of the tarp. This took only a moment to do. Then he returned to the lane and looked to his right. The wolf was headed off toward the outskirts of town at an easy trot. It glanced back only once; the look it cast in his direction seemed to Carlos not the least fearful. *I've finished my business here*, it seemed to say.

Diego, blurry-eyed from having just been awakened, poked his head out of the hayloft where he had constructed his living quarters. He grabbed a coat, jumped down, and spoke in a calming way to the horses, all three of which were pawing at the ground and moving nervously in their stalls. "What set them off?" he asked.

"Those gusts of wind didn't help any. You heard how they loosened the tarp and made it flap, which is enough to scare any horse out of its wits. And you know they're always on the alert for whatever might want to eat a horse. They also probably sensed the presence of a predator, a large wolf that was coming down the lane toward the house from the south."

Diego looked startled, but his voice was steady as he commented neutrally, "It's unusual for a wolf to come inside the town limits."

"Unusual is the right word," Don Carlos agreed. "Once I came out in the lane, it went away. The horses are still nervous. It might help settle them down if you and I distracted them with grain."

That chore complete, Diego climbed back up to his loft while Don Carlos went into the kitchen and made his own breakfast.

He reflected on the wolf incident. Was it an ordinary wolf, or was it possible that the wolf's actions were being guided by a witch or sorcerer who had taken possession of it? Or was it a shape-shifter, perhaps even Leandro, who had approached the house to test whether Carlos was a brujo who would use sorcery to drive it off? In any case, he congratulated himself on having kept his brujo skills hidden, giving the wolf, whatever it was, no clear sign of his secret identity.

Having finished his breakfast, he stood up. His head began to spin. Cautiously, carrying his dishes, he walked toward the sink. A step away from his destination he lost his balance and dropped his dishes, which shattered into dozens of shards. He bent to pick them up, and when he straightened he struck his head on the edge of the counter. "Damn!" he swore out loud. He backed away from the counter and stepped on a large shard. He lost his balance again and staggered backward toward a chair that he almost knocked over as he sat down on it. Gordo, who'd been curled up in a corner, jumped to his feet and stared at Carlos with anxious eyes.

He felt exceedingly strange. The confrontation with the wolf, he thought, must have caused this mental and physical state. He didn't like it at all. He had not received any physical blow, so he must, he concluded, have been assaulted by some non-material mental force or energy. He quickly searched his past lives for any remotely similar experiences. The only one that came to mind was an encounter in his second life with an African witch doctor who had laid a spell on him that made him very sick. But he hadn't understood the witch doctor's magic, so that gave him nothing to go on.

Even if he did not understand the metaphysical cause of his condition, the physical effects could still be observed, and conclusions possibly drawn. He settled back in his chair to examine his physical state. The first thing he noticed was that he was listing to the left, so much so that he might have toppled over had he not constantly pulled himself upright. His second observation proved more important. He sensed that his body was out of kilter. It was almost as though he had two bodies that didn't quite coincide. One was clearly his physical body, but the other body — at least that's what he called it for want of a better word — was more like a shadow or a transparent sheath that surrounded his physical body. He found that he could see as well as feel it. It projected out about two inches to the left and wasn't visible at all on his right side. This undoubtedly accounted for his tendency to fall to his left.

But what was this shadow body? It didn't resemble the auras Don

Serafino had trained him to discern in people, animals, and inanimate objects. Neither was it like the golden halos that had surrounded Zoila and him when they'd completed their Tantric chakra meditation. It was something else, certainly non-material, and for want of a better word he labeled it his energy body. Somehow the wolf, or the magician, witch, or sorcerer who was manipulating the wolf, simply by confronting him at such close range, had jarred his energy body out of its correct alignment with his physical body.

At the very least, he believed what he was thinking made sense, and he was compelled to conclude that he had encountered some malign force that was in command of a technique or weapon that was different from his own arsenal of powers. This was not a happy thought. Moreover, there were still unanswered questions — who or what was affecting his energy body, and what antidote could he apply to improve his current state and literally pull his two bodies back together?

Responding to the second of these questions, he decided that what he needed was an activity, a project that would focus his attention and get him out of town.

At that very moment Diego came in the back door to the kitchen. A look of surprise came on his face when he saw the pieces of broken pottery strewn on the floor. Before he could ask, Don Carlos said, "I tripped over something, dropped my breakfast dishes, and hit my head on the counter. I'm sitting here to clear my head."

"Are you going to be all right?" Diego asked, bending down to collect pottery shards.

"Definitely, though I think a ride in the country would do me a lot of good, and I hope you'll come along."

"What about Mass? And weren't you going to go to the entertainers' performance on the plaza this afternoon?"

"Inéz doesn't have time to attend Mass this morning, so I've decided to skip it too. I'll miss the entertainers' public performance at noon, but I have an invitation to a private entertainment tonight that ought to be even more fun. So what's your answer? Are you free to join me for a ride in the country today?"

A slight hesitation showed on Diego's face. Carlos knew what that was about. "Don't worry, we'll be back shortly after mid-afternoon, which will leave you time to visit Ana at the Presidio and still get home in time to cook dinner. I'm just as interested in getting back sooner rather than later to attend the performance that Leandro and the two dancers will give at the Trigales house tonight."

Carlos smiled at Diego's evident relief at not having to choose between two of his heart's desires. The young man finished picking up and disposing of the broken dishes and headed for the stable to saddle Eagle and Alegría. "Put the pack frame and some sacks on Pepper," Carlos called after him. "We're going to be bringing some desert rocks back with us."

In response to Diego's questioning look, Carlos said, "I'll explain about the rocks after we're on our way." Diego left the kitchen and Carlos went to his bedroom, still feeling a bit unsteady on his feet, and changed into his riding clothes.

Once Don Carlos and Diego reached the outskirts of Santa Fe, Carlos described his plans. "I hope to achieve two objectives today. The backpacks and our saddlebags are for carrying a type of white stone I've been wanting to collect to decorate the exterior of our house. I say 'decorate,' but the true purpose of these embellishments is to create a shield of protective positive energy around the house. This morning's strange incident with the wolf made me decide to start the rock-gathering project today. The second purpose, not entirely unrelated to the first, is to start collecting items for a medicine pouch for you."

Diego digested Carlos's statement in silence for a while before saying, "May I ask some questions?"

"Of course. I expect you to have questions."

"You specified a white stone. I don't know of any in the area."

"They're located in only one place, which Eagle and I found not long after I moved here."

"What is this rock?"

"It's called chalcedony. It has a long history, dating back to the High Priest of the ancient Hebrews, who wore a breastplate with twelve stones, one of which was chalcedony. I don't know what power was attributed to chalcedony thousands of years ago, but my sources say that it has protective properties due to its capacity to absorb and deflect negative energies. Based on that fact, it should be perfect for our purposes."

"Are we looking for rocks of a certain size, or will any size do? And how many will we need?"

"What we're hoping to collect are stones about as big as a man's fist. We'll probably have to dig out some larger pieces and break them into the desired size, which will mean that they'll have rough edges. Once we get them home, we'll put them at the base of the exterior walls at spaces of perhaps two feet and do the same on the edge of the roof."

Diego was astonished. "Whew! That's a lot of rocks."

"True, but we don't have to do it all today. My plan is to space the first batch we collect at even intervals around the house. Initially, they'll be fairly far apart. We'll fill in the gaps later as we collect more rocks in future trips."

"What about the medicine pouch?"

"That's trickier because it's personal. An object that's suitable for one man's medicine pouch might not be for another's. Nevertheless, I'm confident that you'll know you've found a power object when you do."

"Have you ever done this?" Diego asked, in what seemed to Carlos to be all innocence.

"Never."

"And you're supposed to help me?"

"Have a little faith, Diego. I have skills that may come into play. That stand of trees ahead is where we'll turn off the trail to the north into those low hills. The trail's rather narrow; let's move in single file."

Don Carlos and Eagle took the lead. They entered a canyon and picked their way forward on a faint path that wove through boulders and brush. Soon they came to a place where the canyon widened out and a grassy bank was visible to their left. "Let's stop here," Carlos proposed, and they dismounted, tethered their horses, and drank some water from their water bags.

Carlos sat down with his back against a large boulder. He said nothing. Finally, Diego's curiosity got the better of him, and he spoke up. "Are you going to sit there all day?"

"What I suggest," Carlos replied, "is that you sit down too and get to know the spirits of this particular spot. Perhaps they can lead you to your first totem object."

Diego, clearly perplexed, sat down and asked, "How am I going to get to know the spirits of this place?"

"Hush. Spirits of such places can be very shy. They won't come out unless you're very quiet. Think of becoming as still as a rock. Better yet; become a rock."

Don Carlos began to do as he'd advised. Of course, he had many lifetimes of experience at Watching and the silence it entailed, and as a result, he soon was breathing slowly and only rarely blinking an eye. To a casual observer he would have looked like a man-shaped rock. Out of his peripheral vision, he could see that Diego was doing a good job of following his example.

Once the silence settled in, it became apparent that there was a lot of life in the place. A red-tailed hawk circled overhead; small birds of various types flitted through the underbrush; insects buzzed around, and lizards dashed in and out of view. Carlos wondered which animal would approach Diego.

To Don Carlos's great surprise, the first magical being to speak was a mesquite bush right next to Diego's head. "I hope you're not here to cut my limbs. Can't you find other sources of firewood closer to your homes?"

Don Carlos said nothing. He wanted Diego to speak and nodded gently to his young friend that this was his show.

"No," Diego finally said. "We didn't come here for firewood."

"That's a relief," the mesquite bush replied. "You can see from looking at me that several limbs were cut off by Natives who camped here. If not firewood, what are you after?"

"My friend and I hope to collect pieces of white rock to decorate our house in Santa Fe, and I'm hoping to find fetishes for a medicine pouch I'm starting."

"Aren't you a little old to be starting a medicine pouch? Most seekers who visit here on vision quests are much younger."

"I'm an orphan who didn't have a proper upbringing because I lived in a town that had no medicine man to guide me."

"Who's that fellow over there? He looks like a Spaniard. Can he be trusted?"

"Absolutely. He's a good friend. He brought me here because he said this would be a good spot to start my search and also a place where there are white rocks."

"Hmmm. Most unusual. If he knows where the white rocks are I'm impressed. They're difficult to find. Of course, as a plant I can't move around, but birds, lizards, mice, and other neighbors of mine keep me well informed."

"My friend knows where to find the rocks. I wonder if you can advise me about finding a fetish."

"Usually that's something you do on your own, but since you're at the disadvantage of being off to a late start and having no one to turn to except a Spaniard, I'll give you a hint. Walk up the canyon beyond this spot. Watch the ground. There's a rare and powerful object fairly near here. I won't tell you what it is, but it once belonged to a medicine man with great powers who died near the top of the ridge. Flash floods have washed it down into the canyon. That's all I can say, if it's to be a discovery of your own."

Diego jumped up, eager to get started. "Go very slowly, Diego," Don Carlos advised. "The quest you're on requires a steady mind, a patient heart, and clear vision."

"That's excellent advice," the mesquite plant declared, "especially coming from a Spaniard. A Spaniard who's wise in the ways of the spirit world! I've never heard of such a thing."

Don Carlos said nothing as Diego moved up the canyon at a slow pace. He refrained from conversing with the mesquite plant, feeling that Diego and the mesquite plant had a special relationship on which he shouldn't intrude. For a long time he could hear Diego creeping through the underbrush and hoped his young friend's search would be successful. He considered transforming himself into a pack rat and showing Diego the way, but rejected the idea. This had to be Diego's discovery.

While he was waiting for Diego to return, a ground squirrel came out of its hole and struck up a conversation. "What brings you here?" the squirrel asked.

"I came to collect some white rocks, and, just so it won't alarm you, I'll probably have to return several times. Don't worry. My friend and I will be careful not to step on your burrow."

"Thank you. Not everyone who comes here is so considerate—probably because they don't even notice where I live. By the way, what's your name?"

"In Santa Fe I'm known as Alfonso. What's yours?"

"Roberto. Look, I'd like to talk more, but I need to collect seeds. My girlfriend is about to have a litter, and our stored seeds have almost run out."

"I'd be glad to help you collect seeds, if you'll point out the kind you favor. I have nothing else to do while I'm waiting for my young friend to return."

"That's kind of you," Roberto replied, and he showed Carlos the three types of seeds he liked. With Carlos foraging in the area, apologizing to plants whenever he harvested seeds from them (always leaving a few so that they could propagate), he and Roberto soon had collected a big pile of seeds to store and consume later.

Diego returned with a huge smile on his face, his aura aglow with pulsing gold light. "I think I found the object the mesquite plant told us about." He opened his hand to show Don Carlos a brownish projectile point in perfect condition. "What do you think?"

"Beautiful. You're off to a great start. Did you notice the white rock quarry while looking for this treasure?"

"No, I was looking at the ground and under bushes all the time. But wait. I did see a few chips of white rock on one bank that looked as though they'd weathered out of the canyon wall from some place higher up."

"Let's go and have a look," Don Carlos said. "I'm sure you're on the right track." Diego led the way to the place where he had found the chips, which had broken off from an outcrop nearly sixty feet up the canyon wall. The two men climbed to the outcrop and started collecting rocks by using small picks to knock off large chunks of chalcedony, then breaking them into fist-sized pieces with a hammer Carlos had brought along. In less than an hour they had more than enough white rocks to fill their sacks and saddlebags. To get the stones to their horses was another matter, but Don Carlos, having foreseen this problem, had brought a rope. The two men filled sacks at the quarry site and used the rope to lower them to the canyon floor.

Before loading the rocks on their horses, they ate the rest of the food they had brought along. "Eating so fast isn't ideal for digestion," Don Carlos remarked, "but if we don't start back soon we won't get to Santa Fe in time for everything we hope to do this afternoon."

They quickly loaded the horses, Pepper in his role as a pack horse having to bear the heaviest load, and mounted up. Theirs was a very happy two-person, three-horse caravan. Diego, not surprisingly, was walking on clouds. His trip with Diego had fully restored Don Carlos's normal good spirits, leading him to sing a *verso popular* he'd learned since coming to New Mexico.

> Four little white doves
> Sat in a rosemary bush,
> Singing to each other:
> There's no love like the first.

The song made him think of Inéz. He did not pause to wonder how she could be his first love. Not until much later did he realize that this was true.

12

Kisses

Less than a mile from the outskirts of Santa Fe, Carlos and Diego heard someone hailing them. It turned out to be Mara and Selena approaching from a side road. The women looked marvelous in their riding breeches and coats with red scarves at their necks. The two were full of life, laughing and waving. "Hello, Alfonso, Diego," Selena said when the two dancers pulled abreast of them. "What have you been up to?"

The truth, at least an edited version of the truth, is often the best answer. "We've been collecting white rocks," Carlos told her, "to use to decorate the exterior of our house. We've lived in it more than two years without making it prettier. But you'll be glad to hear that we started out early this morning so as to get back to Santa Fe soon enough for me to attend your performance tonight."

"You missed our noon show on the plaza," Selena said, her tone reproachful but her manner flirtatious.

"I'm sure it was splendid," Carlos replied, "but by waiting for tonight's show, I've planned to see what's sure to be even better."

Selena nodded, apparently not too bothered by his having missed the earlier performance. "Yes, you'll find tonight's program truly special," she agreed airily. Then she added, "We saw you head out of town and wanted to come along, but of course we couldn't follow you until after our performance. We tried, but we failed to catch up with you."

"But you have caught up with us," Carlos pointed out, nudging Eagle to begin walking again.

"How about a race to the first house at the edge of town?" Selena proposed.

"Eagle loves to race," Carlos replied, "but right now he's loaded down with rocks in his saddlebags."

"Why don't you give your saddlebags to Mara? Then the two of us can race, and Mara, Diego, and the packhorse can come along at a reasonable pace. Or maybe this is another time when you'll find some excuse not to take a chance."

This rankled. "All right," he said, unwilling to let it go. "I'll take your dare," and he maneuvered Eagle over to Mara, got off, and transferred his saddlebags to her. By the time he remounted and turned back to start the race, he saw that Selena, who was looking over her shoulder with a grin on her face, had taken advantage and started without him. "Cheater!" he called after her, but he didn't really mind, having great faith in Eagle's competitive spirit. Eagle hated to be behind, and he never failed to forge ahead in a race. With a determined look to his ears, Eagle set about closing the gap between himself and Selena's mount. Eagle steadily gained on Selena, and with a quarter of the distance remaining, he passed the other horse, at which point Carlos let out a triumphant whoop. Selena spurred her horse vigorously, but they lost still more ground.

Carlos and Eagle reached the house that was the finish line well ahead of Selena and turned to watch her approach. Soon Selena pulled to a halt next to Don Carlos, so close that they could easily have touched. "All right," she declared, panting, "you win. What must I forfeit to you?"

"I think it's too late to speak of forfeits or prizes. Once the outcome is known, there's no risk in betting. And risk is what taking a dare is all about, wouldn't you agree?"

Not willing to give up easily, Selena replied, "I lost, and as a matter of honor I put myself entirely at your mercy, trusting you to choose wisely."

Carlos observed to himself that in another time and place he would have had a variety of ideas about how to take advantage of her open-ended offer. In the present, however, he contented himself with saying, "I know you think I'm a strange fellow, but the truth is that I do some things, our race for example, for pleasure alone with no thought of any other reward."

"Very well, if that's how you want it, and it's an admirable viewpoint. But you're getting deeply in debt to me. You already owe me a kiss, and now you owe me the satisfaction of having my offer of a forfeit accepted."

The arrival of Mara and Diego with Pepper in tow saved Carlos from having to make a further reply. Carlos retrieved his saddlebags from Mara and wished the entertainers well. The two pairs went their separate ways, with Selena calling out a cheery, "Until tonight!"

"What did you think of Mara?" Carlos asked Diego when they were alone again.

"She seems nice, kind of sweet and very pretty, but Ana is more my type."

"Good choice," Carlos replied. "And we're back in plenty of time to rendezvous with Ana and Inéz at their respective homes. Let's unload the rocks, get cleaned up, and go find our lady friends."

"Where do you want the rocks put?"

"In the corner of my bedroom."

Diego was obviously surprised by Carlos's direction to put the rocks in his bedroom, and Carlos felt it necessary to provide a sketchy explanation. "The rocks," he said, "aren't ready to be put out. I need to work with them some"—a vague statement, but Diego didn't ask for more details. They quickly built a rock pile in Carlos's room. A fast wash-up and they were off to visit Inéz and Ana.

Carlos found Inéz seated at a table next to a window in the Beltráns' kitchen, doing some sewing. She was watching for him and smiled as he entered the room. He welcomed the smile, but thought he detected a disturbance in her aura. "How did your tutorial with Elena go?" he asked cautiously. "Your aura seems a bit—"

"Frayed?" she finished for him. "Your aura-reading skills are good. Nothing bad happened during Elena's lesson. The tutorial, the Elena part, went well, but there was an incident at the end that was unfortunate."

He pulled up a chair and sat down at the table across from her. "Tell Alfonso all your troubles," he said.

"Here's what happened. Elena and I were having a good session. She's grasping the technical aspects of fencing and the spirit of the art faster than one might expect, given that she's never been physical in the past. I'd become very warm from an hour of vigorous exercise and took off my padded shirt, as I sometimes did with you in hopes you would take some notice. Obviously, that wasn't a factor with Elena.

"We returned to fencing, and both of us were getting sweaty and breathing hard. Following my example, Elena took off her padded top, stripping down to a black corset not unlike mine, but she's plump and more bosomy than I am.

"We were almost done when I sensed that someone was watching us. It was Leandro. Later, Elena's mother told us that Leandro had come by to collect the payment she'd promised him for last week's performance. While she left the hallway to get the money, he heard the sound of our fencing bout and wandered into the patio."

"And?"

"Oh, dear. Well, he had stopped about twenty feet behind me. Before I turned around to see who was standing there, Elena, poor kid, spotted him, let out a little eek of dismay, and rushed to cover herself with her padded top."

"Too bad."

"It could have been worse, except Leandro quickly averted his eyes, said 'Excuse me,' and turned and left the patio."

"That's not the worst possible outcome."

"I agree, and I admit that Leandro handled it in a gentlemanly way. Still, I felt badly for Elena, who was very embarrassed. And it left me a little rattled, as you noticed. I feel better, having told you. So now, you tell me how your day has been going."

"Three incidents are worth mentioning. First, Diego and I had a very successful trip into the countryside. I was waiting for a magical animal to speak to him—there were plenty of candidates in the canyon where we stopped—but instead a mesquite bush spoke to him and told him approximately where he might find a fetish. He went off as instructed and found a fine projectile point, an object that the mesquite bush told him had belonged to a powerful medicine man."

"Diego must have been excited."

"He was, but that wasn't the end of our adventures. On the way back, we met our favorite dancers, Selena and Mara, mounted on horseback and headed in our direction. We exchanged a few words, and then Selena challenged Eagle and me to a race.

"She cheated and got a head start by not waiting for me to get mounted again after I had unloaded my saddlebags, which were full of rocks that Diego and I had collected. But you know Eagle, he wasn't going to be left behind and he soon caught and passed Selena. At the end Selena congratulated me and offered me what she called a 'forfeit' for having lost. I didn't take her up on her offer."

"I doubt that your failure to do so will discourage her from flirting with you."

"Probably not. And the third thing I wanted to tell you about also involves her, although in this case she was not pursuing me. Rather the reverse, if anything, which made me uncomfortable. It was a dream I had last night. In the dream I found myself in a hallway and, without thinking twice about it, walked through a wall at the end of the corridor. I came out on a balcony overlooking a bed in which Selena was asleep. Then I felt disloyal that she showed up rather than you in my dreams."

"You're being silly. Selena has been on your mind, so it doesn't surprise me that you dreamed about her."

"I don't know. Maybe I sent my dreaming mind to spy on her and the Trio. But she was just innocently sleeping."

"Perhaps the Trio have nothing to do with the danger you sense," she suggested quietly.

"Perhaps not," he agreed. "Well, we'll see all three of them tonight, and I look forward to seeing you there too." He pushed his chair back and stood up. She gave him another smile and he let himself out the door.

Don Carlos dressed in his Sunday best for the Trigales's housewarming party. His knock at the door was answered by a butler who ushered him down a hall to a *sala* that was one of the largest in Santa Fe. Two full-length portraits—one of a man, the other of a woman, both in aristocratic attire—hung on the room's main wall. These, Carlos assumed, must be ancestors of Raul Trigales. It didn't surprise him that Raul had such forebears and had brought their portraits with him on the fifteen-hundred-mile trek from Mexico City to Santa Fe.

Carlos could see that the house's interior decorations were still incomplete. The family probably hadn't yet had time to acquire all the rugs and storage chests that would have been normal in an upper-class residence. He did notice, however, that unlike his own miscellaneous collection of chairs, the Trigales family had eight well-matched chairs set in a row against the back wall for the performance to come. Cushions were placed on the floor for the children. Carlos moved to the back of the room and sat down.

Most of the guests were already there. Javier and Cristina Beltrán, their daughter Elena, and Inéz were listening with interest to a story being told by Raul Trigales, who had a very engaging way of speaking, and Bianca Trigales was trying to get her four children to settle down. "The performance is about to start," Bianca was saying to them. "Please behave yourselves." The four sat down, although they continued to squirm with youthful energy.

Dr. Fabio Velarde entered at that moment and took a seat next to Carlos. Inéz came over and sat on Carlos's other side. The rest of the audience arranged themselves on the remaining chairs.

Leandro, dressed in a red sash, tights, and a loose yellow shirt, strutted in, paused in the center of the room, and introduced the evening's entertainment. "This is a very special program," he began, "one we have planned specifically for this occasion. It will consist of three parts. In the first part my friends Selena and Mara will amaze you with their incredible flexibility, strength, and fearlessness. While they change costumes, I will entertain you with a demonstration of magic. In the third and final part of tonight's performance, the ladies will return and dance for you. In each of the three parts we will invite some of you to join us in the performance. And now for part one!"

Mara and Selena came in. Their white tops had long tight sleeves and snug bodices, and instead of skirts they wore yellow and blue pantaloons gathered at the ankle. Their feet were bare.

Upon reaching the center of the room, the two dancers bowed and then sank to the floor. They crossed their legs, each putting her left foot on her right thigh, and once it was in place, bringing her right foot over to place it on her left thigh.

As they held this position, Leandro invited the children in the audience to attempt the same pose. All four Trigales youngsters scrambled to try it. As the entertainers beamed appreciatively, all four managed to put their legs into the correct position.

"Good! Good!" Leandro exclaimed. "Now comes the truly challenging part. Watch closely and see if you can duplicate the movement that Mara and Selena will now demonstrate."

The two women bent forward and inserted their hands, forearms, and elbows into the space between their thighs and their calves. With their torsos now extended flat over their legs, they worked their hands upward until they could touch their ears. Then, using their stomach muscles, they carefully lifted their folded legs off the floor and balanced on their buttocks.

"Would any of the volunteers like to try this second stage of the pose?" Leandro asked. The four kids who'd gotten into the original seated meditation pose tried it, but all four toppled backward, unable to balance and remain upright. The audience and the children all laughed uproariously as little bodies rolled around like ninepins.

"Let's try another variation," Leandro suggested. "Come back to the original seated pose, and try to copy Mara and Selena."

Resuming their original seated pose, Mara and Selena again inserted their arms into the space between their thighs and calves until their arms up to their elbows were out of sight. With a deep breath, each of them straightened her elbows and raised her body above the ground, balancing on her hands while looking at the audience.

Carlos was impressed and resolved to try it at home.

The Trigales children attempted to duplicate this pose without success. They lacked the necessary strength, but they received a round of applause for their efforts.

The last demonstration of acrobatics was announced by Leandro as "The Art of Motion." With a gesture, he invited Mara to come to the center of the room. Selena took a position about four feet to one side of her, and Leandro moved until he was another four feet away from Selena. He clapped his hands twice. Mara made a deep bow, then placed her hands on the floor shoulder distance apart. With apparent ease she lifted both legs straight up until her body was vertical and she was balanced in a handstand. She remained motionless for perhaps twenty seconds while the audience seemed to collectively hold its breath. Then she slowly lowered her legs until her toes touched the floor, bent her arms, and made a triangle of her hands and her elbows. She placed the top of her head in the center of the triangle and lifted both legs into a headstand. Once her legs were straight she began to move each leg slowly back and forth in a scissoring motion.

At that moment Selena arched her back and bent backwards until her hands touched the floor behind her. She shifted her weight to her hands and lightly swung one leg up after the other, touched down, stood upright, arched and bent backwards again, beginning to make a circle around Mara with slow repeated arcs and slowly scissoring legs.

With Selena circling Mara in clockwise direction, Leandro began slow cartwheels in a larger circle around Selena in the opposite direction.

It was visually a dance of upended legs, but Carlos, watching intently, was fascinated by each dancer's spine—Mara's vertical and motionless, Selena's radically extending and flexing backward and forward, and Leandro's flexing and extending sideways. He wondered if it was his imagination or if the chakras of each spine pulsed and glowed with each performer's movements, and if they were aware of these energy centers. He knew he lacked the physical flexibility to do all these movements, but he wondered if, to the degree he could duplicate them, he might learn a new method of energizing the chakras.

There was no doubt that the performance of "The Art of Motion" changed the energy in the room from a state of general merriment to an absorbed, quiet focus on the Trio's rhythmically alternating legs. When the performers, with no visible signal, simultaneously stopped, the room was filled with a hush. Mara silently came down from her headstand, stood upright, and all three dancers bowed.

"Thank you," Leandro said, breathing deeply and smiling. He nodded to Mara and Selena and they left the room. "While the ladies are changing their costumes, I invite you to join me in an exploration of the mystery of magic. Once again, I need four volunteers, preferably children, each of whom must invest one real in hopes of doubling their money, so that as a group they would get eight reales — one peso — back. Do I have any takers?"

The Trigales kids appealed to their father and their Uncle Javier for the money and each came forward with a real. Leandro took the coins and organized the children into a line facing the adult onlookers with their backs to him.

"We will start the fun by investing the total of four reales I've been given and seeing if we can make a profit." He showed the coins in his hands, then closed his hands and spun in place for several counterclockwise circles, moving his hands up into the air, down to his waist, up to his head, back to his waist, and finally out to either side. When he at last stopped, he opened his hands. The two reales he had held in each hand had disappeared and were replaced by two four-reales coins.

"Look at that," he said to the kids in feigned amazement and joy, "after barely five minutes your money has grown to twice its previous value." With a mischievous grin he said, "Tell your parents that if they want to get rich quick, they should give Leandro the Magician all their money. The only thing I can't guarantee is that I'll still be in town the next day!" This got an appreciative laugh.

Closing his hands around the two coins he was holding, Leandro told the audience, "The trouble with investments is that you can lose as well as gain. Just a moment ago you each seemed twice as well off than you were five minutes earlier. Now, however, I fear that your two four-reales coins have disappeared" — whereupon he opened his hands, found them empty, patted the red sash around his waist, groped in his shirt pockets, scratched his head, and looked dismayed. "Oh dear! I can't find the coins. An evil genie must have stolen them." He appealed to the children. "I know you've been watching me closely. Did you see what happened to the coins?"

The children looked puzzled and shook their heads.

"I think the thing to do is for you to search me to see if you can find the coins. Here I am; just bear in mind that I'm terribly ticklish."

The four children swarmed over him, and Leandro pretended to be knocked to the floor, where he writhed in agony due to their searching — poor ticklish man — under his sash, in his hair, and in his shoes, causing Leandro to cry out in dismay, "I must really get out of this investment business; it simply gets too personal."

Finally, the kids gave up, and Leandro rose to his feet. "I'm so sorry about your reales," he said, with a mournful face. But then he brightened. "I see what happened to the coins. You've been hiding them from me all along! You just wanted to torment me with your tickling." And he reached behind Anton's ear and pulled out a two-reales coin, repeating the process until he'd found a coin on each of the children, eight reales in all. He distributed the reales to his little assistants.

"Let's have a round of applause for the wonderful Trigales children," he said, a request that seemed to make Leandro even more popular than he'd been previously.

"Now it's time for the adult portion of the evening. The children are to be excused to prepare for bed, although we've arranged a treat for them. Señorita Elena Beltrán has agreed to tell Constanza and Carmela a bedtime story she remembers from her childhood, and Dr. Velarde has promised to do the same for Cristofer and Anton." The Trigales children stood up and followed Elena and Fabio out of the room.

The adults who'd remained in the room took a short break for refreshments while waiting for Elena and Fabio to return from their story-telling duties. Once they came back, Leandro resumed his introductory remarks. "Ladies and gentlemen, what you are about to see is an exceptional display of dancing. This dance, which will surely amaze and entrance you, as yet has no name. Here they are again, the lovely Mara Mata and Selena Torrez."

Mara and Selena emerged through a side door, holding themselves very erect and moving with a stylized elegance. They were wearing identical dresses, both high-necked and dark green, with ankle-length skirts that were flared and slit on the left side so as to expose that leg up to the knee. The dress material was clingy, as though glued by static to the dancers' bodies.

Mara and Selena commenced the dance in a formal position, their bodies touching, their heads lifted and tipped back, one leg slightly extended to the side. Selena was the leader, the male, and Mara took the part of the woman. Leandro struck the floor with the *seco* pole and the movements of the dance began.

As in their troupe's presentation of *Duende*, there was no accompaniment except Leandro's beating of the *seco* pole on the floor. The rhythm of the Unnamed Dance was entirely different from that of *Duende*. It moved forward in bursts—a few moments of rapid motion followed by several in which the dancers briefly stood absolutely still. Nearly every movement struck Carlos as highly eroticized. Their bodies moved together sinuously, their legs often seeming to entwine. Selena frequently bent Mara backward in a pose of sensual abandon. Through much of the dance, the two women looked deeply into each other's eyes.

Inéz whispered to Carlos, "Be prepared for when Leandro asks us to participate in the next part of the performance. Which one do you want: Mara or Selena?"

"What makes you think Leandro is going to ask us to choose one of them?"

"You're not the only one with intuitions. What's your answer to my question?"

As Carlos and Inéz were whispering to each other, the dance ended with Mara arched in a backward bend, supported under her torso by Selena's forearm. Selena then lifted Mara nearly upright. Mara curled her arm around Selena's neck, drew her forward, and they kissed.

"You choose," Carlos whispered back. "If I make the wrong choice, you'll make me suffer for it later."

"I insist that you choose."

"All right. My choice is Mara."

"Good. That's how I would have chosen for you."

Leandro's voice broke into their whispered conversation. He was announcing that, as promised, there would be audience participation in a second performance of the dance. "If it's all right with everyone," he said, "we would like to invite two members of the audience whom we've come to admire greatly—I refer to Señora Inéz de Recalde and her friend, Don Alfonso Cabeza de Vaca—to join the next dance."

Turning to Carlos and Inéz, Leandro asked, "Are you willing?"

Carlos put on a puzzled look. "Are we to dance with each other?" he asked.

"It would be better if you danced with an experienced partner, not that I doubt your ability to dance beautifully with each other. But since you'll be performing the Unnamed Dance for the first time, you'll surely benefit from having a guide who's familiar with the movements and rhythms. Please choose which of the dancers you'd like to partner with."

Turning to Inéz, as though they hadn't already discussed the matter, Carlos asked in a voice that could be heard by everyone, "Inéz, shall I choose first or would you prefer to?"

"I'm content to defer to your choice."

"In that case I will dance with Mara Mata."

"Good," Inéz replied. "I was hoping to dance with Selena."

Don Carlos met Mara at a point halfway between where the dancers had been standing and he'd been sitting. She looked him directly in the eyes and positioned her arms to adopt the dance posture of couples. Then she gave him simple instructions. "Put your hand on my back, placing it firmly on the lower part of my rib cage; you need to hold me close to you." Demonstrating the degree of closeness by pulling their lower ribs together, she added, "Now step a little to your right, so your left hip is facing my right hip. This will enable us to step between each other's legs. The steps are simple; the connection of our bodies will tell you how to move, as will our eye contact."

Leandro began to beat the cadence of the dance. The first beats were slow: two beats, two more, then a long pause. Following Mara's slow steps, Carlos's body soon intuited the pattern, and as the beat gradually quickened, he easily matched his steps to it. Maintaining their intense eye contact, Mara whispered to him, "This is a Gypsy dance, a public performance of smoldering passion that you must embody."

Carlos felt Mara's words register somewhere else than in his conscious mind. Something in him said *yes*, and he gave himself to the movement of their two bodies, now united from pelvis to lower ribs. His body felt molten, fluid; his second and third chakras pulsed and glowed. There was a fleeting memory of his Tantric union with Zoila, but this was different—hotter, more obliterating.

Abruptly the fast, irregular beat of the *seco* pole stopped. Carlos found himself holding Mara around the waist as she dropped backwards, her head flung back. They were somehow perfectly balanced and able to remain immobile for several seconds after the beat stopped. Then she planted one foot underneath her and raised her head and torso until she and Carlos were close enough to kiss.

Carlos was nearly overwhelmed by his desire to kiss her. The word *inflamed* passed through his mind, seeming to come out of nowhere and name all his feelings. "*A public performance of smoldering passion,*" Mara had said. For a timeless moment they held each other's eyes, breathing heavily from their exertions. Then—and he knew it—the performance was over. As if by unspoken agreement, there was no kiss.

Mara smiled, and with a nod of her head directed his attention to Inéz and Selena, who were embracing. "It looks to me as though they don't want to stop," Mara remarked.

"They certainly seem to like each other," Carlos offered.

"At the very least, they seem to like embracing each other," Mara replied.

The small audience — the Beltráns, Raul and Bianca Trigales, and Elena Beltrán and Fabio Velarde — had been applauding the performance. Fabio and Raul shouted, "Bravo!"

Carlos turned to Leandro and said, "I trust we didn't ruin your show,"

"Certainly not," Leandro replied. "The two of you are naturals. It wasn't difficult for you to get into the spirit of the dance. My only complaint," Leandro told them, "is that Alfonso and Mara didn't kiss at the end." He was evidently prepared to tease them, but Mara shot him a look that warned him off. Just at that moment Inéz noticed that Elena had approached and was hovering in back of Selena. "What did you think, Elena?" Inéz asked her.

"I loved it," she replied, "and I would have loved to join in the dance, though I'm not sure my mother would approve."

Leandro sized up the situation quickly and replied, "I meant to apologize for intruding on your fencing session today. That was rude of me, and I regret any embarrassment I caused. In the light of that fact, I feel I owe you a dance. I hope there will be an opportunity for us to dance together while my friends and I are in Santa Fe." He took Elena's hand in his, bent over it, and gallantly kissed it. She blushed, but she didn't pull away.

The four dancers, still suffused with the spirit of the dance, looked on with appreciative eyes, and when Leandro straightened, the four others quietly applauded. "May the goddess of love smile on you all your life," Leandro told Elena. Tears of happiness came in her eyes, and she said simply, "Thank you" before turning away and walking over to where her parents were standing.

"That was lovely of you, Leandro," Inéz told him.

"It was a pleasure, I assure you, but be forewarned that you, too, are among the beautiful women with whom I hope to dance."

Inéz took his statement well. "Perhaps some day, but you need to realize that Don Alfonso is first in line for the next dance."

Leandro bowed politely. "I will wait my turn."

By this point everyone else — the Beltráns, Trigaleses, and Dr. Velarde — had gathered around. Enthusiastic words about the night's performance were spoken by all.

"The pleasure was ours," Leandro replied, "though perhaps I should say that the intimate circumstances of tonight's show enabled us to perform in ways — especially the passionate nature of the Unnamed Dance — that we couldn't for a more general audience, such as the one we entertained on the plaza earlier today."

Raul Trigales answered the implicit question in Leandro's statement. "Rest assured," he said, "that we enjoyed your performance immensely." Everyone else seemed to agree.

A brief period of small talk followed until Carlos, nodding in Inéz's direction, announced, "It's time for me to walk my friend to her home." Turning to Leandro and the dancers, he added, "Thank you, all three of you, for a memorable experience."

"Nicely done," Inéz told him as he walked her back to the Beltrán residence. "I wasn't sure how you would take his announcement that he aspired to dance with me."

"I expect he had the Unnamed Dance in mind," Carlos observed neutrally.

"I expect he did," Inéz replied. "Wasn't that dance an amazing experience? So very sensual. I enjoyed dancing it with Selena, but I don't think I would want to dance it with any man but you." She looked at him questioningly.

"You mean, how did I feel dancing with Mara?"

She nodded, not taking her eyes off him. "Leandro said you didn't kiss her."

"No," he replied, but seemed unable to go further.

"I'm glad," she murmured. "I would feel deeply distraught, betrayed even, if you fell in love with her."

"Not a chance!" he protested.

Inéz seemed satisfied, but she immediately added, "Just don't make promises you can't keep."

13

Discoveries

"*D*on Alfonso! Don Alfonso!" Someone was calling him and knocking on his bedroom door. Carlos cracked one eye and saw that the sky outside his window was still dark. Another dream, he decided. Dreams that interrupted his sleep were getting annoying. Besides, he didn't feel like getting up to meditate yet. He was still tired and rolled over preparatory to going back to sleep.

"Don Alfonso! Don Alfonso!" came the voice, more insistently. "You said we should start for the Spirit Ledge by daybreak. It's almost time."

Damn! It was José. "I'll be there in a moment," he shouted, swinging his feet out of bed and instantly wishing he hadn't moved so quickly. He felt woozy and, what surprised him even more, he didn't feel the buoyant energy with which he usually met a new day. Hurrying to join José, he tossed off his sleeping outfit, put on a shirt and pants, and headed for the door, picking up his boots on the way.

He opened the door between his bedroom and the kitchen and found José standing there with a candle that dimly illuminated the room. "Sorry, Don Alfonso," he said. "I thought you'd be up by now. If you want to sleep in, we can take our trip another day."

"No, I'm ready any time," Carlos assured him. "You've asked for a mid-week day off, and we shouldn't waste it. Go saddle Eagle and Alegría. I'll be along as soon as I grab a bite to eat."

Pedro came into the room just as José left. "What," he asked, "was that racket about? I was fast asleep until the shouting and banging began." Stopping in his tracks, he looked closely at Carlos. "What's the matter with you? Are you sick? You look like something Gordo dragged in." From his sleeping pad in the corner of the kitchen, Gordo was watching Carlos with a look that seemed to agree with Pedro.

"I'm not sick," Carlos protested, "just a little tired—really dragging, if you must know."

"That's not like you," Pedro replied. "You're seldom sick. You probably don't even remember what being sick feels like."

"You're full of confidence-inspiring observations, Señor Gallegos. No, I just feel lethargic, though I'm puzzled as to why. All I did at the housewarming party was watch Leandro's magic tricks and dance with Mara."

"Mmm," Pedro said. "Dancing with Mara might leave a man exhausted."

Pedro's comment surprised Carlos, but he dimly wondered if Pedro might be right. He shook his head, trying to clear it. He vaguely remembered dancing very fast with Mara—no, that was a long time ago, with Selena. Last night he had danced with Mara, to the *seco* beat, but he had only the foggiest memory of what the dance itself had been like. There seemed to be a large, dark hole in his memory, a hole that throbbed with violet light at its very center. He realized that he had a major headache.

Carlos splashed some cold water on his face, gulped down some cold stew, pulled on his coat, and headed outside to the stable in back of the house. He began to feel better in anticipation of getting into the high desert country and drawing on the energies of that environment to restore him. José had their horses ready to go, so they mounted up and headed off.

The ride north from Santa Fe to the Spirit Ledge proved as restorative as Carlos had hoped. Upon arriving at the mountain pool below the cliffs, Don Carlos and José unsaddled their mounts and staked them on long tethers to graze.

Don Carlos described José's task for the day as Old Man Xenome had outlined it earlier. "The shaman," he told José, "must learn to become sensitive to the subtle energies of places, animals, and people. Ordinary people look at this place and see only the surface of things: a pool, a grassy bank, trees and shrubs, a few birds flitting about, and a steep cliff overhead. A shaman, who is attuned to the deeper levels of reality, sees the life forces that pulse through everything.

"Your task today is to begin honing your capacity to see those deeper levels. Once your skills as a shaman become refined you'll be able to locate the special features of this place without any hints from me, but today I'll tell you about the spot you're to find. On the cliff above us, there's a deposit of crystals—large numbers of them in various colors. That site has long been known to medicine men, and when we finally reach it, you'll see evidence that they have used it for vision quests. The only instruction I'll give now is to look around. Can you see—remember you are developing a special kind of sight, the shaman's vision—where the crystals are located? I'll leave you to that task and take a nap. I'll check on you later."

Don Carlos slept for an hour, enjoying a restful, dreamless sleep. As he awakened an image came to him of Inéz from the time they'd had a picnic at the pool below the Spirit Ledge. Memories of their delight in the splendors of the place—the multi-colored auras of the plants and animals, the glory of the sunlight, and the warmth of the pool—filled him with great peace and happiness.

After a few moments he got up and went to see how José was progressing. Not too well, it seemed. "You told me," José said, "that the crystals are on the cliff above us. I've been looking at the cliff—standing back from it as far as I can get, and also going up close to it and looking up as far as I can see, but all I'm seeing is what you called the surface of things."

"You must be patient with yourself, José. If the shaman's sight came quickly or without any training, then everyone would see beneath the surface of things. And, by the way, the surface of things isn't to be disdained. However, since we hope to get back to Santa Fe this afternoon, we don't have much time to spend here today. Let me give you a hint. I'm guessing that you have a special affinity for spirit beings that reside in plants. If I'm right about that, then what you need to do is to look around for a few minutes and ask yourself which of the plants here has a quality that you find in some way special. Don't try too hard. Let the discovery be as spontaneous and unplanned as possible."

José, in a move that told Don Carlos the young man had good natural instincts, sat down on the bank near where Eagle and Alegría were grazing and let his gaze move slowly over his surroundings. Eventually he announced, "That gnarled piñon tree up on the cliff that's growing out of a crack in the rock seems—heroic."

"Excellent!" Carlos exclaimed. "You couldn't have chosen better. That piñon is special. Consider this. The seed from which it sprang fell in an unpropitious place—a place with little soil and almost no space for its roots to spread. Most men might say it's stunted, but you chose a better word: gnarled. Given that it's been shaped by the hard circumstances of the unpromising place in which it landed, your choice of the word heroic is good. Unlike men who are defeated by adversity or give up when facing a nearly insurmountable challenge, your piñon has persisted and even prospered. Consequently, that piñon has powerful soul energies that in a human being we would call endurance and wisdom. Climb up there and see if your piñon friend will give you advice on finding the Spirit Ledge."

José immediately followed Don Carlos's directions. He climbed up to the piñon tree, sat down next to it, and stayed there for the better part of an hour before climbing back down to report to Carlos. "I heard the old tree speak to me," he said, "in something more like an inner voice than a sound. It told me to sit here and scan the cliff with my peripheral vision until I see a place that's different, marked by a glittering light."

Having received proper instructions—Carlos knew the piñon's advice was good, since he had often used the same technique successfully—José spotted the Spirit Ledge in less than ten minutes. Eagerly, he climbed up the steep slope, followed by Don Carlos, to the place where the crystal deposits were located. At Don Carlos's suggestion, they walked slowly around the site to see the various colors and shapes of crystals found there. After they'd toured the whole area Don Carlos took a small pick out of his knapsack and told José that he could collect some samples to take back to Santa Fe. "Take no more than one of each color. We show respect for the crystals and this place by being sparing in what we take. Also, apologize to the crystals for any discomfort you cause them when you dig one out."

After a brief silence, José said, "I don't need any. I think I'd rather leave them here."

"That's fine too," Carlos assured him. "The other thing you should know is that this site has been visited by shamans for many years. You can see where they've carefully removed one or two crystals for their healing work. Also, look at the cliff wall that forms the back of this ledge. Do you see a shallow recess in the cliff wall?"

It took José a few moments to locate the spot. "Yes," he exclaimed. "There seems to be a red and black outline of a hand on the back wall."

"Exactly. Go over there and sit below the image of the hand. It will help attune you to the power of this place. I'll go off on my own business and return in about an hour." José nodded that he would do as Don Carlos said.

Don Carlos immediately set about to pursue a plan of his own. As soon as he was well out of José's sight, he undressed and transformed himself into a red-tailed hawk. It was a windy day, and he soared into the air, making the gusty wind currents into his playground: swooping back and forth in swift curving passes near the cliffs, surrendering himself to sublime aerial maneuvers, and delighting in all the forms of virtuosity the hawk's body allowed. Although he was playing at flight, he was simultaneously engaged in serious work, since every expression of the hawk's formidable powers of flight strengthened his brujo energies.

He would have been happy to continue his day as the hawk-Carlos had he not spotted the den occupied by Inéz's skunk friend, Elvira. Landing on the lower limb of a pine tree near the pool, he changed into his human form and dropped to the ground. He wanted to call on Elvira, and he wondered what animal form to transform into to make his visit successful. He decided a female skunk would be the least threatening form to take. He effected the change and waddled over to the mouth of her den and called, "Elvira!"

Elvira answered from inside her den. "Who are you?"

"I'm new in the area," Don Carlos replied, "a bruja in skunk form."

"What do you want? I have no intention of coming out of my den in broad daylight."

"I have a question to ask."

"That's fine. Just don't try to enter my den."

"Don't worry. I have no intention of doing so. I am visiting the area on behalf of a brujo who comes here now and then, once with a woman friend of his."

"I remember her," Elvira replied. "Nice person, and she and her friend make a nice couple, allowing for their strange habits—taking their pelts off to swim in the pool—and the fact that humans aren't good-looking in comparison with skunks."

Don Carlos winced at Elvira's judgment about his and Inéz's appearance, but he supposed beauty was in the eye of the beholder. He began explaining what he wanted to know. "My brujo friend is from far south of here. Recently he's seen some strange things that worry him. In the last week alone he's encountered spirit animals of a menacing type. One was a large black wolf; the other was a flock of turkey vultures. Is there any information circulating among the local animals about these entities?

"We've heard rumors," Elvira responded, "and Cousin Coyote even went to a farm near the place called Santa Fe to talk with the mice and squirrels there. As you might imagine, since Cousin Coyote likes to eat mice and squirrels, they stayed in their holes when they talked with him, and that made their answers hard for him to hear. Cousin Coyote—his name is Che— reported that the creatures he talked with said that one day they'd seen a large flock of turkey vultures circling low above the town and then, shortly afterward, a wolf that was trotting toward the town center early one morning, which is strange because wolves and turkey vultures usually avoid towns. No one knew much about these entities, but all the mice and squirrels seemed to think that they are spirit animals, apparitions rather than flesh and blood. Che came away with the impression that these black entities had arrived in the area only recently. They definitely aren't the witches or demons from around here that are well known to us."

"Could the wolf be a sorcerer who's a shape-shifter?"

"Possibly."

"How many such dark entities have invaded the area?"

"You are asking many questions," Elvira replied, "to which there are no clear answers."

Don Carlos would have lingered, but he needed to get back to José. In quick succession, he thanked her for her help, changed from a skunk into a blue jay, flew to the Spirit Ledge where he'd left his clothes, and returned to human form. He found José seated below the painted hand with a contented look on his face. "I gather," Carlos said, "you've had a good time."

"Yes, I have, Don Alfonso. As I sat here waiting for you to return, everything got very quiet. I didn't hear even a bird call until a minute ago. Although I didn't think I should leave this spot while you were away, something made me want to get up and look for a special crystal. The impulse was so strong I felt I shouldn't ignore it."

"You did exactly what a shaman ought to do, José."

"Thank you. Let me show you what I found."

José held out his fist and opened it to reveal a clear crystal that sparkled in the mid-day sunlight. Most striking of all, it was a double crystal, with a perfect point on each end. "That's special, José, a treasure. Do you know who or what guided you to the crystal?"

"Guided me? What do you mean?" José asked uncertainly.

Don Carlos leaned very close to José and spoke in an almost inaudible whisper. "There is nothing to worry about," he assured him. "Trust me and do precisely what I say. Don't move until I signal you to do so. Do you remember a small piñon tree on the right side of the ledge—one that's even more gnarled than your spirit friend down the slope?"

José nodded his head ever so slightly.

"All right. In a moment I'll wink my eye, and at that very instant I want you to turn your head as fast as possible in the direction of the tree and fix your gaze on its skinny trunk. Tell me what, if anything, you see." With this Carlos winked his eye, and José rotated his body with lightning swiftness and looked at the tree.

"Did you see anything?"

"There's nothing to see; just a gnarled piñon tree."

"Of course, there's nothing now, but did you see anything else besides the tree for even a instant? If you didn't, that's all right; you'll have many more days to practice your craft."

Shyly, José replied. "For a fleeting moment I thought I saw the shadow of a man. The shadow vanished instantly, and I doubted that I'd seen anything."

"Good! You don't yet realize what a magnificent accomplishment that was on your part. What you saw was the spirit shadow of the shaman who left his handprint on the wall behind you. He also guided you to that extraordinary double crystal you're holding in your hand.

"As for this place, you must return here often. In time, perhaps, the ancient shaman will show himself to you more plainly, possibly even speak with you. He is, from what I saw, a member of the Ancient Ones' generation, a shaman who lived to be nearly one hundred years old. Tell your teacher Xenome what you saw. He will be glad for you."

"If you saw the Ancient One, you must be a shaman too, Don Alfonso."

"Don't leap to conclusions, though I admit I have some skills that might seem to suggest that I'm a Spanish shaman."

"Is a Spanish shaman different from a Pueblo shaman?"

"I hoped to make you laugh at the notion of a Spanish shaman. Remember what I told you when you first asked me whether I was a shaman?"

"You answered with a question, asking whether I'd ever heard of a Spaniard who was a shaman."

"Exactly," Carlos replied. José looked at Carlos quizzically but seemed to realize that a further clarification would not be forthcoming. He's a good man and an excellent student, Carlos thought to himself.

The two seekers' ride back to Santa Fe was uneventful. At the town's outskirts, they went their separate ways, José making a quick stop at Carlos's house to leave Alegría there and then continuing on to the blacksmith shop where he was working as an apprentice. Carlos rode directly to the site of the house that he, Pedro, and Diego, with some help from their Tesuque Indian friends, were building for Dr. Fabio Velarde.

"Things are going very well," Pedro told him when Carlos rode up. "We luckily found enough adobe bricks and large timbers to complete two rooms and get a roof over them by next week. Dr. Velarde saw our plan and liked the idea of a courtyard house with the courtyard opening to the southwest, which gets the strongest sunlight. He can live in the two rooms we'll complete first. We'll build the other wing as soon as the weather warms up and we can make adobe bricks."

"Excellent," Carlos replied, feeling very pleased that a day that had started badly was going so well. He no longer sensed any of the lethargy he'd felt when he woke up.

Telling his friends to keep up the good work, he rode home, unsaddled Eagle and turned him out, and walked to the Beltrán house in hopes of visiting Inéz before she gave Elena her next fencing lesson. His timing was perfect. Inéz had changed into her fencing outfit and was checking some kettles in the hearth. Turning to him, she said, "How lucky that you should come along just now."

"No, the good fortune is all mine to be welcomed by such an entrancing woman."

"If it's enchantment you're after, I fear I can't rival the two dancers who are trying to bewitch you. And before you attempt some sort of witty repartee, allow me to invite you to come to Elena's lesson today. I think it's time for her to see a demonstration of high-quality fencing, and I'd like you to fence with me—unless, of course, you prefer to let me fall into Leandro's clutches."

"Has he been after you recently?"

"I haven't seen him since last night. He and his two beguiling companions are out of town today."

"Any word on why?"

"Their fame has spread. Some people from Francisco Trujillo's ranch heard about their entertainments in Santa Fe, and they offered Leandro and the dancers a tidy sum to do several performances for their friends and neighbors. That's all I know. Now let me show you the fencing strip."

Inéz took Carlos by the arm and steered him through the Beltrán house. Elena's mother met them at the door to the patio. After Inéz explained why Carlos was along, Cristina smiled and said, "What a treat for Elena. She's waiting for you on the fencing strip."

Elena's face lit up when she saw that Carlos was with Inéz and Inéz told her what she had in mind for the day's session. "Let's get started, Alfonso," Inéz said, directing him to some foils lying on a wooden chest.

"Where did you get these?" he asked, astonished. "They look like mine; in fact, they are mine."

"You are the victim of a conspiracy hatched by Pedro and me. Pedro brought them over earlier when I told him I hoped you'd be able to join Elena and me today."

The bout commenced. Carlos found that his skills were a bit rusty at first, and Inéz also seemed out of practice. Although she'd been doing basic exercises with Elena, it had been a long time since she'd had a chance to test herself against a skilled opponent. They were both aware that they weren't meeting their highest standards, but when they missed an obvious move defensively or offensively, they laughed at their errors. "We'll be warmed up soon, Elena," Inéz announced, "and then you'll see sparks fly."

"I'm already impressed," Elena replied happily. "Don't worry about me."

A little while later, Carlos said, "I think we're close to being competent again. Why don't we establish some parameters for our bout? Let's see who gets the most hits in ten exchanges."

"Fine by me," Inéz replied.

Having a framework within which to test their skills heightened the intensity of their competition. Out of ten exchanges, Carlos scored seven hits and Inéz three. Remembering that he often won nine of ten in past bouts, Carlos asked, "Have I gotten that much worse, or are you so much better?"

"You know very well that you're still not performing at your highest level. Let's do another ten."

Of the next ten hits, Carlos won eight, although at least half of them were hard won, the end result of brilliant exchanges. One of the two hits that Inéz scored came on the next-to-last exchange. "If we had started counting after the eighth point," she said with a smile in Elena's direction, "we would be tied: one hit each."

"That being the case," Carlos proposed, "why don't we fence for one more hit, with the winner taking all?" He knew that his words would remind Inéz of a memorable bout they had had shortly after they'd met a year and a half earlier.

"And what will you claim as your prize, if you win?"

"I'm a man of modest habits and demands," he began, a statement that made Inéz laugh. "All I will require if I win the exchange is a kiss from my opponent. And what prize would she claim, if she wins?"

"We would spend my night off with Pedro and María, and you would tell us some stories from your youth that we've never heard. But you tend to win such a high proportion of exchanges that I should probably do something to even the odds."

"The last time you tried that, it didn't work."

"I know, and we shouldn't ever repeat ourselves."

"I agree," he said. "As the old saying goes, you can't step in the same river twice."

She smiled. "You can if the river is frozen, though that scarcely seems to apply to us. Let's get on with it and see who wins. To give me a shadow of a chance, restrict your hits to the middle of my torso."

"As in the past, placing that limit on my hits gives you a significant advantage."

"All's fair in love and war, or so they say, and our bout is a curious combination of both. You haven't said you'll accept the rule I've suggested." Smiling, Carlos agreed.

With those ground rules in place they began to fence. The bout quickly became an extraordinarily intense contest. Both Carlos and Inéz fenced with great skill. Neither seemed able to gain an advantage over the other. At times Carlos drove Inéz back to the far edge of her end of the fencing strip, only to have her launch a furious counteroffensive that drove him back in the other direction. Three times they met in a stalemated position at the middle of the strip, their bodies pressing against each other, their faces mere inches apart. The third time that they found themselves locked eye to eye, Carlos couldn't resist saying, "Had you worn that perfume of yours that sometimes brought me close to fainting, you would have won by now."

Speaking in a whisper so that Elena could not hear, she said, "My mistake, but just to raise the stakes a bit, I propose that you be allowed to use your special vision, as I will do with my similar powers that you've been training."

As the two combatants separated again, Carlos, now free to use his sorcerer's vision and to benefit from anticipating his opponent's next move, was struck by how the two of them were suffused in the warm, golden luminescence of their auras. His had expanded to envelop nearly the whole length of the fencing strip, and Inéz's extended nearly as far, with the result that where their auras overlapped, the golden light was doubly intense. The atmosphere was electric, but then, with a suddenness that surprised both of them, Carlos's creativity led to a breakthrough and he scored a touché on Inéz's padded vest just below her left breast.

All action ceased, and, exhausted, they lowered the tips of their blades to the floor. Clasping her torso where his weapon had touched home, Inéz declared, "You have pierced me through, straight to my heart."

Reacting to the look of alarm that came on Carlos's face, she laughed and said, "No, Alfonso, you haven't hurt me. My reference was to a metaphorical piercing."

She lowered her sword and walked slowly over to him. "Claim your prize."

They stood face-to-face, warm and breathing heavily from their exertions. For Carlos it was the experience from the end of the dance with Mara all over again, except that this time he acted on his desire to kiss his partner. He gently lowered his mouth to hers and they kissed. The kiss continued for a long moment until Inéz made a sound like "Mmm, mmm" and drew back slightly, turning her eyes away to direct his attention to Elena, the solitary witness.

Regretting the necessity, but agreeing with Inéz that discretion required that they stop, he softly voiced his feelings toward her. "You are magnificent," he said.

She looked at him, her eyes tender, and replied, "It's been too long since we've fenced." Then she addressed Elena, "What did our one-person audience think of all that?"

"The fencing was extraordinary! Such virtuosity! And your final embrace was beautiful beyond words. Such love!"

Having said this, Elena's eyes filled with tears. "Don't mind me," she said, as they went to comfort her. Addressing herself to Inéz, she said, "I know I'll never find anyone who loves me as Don Alfonso loves you."

"There, there," Inéz murmured consolingly, taking her student in her arms. "Dear Elena, there's no predicting where or when one will find love. Your moment will come some day. I know it."

14

Transitions

The rest of the week after what Don Carlos came to think of as "The Kiss" passed in a blur. Buoyed by the memory of kissing Inéz at the end of their fencing bout, he was in a very good mood. Every day he had stopped by the Beltráns' in hope of finding Inéz available for a stroll or at least a talk. He had no luck at all. She was always busy. On Wednesday she had explained a bit impatiently, "There are many formal dinners in town because several leading members of Santa Fe society, including Governor Villela and his wife and your stepbrother and his wife and son, are departing with the supply caravan at the end of this week. I've been asked to help prepare a special dish, usually an appetizer or a dessert, for nearly every dinner. All these extra demands on my time are running me ragged."

On Friday it occurred to him to wonder who was hosting these dinners, and he cornered Inéz long enough to ask her.

"Let's see. The Peraltas held one for the Villelas. The Cabreras held one to welcome the Presidio's new commander, Captain Posada. The Mendozas threw a big party for everyone with an official post—the Peraltas, the Villelas, the Archuletas, the Cabreras, the Posadas, and your stepbrother and his wife."

"The Mendozas? Aren't they that old Santa Fe family that's somehow related to Juan de Oñate, the first governor of New Mexico province?"

"Some sort of cousins," Inéz replied. "Cristina has been filling me in on all of this. The Mendozas are a politically powerful and very wealthy family who have returned to reclaim property they abandoned when they fled town as refugees from the Pueblo Revolt twenty-five years ago. Cristina said that they brought five wagonloads of furnishings with them to their big hacienda overlooking the north acequia. She added that the way they've furnished their residence carries a clear message that they intend to reclaim their former position at the top of Santa Fe's social pyramid."

"I note that I wasn't invited to any of these affairs."

"Don't lose any sleep over that," Inéz replied. "You don't particularly enjoy formal dinners, and you don't have social ties to the Peraltas, and the Mendozas are returnees who don't know you at all."

"I have a feeling there's more to it than that."

"That may be. I wouldn't know. I don't have time for idle gossip."

"I'm busy too," he said. "Diego and I plan to take several trips into the country this week to collect more white rocks, and Pedro and I have been working long hours on the house we're building for Dr. Velarde. José says that Rubén and Lázaro, his cousins from Tesuque Pueblo, and two of their friends are coming today and tomorrow to help us. We're going to finish the walls for one wing of the house and raise the roof over it, a complicated job that requires all the manpower we can muster."

"You really must go," Inéz declared. "It's even possible that another reason why you're not getting invited to this week's banquets is that you have a romantic relationship with a cook. For people like Pilar Peralta and the Mendozas that's unsuitable behavior for an upper-class Spaniard, definitely *déclassé*, as the French would say."

"I didn't know you knew French."

"Out!" she exclaimed in mock exasperation, pushing him firmly toward the door. "I have to get back to work."

What Inéz had suggested about the attitude of some upper-class Santa Fe residents toward him didn't come as a complete surprise to Carlos. As he reached the plaza he was still mulling over its implications when he heard someone hailing him, "Don Alfonso! Over here!" It was Leandro, who was coming toward him at an angle but headed in the same general direction. They shook hands and started walking together toward the south part of town.

"Welcome back," Carlos said. "Did you have a good trip to Trujillo's ranch?"

"Yes, Trujillo, his family, and some neighbors were an appreciative audience. And they paid us well, which always buoys our spirits. But I'm concerned about scheduling performances here. I've heard that there are many dinner parties in town this week, and we haven't been invited to perform at any of them. Is somebody spreading stories that we're no fun?"

"I don't know for certain," Carlos admitted, "but if I had to guess, I would say that it's precisely because your threesome is so much fun that you've not been invited to perform at these parties."

"Too much fun? You mean our performances are too flamboyant?"

Carlos clapped Leandro on the shoulder, overcome with friendly feelings toward the three entertainers. "The departure of Governor Villela and his wife and my stepbrother Joaquin Alvarez and his wife will remove two of the leading families from Santa Fe society. The new governor's wife, Pilar Peralta, is, I gather, determined to establish herself as the arbiter of upper-class social life. Apparently she has found an ally in Josephina Mendoza, the matriarch of a very wealthy family that has deep roots in Santa Fe and has just returned to town after twenty-five years in exile due to the Pueblo Revolt. Both Pilar Peralta and Josephina Mendoza are very conservative. Neither of them would approve of a marriage between a son or grandson of theirs and a woman from the servant class, as the more open-minded Villelas did in welcoming my stepsister-in-law's personal maid as the wife of their only son. Another feature of their conservatism is that they regard themselves as guardians of propriety, and your performances are, as you say, too flamboyant, too racy. To top it off, you're pagans."

"Pagans?" Leandro laughed. "I suppose so. As itinerant entertainers, we're more like Gypsies than Catholics. But what about you? I gather you were born into an upper-class family and had a high position in the provincial government."

"Not so high, at least not in their eyes. I held a subordinate post as the governor's secretary, and now I've lost even that status. Also, several aspects of my life don't conform to the Peralta-Mendoza concept of what is required for high social standing. Although I attend Mass nearly every Sunday, I suspect that members of their circle nevertheless consider me a pagan, or at least very unorthodox."

"If enjoying dancing and being open to the spirit of *duende* makes you a pagan, I suppose you qualify as one," Leandro observed. "But is that their only evidence of your pagan proclivities?"

An interesting question, Carlos thought, wondering if Leandro was linking *pagan* to *brujo*. He skirted that possibility by taking the conversation in a different direction. "There is," he began, "one other criterion members of the small coterie of upper-class people who share the Peralta-Mendoza mentality might use to exclude me from their circle, or at least keep me on its margins. You know how significant ancestry is in both Spain and New Spain. At the top of society are pure-blooded Spaniards of noble birth. Not for these families to have even a drop of Jewish or Moorish blood. And in New Spain social superiority depends not only on blood but on where your parents and grandparents were born. Families like the Peraltas and Mendozas, all of whose older members were born in Spain, are considered of higher status than those of us like me, whose parents and grandparents, titled or not, were born in New Spain."

"I don't understand," Leandro said, apparently genuinely puzzled. "Even though your grandparents were born in New Spain, you're still Spanish. Do these arbiters of social rank suspect that your ancestry is tainted by Jewish or Moorish blood?"

"Who knows? But it's surely come to their attention that I'm comfortable socializing with someone like Selena, whose appearance doubtless leads them to suspect that she has some ancestry, either Gypsy or Moorish, other than pure Spanish."

"True enough," Leandro replied, "but may I point out that you haven't answered my question about your possible paganism. I've frankly acknowledged mine, but I don't see any evidence of yours beyond your love of dance and affinity for *duende*."

In the glow of his warm feelings for Leandro, Carlos became more expansive. "It's probably not gone unnoticed—in a town this size nothing goes unnoticed—that I've formed a mentoring relationship with a young Pueblo man, José Lugo, who has aspirations to be a medicine man. That, in the eyes of Catholic orthodoxy, is about as far out on the pagan scale as one can get."

"Interesting," Leandro commented. "I've been wondering about the copper bracelet you wear. It doesn't look like a piece of Spanish jewelry. Both my lady friends were very taken with it."

"The bracelet," Carlos replied, caution returning as he wondered if Leandro had some knowledge of the bracelet's effect on the large wolf that had appeared in town, "was a gift from the Tesuque medicine man with whom José is studying. He's a shaman known as Old Man Xenome."

"Ah," Leandro said lightly, "so you wear a pagan artifact, which I assume must be imbued with power. From that it seems you have some knowledge of Native religion. If so, perhaps you can tell me," he went on in the same disarming tone, "whether the terms medicine man and shaman are synonyms for what we Spaniards would call a brujo?"

"No, quite the contrary," Carlos replied. "Among a medicine man's many roles within his community is responsibility for driving off witches, as brujos and brujas are known. While medicine men are devoted to the health of their neighbors, witches are viewed as malicious and injurious to the community's well-being." Leandro nodded, understanding the distinction.

The two men, who had been walking toward the site on which Carlos was having Dr. Velarde's house built, now reached it and halted in the lane beside it. Pedro and Diego were already at work and waved greetings, but since the Tesuque men had not yet arrived, Carlos decided to keep talking with Leandro. He was curious where Leandro's line of questioning might lead and inquired, "Is there anything else I can tell you about local customs, either Spanish or Indian?"

"One more question about medicine men. I've heard it said that they can transform themselves into animal forms. Do you know anything about that?"

"I've heard the same stories," Carlos replied, "but what you're describing would be equally true of witches, who attack their victims in animal form, often as coyotes."

"Do you have any idea how these transformations are achieved, whether by witches or shamans?"

"No, I don't," Carlos answered quite truthfully. "All I know is that Native shamans reach trance states through fasting, chanting, and ingesting mind-altering plants. But it seems to me a huge leap from altering one's perceptions to actually assuming the form of an animal. I've wondered whether the transformation is imaginary, in the shaman's mind, or whether a shaman truly takes on the shape and appearance of the animal. I don't know, and the secrets of a shaman's training are closely guarded."

"So, assuming your friend José learns to do transformations, you aren't likely to find out how he achieves them?"

"I don't expect to. But Leandro, you seem extremely curious about transformations. Do they figure in your magic or that of the man you call Master?" Dangerous territory here, Carlos realized, but worth treading lightly into it. He sat down on a pile of timbers and gestured for Leandro to join him, which he did.

"As a magician," Leandro began, "I would love to be able to change an apple into a mouse rather than simply creating the illusion that I've done so through sleight of hand, and of course I'm interested in how it might be done. When my teacher began to study magic, he took a great interest in transformations. Initially, he thought the science known as alchemy offered the best avenue to achieving transformations, but despite some successes, he never attained his ultimate goal."

Leandro paused, falling silent as though he felt he'd revealed more than he intended. Carlos prompted him. "I've heard that many serious scholars pursued alchemy, especially two or three centuries ago, and even today. What frustrated your teacher?"

"He read a wide variety of occult texts but found them impenetrable. They contained symbols and formulae whose meaning could not be deciphered. But he believed in the main principles of occult practitioners—that nature is alive, that the universe is a giant organism woven together like a spider's web—and he hoped that if he fully understood all the relationships of nature in all its varieties, material and spiritual, he could control all natural phenomena, including being able to change one form of matter into another."

"Such as changing base metal into gold?" Carlos ventured carefully.

"Some lesser alchemists did have materialistic goals of that sort," Leandro replied. "But in his youth my teacher and his closest allies were in pursuit of something much more profound, which was to discover the laws that govern Heaven and Earth by discerning the correspondences between small, everyday phenomena and the cosmos. His was an effort to attain the furthest reaches of spiritual truth."

Carlos thought about this for a while. "A noble undertaking," he declared without a trace of irony. "But it's not clear to me how an understanding of spiritual truth could enable one to do what shamans are said to do in taking on the form of an animal."

"I also fail to see the connection," Leandro replied, "which is why I'm asking you these questions."

"Once alchemy failed to provide this man you call Master the answers he sought," Carlos asked, "did he give up the study of transformations altogether?"

"Not exactly," Leandro said evasively. "A long time ago, before I knew him, he parted from his own master under unpleasant circumstances and consequently left the circle of other magicians who had once been his closest allies. They went their way, becoming rivals who pursued different methods from his."

"And," Carlos inquired, "what was the nature of your teacher's methods?"

"I'm not at liberty to tell you," Leandro replied. "He's ordered me not to reveal such details to anyone who's not his apprentice. All I can say is that he achieved transformations, but he felt his method was inferior to that of an old rival and one of that man's apprentices. In seeking out Mateo Pizarro, the magician who died mysteriously, I had hoped to learn whether Pizarro had mastered this other, supposedly superior method of transformations."

Carlos was burning with curiosity to know whether the rival of Leandro's master was none other than his own teacher, Don Serafino Romero, and whether that teacher's apprentice was himself, Carlos Buenaventura. But he didn't see any safe way to pursue those details. It was a puzzle, and several important parts of it were missing. He knew—because he himself in an earlier lifetime had been at the scene—that Don Malvolio had died in 1603. He also knew that Malvolio had been reborn some decades later and had taken revenge on Don Carlos, killing him in 1683. And he knew from Manuel Tapia that Malvolio was again in pursuit of him less than a year ago. From those facts it was obvious that Malvolio had learned the art of retaining his consciousness through death and being reborn with that consciousness intact. But nothing Leandro had told him suggested that the man he called Master had lived many lives. To be sure, the possibility remained that Leandro's master hadn't revealed that information to Leandro, or that Leandro knew and was hiding it from Carlos. There seemed no way of knowing for certain whether or not Leandro's master and Malvolio were one and the same person.

"Are you going to talk or work?" Pedro called from the construction site. Their four Tesuque helpers had arrived and were ready to start completing the house's walls and roof.

"Duty calls," Carlos told Leandro, standing up and reverting to his usual social tone. "I've enjoyed our conversation. I hope to hear more, whatever you're free to tell me, of course. I'm afraid it won't be a fair exchange because the education I had with Jesuit tutors didn't go deeply into occult sources. They taught me a little about the philosophy of alchemy but nothing about its practice." Carlos and Leandro shook hands in a friendly fashion and Leandro went on his way. Watching the figure of the retreating magician, Carlos decided that he rather liked Leandro without being entirely sure he could trust him.

The house-raising project went well that day and the next, and by the time darkness set in Saturday night Don Carlos and his helpers had completed a two-room wing of the house and roofed it over. The four Tesuque men had intended to leave immediately, but Carlos prevailed on them to spend the night. Two of them could sleep on the floor of Carlos's bedroom and the other two could share Diego's quarters in the hayloft. They left at dawn Sunday morning.

After seeing them off, Carlos grabbed a cup of coffee before hurrying to the plaza, where the southbound supply caravan was assembling for its departure. He talked briefly with Javier Beltrán, who had eight wagons in line, each of them filled with typical Santa Fe trade goods— raw wool, coarse woolen cloth, hides, and pine nuts. Carlos moved on to wish his old boss, now ex-Governor Villela, and his wife Isabel a safe journey and a pleasant life in retirement in Mexico City.

His next and final stop was to bid his stepbrother and sister-in-law, Joaquin and Francie Alvarez, farewell. Carlos's little nephew Esteban was fussing, and Francie handed him to Carlos and said, "See what you can do to quiet him down. It's your last chance to play uncle for the foreseeable future." Much to his surprise Carlos had some success with the child, possibly because Esteban regarded being held by his uncle as a novelty.

Joaquin came over and told Carlos, "We're sad to be leaving, and there are so many unknowns ahead, both on the trip and after we arrive in Mexico City."

"You'll be fine," Carlos assured Joaquin and Francie, sincerely believing his comforting words. "Francie's parents and the rest of the Suarez clan will bring their considerable influence to bear on your behalf. Also you'll find valuable allies in my sister Fortunata and her husband, Emiliano Alaniz. If the review of your military status goes poorly, you should consider accepting a position in the trading company in which Emil is a managing partner."

"You're most kind," Joaquin replied, "and I know that I speak for Francie too when I say how very fond we've become of you. Please keep in touch by writing, infrequent though the chance is to send letters from Santa Fe to Mexico City."

Joaquin turned to talk with another well-wisher, and Francie held out her arms for Esteban. "I want to add my voice to everything Joaquin said about our love and admiration for you. Separating from you is part of the sadness we feel today." Brightening a bit—she was a cheerful, optimistic person—she added, "Perhaps it would amuse both of us if I shared some gossip I picked up from Margarita Posada, the wife of Joaquin's replacement as commandant. It seems that when they stopped in El Paso del Norte and visited our old friends Rafael and Camila, it was obvious that Camila was pregnant."

"Obviously pregnant? That was fast. How far along is she?"

"Margarita estimated close to six months, and I don't need you to point out that she must have gotten pregnant before they were married."

"Camila the chaste?" Carlos said, mildly shocked. "I'm not surprised that you sound affronted. Obviously, Camila broke your rule against female employees engaging in intimacies while living under your roof."

"I'm not going to berate her now that what's done is done, but if I'd known about it at the time, I would have kicked her pretty pink butt out of the house the next day."

Carlos was always startled when his sister-in-law, the offspring of one of Mexico City's most prestigious upper-class families, expressed herself in a vulgar way, but he enjoyed her occasionally salty language and joined her in laughing at her statement.

Shortly after sunrise the caravan lurched into motion, a long line of wagons, carriages, and riders beginning an arduous trek of many months to Mexico City. Carlos was saddened by their departure, not simply because the Villelas and the Alvarezes were some of his favorite people in Santa Fe, but because they also represented a significant proportion of his partisans among the town's social leaders.

Elena Beltrán had been waving to some friends of hers who were leaving. Now she came over to give a message to Carlos. "Inéz asked me," she reported, "to tell you that she's too busy to spend much time with you today; she's even going to skip Mass. What she suggests is that you poke your head in the kitchen door for a five-minute visit."

Elena rushed off to see another friend, so Carlos hurried to the Beltrán residence and knocked on the kitchen door. "Come in!" Inéz called. As he entered, and before he could say anything, she declared, "I'm at a very delicate moment with this breakfast dish. Let me keep an eye on it while I quickly ask some questions."

"What's on your mind?"

"I wondered why you missed the Trio's performance yesterday during Saturday market. I went in hopes of seeing you."

"Sorry, we were in the middle of putting up the wall and raising the roof for the east wing of Dr. Velarde's future home. We needed all the muscle-power we could muster."

"I suppose that's an adequate excuse, although I was disappointed that you weren't there. Since you weren't, I danced with Leandro."

"Ouch!" he exclaimed. "I'm already feeling low from having seen Joaquin, Francie, and Esteban leave town, and now I learn that you've been dancing with another man, and a handsome fellow at that. Besides, didn't you tell Leandro that you were reserving the next dance for me?"

Inéz gave him a serious look. "Don't tease about that," she said. "The reason I said that was to emphasize that you're first in my heart, something you surely know, or ought to. What man I dance with and when doesn't change that in the least."

"I feel the same way about you," he replied. "So what sort of dance was it? Certainly not the Unnamed Dance?"

"No, they said it was their variation on a new dance from Andalusia called the Fandango. It was quite simple and innocent. Leandro divided everyone who wanted to dance into groups of four. He, Selena, Fabio, and I were one foursome. We held hands and circled first right and then left as Mara alternated between counting the beat with castanets and the *seco* pole. Once we'd circled twice in each direction as a foursome, we broke into pairs— Leandro with me, Fabio with Selena—linked arms with our partner, and circled to the left, then the right, after which we were encouraged to clap our hands quickly three times before joining up as a foursome again. It was quite sweet, and to judge from the smiles of everyone who danced, it was enjoyed by all."

"Did Señor Luna importune you for kisses too?"

"It wasn't that sort of dance, and as Leandro said, they don't do the Unnamed Dance in public places like the plaza."

Since Carlos said nothing in response, Inéz continued her report. "After the Fandango, Leandro called the children up around him—he had a table set up on which he'd placed a basket for donations—and he did a few card tricks that entertained the children and made everyone laugh. Then he got very serious and mysterious—you know what a showman he is—and declared that, unbelievable as it might seem, there exists a creature called the 'Wolfman Spider,' and he promised to show it to us.

"You can imagine the sensation that created! He said that it lived in Europe but he had a specimen right here—not alive, fortunately, because it was very deadly, but he would now show us that it existed. Then, very solemnly, he took a box from the table, carefully opened it, and took out a sealed jar. Inside, suspended in a pale brown liquid, was a large, revolting, hairy spider. The audience gasped and the children shrieked and Leandro pretended to thrust the jar at them, which made them shriek more. Next he changed his style again, held the jar with the horrible spider close to his chest, and in a soothing voice calmed everyone down. Then he announced, very solemnly, that people bitten by this spider would become extremely agitated and involuntarily do a kind of frantic dance, which is known as the Tarantella, the Italian word for tarantula. 'As far as we know,' he said, 'Mara has never been bitten by the Wolfman Spider, but she has agreed to perform the Tarantella for you.'

"Carlos, it was the scariest thing I ever saw. Mara jumped around like a spider. She was so quick, so agile. She shot out her arms and legs; it almost looked as if she had eight of them. What made it scary was the frenzy—it was as if she were possessed. At first there was no *seco* beat, but as her agitation increased Leandro began a beat, and it seemed to help steady her. Her movements began to match the beat and gradually she slowed down. At the end she collapsed in his arms.

"The crowd was silent, awestruck. I wondered if Leandro hadn't gone too far. But then he turned the crowd's mood around again. 'Don't worry,' he said in a cheerful voice. 'Our Mara will be restored!' And he gave her a drink of something. It took a few moments, and the crowd held its collective breath until Mara stood up and smiled and made a graceful bow. 'Back from the brink of death!' Leandro crowed. 'Have you ever seen anything like it?' The crowd cheered wildly. Leandro grinned and handed Mara the donation basket, and she went into the crowd offering it and smiling. Reales poured in. People reached out to touch her, as if she really had returned from the dead."

"That must have been quite a sight," Carlos said. "I wish I'd seen her performance."

Inéz gave him one of her sideways looks. "She interests you, doesn't she? More than the flirtatious Selena."

"It's true that Mara is more mysterious," he began, and he might have gone on, but Inéz abruptly changed the subject.

"Oh, there's one more thing I want to ask you. Do you know what damiana looks like? It's a small shrub with short pale green leaves, though in some seasons the leaves are yellowish brown. In summer it puts out pretty yellow blossoms that have a spicy scent. The trouble is that it's more common south of here, and during winter damiana plants die back due to the cold."

"Yes, I've seen some. In fact, I know that there's a small cluster of plants in the arroyo where Diego and I have been collecting white rocks. They're in a sunny spot that's sheltered from the wind. Perhaps a few are alive."

"Please collect some."

"What for?" he asked, thoroughly puzzled.

"I don't have time to explain. I have to serve this soufflé this very minute. Will you be able to get some damiana soon?"

"Possibly today," he replied. "Since you aren't going to Mass, I'm inclined to skip it too. Diego and I can make a trip to the white stone site."

"Good—the sooner the better."

At that moment a maid entered the kitchen and Inéz said to her, "Please pick up the blue casserole; I'll take the yellow one; we've got to serve this soufflé before it collapses."

"Are you annoyed with me for missing yesterday's show?" Carlos asked.

"Not very," she called over her shoulder as she hurried out of the room.

That wasn't a particularly satisfactory answer, and Carlos found himself regretting having missed Mara's performance. The conceit of a dance that resulted from being bitten by a Wolfman Spider was full of so many troubling possibilities regarding dark energies that he didn't know where to start thinking about them. Deciding that the best antidote to uncertainty was to do something, he returned to his house and invited Diego to join him in an expedition to the site where they'd been gathering white stones.

On the way there he had a chance to ask Diego if he knew what Ana Lugo, the Indian girl he liked so much, was going to do for a job now that her former employers, the Alvarezes, had left town.

"There's good news about that," Diego replied. "The Trigales family needed another maid for their big place, and they've hired her. She starts today."

The trip itself proved entirely satisfactory. They collected several bags of chalcedony pieces, and Carlos found a damiana plant that was in its dormant stage. With apologies to the plant for disturbing its rest, he used his brujo power to get one branch to burst into green leaves and pretty yellow blossoms, which he collected and put in a small bag for Inéz. Best of all, the journey into the countryside calmed him, and he stopped puzzling about Mara and Leandro. Given the short days of January, they were lucky to get back to Carlos's house before darkness fell.

Carlos helped Diego unsaddle the horses and feed them, and together they carried the rock-filled saddlebags into the kitchen. José was waiting for them there, talking with Pedro. Immediately sensing that José had something of importance to tell him, Carlos looked at him expectantly. José reported that he'd been to visit Old Man Xenome earlier that day. He said, "Grandfather Xenome was pleased with my description of our trip to the Spirit Ledge. He called the two-faced crystal I found a strong power object, and he was even more pleased by my having glimpsed the Ancient One. He encouraged me to return often to the Spirit Ledge in hopes of gaining the ancient shaman's trust. His last words to me were a message for you. 'Tell Don Alfonso,' he said, 'that the time has come to spend three days at the lost kiva site.'"

Carlos smiled in satisfaction. "Why not leave tomorrow?" he proposed, and they agreed to start after breakfast.

Carlos sat down at the table and wrote a note. "José," he said, "I want Inéz to know we're going. Please take this to her at the Beltráns' house on your way home and be sure she gets it. I'll see you in the morning."

That night, of all the images from the day—the sight of his family and friends leaving Santa Fe, his brief visit with Inéz, and his trip with Diego to collect chalcedony and damiana—his dream consciousness selected a fragmentary image that he'd heard about but hadn't seen.

He found himself walking on the lane toward the house where Inéz had lived with Dr. Tiburcio, which was now being rented by Leandro, Mara, and Selena. Barely three hundred feet separated his home from theirs. As he passed his neighbor Gilberto Barrera's house, a violet spider jumped into his path, a monstrous spider that had eight hairy legs, a big body, and a head of heavy black hair. He instantly recognized that the spider was Mara.

Mara moved about in an agile way, sometimes seeming to scuttle low to the ground and at other times hopping and skipping in an exuberant manner. She seemed to be leading him toward her house. He followed her, more fascinated than frightened. It wasn't until he was only a few steps from her door that he looked up and saw, instead of her house, a huge spiderweb that filled his whole field of vision. A full moon was visible directly behind the spiderweb. It was just before dawn and dewdrops had fallen and covered the web's strands, creating a luminous display of many moons, each dewdrop capturing the moonlight and transforming it into a jewel.

Carlos woke up before he reached the spiderweb. He hadn't been frightened in the dream, but when he awoke he felt chilled, aware that he still might get caught in whatever web Mara and the other two entertainers were spinning, and that he might not escape with his life.

15

Kachinas

After a big breakfast, Carlos and José saddled Carlos's Eagle and Inéz's Alegría, whom she had said they could borrow any time because she was too busy to ride her. They had arranged to take Pedro's horse Pepper along as a packhorse. On their way out of town they stopped by the Beltráns' to say goodbye to Inéz and found her hard at work in the kitchen.

She didn't seem particularly glad to see Carlos. She didn't bother to stop what she was doing and gave the impression that she was too busy to talk with him. "So," she said, not looking at him, "I gather you're going off for a week to some remote place in Indian country."

Carlos, who was still buoyed up by blissful feelings from their kiss the week before, was taken aback by her chilly tone. Rallying, he said, "That's right. Old Man Xenome sent a message that it was time for José to undertake his vision quest. He gave us directions to a very secret place."

"So no one knows where you're going," Inéz said, turning to face him.
"Well, Xenome does —"
"But it's a secret place, so for all practical purposes nobody knows."
"Xenome gave directions to José —"

"Who will be with you, so it will be a secret from everyone else. And how long will you be gone? Does anybody know that?"

"Xenome said José was to spend three nights there, but we can't say in advance exactly how long the trip each way will take."

"So you're going to an unknown place, through country that is probably full of hostile Natives, and Heaven knows what might happen to you or when or where to send out a search party."

"Sweetheart," Carlos began.

"And don't," she said before he could say anything more, "tell me I'm being irrational. Or that the traders' caravan is also going off on a very long trip and they might meet hostile Natives. For most of them it's not an adventure. It's something they have to do. You don't have to do this."

Carlos looked at her steadily. "Yes, I do," he declared. "I gave Old Man Xenome my word I would do it."

"Well then, go," she said. "But don't expect me to be happy about it. Oh," she added, "and before you go, you ought to talk with Raul Trigales. He's here for breakfast and said he hoped to speak with you soon. You can find him in the dining room through the door to your left." She turned away again and addressed herself to her cooking.

"I'm going to miss you," he said to her back.

She made a sound that might have been a snort, but then relented, turned, and brushed his cheek with hers. "I'll miss you too."

Carlos entered the dining room and found Javier Beltrán and his brother-in-law Raul Trigales conversing intently. They broke off their talk, invited him to sit down, and offered him coffee, which he refused, saying he was about to leave on a trip.

"I've told you," Raul began, "about our plan to acquire a large horse herd to provide mounts and workhorses for the settlers who are coming to the area." Carlos nodded that he remembered. "As a sideline," Raul continued, "I just yesterday bought Barbon's stable. He wants to get out of town, and I don't think many people will be sorry to see him go. But I need someone to run the stable and Javier has suggested your man Pedro Gallegos. I'm asking your permission to approach him."

Carlos's heart sank at the thought of Pedro moving on, but the position Raul had to offer was a good opportunity, especially now that Pedro was married and he and María were starting a family. Despite his private feelings, he was sincere when he said to Raul, "Pedro would be a fine man for the job. He's as solid can be in every necessary category — knowledge of horses, a level-headed approach to life, and dependability. I don't think you could do better. My loss will be your gain."

"That's generous of you," Raul replied. "I'll speak with him soon. The other position I need to fill is that of an assistant cook. My wife informs me that our present cook is feeling overburdened by our large household's demands and wants help. My first choice would be to hire your friend Inéz away from Javier and Cristina, but Javier has made it plain that he'd never speak to me again if I tried."

Carlos knew what he needed to do, and even though he didn't want to, he went ahead. "The next best thing to having Inéz as your cook would be to employ a young Indian man she's been coaching. I refer to Diego Campos, who's been my groom and handyman. I don't feel he's ready to be the head chef, but he'd do very well as second cook."

"If I approach him and he agrees, that would leave you with no household help whatsoever," Raul observed. "I don't feel good about that."

"I don't either, truth be told," Carlos replied, "but I won't stand in the way of my friends bettering themselves, and the positions you're offering are definitely several steps up from the ones they hold with me. If Diego shows any reluctance at all, remind him that a young woman he likes a lot, Ana Lugo, is already in your employ."

"Will that pose a problem?"

"Not unless you object to employing a married couple, which I expect will happen fairly soon, and I say that as someone who sees love as a source of happiness."

"I can see that," Javier replied, "having seen you dance."

"That, it seems," Carlos ventured, feeling that Javier and Raul were allies, "may have led to gossip that has put me on the outs with some of Santa Fe's first families. I notice that I didn't get invited to the dinners given by some of our upper-class neighbors last week."

"We know exactly who you mean," Javier declared, annoyance showing in his expression. "That's their loss, and you might note that Raul and I and our wives weren't invited either. Members of the Peralta circle don't think much of mere merchants."

"And I'm now a businessman," Carlos observed, seeing the situation more clearly than he had previously.

"You are always welcome," Javier assured him, "in the Beltrán and Trigales houses and at our dinner tables."

Carlos expressed his gratitude for their words of friendship, but he left with mixed feelings. He was gratified to have the support of such good-hearted and wealthy neighbors as the Beltrán and Trigales families. But the thought of how empty his house would be without Pedro, María, and Diego was depressing. Only Gordo and me left, he observed.

Once outside, Carlos mounted Eagle and he and José started on their way. By alternating the pace between a brisk walk and an easy trot, they made good time. They continued northward until they came to a three-way fork in the road. The road to their right went to Nambe Pueblo, the straight-ahead route to Taos, and the left-hand road turned west toward San Ildefonso Pueblo. They turned left, rode past San Ildefonso, and soon reached the main ford of the Rio Grande.

Carlos wasn't too worried about Eagle making it across safely, but he was concerned about Pepper, who was loaded with their gear. He told José, on Alegría, to wait on the east bank while he forded the river. Although the current was strong, he and Eagle made it easily. He took a length of rope out of their supplies and doubled back. He secured the rope to one side of Pepper's halter while José held Pepper's lead rope on the other side. Steadying Pepper in this way, the men and horses made it across safely.

They were now on the south side of a small tributary river, and they were heading directly toward the mountains looming ahead. The edges of the mesas and the tops of a line of snow-capped peaks beyond were a glorious sight in the midday sun. The trail they were following passed through canyons that now and then broadened out into small meadows. Wildlife was everywhere. Six deer looked up curiously when the riders came into view, a covey of quail exploded into the air at their approach, and a coyote trotted off to put some distance between itself and the riders.

The south edge of the mesa that was their initial destination now came into view beyond a creek that crossed their route. The creek was no more than a foot deep, but Old Man Xenome had warned them that quicksand sinks would make crossing it dangerous. Using his brujo vision, Don Carlos spotted several such sinks at places that otherwise looked like perfect fords. Finally he located a ford where the footing was solid and led José and the horses across it.

Less than two hundred feet ahead, the slope of the mesa they were going to climb thrust steeply upward. Carlos and José dismounted and transferred some food and blankets from the packhorse to backpacks. They'd also brought fresh water, not knowing whether water would be available on top of the mesa. They loaded a third of the water into their backpacks and left the rest of it along with additional supplies in a cache at the mesa's base.

They then hastily constructed a temporary corral for their three horses, using dead tree branches. These they attached with rope to live trees and tree stumps to make a rough three-sided enclosure. There was enough grassy stubble inside the enclosure to permit the horses to graze happily, and the improvised corral's railings were flimsy enough that the horses could break out and run away if a predator threatened them.

After completing the corral, the two men undertook the most strenuous part of their trip. The mesa wall was nearly a thousand feet high. They picked their way upward, slowed by the weight of their backpacks. At one point they halted to watch as a great blue heron took off from a small pool in the river to the north of them. The big bird rose slowly and majestically from the canyon's floor, flying a spiraling path on the updraft of air currents, each gyre lifting it higher in ever-widening circles.

Once it reached an altitude above the mesa, the heron flew off and Carlos and José resumed their climb. When they arrived at the top, a potential problem remained. Carlos knew that once they walked out onto the mesa itself, it would be difficult to find the exact place where they'd reached the mesa's outer rim. He studied his surroundings carefully to find landmarks to locate that particular spot on the mesa's fissured edge. Seeing none, he and José constructed a cairn with stones to guide them back.

This task complete, they started across the mesa. Though it appeared flat when seen from a distance, the mesa's surface was made up of dips and gullies, and a second mesa rose from the first about a mile ahead. Following Old Man Xenome's directions, they hiked toward a cleft in the second mesa's wall. The cleft, a narrow arroyo caused by erosion, was their route up to the long-abandoned pueblo and the kivas at its center.

After clambering up the arroyo to the top of the second mesa, and building another cairn to mark that spot for their descent, Carlos and José saw their destination ahead. Remnants of stone houses were scattered about, only a few of them with walls more than two feet high. Carlos estimated that the settlement at one time must have had close to a hundred residents. The most remarkable feature of the place was that it had two kivas, possibly an indication that the pueblo's residents had been members of two clans, each with its own ceremonies and deities. One kiva was in remarkably good shape, considering that it had been abandoned hundreds of years earlier. It had half a roof, and the floor of its below-ground room was relatively uncluttered by debris. Carlos assumed, correctly as it turned out, that Old Man Xenome had made many repairs in the kiva during his long stays on top of the mesa.

José scrambled down into the kiva, where he intended to spend the next few days. Carlos helped him move a collection of supplies — food, water, a knife, a small drum, candles, and a blanket — into the covered part of the kiva. Carlos had also brought along a little bag with peyote buds in it, which he told José to ingest with lots of water to avoid getting sick. Bidding his young friend a good voyage on the lake of spirit consciousness, Carlos hiked down off the second mesa, walked back across the first mesa, located the cairn that marked the route to the valley floor, and climbed down the side of the mesa to join his four-legged friends there. They were fine.

Darkness had arrived, and only Don Carlos's brujo vision had enabled him to make the trip safely. His first thought on arriving at the horse corral was to rest after a strenuous day, but his energy level was so high that he transformed himself into a barn owl and flew along the mesa wall, investigating its contours. As always, he found flight an ecstatic experience. After an hour he made a quick trip to the top of the second mesa and José's vision-quest site. He heard faint sounds of drumming and chanting and knew that José was following instructions that Old Man Xenome had given him. Carlos then returned to the horse corral and to human form, rolled himself into two thick woolen blankets, and promptly fell into a deep sleep.

Waking before dawn, he remembered that he had missed his morning meditation on the previous day. He resolved to start Tuesday with his usual meditative practice. He sat up, focused his attention on his body pulse, and soon achieved a state of highly concentrated awareness. He then began to work with his chakras, the energy centers located on or in front of his spine. He felt an unusual sensation in his lower back, as though it was being stroked by a feather or touched by wind. Curious to see what this was, he turned and looked to his right.

Zoila Herrera, his mentor in Tantric meditation who'd died nearly a year earlier, was sitting cross-legged by his side. She was wearing her customary loose top and draw-string bottoms. She smiled lovingly at him. "Zoila!" he exclaimed in astonishment, but apparently she couldn't hear him. She cupped her right hand around her ear and shook her head and then shrugged her shoulders, bursting out in laughter that he could see but not hear. She pointed to her left hand and showed him that she was holding the locket he'd given her when they parted. He was moved to tears. Could it be that she had survived the shipwreck that he and all her friends had assumed had resulted in her death? Was she now entering a dream of his as they had planned to do on their last day together?

Zoila held the locket in her palm and gestured with her left hand that he should keep his eyes on it. She next lifted the locket to chest level and then to eye level. Finally she raised the locket above her head and then moved it behind her head. At last he understood what she was trying to communicate. The locket, even when held behind her head, was still visible. Her body was a transparent shadow; she was a ghost.

Disappointment must have shown on his face because she gave him a reassuring smile. Her lips seemed to form the words, "I'm all right where I am."

Moving his lips as expressively as possible, he asked, "Any advice?"

She nodded. She leaned closer to him and outlined the shape of two letters on the palm of her hand: an "m" and then a second "m."

Puzzled, he mouthed the first words that came to mind: "Mara Mata?"

She shook her head vigorously in the negative. Still in her cross-legged position, she put one hand on each knee with her thumb and middle fingers together, and closed her eyes. He did likewise. He immediately realized what the double m meant. He opened his eyes and mouthed the words, "More meditation." Zoila, who had also opened her eyes, looked very pleased, but to his dismay the outline of her body began to fade and soon disappeared, though not before she blew him a kiss.

Carlos knew he'd been lax in his pursuit of meditation. Although he'd done his chakra practice regularly, he'd done it in a perfunctory way, excusing himself with the thought that without a teacher, he had no way of refining his technique. But Zoila's visit conveyed the message that "more meditation" — the practice itself — was the best and perhaps only reliable teacher. He spent the rest of the day either doing sitting meditation or chores around his camp.

That evening he decided to visit José's vigil site. He transformed himself into an owl and flew to the flat courtyard area next to the kiva that José occupied. Returning to human form, he wrapped himself in a blanket he'd left there. Faint sounds of drumming from José's kiva indicated all was well. Chewing a few peyote buds he'd also left behind, he sat back and waited.

In what seemed a brief time, he saw the area filling up with spirit figures — ghosts, apparitions, whatever one called them. They were engaged in commonplace activities: the women skinning rabbits, plucking feathers off some type of bird, grinding corn, and cracking nuts; men knapping projectile points and attaching them to wooden shafts. None of the spectres seemed to notice Don Carlos, and some even walked right through him, causing him to feel a momentary chill. After an hour the figures faded from sight.

Don Carlos changed back to owl form and flew to his camp. He slept until sunrise, got up, and had breakfast. His plan for today, Wednesday, was to transform himself into bird form and fly across the mesa top looking for mind-altering plants. Ever since his talk with Leandro about shamans using plants in their spirit quests, he'd been thinking about which ones might fall in that category. He'd come up with a short list and had resolved to keep an eye out for samples to collect.

Rather on a whim, he transformed himself into a turkey vulture. He took off, reached an adequate altitude, and caught a gust of wind that carried him directly to a spot where three vultures were circling.

His arrival was not welcomed. He came on the three so suddenly that they shied away from him. Don Carlos called after them, "Don't worry. I'm not an enemy."

The boldest of the group coasted over close to where Don Carlos was hovering and said, "Who the hell are you? You're new to us and a loner, neither of which is a good sign. Did your previous companions chase you off?"

"No such thing," Don Carlos replied. "If you look closely, you'll see that I'm not an ordinary turkey vulture."

Insulted, the vulture declared, "No turkey vulture is ordinary."

"You're right about that," Don Carlos agreed. "I simply meant to call your attention to the fact that I'm not a turkey vulture at all. I'm a brujo who's taken a turkey vulture's form."

"Ah! So I see," the vulture said, taking a closer look at Don Carlos the next time their flight paths brought them near each other. "I've never before seen a brujo around here, or heard of anyone else seeing one for that matter. I don't mean to be impolite, but do you have anything you wanted to ask me? It's difficult to converse on the fly and my friends and I still haven't had breakfast."

"I can help regarding breakfast. Over by that tall tree on the mesa's edge there's a deer carcass, probably a mountain lion kill. That might make a good meal."

"Thank you for that suggestion. Would you care to join us?" the vulture asked.

"No thanks," Don Carlos replied, not finding the idea of eating rotting venison at all appealing. "However, I do have a question I'd like to ask before you fly off."

Considerable virtuosity was required to carry on a conversation while circling as turkey vultures are wont to do. But by maneuvering skillfully, Don Carlos managed to ask the vulture, whose name turned out to be Vito, if he knew anything about the spirit vultures that had shown up near Carlos's house in Santa Fe. Were these vultures, he wondered, aligned with dark energies?

"We'd be deeply annoyed if an evil entity took the form of a turkey vulture. I don't know anything about the vultures you mention. All I've heard is that a brujo has recently been active near a Spanish town south of here. Sorry, that's all I know." He turned and flew off.

Vito's information didn't clarify matters much. The brujo active near Santa Fe might even be Don Carlos, although he wasn't a recent arrival in town.

Before returning to his camp, Don Carlos devoted several hours to searching for mind-altering plants on the mesa top. At one point when he'd landed to investigate a plant that looked like damiana, though it proved not to be, he had a conversation with a honeybee named Bernardo, who said he'd been lured out of his hive by the midday sunlight. "I thought spring had arrived," Bernardo declared. "I guess I'm a hopeless optimist. It's cold out here, and there are no flowers in bloom. It's back to my hive for me."

"It is cold," Don Carlos agreed. "But before you go off, could you tell me about any plants in the vicinity that leave you light-headed after you've gathered nectar from them?"

"I know what you mean," the very agreeable bee replied, and promptly told Don Carlos where to find such plants. Then the little creature, who despite the season and the chilly day seemed delighted to meet a Spanish brujo in vulture form, excused himself and flew off.

Guided by Bernardo's directions, Don Carlos discovered several patches of salvia and datura, and a large peyote cactus plant. The mesa was a veritable garden spot of plants with mind-altering properties. He wondered whether the ancient residents of the site had been attracted by the presence of many vision-inducing plants that could be used in their ceremonies. Or perhaps they'd introduced the plants to the mesa. That afternoon he returned to the area in human form and collected samples of the various plants he'd located.

After flying back to his camp and changing from bird form, Carlos ate dinner and slept for several hours. He set his interior clock to awaken him a little before midnight, the hour at which the nearly full moon would be directly over the mesa. He wanted to return to the site of the kiva where José's vision quest was in progress, both to see how José was doing and to determine whether the spectral figures he'd seen the previous night would be visible again.

They had returned, but with a difference. Tonight the shades of villagers past were no longer engaged in daily chores, and they were dressed in ceremonial clothes. Almost precisely at midnight, the male members of the crowd formed themselves into two lines, a corridor of sorts that ran from the largest house on the courtyard directly to José's kiva. Soon they began stepping in place, lifting first one foot and then the other to the rhythm of a drum, the beat of which made a vibration that Don Carlos could feel. Although he couldn't hear it, the men seemed to be uttering a chant which, from the shapes of their mouths, appeared to be, "Hey, hey, hey, hey. Ho, ho, ho, ho." Even in the silence, the rhythm of this repetitive chant and the stepping dance had its intended effect, and Don Carlos felt himself slipping into a trance.

Five figures then emerged from the large house. The five walked through the corridor formed by the two lines of chanting men. All five wore masks. The first figure in the group had a black headdress with three huge corncobs, two protruding from either side of its head and a third standing straight up in front. It wore a black skirt and green vest—Carlos could see the color, even though the only light was from the moon overhead. It was as though the colors were illuminated from an inner source. The figure held a gourd rattle in its right hand and an object Don Carlos couldn't quite make out in its left. Looking closely at the five masked men, he noticed that all of them carried rattles in their right hands and some other object in their left.

The costumes of the other four figures were, to Carlos, equally exotic. The second figure had a headdress consisting of two horns made of eagle feathers and a collar of green cloth around its neck. The third figure wore brown moccasins, a white skirt, a yellow and brown shirt, and a mask with a two-pronged headdress. It, too, held a rattle in its right hand, and its left hand held a corncob. The next-to-last figure unmistakably represented agriculture, given that its head was in the shape of a squash and its shirt was striped like the common squash from the area.

The fifth and last figure in the line was perhaps the most unusual. It had a headdress of long hair and a red beard that fell down nearly halfway to its waist. Its shirt was plain, tan and unembellished, but its pants were covered with brightly-colored flower blossoms.

The five figures—deified ancestral spirits of the Pueblo people—

marched in a measured way to the entrance of the kiva where José was drumming and one by one went down into it. As the fifth disappeared into the kiva, a sixth costumed figure entered the courtyard. The sixth masked figure's arrival seemed to surprise the assembled crowd. Many onlookers sent startled glances in its direction, and a few of the men who'd formed the ceremonial corridor briefly lost their step. Unlike the first five figures, all of whom wore bright colors and had elaborate headdresses, this figure's shirt, belt, pants, and boots were unadorned and all in the same sand-brown color. Like the others it carried a gourd rattle in its right hand. In its left it held a rawhide whip. It strode across the courtyard and followed the others down into the kiva.

As Don Carlos watched, the ghosts of the pueblo's inhabitants gradually drifted away. Many went into houses. Others sat or stood talking in the courtyard, but as the sound of José's drumming slowed, grew softer, and finally ended, so too the figures of the spirit people moved ever more slowly, grew visually fainter, and finally disappeared altogether. Judging from the position of the moon, Don Carlos estimated that it was about two o'clock in the morning. He suddenly felt very tired, as though what he'd witnessed had sapped his energy. With an effort, he pulled himself together, flew back to his camp, changed to human form, dressed, and prepared to lie down and sleep.

A few moments later the three horses in the corral began to stir restlessly. Suspecting that a wild animal, possibly a coyote or a cougar, was prowling around, he got up to investigate. He'd reached the far side of the corral when he heard the soft footfall of an animal. Simultaneously, his mountain lion bracelet became warm, almost uncomfortably so.

The cause soon became evident. Don Carlos saw a masked figure emerging from the brush near the corral. Its headdress was a dark-brown wig with two clusters of eagle feathers mounted on it. Its earth-colored face mask had turquoise and black circles around the eyes and a broad snout with pulled-back lips that revealed two lines of sharp teeth. Below the mask was a throat piece with small white spots on a gray background, a pattern that was repeated in the spirit-creature's arm bands and leggings and in the apron over its belly. Don Carlos realized that the peyote buds he'd chewed earlier that night must still be having an effect.

The figure stared balefully at Don Carlos. In a deep voice that resembled a growl, it announced, "You have seen things tonight that no one who is not part of the mountaintop village should ever see. But the two animals with whom you spoke, Brother Bee and Grandson Vulture, reported that you seemed to respect this place, its animals, and its spirits, and that is in your favor. Also, I've noticed your bracelet, apparently a gift from our friend Xenome, and that speaks well for you. What's your name?"

"Carlos has been my name through many lifetimes."

The masked figure's body tensed as if in anger. "Then you don't deny that you're a brujo? Surely you know that Pueblo people, whether of the ancient, old, or present generation, are enemies of witches and brujos."

"I've discussed that fact with Old Man Xenome and he's come to trust me because I do not use my brujo powers to injure anyone. On the contrary, I am one of a small number of brujos whose motto is 'Do no harm.' I hope that you would agree, from what you've observed of my behavior in your sacred space, which I found only because Old Man Xenome directed me to it, that I've honored my devotion to that motto and shown respect for the spirits of this place. Also, I have not always been a Spaniard. In several of my lives I was an Indian man."

The masked figure was silent for a long interval, finally speaking as if to himself the words, "Indian ancestry may explain how this Spaniard saw what he has seen." Then, addressing Don Carlos directly, he said, "You're persuasive in what you say, Carlos. My name is Toho. I am the mountain lion kachina, kachina being the name we use for spirit entities that rise from the Sacred Lake to visit Pueblo people. By wearing that bracelet you have taken the mountain lion as your totem animal. You have chosen very well in picking as your ally Toho, one of the most powerful creatures of the earthly and spirit worlds."

Don Carlos felt profound humility in the presence of Toho and, after thanking him for revealing himself, asked, "May I inquire whether the masked figures I saw last night are all associated with a particular pueblo and, if so, which one?"

"That's an excellent question, wiser than I'd generally expect to hear from a Spaniard, even a Spanish brujo. Different pueblos have different kachinas associated with them. All but one of those you saw in the ceremony tonight are found among the Hopis."

"Was that exception the one that seemed like an unfinished sand drawing, lacking in features?"

"Yes."

"What is that kachina's name?"

"We are sworn to secrecy with regard to our names. I revealed mine to you only because we are bonded. Don't interpret my refusal to tell you the names of the others as an unfriendly act. Such knowledge is reserved for initiates, like your friend who inhabits the old kiva."

"I will honor that rule," Don Carlos replied, and the two parted with expressions of mutual respect.

Don Carlos slept soundly until the sun was peeping over the eastern horizon. He meditated for an hour, checked on the horses, and ate breakfast. Refreshed by a good night's rest, Don Carlos was loath to leave a place that fed his soul, but, knowing that he and José needed to start home by noon, he stayed on schedule. He hiked up onto the mesa, carrying a water bag for José that he lowered into the kiva. José didn't speak, but a jerk on the rope and its return without the water bag attached assured Don Carlos that all was well.

He changed himself into a red-tailed hawk and indulged his animal spirits by undertaking a series of aerial acrobatics — long coasting rides on wind currents and dives nearly to the ground from high altitudes. During the latter he further gave vent to his wilder side by producing a series of loud hawk cries that echoed off the canyon walls and that, incidentally, probably scared the rabbits, squirrels, and birds that were typical hawk prey. On a final wide circle, he swung out over the river canyon to the mesa's north. He was astonished to see a herd of wild horses numbering in the dozens grazing in the valley below. Horses hadn't been present in New Mexico until after the Spanish arrived, and this herd was probably composed of runaways that had scattered when Spanish ranchers abandoned their homesteads during the Pueblo Revolt of 1680. It was possible, he thought, that the horses in this herd would become valuable commodities if they could be rounded up and driven south to Santa Fe as part of Raul Trigales's proposed horse business.

But there wasn't time for speculating about the future. It was near noon and time to leave the mesa. He flew back to the kiva site where José was. After changing himself to human form, he dressed, walked over to the kiva, and called softly, "José, time to start back."

Carlos heard various rustling sounds from within the kiva and after a few moments José scrambled out of the kiva carrying his backpack.

Don Carlos was thrilled with what he saw. José's aura was large, bright, and practically throbbing with energy. "I see that your time went well," Carlos observed.

"How can you be sure?" José asked, blinking to get used to being out in the full sun.

"It's obvious. Care to tell me any details?"

"I am sorry, Don Alfonso," José replied. "I'm not permitted to reveal the secrets of the kiva to anyone except Grandfather Xenome. But I suppose it's all right to tell you that I was visited by spirit entities with whom I talked at length."

"Yes," Carlos said. "I counted five masked figures who entered your kiva together, and a sixth who followed shortly thereafter."

José's astonishment was extreme. "You saw them?"

"I saw what I just described. I had chewed peyote buds. They affect one's perceptions, making it difficult to separate what one actually sees from what's in one's mind only. And even if the figures I saw were hallucinations, it's possible that a trance state I shared with you enabled both of us to have the same visions."

"It sounds as though we were having a shared vision," José said. "Were the figures you saw in multi-colored costumes? Although it was dark in the kiva, I could see the colors as though they were illuminated from within."

"That was my experience also. The same was true later last night when a kachina visited me at the camp near our horses. The colors of his outfit seemed to come from inside. A strong bond arose between us."

José's mouth dropped open. "You established a bond with a kachina!" he exclaimed. "Spaniards don't have kachinas; that's something in the Indian spiritual world."

Don Carlos could barely stop himself from laughing. "You keep underestimating me. Why do you suppose Old Man Xenome trusted me to accompany you?"

"Sorry," José apologized. "I didn't mean to insult you for being a Spaniard. You can't help that."

Don Carlos found José's phrase that he couldn't help being Spanish very funny, and he burst out laughing. José, swept along with the spirit of it, joined in.

When they had recovered from their laughter, Carlos turned to practical matters. "We need to return to our camp, pack up, and head back to Santa Fe, with a stop at Tesuque Pueblo for you to talk with Old Man Xenome." They gathered their belongings and started across the mesa.

Don Carlos wondered whether he could get away with one more question. "I'm not asking for specifics," he ventured, "but was your experience complete, or are there some loose ends that need to be gathered up?"

"There are definitely loose ends. Although I learned a lot from my spirit visitors, they didn't tell me what my special role as a shaman is to be. Some medicine men are particularly skillful as healers; others are known for driving off witches; still others are revered because they bring rain. And there are other talents too."

"I'm confident," Don Carlos assured his young friend, "that Old Man Xenome will help you answer your question. The clue may be in what each of the kachinas represents. It seemed to me that the first five might have something to do with agriculture. Most wore green, and one even had a squash for a head. That led me to wonder, is José supposed to serve his people by becoming a farmer?"

José shook his head. "I doubt that. I've lived in towns all my life and most recently I've been a blacksmith's apprentice."

"I'm in no position to know, especially given my status as a Spaniard." (This was said with a playful grin.) "However, I know that change rules our lives, and something tells me that the sixth masked figure—the one in the plain costume—is the key to the future direction of your life. And that kachina carried a rawhide whip, which suggests it had something to do with horses. Ask Grandfather Xenome."

Which is precisely what José did after he and Don Carlos reached Tesuque Pueblo just as night was falling. Only many months later did José feel free to tell Carlos what Xenome said, which was that the sixth kachina, who introduced himself as the Unfinished One, was a horse kachina. Since horses hadn't been a part of traditional Pueblo culture, it was up to José to name him and complete his costume, making him José's personal spirit ally.

Old Man Xenome had words of wisdom for Don Carlos too during a brief conversation they had after José went off to say hello to his cousins. "You and I share the same spirit ally," Xenome said. "That makes me very happy. As for what to do about these newcomers in Santa Fe who worry you, I suggest that you bring the magician to visit me. I'm curious to meet him. After his visit you and I can discuss whether he represents a threat to your well-being. If he's a friend of yours, he'll become a friend of mine. But if he's an enemy of yours, then he's an enemy of mine too."

Carlos and José spent the night at Tesuque Pueblo, rising before dawn to reach Santa Fe in time for breakfast.

16

Secrets

Sitting down to the table for breakfast the morning he arrived back in Santa Fe, Carlos got the distinct impression that Pedro, María, and Diego were all preoccupied with something they weren't comfortable telling him about. Even Gordo wasn't quite his usual cheerful self. After trying to engage his housemates' interest with stories of his successful trip with José, Carlos at last gave in and asked, "What's the matter with everyone?"

A period of silence followed until Pedro said, "The day you left with José, Raul Trigales came around and told us that he'd bought Barbon's stable. Señor Trigales wants me to move in and manage it for him. I told him I'd let him know after I had a chance to speak with you."

Pedro looked so worried that Carlos leaned over and clapped him on the shoulder. "Pedro," Carlos said enthusiastically, "it's an excellent opportunity financially, and there is even an attached apartment that has a large kitchen and two rooms, one for you and María and the other for your baby, if you eventually want him to have a space of his own."

"You mean you'll be glad to be rid of us?" Pedro asked with a wry smile.

"Nonsense! You know better. Gordo and I will miss you enormously. But Raul's offer is a chance that shouldn't be missed."

"I'll still be able to help with the Velarde house."

"That's generous of you, but I don't see that you'll have much time. Based on what you know of the local craftsmen, can you recommend someone who's skillful enough to do the job well?"

Pedro looked relieved. "Orfeo Jiranza is the best possibility. You might have reservations because he's young and has never handled a job as big as a house. But Lucila Archuleta had him do some renovations on Tiburcio's place, and I heard he did good work for her."

"Your recommendation is good enough for me," Carlos declared. Then he turned to Diego and said, "I think you must have something to tell me too."

Diego nodded. "Señor Trigales also spoke with me. He said you told him I'd become a good cook, and he asked me to join his household as an assistant cook. Don Alfonso, I am grateful for your praise, and I have liked preparing meals for the four of us. But cooking for twelve people, or thirteen if I count myself, seems—what was that word you were teaching me? Oh yes—daunting."

"You won't be in charge of it all, Diego, and you will learn. As I told Pedro, though I will miss you, it is an opportunity you should not refuse. You have often expressed your wish to be a chef. And I would think it will be nice for you to work on the same household staff as your friend Ana."

Diego blushed and mumbled, "Yes, that would be nice."

"It's settled, then," Carlos said, beaming at them all.

"Alfonso," Pedro asked, "Who will replace Diego as caretaker for your horses?"

"I'll ask José. We worked well together on our trip. If he moves in here, he'll be closer to the blacksmith shop where he's an apprentice than he is now, living at home."

Turning to Diego, Don Carlos asked, "Please tell me about Inéz. You must have seen her during the week I was gone. How is she doing?"

"I didn't see her every day. She was kind and helpful, the way she always is, but I thought she had something on her mind. I'm sure part of it was that she missed you."

"And the other part?" Carlos inquired.

Diego shrugged. "You must ask her yourself."

"I'll do that," he said, and ten minutes later he was knocking on the kitchen door of the Beltrán place. Inéz called for him to come in, and he found her sitting at a table peeling potatoes.

"Good morning," he said. "I hope you're well," using a fairly formal greeting and feeling strangely shy, perhaps because of the tension of their leave-taking a week ago.

"I'm well, thank you," she replied, matching his tone. "Please sit down," she added, indicating a stool across the table from her. "How did your trip with José go?" she asked.

"We both had adventures, although mine might have been due to peyote-induced hallucinations. I'd be sure they were hallucinations, except that José saw some of the same things."

She gave him a serious look. "You and he may have a deeper connection than you realize. You saved his life when he was falsely accused of murder. Now you're one of his mentors in the Shaman's Way. I suspect your recent journey together confirmed and strengthened those bonds."

"Yes," Carlos said, equally seriously. "But I want you to know that you were also on my mind and in my heart these past four days. Among other things, thinking of you, I asked a friendly bee named Bernardo about where to find vision-inducing plants. No damiana, but salvia, datura, and peyote. The village must have been an important site for religious practice, especially vision quests using those plants."

"A friendly bee," she said in a lighter tone. "Given your past proclivities, it surprises me that the bee was a Bernardo rather than a Belinda."

Relieved that she was teasing him a little, Carlos relaxed and said, "Now, please tell me what you've been up to."

"If you don't mind, I'll keep peeling potatoes."

"That's fine by me," he replied. "Let me help." She didn't object when he picked up a knife and a potato.

She began by saying, "Let me summarize what's been happening. I'm warning you that a lot of my stories involve the three entertainers."

"All the more reason to hope for a detailed account."

She gave him a look he couldn't interpret and replied, "There will be plenty of details."

"To start with"—she broke off. "I don't know where to start. Monday afternoon, I suppose. I had a half-day off—no dinner preparations. I was worried about your trip and upset about your going off and leaving me here to fret about it. I had nothing to do for the whole afternoon. I would have taken Alegría for a ride, but even she was gone—with you. I was just about to go out for a walk—I was putting on my coat—when there was a knock at the front door. The maid answered it, and I heard a woman's voice asking for me. I went to the door, and there stood Selena and Mara.

"I didn't really want to invite them to my room, and since I had my coat on I suggested we take a walk. They said they hadn't intended to come in anyway, and they had something they wanted to tell me about.

"We walked, and they rather hesitantly told me that they had heard that the house where they were living held bad memories for me. 'Bad memories are presences,' Selena said. 'We know rituals for cleansing places where bad things have happened. In fact, we did them as soon as we moved in because we didn't want bad presences there for our sake. But we were also concerned about whatever happened to you, and we wondered if it's possible we could help.'

"My first response," Inéz said, looking up from the potato she had been peeling, "was to be annoyed that they should think I was in need of help, and I tried to decline politely. Selena let me have my say, and then she said, 'My mother was a Gypsy, and Gypsies have many kinds of knowledge. Her special gift was as a healer. These gifts can't be taught, but I watched her work, and I found that I had similar abilities. Mara, too, has them to a degree. Did you know that we are half-sisters? We have the same father.'

"I was so astonished to hear that they were half-sisters that I stopped in the lane—we were right in front of your house at that point—and I turned to look at both of them. They are so different in appearance—they are both exotic-looking, but in such different ways. I couldn't see any resemblances, but I thought their being half-sisters explained something.

"We kept on walking, and Selena continued to talk, and the gist of it was they wanted me to go to their house with them—Leandro was out of town, they said—and let them do a healing ceremony on me. The closer I got to that house, the more I didn't want to go into it, and you" — she shot a glance at Carlos, and then went back to her potato—"you somehow got mixed up in it, I suppose because we had fenced—or I had tried to seduce you—there. This sounds awful, but all of a sudden I couldn't sort out who was tormenting me, you or Loreto. That convinced me that I was in a bad way, and if Selena and Mara were offering me healing, maybe I should accept it. And also" — she hesitated. "Also there was the way Selena embraced me at the end of the Unnamed Dance. It was so...comforting. I can't explain it. I don't want to explain it. But suddenly my resistance was gone, and I went with them into the house."

Inéz finished her potato, picked up another one, and then plunged into her story again. "The minute I walked through the door my heart started jumping around in my chest. I'd never felt anything like that, and my crazy heartbeat scared me. Mara and Selena got me into the kitchen and sat me down. Selena immediately put her hands on the top of my head. I closed my eyes and willed my heart to slow down, and gradually it did. I noticed a pungent smell—incense of some sort—and Mara sat in front of me, took off my shoes, and held my feet in her hands.

"Selena told me, 'We know what's happening to you. You're safe,' and then they began to sing something—not a song, not a chant, but it was very musical. Their voices wove through each other's, on different tones, up and down. It wasn't 'La, la, la'—there were a lot of different syllables, a lot of 'k' and 'ki' and 'l' and 've' and 'ah' sounds. I just listened, following their voices.

"After a while I became very quiet, and maybe my brain put the random syllables I was hearing into words—I seemed to be hearing inside me *quien quiere, que quiere, quiero*, who loves, what loves, I love, or maybe what, who, do you want? The words were very clear—but the meaning wasn't. Even so, it was comforting.

"Finally they stopped singing, and after a while I opened my eyes.

"Mara got up from where she'd been holding my feet, put a shawl over them, added more wood to the fire, and brought me a cup of something hot. Selena lifted her hands from my head and sat on the bench beside me. 'How do you feel now?' she asked. I said I felt much better. I risked a look around. The house seemed to be just a house. Selena seemed to understand. 'The bad presences are gone from the house,' she said, 'but they are still inside you. We did a healing to help free you from them.'

"I nodded and drank some of the tea they'd given me. It had a strange flavor—herbs of some sort. Not unpleasant. It warmed me.

"Selena looked at my hands holding the cup. 'You're not wearing the rose-quartz ring I gave you,' she said gently. I hadn't thought about it. The last time I wore it was at the Beltráns', when we did the Unnamed Dance.

"I began to explain, but Selena interrupted me. 'I know,' she said, 'you think of it as jewelry, for special occasions. It's more than that. It is a stone that heals the heart, and there is a deep wound in your heart. You need to wear it all the time, especially when you come here. We hope you will come again in the next few days. There is another healing we would like to offer you.'

"I agreed. And I thanked them. I felt that something in me had shifted, and I also felt extremely tired. They seemed to sense that. Mara put my shoes back on for me, and they collected all our coats and walked me home. We talked very little on the way, other than to make an appointment for me to come on Wednesday afternoon. When I got home, I went to bed and slept for two hours."

She turned her face toward Carlos and gave him a long, questioning look. "I want to hear the rest of the story," he told her. "Please go on."

"All right." She took a deep breath and released it. "On Wednesday Selena, Mara, and I talked more. They had me sit on the bench again. They gave me some of the same tea, Mara took off my shoes and asked me to take off my stockings, and she brought a basin of warm water and had me put my feet in it. She washed them very gently with soap. It is a lovely feeling to have someone washing your feet with soap!"

Inéz flashed him a smile, then grew serious again. "While Mara was doing that, Selena was talking to me. What she said, basically, was that they did not want to be intrusive, but that it would help the parts of me that needed healing if I would tell them about what had happened. 'The man you lived with in this house,' Selena began. 'He was your father?'

"The truth burst out of me. 'My father sold me to him,' I said.

"They both let out a long breath, like a sigh. 'Our father took us from our mothers and gave us to Leandro,' Selena said. My heart gave a leap, and suddenly I was afraid for them.

"After a moment's silence, Mara declared, 'Leandro is good to us. But we understand the harm that fathers can do.'

"Then I found myself talking about Loreto, and I realized he was sort of an extension of my father, even passing himself off as my father, which I'm sure nobody believed! And pimping me, which was essentially what my father did. A lot of anger came up in me as I was telling the story—my heart began to leap around the way it had before. Selena told me to let what I was feeling move through me, and Mara brought a fresh basin of water for my feet.

"When I was through with my account, they began to tell me something about themselves. Mara told me a little about her mother, who was a dancer, and who had trained her to be a dancer. 'It's not always easy to support yourself, being a dancer,' Mara said looking up at me with a wry smile. Her mother, she said, had 'gone with men for money,' as she put it, on the side. By the time Mara was thirteen her mother was forty, and the men, as Mara said, liked young girls. Several made it clear that they would pay well for Mara's favors. 'My mother,' Mara added, 'did not want to pimp me at such a young age, but we had to make a living, and it was inevitable that she would give in to these men eventually. But before that happened my father showed up for one of his rare visits and told my mother that he was taking me with him. She resisted, and they had a violent argument. I overheard snatches of it. My mother was shouting that she had to keep me because I would soon be earning good money for her. My father yelled back that I was worth more to him than what I could earn for her. They started arguing over how much I was worth. In the end a sum was agreed upon. So,' Mara added bitterly, 'she didn't pimp me, but she sold me. She didn't tell me this, of course. She just said that under the circumstances my life would be better if I went with my father—that I was important to him and he had great plans for me. I scarcely knew him, and I would have resisted, but two days later my mother collapsed and died, apparently of some sort of heart condition. I had no choice then except to go with my father. He assured me that I would be taken care of, but other than that he told me nothing. He was a very secretive man. We traveled for a while, and after a few weeks he brought me to Selena, telling me she was my half sister. Leandro was also there. I was told they were itinerant entertainers, that I would join their troupe, and that they would take care of me. And they have.' She smiled at Selena.

"Selena broke in at this point. 'I will say this very baldly. We are dancers, and we flirt with men to draw them to our performances. But Leandro does not pimp us.'

"I was shocked to hear her say it so bluntly, but I must admit the thought had occurred to me. And I began to feel a sisterly bond toward her. They are so different, she and Mara — physically, I mean. Selena is half a head taller, and very regal, and in my mind's eye I see her as a Moorish princess, veiled except for her dark eyes. Hidden. I think her flirtatiousness is all an act, almost an overdone act. She as much as said that it's part of her job. Mara is more sensual. In one sense she seems childlike, perhaps because she's so small...." She drifted off into unexpressed thoughts for a moment.

When Inéz went on her voice was more matter-of-fact. "Mara," she said, "had finished drying my feet and I had just put my stockings and shoes back on when I heard the front door open and close and Leandro came in. He seemed very glad to see me. His manner was warm but perfectly polite. He said that he'd heard — from Elena, no doubt — that the two of us had had a fencing match. He added that you had asked him not to propose a bout with me until you and I had had a chance to fence, but now that we had done so there didn't seem any obstacle to me fencing with him. And since I seemed to be comfortable now in his house, perhaps we could fence in the patio.

"My first thought was of fencing with you in that patio, and I didn't want to have that memory while I was fencing with him. I also thought the proprieties would be better observed if he came to the Beltráns' fencing strip — Cristina had already told me that she didn't mind if he did. So I suggested that it would be better if he came there and proposed that we meet the next day, Thursday, at two. He was perfectly agreeable."

"You didn't wonder," Carlos broke in, "if this whole business of healing you was perhaps a ploy to get you to go to his house?"

She shot him a surprised look. "No, I didn't," she said. "What they did made me feel a whole lot better. And I didn't go there to fence with him. He wasn't even at home when I was there and didn't come in until the end."

"All right, so he came here. What happened?"

"Well, there was a bit of a mix-up. I was late cleaning up after lunch, and he may have arrived a bit early. In any event, the maid let him in and showed him to the fencing strip and told him to wait there. Elena, apparently thinking that she and I were going to fence, came in a few minutes later. By the time I got to the patio, Leandro was engaged in a tête-à-tête with Elena. I had been feeling more open toward him—I trusted him more—since my visits with Mara and Selena, and here he was, being altogether too intimate with Elena. There was no one else around. I'm afraid I overreacted. I strode over to him, grabbed him by the shirt, and virtually dragged him off to one side. 'Leandro!' I exclaimed. 'You shouldn't be visiting Elena when she is unchaperoned.'

"He protested his innocence. 'You and I had an appointment to fence,' he said, 'and when I arrived, the maid showed me to the patio and told me to wait here. Elena came in looking for you. We were talking, that's all.'

"What he said was perfectly reasonable; it was just the appearance of the thing. But something in me exploded. 'Bah!' I replied, angrily. 'I don't see any need to mince words. You were playing your very charming self to a young woman who's inexperienced in the ways of the world. It's shameless of you to exploit her innocence.'

"He put his hands up and backed away from me a little. 'Inéz, whoa,' he said. He did it very gently, and it calmed me down."

Inéz looked down at the potato she was holding and shook her head. "I don't think I handled things well. Elena obviously heard what I said, and later she seemed withdrawn despite my best efforts to smooth things over."

Carlos let this pass. "Did you eventually get around to fencing?"

"Yes," she said, putting a peeled potato he'd handed her in the pot. "All three of us fenced by turns. He's a lot better than Elena—no surprise there, but I am better than he is, which I think surprised him. He's nowhere close to your level of skill. You would probably score ten hits for every one of his."

"And?"

"And what? Did he try to kiss me? No, of course not. Carlos, this is not about kissing. It's about you and me. It all started with me being upset and feeling abandoned because you had gone off on a potentially dangerous trip. It brought up feelings I thought I'd buried, and talking with Mara and Selena made me see that these feelings are far from dead in me. What Mara and Selena did brought them to the surface, which I think is good, but it also seems to make me very volatile, as when I exploded at Leandro."

She got up to take the kettle they'd filled with potatoes over to a table next to the hearth. "All of this," she continued, "has made me realize that I couldn't live up to Elvira's advice that we could marry if I let you be free.

Here I was, distraught because you and José had gone off to an area where Native war parties might be prowling around. Lacking any way to know you were safe, I imagined all sorts of terrible things."

"Inéz," he said softly. He would have embraced her, except she was on the other side of the kitchen table. "It's all right. I hope that talking about these old hurts with Mara and Selena will be good for you. And don't worry. I'm not pressing you for marriage. If I do, you have my permission to whack me on the head. I'm entirely content with our relationship as it is, though my house is going to feel very empty tonight now that Pedro, María, and Diego are moving out."

"I heard about that." She seemed about to say something more when Cristina Beltrán pushed the door open and entered the kitchen. After a slightly startled look crossed her face as she took in the situation, she smiled in amusement. She was an attractive woman with a full, ever-so-slightly matronly figure, and bright eyes that twinkled with merriment, or was it mischief? Either way, Carlos liked her.

"Not only do we have the best cook in Santa Fe in Inéz," she declared, "but our chef has recruited a handsome assistant. I suppose we'll have to negotiate a salary for him."

"The only return I wish on my occasional culinary efforts," Carlos told her, "is your permission to continue to visit your cook now and then. That's reward enough, and I appreciate the tolerance you've shown in allowing me to stop by regularly."

"You're always welcome, Don Alfonso. In fact, I'm the one who needs a favor done. Teodora Castro, a young Indian woman who used to work for us as a maid, is getting married this afternoon in La Ciénega. Elena is eager to go, but I told her she couldn't because I won't let her make that long ride in open country by herself, and neither her father nor any of his male employees are available to accompany her. She did not take it well and has been sulking all day about being treated 'like a child,' as she put it over and over."

Inéz shook her head and remarked, "If one wants to be treated as an adult, one shouldn't act like a petulant child. I must, with your permission, include a few words about mature behavior in your daughter's fencing lessons."

Cristina nodded. "I would appreciate that. She's very much in awe of you. But she did have her heart set on going, and it would be an honor to Teodora to have her attend, so I wonder if the two of you would be willing to escort her."

"Of course," Inéz replied. "Alfonso is always ready to go on an outing in the country, aren't you?" she asked him. He indicated that he would be glad to do so. "But what," she asked Cristina, "about lunch and dinner for the rest of the household?"

"Javier and I will go to the Trigales's for dinner. Lunch looks as though it's almost ready. And the servants can share leftovers in the evening. I checked the larder, and there are plenty on hand."

Thus it was that Carlos found himself riding south to La Ciénega that afternoon in the company of two attractive women. His companions both rode sidesaddle to accommodate their party dresses. The three of them were in high spirits. They told stories; laughed at bad jokes; enjoyed the winter countryside in which sleeping trees had their own dignity and beauty. They arrived at La Ciénega shortly before the ceremony started. When the bride, beautiful in her wedding finery, saw Elena, her face broke into a radiant smile.

Carlos, Inéz, and Elena found seats on benches in the main hall of the hacienda in which the ceremony was being held, Elena on his right, Inéz on his left. As the wedding party processed down the aisle, he heard a snuffling sound from his right and turned to see its source. Elena was weeping, mopping at her tears with a handkerchief that was too small for the task. He whispered, "What's wrong with you?" and handed her a larger handkerchief of his own to use.

"Weddings always make me cry," she replied. "They are such happy occasions."

Happiness and tears had always seemed somewhat contradictory to Carlos, but he didn't argue the point. He turned to his left to say something to Inéz and was surprised to see tears running down her cheeks. "You too?" he said. "Do weddings always make you cry?"

"I'm crying because I've never been to a wedding before, and I'm feeling that is a big loss in my life, one of many losses."

"What about Camila and Rafael's wedding? Oh yes, I remember you stayed away. But, Inéz, you were married once. Doesn't that count?"

"No," she replied with some heat. "There was no wedding. Hernando and I went to a town hall and registered ourselves as married, using a document that Loreto had bribed a priest to draft and a lawyer to notarize. That was it. No ceremony or priest to bless us."

Carlos was stunned. "Was it a legal marriage then?"

"Only on paper, I suppose, but no one ever challenged the document's validity. Please, let's not talk about it. Doing so will only make me sadder."

Elena, Carlos noticed, had stopped crying and was taking everything in. She's learning our secrets, Carlos observed to himself.

A bigger revelation, one with vastly more serious potential consequences, came on the way back to Santa Fe. The three companions had left the post-ceremony party early, staying only long enough to have light refreshments and watch the newly married couple enjoy their first dance as husband and wife. Elena asked Teodora to excuse them for leaving early. If they didn't, they wouldn't make it back to Santa Fe before dark.

They set as fast a pace as they felt they could, mostly an easy trot. The trouble came at the midpoint of their return trip. Don Carlos noticed them first, three dark-clad Indians on horseback, carrying muskets, lurking in a stand of trees ahead. The three bandits—Carlos knew instantly that's what they were—rode out of their hiding place and trotted in the direction of the three approaching travelers. Inéz gasped in alarm. "Should we turn around and make a run for it?" she asked.

"I doubt that Elena's horse could outrun them," Don Carlos replied.

This was no time to hold back. Don Carlos spurred Eagle forward, a gesture of attack that didn't impress the three bandits, who could see that he was unarmed. They had no way of knowing that he had formidable weapons at his command.

When he was less than twenty feet from the robbers, he asserted his brujo powers, hurling a bolt of invisible energy at the Indian who was riding at the front of the group. The bandit was thrown off his horse and landed heavily. Don Carlos released another bolt at a second bandit with the same results. Both of the fallen Indians lay on the ground, apparently unconscious.

The third Indian, seeing the fate of his comrades, wheeled his horse about in order to retreat. Too late. Don Carlos knocked him out of his saddle with a third blast of invisible energy.

Don Carlos turned around and motioned to Inéz and Elena. "Come along!" he called. "Those bandits won't bother us now." A quarter of a mile later, as they approached a curve in the road, Carlos looked back and saw that two of the bandits were still lying on their backs, while the third was sitting up, holding his head in his hands.

After rounding the curve, Carlos slowed Eagle to a walk, and Inéz and Elena did likewise with their mounts. Some things needed to be said, especially since Elena was staring at him with an awed expression on her face.

"Elena," he began, "I need you to promise to keep this incident a secret, even from your mother. She'd be very upset if she knew you'd been threatened by bandits, and she'd probably never again let you go out for rides in the country. I'll tell Captain Posada that I saw three armed Indians who were probably bandits in this section of the road and that only our good luck in having passed the place where their path would have crossed ours ensured our safety. He'll doubtless send out a patrol to be certain that there are no more Native raiders in the area.

"More important, however, is that you must not say anything to anyone about what you saw me do. Inéz can be your confidante, but it would be unsafe for me if anyone other than you and Inéz knew about what I did."

"But it was astonishing! I have so many questions. Are you a magician or a sorcerer?"

Trying to make light of it, he laughed and replied, "Now and then I have to dig deep and use a fighting technique I learned years ago from an old combat veteran. But most of the time I'm just an ordinary guy named Alfonso Cabeza de Vaca who's in love with your family's cook. Can we leave it at that for now, with you promising to keep this incident a secret?" Still wide-eyed, she nodded yes.

17

Parties

Don Carlos hoped that after the trip to La Ciénega his life would return to normal. But on Sunday morning an extraordinary event occurred that disrupted his usual routines.

Before dawn the sound of rain on the roof of his house awakened Carlos earlier than usual. He got up and decided on doing an extra-long meditation session. He had nearly completed a third fifty-minute period when he heard a shot ring out. It came from the direction of the entertainers' house to the south of his place. He hurriedly put on his boots, grabbed a jacket and his hat, rushed outdoors, and sprinted down the lane toward the Trio's residence. Up ahead he saw Mara with a musket in her hand, staring up at a turkey vulture that was sitting on the rooftop of her house. At his approach, it flew away.

Panting from his exertions, he reached Mara's side. She was wearing a woolen nightgown that covered her from neck to her feet, and it was soaked from the cold rain. Droplets of rainwater were dripping from her hair. She thrust herself into his arms, trembling with fear. "It was terrible!" she cried.

"What happened?"

"The rain woke me up, and it was such a heavy rain that I got up and went to the veranda that surrounds the patio to see. There was a big, ugly black bird perched on the fountain, taking a drink. I ran into the house and grabbed a musket that Selena and I keep in the corner of our bedroom, dashed back to the patio, and fired a shot at the bird. I know my shot was a bull's-eye. I'm an excellent marksman and couldn't miss at that range. The musket ball must have gone right through the bird, but even so it took off. I ran out to the lane to see where it had gone, and there it was, sitting on the roof."

"Hey!" Carlos said, in an effort to calm her, "It's gone now; you drove it off."

"I'm not so sure. Your arrival was what scared it away. This is the sort of thing that Leandro usually deals with, but he's been out of town."

"This isn't the first time a shadowy big black bird has shown up?"

"No, it's happened a lot since we came to Santa Fe. There's something spooky about this town."

Mara was shivering, and he said, "Perhaps you need to go inside and put on something warm and dry."

They went in the front door and saw Selena coming down the hall with a worried look on her face. "What happened?" she asked, as she gathered Mara into her arms. Mara started to describe the bird incident, but Selena, realizing how cold Mara was, said, "Come along, Mara. We need to get a cup of something warm into you. You were very brave to chase off whatever it was you saw."

Carlos excused himself, and both women expressed their thanks for his help. He went home feeling puzzled. The appearance of a black bird that a musket ball couldn't hurt intensified his sense that something dangerous was afoot.

The next morning, Monday, Carlos again woke up well before dawn. That was normal, but the fact that he felt lethargic and anxious was not. He swung his feet over the side of the bed. It was cold in the room, the fire having gone out many hours earlier. Gordo burrowed deeper into the blankets, taking over the place that Carlos had kept warm with his body. "Coward!" Carlos grumbled. "You at least have a fur coat." Gordo looked unimpressed by this information.

Before starting his meditation, he dressed warmly and put on heavy socks to keep his feet warm too. The anxiety he'd felt upon awakening came back. It seemed to have multiple sources. He was worried about the consequences that might result from Elena having seen him use his brujo powers. Even though she was a nice young woman, he wasn't sure she would keep his secret. She'd certainly been quick enough to tell Leandro that he and Inéz had fenced.

A lesser concern was how to reorganize his household now that Pedro, María, and Diego were moving on to other jobs. He still had three horses that needed to be taken care of—Pedro wanted his Pepper to stay with his long-time stablemates, Carlos's Eagle and Inéz's Alegría. Fortunately José had agreed to take on that job. Carlos could manage the chore of cooking his own meals, but eventually he wanted a live-in cook. He wished it could be Inéz, but he knew that was an idle fantasy.

Those domestic details skirted another concern, which was his lack of progress in the quest for wisdom he'd called the Unknown Way. Of late his meditations had been dry. Both his mentors in such matters—Father Stefano and Zoila—had warned him that he might never again experience the ecstasy he'd felt in his Tantric practice with Zoila. The Zoila who'd appeared to him in the dream or hallucinatory vision he'd had on the mesa had told him that he needed to do more meditation. But, he wondered, was there anything more to be gained by the practice of close attention?

José arrived as Carlos was scrambling eggs for breakfast. He was carrying his possessions in two canvas bags. He asked Carlos, "Where shall I put my things?"

"It's your choice, José," Carlos replied. "You can bunk in the small loft above the hay storage area, which is cold this time of year, or you can have one of the rooms on the south side of the house, which are only a little warmer."

"I'll take the hayloft. That way I can keep a closer watch on the horses. I'm sure they're usually all right, but Diego told me about the wolf incident, and I'd like to be nearby if they feel threatened again."

"Fine by me," Carlos said. "Shall I scramble a few more eggs for you?"

"Yes, thank you. After breakfast I'll clean the horses' stalls and then leave for the blacksmith's. I think today my boss is going to let me shoe a horse under his supervision."

Don Carlos had his own agenda for the day, and by the time he'd washed the dishes the sun had risen. Gordo finished his breakfast and, as always, gave Carlos a pleading look in hopes of getting a second helping. "You had a big dish of food," Carlos told him. "Come along with me and walk off some of that fat."

The site where Don Carlos was having a house built for Dr. Velarde was less than two hundred yards from Carlos's place. He arrived to find Pedro, who now lived at the stable next door to the building lot, already there. He was showing Carlos's new carpenter, Orfeo Jiranza, around. The three men shook hands while Gordo entertained himself by sniffing a pile of timbers to see what messages might have been left there.

Don Carlos and Orfeo hit it off immediately. Orfeo's aura was basically a bright golden color, though today it was suffused with shots of gray suggesting some anxiety or doubt. Don Carlos understood the source of the anxiety. The young man had never undertaken a job as large as a house. Carlos moved immediately to reassure him that he wouldn't have to do everything on his own. He, Carlos, would see that he had help at crucial points, and Pedro added that now that he lived next door he could easily come over and give advice or help as needed. Relief was visible on Orfeo's face, and his aura became uniformly golden.

Dr. Velarde, the prospective owner, stopped by briefly and said he was pleased to see how quickly the house was going up.

"What you're seeing is the fastest, most visible phase," Pedro warned him. "Completing the interior will go more slowly."

"I'm not worried," the doctor replied. "I just enjoy coming by every day and watching your progress, but I can't stay right now because I have a house call to make. One of my patients has a headache that refuses to go away."

"Any idea who has the headache?" Carlos asked Pedro after the doctor was out of sight.

"If gossip is to be believed, it's the vice governor's wife, who is said to be a flirt."

"That doesn't sound good for the Cabrera marriage," Carlos observed. "I'll see what I can learn from Señora Cabrera's stepson, Marco, when I visit him later today."

"I'm surprised that you worry about the health of other people's marriages," Pedro said.

"One important rule in war is to know one's enemies even better than they know themselves," Carlos replied rather obscurely.

Pedro's eyebrows went up. "The Cabreras are your enemies?"

"Not the Cabreras in particular," Carlos replied, "but they have ties with some members of Santa Fe society who appear to be trying to ostracize me, and that leads me to want to keep track of what's on their minds."

"I'll bet you," Pedro commented, "these people have noticed that you sometimes take off your coat and work beside common men like me—very unsuitable behavior for a *hidalgo*."

Carlos took this in and had to agree with Pedro. "That, among other things," he said. Without further comment on the subject, Pedro excused himself to go home and Carlos left the worksite to pursue the agenda he'd set for himself, which included going to talk with Marco Cabrera. He had decided it would be petty of him not to stop by the Palace of the Governors to see the man who'd replaced him as the governor's secretary. It wasn't Marco's fault that Carlos's stepfather had gotten him fired.

Before visiting Marco at his office in the Palace of the Governors, Carlos wanted to check in with Inéz. That forced him to take a somewhat roundabout route through the center of town, past the Palace of the Governors, and on to the Beltrán residence. He knocked at the kitchen door, let himself in, and found Inéz sitting at the kitchen table, writing something. "It's a shopping list," she explained in response to his questioning look. "What's on your mind?"

He sat down opposite her. "I'm wondering if there have been any negative repercussions from our encounter with bandits last Friday."

"Elena scarcely knows which emotion to be carried away by. She can barely restrain her curiosity to know more about you, and at the same time she's thrilled to be the silent keeper of our secrets. Any resentment she felt toward me for intervening in her tête-à-tête with Leandro is long gone. In fact, she seems to be giving more credence to my warnings about him."

"That's a better outcome than I expected," Carlos admitted, "although she was quick to tell Leandro about our having fenced, and that has me wondering how good she is at keeping secrets."

"Keeping a secret might give her a greater sense of importance than telling secrets. She wants to be taken seriously, like an adult, like one of us. I know she's curious about my past too, and I'm sharing well-laundered bits and pieces about my life, including a few details about my marriage to Hernando and his sudden death."

"It sounds as though you have everything under control. I've another topic for you. This morning Pedro mentioned that it's his impression that Regina Cabrera, who is an inveterate flirt, has been practicing her art on Dr. Velarde, who is applying his medical skills to whatever condition she claims to have."

"Headaches," Inéz declared. "At least that's what's rumored on the servant gossip circuit. The causes of headaches, you might note, are notoriously obscure. The only evidence a doctor has to go on is whatever his patient tells him. As a result, Dr. Velarde is wearing a path between the place he's renting from you and the Cabreras' residence across the lane from here."

"So it's common gossip already. But I suppose it's none of my business," Carlos said.

"Perhaps it is. Marco Cabrera, for all that he's ended up taking your job, is your friend, and any disgrace his stepmother brings on the family would reflect poorly on him. Also, you wouldn't want Dr. Velarde to upset the local guardians of morality and get himself chased out of town, leaving you with a partly built house and no one paying you to finish it."

"I certainly hope this flirtation doesn't become a full-scale scandal, but I don't see what I can do about it."

"One thing you might do, ever so carefully, is to suggest to Dr. Velarde that he doesn't want to get on the wrong side of the town's upper class. After all, look what happened to his predecessor, Dr. Tiburcio."

"Good point," Carlos replied. "Perhaps I can say something the next time I see him that will warn him off."

"Another thing you might do," Inéz continued, "has to do with the damiana I asked you to collect. A curandera told me that damiana is known as 'happy weed' because tea made from it induces a mood of well-being. Might it not be a nice gesture to give Marco a small bag of damiana to pass along to his father and stepmother?"

Carlos gave her a long look, and shrugged, not immediately seeing the point of doing so.

"Why not?" she said. "It might be good for them." Rising from her chair, she put enough damiana in a bag to make several cups of tea and handed the bag to Carlos. "By the way," she said, sitting down again, "I ran into Selena crossing the plaza yesterday, and she said that you and Mara were involved in a strange incident early yesterday morning, about which you've not said a word."

"I simply haven't had a chance to do so yet," he protested. "Would you like me to give you a brief summary now?"

"There's no need, Selena filled me in. I'm sure you find these appearances — the wolf and now twice a turkey vulture — proof that malign forces have invaded Santa Fe. But I'm not so sure. It's surprising to see a wolf or turkey vultures in Santa Fe, but they're part of the natural world in this region, so I favor treating them as such until there's better evidence that they represent spirit entities."

He was tempted to defend his view and offer evidence about the spectral qualities of these beasts, but he contented himself with saying, "I can accept a wait-and-see posture. But we're going to Selena's birthday party tonight and one reason I want to go to it, besides the fact that she and her two friends are fun, is to be on the lookout for anything that might suggest that there's some connection between Leandro and these apparitions."

"All right, and now that you mention it, we need to do some costume planning. Selena told me they enjoy masquerade parties and that we should come in costumes of our choice, or they would provide outfits after we arrive."

"I could go as Cupid, the Roman god of love, but he's usually depicted as naked and it's not the season for running around without clothes on."

"I'm sure Selena would enjoy seeing you as Cupid. I'm planning to come as Cinderella, a fairy-tale character whose social status resembles my present station in life."

"A scullery maid who's unappreciated by all and sundry? I hope that's not how you truly feel. And where did you hear that story?"

"It was in a book that one of Loreto's clients, a Frenchman, gave him before we left Spain. Tonight, if you're willing, your role is to come as the prince who tracks down Cinderella using a glass slipper she lost at a ball she attended. But how did you hear the story? The French book Loreto received was published only a few years ago."

"My Jesuit tutors weren't all work and no play. One of them had us read folk tales from all eras, from ancient times to the present, and we read the Cinderella story in French. I will do my best to dress in a princely fashion."

"Good. You'll come by at nine o'clock?"

He rose from his chair. "Yes, that sounds about right. I'll see you then."

He let himself out the door, and a short walk to the Palace of the Governors brought him to the building where he'd earned his living for two years. A sense of relief came over him when he didn't experience any residue of negative feelings as he entered the hallway that led to his former office.

Marco looked up from his desk as Don Carlos let himself into the secretary's office. "I'm surprised to see you here," Marco said. "I thought you told me that you wanted nothing to do with this place."

"That was small-minded of me, Marco. Sour grapes. Please forgive me. I've relented on the matter of staying away and thought I'd stop by to say hello. Everything's going well in your job here, I trust?"

"Yes, although it's not what I expected to be doing when we were young men growing up in Mexico City. My only ambition then was to court a rich man's daughter, marry her, and live a life of leisure with her dowry and, later, with her inherited estate."

"Likewise for me," Carlos admitted. "My father was sufficiently well off that I might have managed a comfortable bachelorhood had circumstances not changed—his death and my mother's remarriage being the main reason I'm now a resident of Santa Fe."

"May I frankly say," Marco ventured, "that I was surprised when I heard that you had abandoned your right to inherit the title of marquis and your estate."

"The title didn't seem meaningful without the money, and there was little left because as my guardian, my stepfather had spent most of my inheritance on two of his sons."

"I see. But Alfonso, don't you have any legal recourse?"

"I'm leaving that to my sister, whose son is now the heir to my father's title, and Fortunata's husband, Emiliano Alaniz, is, as you know, both wealthy and influential. If they decide to take my stepfather to court, he'll find that he has formidable opponents." Marco nodded that he understood.

"Now that I've described my personal situation," Carlos continued, "may I raise a delicate topic that involves a tenant of mine?"

Marco looked uncomfortable. "Dr. Velarde and my stepmother," he said. "Your reference wasn't difficult to guess. Everyone has probably noticed. It's an unhappy situation that echoes her unfortunate behavior in Mexico City."

"Do you mind telling me about that?"

"No, in fact I appreciate having someone in whom I can confide. What happened is this. My father and mother had a cold marriage. I say that without knowing anything of their relationship when they were first married. However, by the time I was old enough to notice, I became aware that there was no warmth between them. They always had separate bedrooms and never, to the best of my knowledge, shared a bed. Perhaps this may have been partly my father's fault. He's a very cerebral man and may not have known how to elicit a woman's interest."

"If a wife rejects her husband's attentions," Carlos observed, "it can have bad results. But, if I may speak frankly, your stepmother doesn't strike me as likely to be cold in that way."

"Quite the opposite," Marco declared, "and therein lies the problem.

My father and Regina, as I call my stepmother, met through a mutual friend. When my mother died, it soon became plain that Regina had set her sights on marrying my father. She's vivacious and seductive, and I confess that, because she and I are almost the same age, I had some hopes for a love affair with her, which she didn't encourage. Given her charms, her campaign to win my father soon triumphed, and in the first year of their marriage, it was obvious that there was passion between them. But Regina couldn't give up flirting and eventually she became involved with a wealthy neighbor, a married man. She made almost no effort to be discreet, and being publicly known as a cuckold became too much for my father to bear. He sought to escape, and his primary reason for accepting a post in New Mexico was to separate his wife from her lover and himself from the knowing looks of his friends. Now she is flaunting her flirtatious self again, and it has embittered my father toward her."

"Don't give up too soon," Carlos said. "I have an idea or two for dealing with the situation."

"I would be exceedingly grateful for anything you can do," Marco replied.

"I will talk to Dr. Velarde and explain that he may be making a huge mistake professionally and socially if he persists in flirting with your stepmother. His predecessor was driven out of town for behavior unbecoming a doctor. That could happen to Dr. Velarde too, and I intend to tell him so.

"My other idea is to help your father and stepmother take more pleasure from each other's company. Are there any special occasions coming in your family — your father's or stepmother's birthdays, or their anniversary, something of that sort?"

"Their third anniversary will be this coming week. I've been dreading it, not knowing how to make it a happy occasion."

"I have a suggestion for a present you might give them. I've brought you a bag of desert herbs I gathered. They can be used to make tea. I haven't tried it myself, but it's called 'happy-weed tea,' and it's said to induce a pleasant and amorous mood. Now precisely how you plant the idea in both your father's and your stepmother's heads that they might drink this tea before bed and reminisce about their wedding day is something I must leave to you."

Marco practically fell over himself in expressing his gratitude, and as Carlos left the room he could tell that Marco was plotting how best to make a success of the forthcoming anniversary party.

That evening Carlos arrived at the Beltrán house precisely at nine o'clock. Noting that the kitchen lights were dark, he went to the front door and knocked. To his surprise Elena rather than a servant answered the door. She struck him as being excited, and without thinking twice about it he leaned over and brushed her cheek with his in a formal kiss. She blushed in pleasure and ushered him into the *sala*. "Inéz will be ready any minute," she said. "You'll be amused by her costume. You certainly look properly princely."

Inéz stepped into the room before he could say anything. Her costume consisted of a long-sleeved muslin blouse, a front-laced bodice of coarse fabric, a long apron, and a skirt that was ragged around the hem. She had pulled her curly hair back into a severe bun that was tucked into a servant's cap. Two short marks, lines of ashes, showed on her cheek and forehead. Obviously, this was an overworked and badly treated scullery maid. She handed a cloak that she'd had over her arm to Carlos, who placed it on her shoulders. Turning to Elena, she said with a happy smile, "Don't wait up."

As they crossed the plaza, Carlos commented, "You're even more sparkly than usual tonight. Is that the result of something other than anticipation of a night with our wanton Trio?"

"A girl must have some secrets," she whispered conspiratorially in his ear, incidentally permitting him to smell the seductive perfume that she sometimes wore when she wanted to set his head spinning.

"Damiana!" he exclaimed. "That's it! You've been drinking happy-weed tea."

"Drat!" she replied in feigned exasperation. "The trouble with being courted by a brujo is that a woman can't have any secrets."

They continued to talk in this playful manner until they arrived at the front door to the Trio's house. The door was ajar and Carlos's knock was sufficient to swing it fully open. The entryway was dark, and as they tentatively stepped in, a hand with a candle popped out from a side room, followed by a mask-like face. Its lips had been painted green and green paint surrounded its eyes, but they immediately recognized that the face greeting them was Mara's. "Welcome to the Casa de Amor," she announced, "where tonight you will share with us a voyage into the realm of magic and mystery. Follow me."

Carlos and Inéz followed as Mara turned and skipped into the adjoining room, which was illuminated by candles set in wall sconces. "I've never been in this room," Carlos commented.

"It's the *sala*," Inéz told him, "seldom used in Loreto's time here because we never received guests. The kitchen is through the door at the other end."

Leandro rose from a chair and stepped forward to greet them with a bow. He was wearing a loose gown that reached to the floor and was covered with strange symbols, which Carlos recognized as being drawn from alchemists' texts.

"May I guess what you've chosen to be for tonight?" Carlos asked.

"Of course," Leandro replied, apparently pleased to be asked.

"It strikes me that you have chosen to stay close to your known identity by dressing as a magician, or possibly as an alchemist who is, by the nature of his practice, also a magician."

"Why do you suggest that I'm an alchemist?"

"Your gown is covered with symbols from occult lore. I see signs for Alpha and Omega, the Sun, the Moon, an Egyptian pyramid, symbols of the Zodiac, including Pisces, Aries, and Taurus, and representations of planets, among others Mercury, Venus, Jupiter, and Saturn."

"It sounds as though you have studied alchemists' texts. Is that the case?" Leandro asked

"No," Carlos replied. "But my Jesuit tutors taught me the Greek alphabet and introduced me to medieval astrological symbols of the planets and the Zodiac."

"Sometimes," Inéz sighed, "I think his very orthodox Catholic parents would have been quite upset had they known what those priests were teaching him."

"Perhaps so," Carlos said with a laugh. "One more question, Leandro. Your robe seems to have some antiquity. Does it have a history you'd care to describe?"

"Only that it once belonged to the teacher I call Master and that it had been handed down to him from earlier generations of magicians. He gave it to me when he abandoned the study of alchemy."

"What about me? What about me?" Mara burst out in a sing-song chant. "Who am I? Who am I?"

Now that Carlos and Inéz could see Mara clearly they saw that she was wearing emerald-green tights and a snug bodice in the same green color as her face paint. She wore a band around her head from which short wires of some sort stuck up, each topped by a green stone. "What about me? Who am I?" she demanded.

"To judge from all the green in your costume," Inéz guessed, "you're some sort of wood sprite—an elf, fairy, or pixie—and, even though it's mid-winter, you represent the spirit of spring."

"Good guess, close to the truth," Mara declared. "Also I'm celebrating my birthday too, not because it's today, it isn't, but because it comes in early summer."

"And when is your birthday?" Carlos inquired out of politeness.

"June 21st, the summer solstice."

The coincidence of his birthday also falling on June 21st startled him, and he asked, "And what year was that?"

"1688, of course," she replied. "Wasn't that the most important year ever to be born?"

Carlos was amused. "I certainly agree that June 21st is an auspicious birth date. That's the same as mine."

"Oh goodie!" Mara exclaimed, once again skipping around the room. "That must make us soul mates. I've always wanted to have a male soul mate."

"That's an astonishing coincidence, adding a mysterious subplot to our evening," Leandro said. "But tell us, dear guests, what do your costumes represent?"

"We're characters from a fairy tale," Inéz replied. "I'm Cinderella, a scullery maid who, with the help of her good fairy godmother, meets Prince Charming here, and after significant obstacles are overcome, they marry and live happily ever after."

"Is this a story you can tell us later, perhaps through mime and a few words?"

"That would be fun," Inéz replied. "But where's the person whose birthday this party honors?"

"You mean Selena, Queen of Isla de Amor, the enchanted island on whose shores you've just arrived. She is making her grand entrance behind you."

Carlos and Inéz turned to see Selena in her royal costume. Her floor-length dress was pure white and covered with clear crystals that glistened in the candlelight. In her right hand she held a wand that she raised and pointed at Leandro. "Great Alchemist, I command you to cleanse this room of all malign spirits, leaving behind only those entities that will enhance our celebration with pleasant feelings."

"Can't the remaining spirits be a little mischievous?" Mara asked. "There's no fun without a little mischief."

"Very well, nymph, as you wish," Selena agreed with a benign smile.

Leandro set to work immediately, raising his hands and chanting a spell

194 ———————

in a language Carlos couldn't understand. He supposed it might be from an ancient Babylonian or Egyptian text utilized by alchemists, but that was pure speculation on his part. When Leandro stopped chanting, Selena declared, "Let our revels begin!"

"Me first! Me first!" Mara demanded.

"Very well, dear sister sprite," Selena said.

Mara skipped around the room one more time, touching each of the other occupants lightly on the arm as she passed him or her. Her childlike exuberance was beguiling. She went to the far side of the room, where, Carlos noticed, a thick, twisted rope attached to the center beam of the ceiling was anchored to a hook on the wall. As Mara freed the rope he could see that the end of the rope had been pulled through a hole in the center of a wooden disk about a foot across. The disk was fixed in place by a knot, and a tail about two feet long dangled beneath it.

Mara straddled the rope, using the disk as a seat, and wound her legs around the rope's tail. She pushed off and swung across the room, singing unintelligible words in a strange, high-pitched voice. Propelling the rope with strong, undulating motions of her body, she made it swing in arcs the width of the room, occasionally turning from side to side by twisting her body, first clockwise and then counterclockwise. Spontaneously the onlookers began to clap rhythmically, and Leandro added the beat of the *seco* pole.

Finally Mara let the momentum of her swinging subside. Still on the wooden seat, she touched the floor with her toes and said, "Now I am in another world, and I will tell your fortunes. I will begin with Inéz."

Inéz, casting Carlos a questioning look, stepped up to Mara, who took both of her hands in hers, leaned forward, and whispered into her ear. When Inéz returned to Carlos's side her face was unreadable. "Alfonso," Mara sang. She whispered in his ear, and he listened. He then went back to the others and Selena came forward, and after her Leandro. There was a whispered colloquy between Mara and Leandro. Leandro left, looking satisfied. Alone on her seat in the middle of the room, Mara gave a big smile, spun her feet about so that the rope twisted wildly, and sang joyously and very clearly,

"Merrily, merrily shall I live now, under the blossom that hangs on the bough!"

With her foot she stopped the swinging. "Now," she asked gaily, "Who am I? What am I?"

Inéz, who had been watching thoughtfully, declared, "You're a sprite whose home is in the air."

Mara dismounted from the seat and carried it over to its anchor in the corner. She walked back to Inéz and lightly stroked her face with her hand. "Yes, yes," she whispered sibilantly, seemingly still in a trance. Then she kissed Inéz lightly on the cheek, marking her with a smudge of green.

A few moments passed in silence. Then Selena, as if announcing another act, said, "Now it's time for Cinderella and Prince Charming to tell their story."

"Very well," Inéz said. "I will narrate and Prince Charming will, for once in his life, follow my directions." This caused laughter and a shift of mood all around.

"As you can see," she began, "I am a scullery maid. In the first scene I am washing my evil stepsisters' clothes and emptying their chamber pots. I have heard that Prince Charming is holding a ball and intends to choose a wife from among the girls with whom he dances. I dream of going to the ball, but I know it's an impossible fantasy." She mimed an upward look, hands clasped under her chin.

"Then my Fairy Godmother appears in the washroom and says she will help me go to the ball!" Inéz exclaimed. Selena, picking up on her cue, stepped toward Inéz and touched her wand to Inéz's head.

Inéz immediately began to tug at her drab work clothes. She unlaced her bodice and untied her apron and threw them behind her. Selena helped her lift the old blouse and ragged skirt over her head. Underneath was a close-fitting apricot-colored gown. Inéz pulled off her servant's cap and loosened her hair from its bun. "Now it's off to the ball, at which I can stay until the clock strikes midnight. But if I don't leave before the clock stops striking, I will return to my previous condition."

Taking Carlos by the hand, Inéz continued, "The prince dances with many beautiful young women before he gets to me. He takes me in his arms, and we dance. Would you, Leandro, beat out a rhythm for us with the *seco* pole?"

Carlos and Inéz faced each other and stepped into the Spinning Dance. It wasn't long before Carlos began to get dizzy. "We'd better stop soon," he told her, "or I'll topple over like the kids did." She smiled in agreement, and they fell into an unsteady embrace, still in motion, even though they were standing still.

"Kissing! Kissing!" the airy sprite Mara called out.

"That's supposed to happen later," Inéz declared, "but since it's during the dance that the prince falls in love with Cinderella, I suppose it's all right." They exchanged a light kiss.

"The rest of the story goes like this," Inéz said. "The clock begins to strike midnight, and Cinderella knows she has to leave before it's struck twelve times."

Mara sat bolt upright and begin to toll like a bell, "Bong, bong, bong, bong...."

Inéz laughed and resumed her story. "Cinderella runs off, losing a slipper in the process." She ran toward the door, kicking off a shoe as she went. Carlos, recognizing his cue, picked it up. "The prince," Inéz went on, "not having learned her name, searches the whole kingdom for her, and he tries the shoe on many young women's feet, all of them hoping it will fit." Carlos approached Mara and Selena with the shoe. "Of course, it doesn't fit any of them. Finally, in spite of Cinderella's stepsisters' efforts to prevent him from trying it on Cinderella, the shoe fits." Carlos knelt in front of Inéz and slipped her foot into the shoe. Inéz beamed and said, "They marry, and live happily ever after."

The Trio broke out in cheers and applause. "You two definitely have talent," Leandro told them. "You can join our troupe any time you want. Now, I suppose, it's my turn, and I can make my presentation while we're seated and having wine and eating whatever food's available. They moved to a long table at the side of the room and sat down.

They passed the next hour amiably, drinking wine and enjoying tapas the Trio provided. Eventually, after everyone had become a little tipsy, Leandro announced, "I'm ready to take my turn."

"I was struck," he began, "by Inéz's choice of Cinderella, a story of a young woman's transformation. I've had a longstanding interest in transformations. I believe the alchemists had the right idea when they argued that transformations are natural, part of everyday life. Water can become steam or ice; a tiny seed can become a huge tree; we burn wood and it becomes fire, smoke, and ash; a man and a woman come together and nine months later a baby, a totally separate being, comes into the world. Miraculous transformations are always there for those who have eyes to see."

"That's a lovely description of the miraculous," Inéz said.

"Yes," Leandro continued, "but you'll notice that all the examples I've given conform to laws of nature that the alchemist doesn't control. The great challenge the alchemist faces is how to achieve mastery over those laws, which would be a triumph that would open endless vistas for intervening in the world in creative ways."

"Also in malign ways," Carlos couldn't restrain himself from saying.

"That's true," Leandro agreed. "The power to do anything is in and of itself neutral and can be used for good or ill. But I'm confessing to the limits of my magic and my frustration at those limits. That's why I asked you, Alfonso, whether the Pueblo medicine man with whom your young friend José is studying would be willing to talk with me about transformations."

"As a matter of fact," Carlos replied, "I asked him last week, and he said he would like to meet you. Let's agree to visit him later this week, weather permitting."

"Good!" Leandro exclaimed. "Perhaps I will learn more. But tonight I would like to try an experiment in the possibility of achieving mental transformations by asking one of you to allow me to attempt to transform your mental state. Since mental states are invisible, we will have to rely on the report of the individual who agrees to be the subject of this experiment. In the interests of maximum objectivity, Alfonso or Inéz would be the best subjects, because if they experience no change in their mental state, they can be depended upon to candidly report that fact."

Leandro gazed at them benignly, and Carlos and Inéz exchanged a questioning look, each, apparently, running though a quick accounting of the possibilities. Before Carlos had had time to finish his internal assessment, Inéz volunteered. "I will be your subject." She also shot Carlos a look that said, Don't argue.

Pleased, Leandro clapped his hands together. "How generous of you, Inéz," he said warmly.

Mara and Selena had already risen and were beginning to clear off the table. When it was bare, they took two thick blankets, folded lengthwise, and spread them over the edge of the table facing the center of the room. Leandro instructed Inéz to sit on the blanket, slip off her shoes, swing her legs up, and lie down. Once Inéz had done so, Mara took another, lighter blanket and placed it over Inéz from her chest to her feet.

"You needn't be alarmed," Leandro said to Carlos, as if reading his thoughts. "No harm will come to her. My intentions are only good. I will not so much as touch her."

Carlos's conflicting thoughts so blocked each other that they left him speechless. Inéz turned her head, looked into his eyes, and assured him. "Alfonso, this will be interesting. I'll be fine." With that she shut her eyes.

Leandro stepped to the end of the table and raised his open hands, palms downward, in the air above her feet. He remained like that, motionless, for the time it took his audience to take several breaths, and then he slowly moved his hands upward and outward. After several more long moments he brought his hands together again, now over her lower legs, and higher in the air than before. He then moved around to the front edge of the table, held his hands about a foot in the air above her waist, and repeated the expansive gesture he had done before. Carlos noticed that all five partygoers were breathing in unison.

Leandro then moved to the area above Inéz's throat, and finally to her head. The expansive motions he made above her head were the largest of all, his arms extending to their full length to each side and then over his head. Finally he lowered his arms—everyone let out a collective breath—and with his right hand he stroked the air above her body in one sweeping movement from her head to her feet. He stepped back from the table. Inéz opened her eyes. "Oh," she declared. "That was wonderful." Slowly she raised herself to a sitting position.

"Report," Leandro said, smiling. "Did something happen?"

"Oh," Inéz repeated. "I would say 'Where am I?', except I know where I am. But I went somewhere else."

"Can you describe this 'somewhere else'?" Leandro asked.

Inéz thought about it. "No," she said at last. "It's not a place. It's a...different state. Wasn't that the word you used, Leandro, a change in a person's mental state? Well, it was a different state, whatever that means. It was lovely." She gave everyone else—Carlos, Mara, Selena—a wide smile and got up from the table. "Thank you all," she said, as if they had played a part in her mental transformation.

Leandro took charge again. "Now it's time for our beautiful queen to make her contribution to the celebration. What does your majesty wish?"

Selena looked around and said, "I believe four of us lost our mothers years ago, and I would like to hold a séance to try to contact one of them. Let's move the chairs to the center of the room so we can sit in a circle, and I will guide us on a passage into the spirit world."

Rearranging the chairs took very little time, and everyone settled down in a small circle. "Let's join hands," Selena suggested. Carlos, who was seated between Mara on his left and Inéz on his right, felt warmth flow between his hands and theirs. Selena had snuffed out all but one of the candles. That candle and the dim glow of the fire in the fireplace were now the only illumination in the room. "Please bring an image of your mother to mind," Selena told them, "and I'll invite her to join us. We'll see who we contact."

After a period of silence, Selena spoke. "Mother, beloved mother, are you there?" This she repeated numerous times until a strange thing happened. A flash of light, or perhaps a ghostly shadow, a white, transparent shadow, crossed the room behind Selena. Had Carlos not had his recent experience of conversing with Zoila in a dream or hallucination, he might have dismissed the ghostly shadow's passage as an illusion or perhaps as something Selena had arranged, though he couldn't tell how she might have done so.

Selena, her eyes closed, announced, "I feel a presence. Will you speak with us?"

There was silence. "Please speak to us," she said in hushed tones. "Give us a message. Wait!" she added, "I sense that you're not a woman but a man. Is that so?" Then she fell back in her chair and in a totally different voice, a male voice, said, "I am seeking Carlos. Is he there?"

"Who is Carlos?" Selena asked in her normal speaking voice.

The male voice came again. "He was my student many lifetimes ago. I have a message for him."

"There is no one here named Carlos," Selena replied.

"But there is," the male voice came. "I sense his presence."

Everyone looked at Selena, who remained in a trance. Carlos shrugged and gestured with his head toward Leandro. Leandro shook his head. Mara looked at Inéz and the others and mouthed the words, "Not me," and for further emphasis put her hands under her breasts to indicate that she certainly was not a man. Inéz, who originally had looked alarmed, laughed out loud at Mara's gesture.

Selena opened her eyes and reproached Inéz. "You have broken the spell."

Contrite, Inéz replied, "I'm sorry, but Mara made me laugh, and there isn't anyone here named Carlos. I don't know anyone by that name in Santa Fe."

Carlos admired the way that Inéz lied so baldly. He supposed that her life with Loreto had required her to feign all sorts of emotions and deny all sorts of truths.

Leandro looked disappointed. "We've never before gotten so far into a séance," he said. "We not only saw a flash of ghostly matter pass through the room, but Selena briefly contacted a spirit who was seeking to reach someone."

Inéz reached over to take Selena's hand, which was resting on the table next to her. "Dear Selena, I apologize for laughing. It's just that everyone looked totally puzzled and your impish sister Mara made a gesture that broke the spell for me."

Soon the party was breaking up. Selena declared that it was the best birthday party she'd had for many years, and everyone exchanged hugs—very firm hugs, no holding one's body away from one's partner during the hug. Everyone, except for Leandro and Carlos, exchanged kisses too.

As Carlos walked Inéz home, they spent a few minutes in a pleasant silence, each mentally reviewing the party. Then Inéz said thoughtfully, "Did it worry you that Selena asked for Carlos in her trance?"

"I don't think so," he replied. "No one seemed to take it seriously. You vigorously denied knowing of any Carlos in Santa Fe, Mara cupped her breasts to indicate it couldn't be her, you burst out laughing, and that broke the mood. The evening ended on a very positive note."

"I think so too. But can we talk about it more in the morning?"

They had reached the Beltráns' front door, which Inéz opened. Before ducking inside, she kissed him on the mouth. "I love you so much," she said. "Now if only you'll be careful."

He wanted to ask what, specifically, she wanted him to be careful about, but she slipped inside without giving him a chance.

18

Entangled

He woke up later than usual, closer to five than four. Even then he'd had barely three hours to sleep since getting home from the Trio's party. He broke with his meditation routine, getting up immediately, dressing, and heading out the door from the kitchen into the lane that ran beside his house.

Gusts of wind made the cold air feel even colder, and Carlos pulled his overcoat tightly around himself against the chill. Halfway across the plaza he looked back. To his surprise Gordo was following him, apparently having abandoned his normal practice, which was to burrow under the blankets until Carlos got a fire started to warm the room. He waited for Gordo to catch up, and the two of them continued on together to the Beltrán place, where they paused outside the kitchen window. Carlos could see Inéz kneeling at the kitchen's big hearth, laying a fire. He went to the door and tried it, but it was locked. Inéz came to open the door, and Gordo burst in. Reaching down to pat him on the head, she glanced at Carlos and said, "Look what the dog dragged in."

"A locked door—that's a change," Carlos observed.

Moving back to the task of arranging firewood in the hearth, she replied, "Yes, we had a break-in while you and José were on your trip to the mesa. The thief stole food from the larder, not a lot. I suppose he was a hungry person. I would give such a person a meal, if asked, but I don't want anyone to take advantage of unlocked doors."

"That kind of break-in is unusual for Santa Fe. Many people would feed a hungry person. Would you like me to help lay the fire?"

"No, thank you. One of the grooms should have done it. I suppose they forgot whose turn it was. All of them will hear from me when they get up, and they should be up to feed the horses about an hour from now. You'll have to be gone by then. The servants mustn't find you in my kitchen so early in the morning. They'll assume that you spent the night, and I can't have anyone concluding that I've violated the conditions of my employment."

"Would that I could have spent the night." She gave him a sharp look, and he denied that he'd seriously expected to do so. "Don't worry," he told her. "I don't want to get you in trouble."

She stood up and wiped her hands, satisfied that the fire was going well. "Since you're here," she said, "I want to talk more about the party. Last night I was still caught up in its buoyant mood, and I think you were too. But in the cold light of morning I wonder—Selena in her trance asking for 'Carlos' in a masculine voice—does that mean they suspect you *are* Carlos? That Leandro's master is actually Malvolio, and he has sent Leandro to find Carlos?"

"Well," Carlos replied, "that is certainly the worst case possible. But the male voice that called my name sounded like the voice of my old mentor Don Serafino. My recent experience of Zoila coming to me forces me to be open to the possibility that Don Serafino spoke through Selena. It couldn't have been Malvolio—he's not dead. But perhaps it was only Selena pretending to speak in a male voice."

"Which would mean," Inéz pointed out, "that they are looking for Carlos, and possibly suspect he is you."

"Mmmm," said Carlos, noncommittally. "Possibly, but everything else that happened last night inclines me to trust Leandro. He seemed to be very open about his interest in transformations, and about wanting to visit Old

Man Xenome. And even though he's secretive about his master's practice, his description of the kind of person his master is doesn't fit with the ruthless Malvolio I encountered in two past lives."

Inéz thought about this. "I suppose you're right. Whatever Leandro did when he worked his mental transformation on me was very calming, very pleasant—not mentally invasive or anything like that. Still, the name Carlos being spoken in that group—it makes me think that we have to guard your brujo identity more carefully than ever. For my part I'm going to see what I can do to keep Leandro and Elena separate. Elena knows too much."

"You suggested earlier," Carlos remarked, "that you thought she could keep what she knows secret."

"Yes, I did," she replied, moving to a shelf and picking up a sack of cornmeal. "But I think she's infatuated with Leandro and hinting that she knows secrets about you would certainly be a way of getting his attention."

"I don't see how you can keep them apart, any more than you and I can suddenly become less friendly with the Trio."

"I'll try to keep Elena loyal to me; maybe that will help. As for the two of us and the three of them, I suggest we enjoy their company while remaining careful. There's no reason, for instance, why you and Leandro shouldn't visit Old Man Xenome together, or why I shouldn't continue to fence with Leandro or visit with Mara and Selena."

"What about dancing with Leandro?"

"Will you stop fussing about that!" she said, making a dismissive gesture with her hand. "Leandro is a professional flirt. Most girls like the attention, and he's very handsome besides. It's like what Mara said about Selena. It's just a game to him; it doesn't mean anything."

She was silent for a moment, thoughtful. "The dancing, though—the *duende*. That's more than a game. I think it can stir something real. My dancing with Selena—you might have cause to be jealous of that. Or I might, of your dancing with Mara."

Carlos was astonished. He had thought Inéz was jealous of Selena's flirtatious attentions to him, and it had never occurred to him to be jealous of Selena and her. And for the most part he had forgotten about the intense effect on him of dancing the Unnamed Dance with Mara. "That's a whole new way to look at it," he commented at last. "I never thought...."

"What?"

"Never mind," he replied, pulling himself together. "Let me raise another question before you throw Gordo and me out of your kitchen."

Gordo, as he always did when he heard his name mentioned, raised his head and wagged his tail happily.

"What's this other question of yours?"

"It's a simple question. What do you want?"

"There's nothing at all simple about that. Answer for yourself first."

"It's not fair of you to turn the tables on me like that, but I'll prove my good faith by complying. It's not," he began, "a simple question for me either; in fact, my lack of a clear answer nags at me constantly. My past preference has been for living from day to day, and that approach has generally served me well. The problem is that the day-to-day approach leads me to go along as merrily and superficially as Mara did in her sprite dance.

"I thought that Zoila had introduced me to a deeper reality and that I'd become committed to pursuing it. But I've begun to doubt, not that it happened, but that I will ever find it again. I'm certainly not making any progress in my meditation practice, although both Zoila and Father Stefano warned me that that might happen. And for the past few weeks, ever since I first perceived that darkness was descending in my world, I've been distracted by ill-defined threats—Malvolio, possibly the Trio, spirit wolves and spirit turkey vultures, and the rest.

"What do I want? Most of all I'd like peace to descend so that I can be free to focus on what I know is real, my relationship with you. All these other worries keep intruding on that."

"What," she asked thoughtfully, "do you think our relationship is, and what do you want it to become?" She'd stopped measuring out the cornmeal and was looking at him with the utmost seriousness.

"I feel," Carlos said, "that I am your closest friend, and I love you more all the time. That's the present, as I see it. The future is less clear. At first I held back, wondering whether brujos marry. I've come around to believe there's no reason why they shouldn't. But will you be able to overcome the reservations about marriage you expressed during our picnic at the Sacred Pool?"

"Damn!" she exclaimed softly. "If you keep on like this, I'll be so conflicted I'll cry. You've gone from talking about a loving friendship to mentioning marriage. I've told you that's out of the question for now, possibly forever. I spent years having nearly every choice in my life dictated by a tyrant. You're no tyrant; you're kind and generous and solicitous of my needs. But the biggest of my needs right now is to find out who I am when I'm free to pursue my deepest inclinations and talents. That's my version of a quest on what you called the Unknown Way. I treasure your companionship and support. I don't want to try to do this without you, but marriage isn't part of that picture for me."

"Do you see any prospect that we might live together as lovers without marrying?"

Inéz seemed to Carlos to find this a deeply troubling question. Her hands trembled, and for a moment she was unable to speak. "All right," she said at last, "I'm going to tell you things about myself that may hurt your feelings, though I hope not. But before I do so, I need you to answer one more question about what you want."

He felt considerable trepidation, but he replied, "Go ahead."

"Do you want children?"

"I've never had children in any lifetime, including this one."

"That's no answer!" she exclaimed.

"I've never thought about whether I wanted children."

Clearly annoyed, she shot back, "That's not an answer either!"

He tried to give her a full and honest response. "I never thought of having a child of my own," he replied, "but last night when Leandro described the miracle of a child's birth as the result of a man and a woman coming together, my first thought was that I'd never experienced the miracle of being a father. You've as much as said, and I've as much as admitted, that my behavior in my past lives, and my present life also, has been immature. Having a wife and child might be a source of greater growth for me than hours and hours, possibly years and years, of meditation."

Inéz wiped a tear from her cheek. He started to move toward her to take her in his arms and comfort her. "No, don't embrace me; that would cut off an exchange of hard truths, and I have more to tell you. For one thing, I'm not sure that I can have a child. Loreto forced me to have relations with dozens of men, and I never became pregnant."

"I assumed you were taking some sort of precautions."

"That was scarcely ever possible. And wait. I have one more truth to tell you, and it's the hardest truth of all to share. I've told you that except for a few times with Hernando, sexual activity was horrible. I learned to separate myself from what was being done to my body. My consciousness literally hovered above the bed in which the act was taking place; it was happening to someone else, someone I didn't even care about. That was useful to my emotional survival, but the result was that the body parts most intimately involved died to feeling. I treasure being held, kissed, and stroked, but I don't believe I'll ever be able to fully enjoy love-making, and I feel that my inability to do so would be terrible for both of us if we ever became lovers."

He was stunned, but he rallied to say, "I had no idea."

"I know you didn't. It's too hard to talk about."

"But that one memorable day when you asked me to bite your neck and you—"

She cut him off. "I know what you're wondering. My sigh expressed my great happiness at being held lovingly. That was all, and everything."

Carlos was going to comment, but she cocked her head toward the door to the inner hallway and whispered, "Someone's coming; you must leave immediately." She nudged Gordo, who was napping in front of the fire, with her foot and said, "Get up, you lazy mutt!" She scooted him toward Carlos, who was already holding the door open. Gordo scrabbled awkwardly on the kitchen's tile floor, a funny sight that forced Inéz and Carlos to smother their laughter. Carlos and Gordo made it out the door and closed it behind them before anyone else came into the kitchen.

He walked home slowly, mulling over the many thoughts raised by his conversation with Inéz. He felt solemn—not depressed, simply pensive. He understood better now Inéz's reservations about marrying him and also her unwillingness to move in and become his mistress. Her comment that she loved being held, kissed, and stroked was a welcome admission, but he'd known that already. He wondered, however, about the long-term impact of not moving on to greater intimacies of the sort he'd enjoyed in all his lifetimes with his mistresses.

It was just after dawn when he reached his house. He spent an hour meditating and then had breakfast with José, who left immediately afterward for his job as a blacksmith's apprentice. In the absence of anyone besides himself and Gordo, the house seemed very quiet. Too quiet. He knew he needed some activity, and he decided that the project he most wanted to pursue was positioning the white rocks he had collected with Diego along the edge of the roof and at the base of his adobe house's walls. For the past two weeks the rocks had sat in a pile in the corner of his bedroom. On top of the rocks he had placed the mountain lion bracelet that Old Man Xenome had given him. He hoped that the rocks would absorb positive energies from the bracelet and become a protective shield around his home. Now he began putting the stones in thick canvas bags.

By mid-morning he was ready to start the outdoor part of the job. He set a ladder up against the side of his house above the veranda and the seldom-used front door. He then made numerous trips to haul bags of stones to the roof. Next he measured a series of regular intervals along the edge of the roof and began to distribute the rocks. His first distribution left more space than he wanted between each stone, so he brought more stones up to the roof from his bedroom. These he began to arrange at closer intervals all the way across the front roof and then the top of the north wall (the one closest to the plaza), and finally, by late afternoon, he finished laying out stones on top of the west and south walls of the house.

That evening he felt underslept from the previous night, the night of the Trio's party, and catching up on rest seemed like a good idea. After a quiet dinner with José, who was lost in his own thoughts, he went to bed much earlier than usual, only a few hours after dark. It was the first week of February, and nightfall still came early.

The next morning he awoke and returned to his usual routines—an early meditation, breakfast with José, a stroll to the house Orfeo was building for him, and a talk with Pedro, who had shown up to see if Orfeo needed any advice. Carlos stayed all day to work with Orfeo. In mid-afternoon the happy thought came to him that he would see Inéz that night at the show the Trio was going to perform at the Trigales residence. He had agreed with Inéz that he would come by for her at eight o'clock and escort her to the entertainment, and he was especially looking forward to the walk from the Beltráns' to the Trigales place, which would allow him to have her to himself for a little while.

It was not to be. That evening, as he left his house to go to meet Inéz, he saw the three entertainers coming toward him down the lane. Selena called out to him, "We're in luck! We'll sweep you along with us."

"I thought you would be there earlier," Carlos replied.

"We're a little late," Leandro admitted. "It will work out fine. We'll swing by the Beltrán place, collect Inéz, and the five of us can arrive at the Trigales's together. Just as a wedding can't start until the bride arrives, a performance can't begin until the entertainers show up."

Leandro threw his arm around Carlos's shoulders, and Selena took Carlos's free arm in hers. "If I don't get a kiss from you tonight," she announced, "I'll be very disappointed." Mara walked in front of them without saying anything.

They went to the front door of the Beltrán house. Inéz was watching for them and came out to greet them.

As one of the largest houses in Santa Fe, the Trigales residence offered performers a spacious stage for entertaining in the *sala*. Chairs had been moved to one side of the room, leaving a big area empty of furniture. Apparently all the expected guests had now arrived—among them, Carlos and Inéz, Javier and Cristina Beltrán and their daughter Elena, Dr. Fabio Velarde, and the hosts, Raul and Bianca Trigales and their four children, Cristofer, Carmela, Constanza, and Anton.

Leandro discarded his winter cloak and displayed his colorful performance outfit—tights and a jerkin with two-inch-wide vertical stripes of red, blue, yellow, and white running from neck to toe. He stepped to the center of the open space and announced that the performance was about to begin. "Ladies and gentlemen, boys and girls, please take your seats." The adults settled back into chairs, and the four Trigales children plopped down on the floor in front of their parents. "What you will see," Leandro continued, "will be an amazing display of art and magic, not that the two, properly understood, are entirely separate. Both magic and dance share a spirit of enchantment we call *duende*. Our program will divide into several parts. For the first, these four little charmers"—he gestured to the Trigales children—"will amaze you with a demonstration of magic that I've taught them. After their performance, our quartet of apprentice magicians will depart for bed and the adult portion of the entertainment will commence."

Leandro nodded in the direction of Cristofer, the oldest of the Trigales children, who stood up. "I am to introduce the magic trick my brother and sisters and I will do for you. We are going to use a deck of cards that Señorita Selena Torrez has loaned us for the occasion. As you'll see, the cards are more interesting than those in normal card decks."

Cristofer then laid all the cards on a low table that had been placed in front of the adults. Carlos instantly recognized that it was a Tarot deck. Instead of the standard Spanish forty-card deck's suits of swords, cups, coins, and clubs, the Tarot deck's suits consisted of wands, cups, swords, and pentacles. There were fifty-six cards from those suits, and twenty-two more face cards with unique figures on them. Some—the Devil, Death, the Tower of Destruction, and the Hanged Man—struck Carlos as alarmingly ominous, but Cristofer cheerfully announced that he and his brother and sisters would use only a few of the extra face cards. They had chosen nine of their favorites: the Magician, the High Priestess, the Empress, the Emperor, Lovers, Justice, Temperance, a Star, and the Sun.

Cristofer collected these nine face cards and handed them to Anton, his little brother, to shuffle. With an excited grin on his face, Anton did an expert job of shuffling the cards sidewise. "He's been practicing and practicing,"

Cristofer reported, "driving the rest of us crazy."

The game that followed required someone to be blindfolded and someone else to draw a card. One of the twin girls, Carmela or Constanza — Carlos still couldn't tell them apart — placed a blindfold on her sister. Anton's Uncle Javier drew the Emperor card and, following Cristofer's directions, held it up for everyone to see. Javier placed it back in the deck and Anton shuffled the deck again. He handed the cards to Cristofer, who laid the nine cards, face up, on the table and told his blindfolded sister, Carmela, that she could take off the blindfold. She stared at the cards and made a great show of moving her hands across them before finally picking up the very card her uncle had chosen.

This process was repeated three times, and on two of the three times Carmela or Constanza, who took turns wearing the blindfold, pointed to the correct card on the first try. The only exception happened on the third round, when Constanza started to make an incorrect choice and little Anton, to everyone's amusement, couldn't contain himself and blurted out, "No! No!" Constanza then reconsidered and selected the correct card. It was a delightful show, made even more enjoyable by the pleasure the children took in their success. At the completion of their magic trick, the four youngsters took a bow to hearty applause.

Their mother, after congratulating her children on their skill as apprentice magicians, told them it was time for them to get ready for bed. Off they went, chattering happily among themselves.

Leandro took center stage again. "My lovely friends, Mara Mata and Selena Torrez, will now begin the adult portion of the night's entertainment by performing an exotic dance from the northern shores of Africa. It combines folk elements from Moorish, Gypsy, and even more ancient traditions, and we believe the meaning of the dance is a celebration of the source of life. You will notice — you will not be able to help noticing — that the source of the movement in the dancers' bodies is their bare abdomens."

A murmur went through the audience as the sound of tinkling anklets and bracelets was heard and the dancers entered from a side room. They were barefooted, and they wore finger-cymbals that they struck together in an irregular rhythm as they slowly swayed, hips leading, to the center of the floor. Their loose, rust-colored, gauzy trousers hung from their hips, and their gauzy shirts were tied just under their breasts. As Leandro had promised, their navels were on full display, their abdominal muscles subtly moving in circles. Their faces were veiled from just beneath their kohl-accented eyes to below the chin.

Inéz playfully put her hand over Carlos's eyes and whispered in his ear, "This is more than a mere mortal man should see."

"So I noticed," Carlos replied, "before everything went dark."

Leandro picked up a recorder-like wooden instrument from a nearby table. Raising the mouthpiece to his lips, he produced a low, hollow, breathy sound that rose and fell in a long, haunting line. He paused, as did the dancers. They stood several feet apart, facing the audience. For a moment they assumed a posture that seemed both utterly foreign and strangely classical, one knee bent with the heel raised, hips thrust to the side, one arm half-raised, the other hand dropped and the arm lifted at the elbow.

Leandro resumed his haunting tones, and the dancers began to move, independently of each other, their gaze on the audience, in graceful, sinuous motions that originated in their torsos and undulated out to their fingertips. Leandro's music had no beat, and the dancers' movements had only flow, interspersed with pauses of both music and movement. Each time the music resumed it seemed as though the level of intensity increased and the dancers drew the audience more deeply in.

It's *duende*, Carlos thought, fascinated. You can't stop looking at them, at the moving center of their bodies, like watching a spiral go round and round and drawing you into its center. At the same time in his peripheral vision he was acutely aware of the movements of the dancers' arms and legs—the dancer closest to where he sat was Mara—and of the stillness of Mara's head and the steadiness of her gaze, which sometimes met his in a disturbing way, as if it pierced him. To the heart—the thought came unbidden, but there it was.

The music paused again, and the dancers stood still. Leandro put down his instrument and picked up the *seco* pole and began a rapid, erratic beat. The dancers' movements—their almost languid suppleness—changed. They turned to face each other and, finger-cymbals clashing, they began a rapid dance, diving forward and back, side to side, brushing each other's shoulders, facing each other and working their hips as if in competition to demonstrate which of them could outdo the other. Their eyes blazed, their movements and the *seco* pole's beat grew faster and faster until at last the beat stopped and they threw up their arms and then collapsed on the floor. The audience burst into simultaneous applause and laughter, and the dancers stood up and, smiling and breathing heavily, took their bows.

Carlos, still clapping, turned to Inéz next to him. "They continue to amaze," he said.

She gave him a look he could not read. "Mara," was all she said.

Leandro announced that there would be a brief break in the program while Selena and Mara changed their costumes. Bianca Trigales invited everyone to enjoy the wine and refreshments to be found on a table in one corner of the room. From the volume of talk, it was clear that everyone was having a good time. Carlos overheard many expressions of amazement. "Enthralling!" "Riveting!" "Did you ever see...?"

Carlos noticed that Leandro was standing alone across the room. He picked up an extra glass of wine and carried it over to him. "Would you like some wine?" he asked.

"No, thank you," Leandro replied, showing Carlos that he was holding a small flask. "I have a special concoction in this flask that gives me energy for the next event, which I will do solo and unaccompanied."

Leandro then signaled that he had an announcement. Everyone returned to his or her seat.

"While the women dancers are changing," he said, "I am going to perform a feat I guarantee you have never seen before. I will spin in place so fast that the colors of my outfit will blend into a single color. It will be somewhat—but only somewhat—like the spinning of a child's top, and hence I call it The Top."

Leandro assumed a position standing in the middle of the open space that was serving as a stage. He began to pirouette, at first slowly, then faster and faster, balanced on the ball of one foot and propelling his spin with the other. It seemed to Carlos that Leandro was spinning faster than was humanly possible, and he had no idea how he could do it. Had he, Carlos wondered, accessed some power unknown to Carlos, perhaps through whatever was in the drink he'd taken?

Leandro spun so fast that the colors of his outfit blended into a single color that seemed to rise up like a flame. His aura was unlike any Carlos had ever seen—very bright, but shattered into tiny pieces, like a broken mirror reflecting light. Carlos could see that all the onlookers were transfixed at the sight, and when Leandro's spin gradually slowed to a stop, it won a round of wildly enthusiastic applause. Leandro was breathing rapidly and his face was darkly flushed. It seemed to Carlos that there was a kind of hyper-excitement about him.

After taking his bows Leandro invited the audience back to the refreshment table for a break while he changed. It was only a few minutes until Mara and Selena entered the room, dressed now in calf-length skirts and shoes with curved heels. They swung their skirts and did little dance steps to the center of the room to gain everyone's attention. "We are," Selena announced, "again going to do what we call the Unnamed Dance, which many of you will recall from two weeks ago. The steps are quite simple, not much different from walking: two slow steps forward (or backward for the woman), two quick steps to the side. The essence of the dance is released from the closeness of the partners' bodies." She took Mara into the dance position, their torsos in close contact on one side from rib to hip. "Let the movement come from this contact," she said. "Watch us. It goes like this."

Selena and Mara began to dance. Their moments dramatized attraction and tension between two partners. Quick movements were followed by abrupt halts, the halts followed by advances and retreats, each of which heightened the dance's aura of danger and passion. The dancers' hard heels took the place of the *seco* pole, beating out a dramatic rhythm. Carlos, watching intently, felt himself being drawn into the dark mystery of the dance. He did not want it to end.

At last Mara let her body arch backward to be supported by Selena in the final movement of the dance. They held the pose for a moment and then stood and received their applause. Leandro, who had changed out of his striped costume and was now wearing black tights and a loose black shirt, entered the room. He invited the audience to stand and asked them to form couples. Selena immediately paired herself with Carlos and Leandro approached Inéz. Mara moved to the side of the room and took up the *seco* pole.

Carlos took his position with Selena while at the same time trying to look over her shoulder at Inéz and Leandro. It was not possible to keep them in sight. Other couples moved between them, each couple going in a different direction. In the pit of his stomach Carlos had an irrational feeling of dread. Nevertheless, he tried to pay attention to Selena's subtle guiding movements. He evidently did not do a very good job, because when the dance ended and Selena arched back in his arms, she looked at him and said, "What's wrong with you? You're so distracted."

He brought her upright and saw her attention immediately shift. She was looking over his shoulder. "Something's wrong with Leandro!" she cried. Stepping out of his embrace, she hurried over to Leandro, who was flung back in the woman's position at the end of the dance, supported at the waist by Inéz, who looked frightened.

There was a general hubbub of voices and everyone began to crowd around, although Leandro was helped to stand up by Inéz and appeared to recover. "I'm all right, I'm all right," he was saying. "I must have overdone the spinning and just now it caught up with me. Yes, I'm fine." Someone handed him a glass of water, which he drank, and he composed himself. "A more dramatic end to the evening than I had planned," he declared. With his professional manner back and speaking to the crowd, he added, "I want to thank our generous hosts...."

Carlos tuned out the conventional social niceties and moved to Inéz's side.

The night's activities were coming to a close. After Raul Trigales had thanked the Trio profusely and vowed that they'd get together again, the other guests began to don their cloaks for the walk back to their homes.

Bianca came over to speak with Leandro. "You were so good with the children," she said. "Everyone could tell how excited they were about doing one of the tricks you taught them. They are pestering me no end to let you take them out of town to perform at Trujillo's ranch. I may have to capitulate. Let's talk further."

Taking advantage of Leandro's being slightly detained by Bianca, Carlos helped Inéz into her cloak and hurried her out of the house. "I must talk to you alone," he whispered into her ear. Inéz, somewhat to his surprise, asked no questions and followed him out the door.

The bracing night air was refreshing. They had walked for several minutes before Carlos trusted himself to speak. "There's something wrong with Leandro," he said.

"I know," she replied. "I could feel it dancing with him. It wasn't his usual dramatic flirtatiousness—he seemed like a beast to me. I felt like he was going to rape me. I know that the Unnamed Dance is a sort of sexual preliminary, but Leandro was different this time—I had to do what I told you I used to do with those other men, remove my consciousness from my body and watch disinterestedly from overhead. At the end, when he fainted, I had the presence of mind to catch him. But he fainted as if he had—you know—"

"I know," Carlos said softly. "How horrible for you."

"Yes, it was. Thank God it's over. But what did you see that made you say there's something wrong with him?"

Carlos told her, briefly.

Javier, Cristina, and Elena, who had been walking more quickly, caught up with them, making it impossible to continue their conversation. "Wasn't that splendid!" Cristina exclaimed. "The children were so good, the dancers so amazing, and the speed at which the magician turned in place was astonishing."

"I particularly enjoyed that Moorish-Gypsy dance," Javier declared.

"I could tell," Cristina said, giving him an affectionate pat on the arm, "and if I had been smart, I would have put my hand over your eyes the way Inéz covered Alfonso's. You'll dream about those women's figures all night."

"Not true," he replied. "The best part of the evening was dancing with you," a statement she rewarded with a smile.

"I enjoyed the dancing too," Elena chimed in, "even though the doctor shows no sign of finding me the least bit interesting."

"Are you interested in him?" Carlos asked.

"I'm not interested in any man who's not interested in me," she declared firmly.

"Good for you!" Inéz exclaimed, with a forcefulness that surprised Carlos.

Cristina's reaction was more pensive. "My little girl," she said, "is growing up."

They'd reached the Beltráns' front door and said good night to each other. Carlos continued on home, deeply troubled by what he'd seen.

19

Masquerade

Carlos slept for less than three and a half hours that night and got up at four o'clock. Gordo rolled over and went back to sleep, snoring softly. Carlos built a small fire to take the chill off his bedroom, tucked a low cushion under himself, and began to meditate. He felt mentally ragged and badly underslept, as if his nerves had been scraped raw. He decided against doing his chakra practice and opted instead for the simple meditation of watching his breath and letting whatever was disturbing him emerge.

He let the events arise and be present in his awareness without directly questioning them—the dreams of darkness approaching, the spirit wolf and spirit vultures, the dinner with the entertainers in which something like a ghost seemed to pass through the room, Selena asking for Carlos in a trance voice, Mara in a trance whispering his fortune, Inéz's confession of her feelings about their possible future, and the display of something like another personality in Leandro.

Then the images began to swirl like bits of leaves picked up in a summer dust devil running across the ground, spinning, spinning. Leandro's spinning like a top last night, the Spinning Dance Carlos had done with Selena when the entertainers had first arrived, the Unnamed Dance that followed it with Mara, the erotic vortex into which that dance had drawn him, what Mara had whispered to him in her swinging-induced trance, "Your fortune and mine are one and the same." They had the same birthday, he remembered; was that all she meant? Then all of his other thoughts seemed to blow away, and the one image left was of Mara's triangular face and her violet eyes. He was suddenly flooded with erotic desire for her, and it occurred to him that he had somehow been bewitched.

With an effort, he pulled himself out of his meditative state and back into rational consciousness. Quite a bit of time had passed; dawn was lightening the sky outside his bedroom window. He stood up. The swirling images in his meditation and his being sucked down into their vortex told him clearly and unmistakably that not only were the darkness and the spirit wolves and vultures connected to the arrival of the entertainers, but that they were presenting him with something far more complex than he had imagined at the outset. If the entertainers had spun a web, he was in it, and he would have to participate in the design that emerged.

Though the meditation had been almost hallucinatory in its power, he felt clarified and strangely strengthened by it. He told himself, be watchful with Leandro; be on guard against Mara's erotic appeal; as for Selena—it was she who, in a trance, had asked for Carlos—he had no idea what she might know, or suspect. Careful, careful, he told himself. Friendly, but careful.

Carlos then put the meditation and the events of the previous night out of his mind and attended to the needs of the day. First breakfast for himself and Gordo, after which he checked on José, who had just gotten up. He helped José feed their three horses and turn them out in the corral. The next order of business was getting down to business. He walked to the building site where Orfeo Jiranza, his carpenter, was setting out the lines along which adobe walls for a second wing of the house would soon be rising. He appreciated the handsome young man's dedication to his work and the joyful way that he accompanied himself by singing New Mexican folk songs. He seemed to have an endless supply of songs and verses, and when Don Carlos had the time, as he did this morning, he always asked to be taught at least one of them.

He fell into work alongside Orfeo, and as Orfeo sang a verse Carlos listened and tried to sing it with him as he repeated it. "These *versos* or *coplas*, as they're called," Orfeo explained after they had sung many repetitions, "are very old. They were brought to New Spain from the old country with little or no revision, and they're extremely popular in New Mexico."

Carlos worked and sang with Orfeo the whole morning. As noon approached he was about to call it a day when Dr. Fabio Velarde, the house's future owner, showed up. "That was a fascinating, I might even say magical, entertainment last night," the doctor remarked. "I couldn't take my eyes off those two dancers. Images of them floated through my head all the way home."

"Such images can be very persistent," Carlos agreed, somewhat wryly. "But may I change the topic, and ask how your practice is going? You will doubtless understand my self-interest in the matter, since a large portion of your income will end up in my pocket for building this house."

It was Fabio's turn to laugh. "So far, it's very good. As the only physician in town, I'm keeping busy, although I do have some competition from Native healers."

"How's that?" Carlos asked.

"The vice governor's wife, Regina Cabrera, was my patient. She had a persistent headache that I was treating on a daily basis. But she was given an herbal tea from a local curandera and it made the headaches go away. She hasn't asked me to visit her since."

"Pity," Carlos said insincerely. "But it may be just as well. Perhaps I shouldn't say this, but a word to the wise...." Fabio looked a little nonplussed. Leaning close to him, Carlos whispered, "People were beginning to talk."

"Oh," Fabio said. "Yes, I suppose.... You're right, of course. One's conduct must always be professional. Ah...thank you," he concluded.

To ease the moment of awkwardness, Carlos gave him a big grin and a conspiratorial wink. Fabio smiled back, feeling less that he had been warned than that his manhood had been validated.

After Fabio went off on his own business, Carlos walked the short distance back to his house and noticed that the white stones he'd placed on the top of his house's walls weren't all evenly spaced. He decided to make rearranging them his afternoon task, and after a short break for lunch he got the ladder from the hayloft, climbed up on the roof, and began to space the stones out more precisely, working around the house from the front or west wall until he was rearranging stones on the southeast corner. From this vantage point he could see the Trio's rented residence to the south and the lane that ran from his house to theirs.

It wasn't long before Leandro and Selena came up the lane, walking quickly. "You look purposeful," Carlos called from the rooftop. They stopped, startled, not having seen him because he'd been bent over, picking up stones from a small pile of extras he had stored on the roof.

Leandro collected himself and said brightly, "How nice to see you, Alfonso. Good morning. Yes, we're on our way to the Trigales house. I'm to teach Cristofer and Anton more about magic, and the twin girls want Selena to give them dancing lessons. And I'm glad we've found you, because Mara is at home making a big pot of stew, and we wanted to ask you and Inéz to share it with us."

Carlos thought fast. He doubted that Inéz would consider accepting an invitation to dinner tonight, so soon after Leandro's disturbing behavior last night, and after their having agreed to exercise great caution with regard to the Trio. To gain time before he answered, he climbed down the ladder, turning his head toward Leandro and Selena and expressing thanks for the invitation as he did so. But once on the ground he proposed an alternative. "We were your guests," he pointed out, "for Selena's birthday party only three nights ago. If anything, it's our turn to entertain you. How about here, tomorrow night, assuming Inéz can make it."

Leandro and Selena conferred, then agreed. "Good," Carlos declared. "Here, tomorrow, at eight o'clock, unless you hear otherwise from me."

Leandro and Selena waved and continued on to the Trigales house. Carlos dashed into his house, changed his work shirt, gave Leandro and Selena a few minutes to get ahead of him, and then hurried off to the Beltrán place to speak with Inéz. She was finishing the after-lunch clean-up when he knocked and let himself in. "I need to talk with you," he said without preliminaries.

Quickly he filled her in on his sense from his morning meditation that their involvement with the three entertainers had brought them into different difficulties and dangers than they had originally anticipated. "I know you're furious at Leandro for what happened last night," he said, "and you have every right to be. But I think we have to keep on appearing to be friends with them—friendly but even more on our guard. We had already agreed on something like this—a masquerade. I'm simply suggesting we continue it, with even more watchfulness.

"Something" he continued, "is going on that I don't understand—something in addition to Selena in a trance asking for someone named Carlos. Leandro underwent some sort of bizarre transformation last night when he did those superhuman spins, then danced in that beastly way with you, and then fainted. It's possible he may not even remember it. I saw him a few minutes ago, and he seemed his normal friendly self, and even invited us to dinner tonight."

Inéz gave a little gasp. "Surely you didn't—" she began.

"No, I said I needed to talk with you first," he replied. "And I decided to take the offensive and invited *them* to dinner, tomorrow night at my house rather than tonight at theirs."

"I don't like it," she said, clearly annoyed. "I thought we were trying to avoid becoming too entangled with them; yet you've invited them to your place tomorrow, which is only four days after Selena's birthday party and barely two since we danced with them at the Trigales's. That's something nearly every other night."

"You're right, of course," he acknowledged, "but we owe them a dinner after Selena's birthday party, and we can control events better on our own ground."

Inéz was silent for a few minutes.

"You can be chilly toward Leandro if you like," he added. "Keep him at arm's length. Would you be willing to do that?" he asked.

"I can be quite chilly," she replied. "But what about you? Shouldn't you display some jealousy—or even some outrage—at Leandro's behavior toward me last night? Can you—should you—carry on as if you didn't notice? And what about Selena's very obvious attentions to you? And even more so, what about Mara and her violet eyes? Don't tell me you haven't been attracted!"

The tone of her voice, as well as her words, told him that she was angry. He would have protested, but he recognized the general truth in her words, and his new awareness from his morning's meditation of his intense erotic feelings toward Mara inwardly shamed him.

"For myself," he replied as gently as he could, "I will maintain the pretense that nothing happened other than Leandro suffering a mildly embarrassing fainting fit, so I have nothing to be jealous or outraged about. In other words, I think we should carry on as normally as possible, while being on our guard."

Inéz gave him a slightly dubious look. "All right," she told him. "I will do my best to be civil. But I will kill you if you betray me with Mara." She tried to say it lightly, but Carlos heard the feeling behind it.

"My dearest Inéz," he assured her. "I promise you."

The next day Carlos prepared chili and cornbread as the basis for a simple evening meal. Inéz arrived a few minutes early and helped him set the table. The Trio arrived shortly thereafter. Without any further preliminaries, Carlos began to serve dinner, aided by José. He was amused to note that Inéz had once again managed the seating of guests so that neither Mara nor Selena was next to him. He and Leandro occupied the ends of the table; Inéz sat on Carlos's right and José on his left with Mara across from Selena at Leandro's end of the table. Selena immediately fell into her usual behavior and began flirting with José, remarking how fortunate Carlos was to have such a handsome young man to help him with his horses. José looked hopelessly embarrassed, and Selena told him he looked even more handsome when he blushed. "I'll bet all the local girls are competing for your attention," she declared.

Leandro, friendly and open as usual, also directed his attention to José, and expressed his interest in José's training as a medicine man. "Don Alfonso and I are going to visit your mentor, Old Man Xenome, tomorrow. Can you go with us?"

"I regret that I can't," José replied. "I'm apprenticed to a blacksmith, and my boss is already annoyed with me for taking so many days off. I've got to keep him happy."

"Can you tell us anything about your training with Old Man Xenome?" Leandro asked.

José looked uncomfortable. "No, that's between me and him. But since he's said he wants to meet you, I suppose he may tell you something about what a medicine man does, if not how he does it."

Carlos, wanting to get José off the hook, turned to Selena. "The new dance you and Mara did at the Trigales's party—the one where you veiled your faces and exposed your navels," he said with an appreciative laugh, "can you tell us where you learned it?"

"I learned it as a child in Spain," she replied. "My mother and I lived on the outskirts of Seville, in a district called Triana, where many Gypsies and other poor people lived. Many hundreds of years ago the Moors ruled southern Spain, and though they were conquered and driven out long ago, Seville's most beautiful buildings are in the Moorish style and a lot of Moorish culture was absorbed. Actually, as Mara told you, I probably have Moorish ancestry, although my mother was a Gypsy. Among the poor people in our district were some who were also of mixed Moorish ancestry, though they were Catholic, like everyone else. As we were all outcasts, we were more or less friendly with all our neighbors, and we taught them some of our Gypsy songs and lore, and we learned some of theirs.

"The local girls learned the Moorish dance that Mara and I did beginning when they were thirteen or fourteen. When I was that age I had a friend who knew how to do it, and she taught it to me. She told me that it was a woman's dance, taught to girls to loosen and widen their hips to make childbirth easier, and was strictly not performed for men. I expect," Selena added drily, "that in non-Moorish countries that has changed. As for us, we are entertainers. Like magpies, we pick up whatever we find along the way that is shiny and attractive and will delight an audience."

Inéz spoke in a carefully neutral tone. "Perhaps while you are here you will teach me that dance."

Carlos watched and listened, trying to gauge what was behind Inéz's request.

"Speaking of learning things," Leandro asked Carlos, "where and with whom did you study fencing?"

Carlos thought of the beautiful woman fencing master, Celeste, under whose tutelage his skills in the art of fencing rose to new heights in his first life as a brujo in the 1530s, but he wasn't about to reveal his past lives to Leandro. "Growing up in Mexico City," Carlos said, "I studied with the greatest master of our time, Don Ignacio de Tortuga. He had taught for many decades in Spain before coming to Mexico City. He's a skilled teacher and, along with one of my Jesuit tutors, was my principal mentor."

"Was he, this Don Ignacio, your equal in fencing?"

"Initially, he was much superior to me. In time, however, I became a better fencer. He told me that when the student exceeds his master, the student should set off on his own, and I suppose I've done so by coming to Santa Fe, though not with the intention of separating from him. As long as I was in Mexico City, I regarded him, and even now still do, as my mentor and friend."

"An inspiring story," Leandro commented, "and should I find myself in Mexico City, I will make a point of seeking him out."

Carlos was curious about the implications of what Leandro had said regarding the possibility of finding himself in Mexico City and asked, "From what you just said, it sounds as if you plan to travel there sometime. Is that so?"

"I don't know precisely when we'll get to Mexico City," Leandro replied, "but we've always been itinerant entertainers and will probably be on our way soon. When we do leave Santa Fe, it will be with regret at parting from you and Inéz. More than anyone we've met in our travels, the two of you feel like comrades, but the practical fact is that winter isn't a good season for us to be in Santa Fe. Except for a few unusually warm days, the cold weather has made outdoor performances, always one of our main sources of income, not possible, and although we've been welcomed by the Beltráns and the Trigales family, too many other doors among the town's wealthy residents have remained shut to us. After I take the Trigales children on the trip that I've promised them to Trujillo's, the three of us will probably leave for warmer climes."

Carlos got up and put more wood on the fire. "We will make you a little warmer," he said, "to keep you here a little longer." As he did so, he observed to himself that the evening's atmosphere seemed to be a natural continuation of the friendly ambiance he had felt at the end of Selena's birthday party four nights earlier.

Remembering the heart-opening effect of the folk song Orfeo had taught him the day before, he made a deliberate decision to move the evening even more in the direction of expansiveness and good feelings. He was aware that he was perhaps tempting fate—or perhaps, he hoped, disarming it. He went back to the table and sat down.

"I have something," he said, "I want to teach you. My carpenter, Orfeo, knows many folk songs from Spain called *coplas* or, here in New Mexico, *versos.*"

"When I was a child in Spain," Selena broke in, "my mother often repeated *coplas* to us at bedtime. Every boy or girl I knew could recite some. All *coplas* are very romantic. Not waiting for Carlos to comment, or to share the *verso* he'd been about to sing, she said, "This is one of my favorites."

Antenoche fuí a tu casa
y vide luz en tu ventana;
era la luz de tus ojos,
lucero de la mañana.

When she finished, José, to everyone's surprise, began to sing a *verso* he later told them he had learned from his mother.

Dicen que lo negro es triste,

yo digo que no es verdad;
tú tienes los ojos negros
y eres mi felicidad.

"Oh!" Mara exclaimed. "That's lovely! Sing it again, so I can learn it." José sang the *verso* again, and Mara, Selena, and Leandro hummed along.

"Again, José!" Mara said, and the other three sang the words and added harmony.

"Give us another," said Selena, and José, warming to the appreciation, acquiesced. The three entertainers quickly picked up the melody and added harmonies. Carlos did his best to follow and learn the new *versos*, and, when José seemed to run out, Carlos at last had a chance to share the *verso* that he had learned from Orfeo:

Arbolito enflorecido,
verde, color de esperanza;
mi corazón no te olvida
ni de quererte se cansa.

"Every heart has its song," Mara remarked. "If you just open your mouth and let song come out, and let your voice make sounds that are not words, and we all do it together, it will be beautiful."

She began to sing in this meandering, wordless way. Selena and Leandro joined in. Carlos found it haunting and beautiful. He opened his mouth and with some difficulty let his unguided voice come out. He noticed that Inéz was making an effort to do the same. The six voices wove around each other, rising and falling, approaching harmonies and finding strange dissonances that were compelling, instantly moving on to other unexpected joinings and partings. After a while Carlos noticed that one voice was singing words, or so it seemed; what Carlos heard was "in your arms, even death is sweet." The words disappeared and finally, as if in mutual accord, all the voices trailed off.

Out of the ensuing silence Inéz said, in a soft voice, "The three of you work magic, don't you? Even music can be a kind of *duende*, casting a spell. It makes one forget oneself. It joins people together." She took the hands of Carlos and Selena, the two next to her, and the rest joined hands for a moment around the table. Then Leandro, releasing his partners' hands, stood up, and the evening was over.

20

Trouble

After breakfast Carlos saddled Eagle and rode down the lane to the house where the Trio was staying. He was very interested to hear what Old Man Xenome would say to Leandro and what he, Carlos, could learn about the magician from spending time with him. Up ahead, Leandro came around the corner of the house on his big black stallion and fell in step beside Carlos and Eagle. After mutual salutations, they rode on in silence. Neither of them seemed to feel like talking, and that was fine by Carlos. He was soon lost in his own thoughts.

Primary among those thoughts was the question of what it meant that the three entertainers might soon leave Santa Fe. If they'd been searching for a powerful brujo who may have caused Mateo Pizarro's death, had they given up on that goal? And had they been sent to find a brujo named Carlos and abandoned that mission as well? That he was drawn to them was beyond question, but he reminded himself to remain on his guard.

Many miles into the ride, Leandro broke the silence. "I don't like the cold, but I find the winter landscape and the absence of human habitation strangely invigorating."

"I couldn't agree more," Carlos replied. "When I used to work day after day at a desk in the governor's office, I became dull and lacking in alertness. A long ride in the country on horseback always re-energized me."

"It seems we have much in common," Leandro observed.

"What particulars do you have in mind?" Carlos asked.

"The old trio of manly delights — wine, women, and song — would be a good starting point. To those I would add dancing, though perhaps that's simply another aspect of song. I don't know you well enough to be certain about much else, except I sense that you're interested in true magic, and your response to the natural world indicates that you have a desire to learn more about the laws of nature."

"You make me sound like a thinker, but I've always been more a doer than a thinker."

"I notice," Leandro pointed out, "that you didn't say anything in response to my suggestion that you're interested in true magic."

"I thought that was obvious," Carlos replied. "Why else would we be making a long ride on a cold day to visit a medicine man, if both of us didn't have an interest in the occult? I'm curious to see what he'll have to say to you. Frankly, I was surprised that he asked to meet you."

"I was too. From what José said, it seemed that the shaman pursues an esoteric practice, the rules of which are not shared with outsiders."

"All the more reason to see what he says," Carlos declared, spurring Eagle into a trot in order to reach Tesuque Pueblo as soon as possible.

Carlos and Leandro arrived at their destination in mid-morning. They left their mounts in the corral behind José's cousin Lázaro's house and walked to Old Man Xenome's one-room home. Greetings were exchanged, and Carlos gave the old medicine man the gifts he'd brought him—a bag of good tobacco, another bag with herbs Inéz told him were rarely found in this region of New Mexico, and a small copper kettle. "If you don't want the kettle for itself," Carlos told him, "you can always have it cut up and melted down for some other purpose."

Old Man Xenome said he was grateful for the gifts that Carlos and Leandro had brought. He filled a pipe with some of the tobacco Carlos had given him and passed it around. A wordless ritual of sharing a pipe followed in which each man was left to his own thoughts—alone together, was how Carlos put it to himself.

Out of respect for their host, Carlos and Leandro waited for him to speak first. Finally he did so. He was, as he'd always been with Carlos, direct. Looking at Leandro, he asked, "What is it you want to know about a shaman's practice?"

"I am, as Don Alfonso has doubtless told you, a magician by trade. I amaze my audiences with tricks that seem to defy nature—marbles that disappear from under cups, coins that are found in an onlooker's ear, a handkerchief that's retrieved from an empty box. The common theme that runs through each of these is some sort of transformation: a solid object vanishes, coins and handkerchiefs appear out of nothing."

Xenome seemed to be enjoying himself. He laughed and declared, "This old medicine man would like to see you do such things and to learn how you do them."

Leandro smiled back. "Those effects," he said, "are accomplished through sleight of hand, a marble that's gathered up and put in a pocket, a coin that's slipped from a sleeve and transferred to a person's ear so swiftly that it seems to have been found there. But those are, as the word 'tricks' suggests, just that—tricks that give the appearance that a transformation has taken place when in fact it hasn't.

"But," he continued, "I have always hoped to practice what I call true magic, magic in which a true transformation takes place, in which one form is changed into another. And I'm under the impression that Native shamans achieve such transformations."

Xenome interrupted Leandro. "Have you," he asked, "any personal experience of what you call a true transformation?"

Leandro looked a little uncomfortable and glanced at Carlos with concern, but he plunged ahead. "Yes," he replied, "I have experimented with a method of transformation that produced some success. For many years I had a teacher who had studied a science called alchemy. Like all alchemists he observed that many transformations happen in nature. Water has a solid form, ice, and also a gas-like form, steam. These changes, he said, all required the application of some outside force, an obvious example being changing water into steam by subjecting it to heat.

"What this information led my teacher to believe was that a man could change his form, if only he knew what outside force to apply. The most obvious, he believed, was finding a liquid a magician could drink that would cause his form to change, at least as long as the effect of the potion continued. He and I created just such a concoction, and when I've drunk it, for a time, at most an hour or two, changes take place in my body."

"What sort of changes?" Xenome wanted to know.

"The changes are both good and bad. On the good side, my muscles become stronger, and, as Don Alfonso observed the other night, even a small sip of the potion enables me to spin on one foot at an incredible speed. If I drink more of it, my body temporarily grows larger and my strength increases to the point that I can run faster and for longer distances than normal men without tiring. But there are bad effects too. Imbibing even a small amount can cause my facial appearance to become grotesque, and I am often caught up in aggressive feelings—a willingness, even a desire, to act violently."

"Perhaps," Xenome remarked in a neutral way, "the method does violence to your body, and your body, violence having been done to it, wants to strike back at someone or something."

"You may be right," Leandro agreed. "In any case I believe there must be a better method of transformations, one that would retain the positive effects without the bad ones. Is there anything you're willing to tell me about the Shaman's Way that might help me to that end?"

Xenome's wrinkled face softened. "Your ambition is a good one. Unfortunately, the rule is that shamans must not reveal their secrets to anyone who is not an apprentice, and you are not likely to become my apprentice. I am an old Tewa medicine man close to death, and you are a young Spaniard with no background in the ways of Pueblo people.

"What I can tell you," Xenome continued, "is about the transformations achieved by an Apache witch who was a danger to my people and with whom I once contended. This bruja's method was quite different from yours. Perhaps you can adapt this witch's method of transformation for your own use."

Carlos was no less eager than Leandro to hear Xenome's description of the method an Apache witch used to achieve transformations. Did it, he wondered, resemble the technique he'd mastered? He leaned forward and listened intently. From Xenome's smiling glance in his direction, he could tell that the old Tewa medicine man was aware of his interest.

"Over several years of battling this bruja," Xenome began, "I learned much about her black magic. Before she could do harm, she had to prepare her powers, which meant that she first had to shift her mind to a trance state. To do so, she used various methods in combination — ingesting vision-inducing plants, chanting for many hours, and calling on a spirit ally to aid her. I believe the spirit ally, a demon, was essential to her magic. The witch would call this demon, and the spirit ally's mind and the witch's would join. You could say that a transformation of the witch's mind state had to precede all other transformations."

"May I interrupt and ask," Leandro said, "whether the witch controlled the demon, or was it the other way around?"

"That is a good question," Xenome replied. "Perhaps the witch controlled the situation at first, but to obtain a spirit ally she had to open herself to the demon — invite it in — and the power the demon gave the witch had dangerous effects. She became intoxicated with power, craved even more power and eventually surrendered to the ally's malign nature. Her condition became like that of a person who can never be without liquor."

"So you would not advise opening oneself to a spirit ally?" Leandro asked.

"I'm not saying that. A spirit ally could be sought, but only with great caution, not rushing the process of self-purification prior to opening oneself and then, upon meeting an ally, cutting off future contact if the spirit ally is demonic rather than benign. A Pueblo seeker would be guided by the stories in our tradition that distinguish between benign and demonic allies. That's all I wish to say on spirit allies.

"Returning to the topic of transformations," Xenome continued, "once deeply in a trance, the Apache witch could transform herself into other forms that a person in an ordinary mind state could perceive. I believe this worked best when her effort was fed by a strong emotion, usually anger or hatred. My enemy, this witch, made her victims sick by frightening them with a voice they heard in the wind or by appearing to them in animal form—her favorite was a coyote—who cast an evil eye on them. She injured many residents of this and a neighboring pueblo before I succeeded in driving her off."

"When she appeared to them in animal form," Leandro asked, "did she somehow take possession of the coyote's mind and body, or did she change her own body into that of a coyote?"

"You have put your question in a wise way," Xenome replied. "The word 'possession' was well chosen. When this bruja wanted to move about and threaten people as a spirit coyote, she used a normal coyote as the host for her magic, taking possession of that animal and bending its behavior to fit her intentions."

Clearly this was a very important point in Leandro's mind, and he pursued it. "So, if you or I observed a spirit coyote, would we find the bruja's body elsewhere in a trance state?"

"Exactly," Xenome said, "and that's how I finally identified this witch. I saw her coyote self attacking a young woman and found the bruja lying in a trance many miles away."

"This bruja's method, therefore, was mental rather than physical?" Leandro inquired.

"Yes."

"But aren't there shape-shifters—brujas, witches, sorcerers, whatever one calls them—who can transform their own bodies directly into other animal or human forms?"

"Yes, and into inanimate forms, though that is said to be even more difficult, and from what I know, true shape-shifters are exceedingly rare. In all my nearly seventy winters, I have heard of only two such individuals. One was even older than I am and is probably dead, and even if she were still alive, I doubt that she'd still have the personal power to work her magic any longer. I have no direct knowledge of how she was able to change her form from human to animal. My only conversations with her left me with the impression that being a true shape-shifter was a gift, not something that could be taught."

Don Carlos was nearly overwhelmed by thoughts. Xenome's statement that being a shape-shifter was more a matter of a natural talent than a skill that could be learned comported perfectly with what Don Serafino, his own guide to the Brujo's Way, had told him many lifetimes earlier. His experience also confirmed Xenome's words that true shape-shifters were few in number. In fact, in the course of his five previous lifetimes as a brujo, he could count on the fingers of one hand the shape-shifters he had met.

Don Carlos was jolted out of his reflections by Leandro asking another question. "Do you believe," he asked, "that it's a waste of time for me to try to learn about transformations?"

"Not at all!" Xenome insisted. "The pursuit of learning is always good. Also, though it may be the result of the partial transformations you have achieved, I see signs that you may have the capacity for a more complete transformation of your ordinary human form, perhaps even the ability to take on animal forms."

"What is it you've seen?" Leandro asked.

Xenome laughed. "You must allow this old shaman to keep some of his secrets, although I'll admit that before you and Don Alfonso arrived, I smoked a vision-inducing plant's roots and sang an ancient chant. With my improved vision, I saw in you gifts of which you're apparently not aware."

"But what gifts?" Leandro asked, clearly wanting more specificity.

Xenome drew himself upright and said with great authority, "Listen to me carefully. All you need to know to pursue deeper transformations is found in a single sentence. You are not as solid as you think you are."

Xenome's statement was made with a ring of finality to it, indicating that he would say nothing more on the topic. Don Carlos was impressed that Leandro apparently understood and asked no more questions. He thanked the old medicine man profusely. Xenome replied by wishing him well. Then he excused himself, saying that he'd found their talk very interesting, and now he needed to rest.

Don Carlos, his brujo awareness strengthened by the combination of the wild landscape and Xenome's teachings, had nothing particular that he wanted to say to Leandro as they started back for Santa Fe. Leandro too seemed lost in his own thoughts and didn't speak until about an hour after they'd left Tesuque Pueblo. Finally he asked, "Old Man Xenome said that all I need to know is contained in a single sentence, 'you are not as solid as you think you are.' What do you think he meant by that?"

Don Carlos thought he knew precisely what Xenome meant, but he was not about to say so. "Xenome often says things that are beyond my understanding," he replied. "And that was a very personal message he gave you. I believe that you are the one who must penetrate its meaning."

"I suppose you're right," Leandro said. "But at the moment it only mystifies me."

What Don Carlos thought Xenome had seen, and what Carlos too could see, was that Leandro's aura was a constantly shifting configuration of various shades of brightness that swirled about like clouds driven by the wind. There was nothing stable about it. Carlos wanted to offer something to Leandro without admitting that he could read auras, so he simply said, "Perhaps the point he's making is that although you look solid, as we all do, we're somehow less solid than we appear, looser around the edges. For example, you said that when you drink a large dose of your transformation concoction, your shape changes. That wouldn't be possible if you had the solidity of a stone or piece of metal."

Leandro nodded, not totally satisfied, it seemed to Carlos, and returned to his own thoughts.

Carlos shifted his attention from Leandro to the countryside through which they were passing. Even though it was midafternoon in mid-winter and the colors were muted by the grayness of the day, the landscape was, as always, profoundly beautiful to him. But a wind had sprung up, noticeably increasing the chill, and he encouraged Eagle to quicken his pace. They alternated between a faster and a slower pace for an hour, and as they approached the ford where the road crossed the north irrigation ditch, Carlos remembered that a strong current in the ditch had recently shifted some stones in its bed and perhaps made the footing treacherous. He called back to Leandro, "Let me cross first to be sure the ford is completely safe. If it is, you can take the same route."

Carlos and Eagle had reached the middle of the irrigation ditch when a large coyote—from its behavior Carlos thought it must be rabid—charged out of a clump of brush on the bank toward which Carlos and Eagle were headed. As the beast lunged at them, Eagle made a prodigious leap to the side. The weight of Carlos's body suddenly lurching to the right, combined with a loose cinch, made the saddle slip a quarter of the way around. Carlos was thrown on his side into the ditch.

Eagle turned, reared, and lashed out with his front hooves at the coyote, which continued its attack on him. Don Carlos reacted instinctively. He raised himself to a sitting position in the water and released an invisible burst of sorcerer's energy at the charging animal. The creature let out a yelp and was propelled backward. It scrambled to its feet and launched another attack. Don Carlos, prepared this time, sent an even stronger burst of energy at the coyote, and it tumbled backward with such force that it crashed against the irrigation ditch's bank. It screamed in pain and anger and retreated, limping badly.

With the coyote's departure, Eagle calmed down and climbed to the top of the bank, where he waited for his master to collect him. Carlos clambered out of the ditch, dripping icy water and certain that he was going to be bruised and sore in the morning. Leandro's horse had been alarmed and had reared, but Leandro had gotten him under control, spurred him forward, and crossed the ditch to Carlos's side. "You didn't learn that from your Jesuit tutors," he remarked.

Trying to make light of what Leandro had seen, Carlos replied, "Definitely not. When I was growing up, one of the grooms who worked for my family was a tough ex-sailor named Sánchez, a veteran of military service and of many battles at sea in which he claimed to have killed dozens of men. I was the only boy in the family, and for lack of other male companionship, I spent a lot of time with Sánchez. Over several summers he taught me the maneuver you just saw—he called it 'the invisible blow'—and by the time he left our employ, I was quite good at it. I could probably teach it to you. You might find it useful in your performances, astounding your audience by knocking something down from a dozen feet away."

"I would like to learn the technique," Leandro said, "assuming we stay in Santa Fe long enough for you to teach it to me." Although Carlos thought Leandro must be trying to figure out how Carlos had done what he'd done, he let the topic drop. He looked at Carlos and said, "You're soaked clear through and must be chilled to the bone. My house will be warm because Mara and Selena have spent the day there. Yours will be cold. Come to my place, and I'll lend you dry clothes and a place in front of a fire where you can get warm."

The fact that his teeth were chattering led Carlos to accept Leandro's offer without hesitation. He mounted Eagle and rode the short distance to the Trio's residence. He slid off Eagle and handed him to Leandro, who had said he would take Eagle to Carlos's place and turn him out in the corral. "Go right in the door," Leandro said. "The girls will help you."

Carlos entered the house, still dripping water. Selena spotted him first. "Holy Mother!" she exclaimed. "What happened to you?"

"It's a long story," Carlos replied. "I'll tell you later. Right now I want to get out of these clothes, wrap myself in a blanket, and warm up in front of a fire."

Mara, who was wearing a simple smock, came into the hallway. "I heard what you told Selena, and I have an even better idea. In addition to wrapping yourself in a blanket, you should warm your feet in hot water. I was soaking my feet in the kitchen until I heard you come in. Go into the kitchen, get your clothes off, and put your feet in the tub of water. There's at least a little warmth left in it, and there's more water heating in the hearth."

Plunging his frozen feet into hot water sounded wonderful to Carlos. As soon as Mara and Selena left him alone, he undressed, wrapped himself in a blanket, sat down on a bench in front of the hearth, and put his feet into the tub of warm water.

Mara returned almost immediately, carrying a shirt and wool pants over one arm. "Leandro's clothes ought to fit you," she said. Picking up the kettle of water heating over the fire, she told him to move his feet to one side of the tub so she could pour hot water in without scalding him. This done, she examined him closely and said, "You're still shivering."

Selena came back into the room carrying another blanket. "I know what to do," she said. "Stand behind him and take one side of his blanket and wrap it around both of you so that the warmth of your body is right next to his back. Then I'll wrap this second blanket around the two of you, so you both will be doubly warm."

Carlos closed his eyes as he felt the warmth and softness of Mara's body against his back. After a while, she asked, "Are you feeling better?"

He said yes, which was true. He had stopped shivering. But he was concerned that there might be a problem due to Leandro having seen him use his brujo powers. He also wondered if he might be taking too much comfort from Mara's body against him and her arms around his shoulders. Inéz would not like this, he thought. Nevertheless, he dropped his head against one of her arms. He drifted into a half-entranced mood akin to the *duende* state he'd experienced when he and Mara had danced together. He raised his eyes to Mara's face and realized that she'd been watching him. What, he wondered, was she thinking?

With no preliminaries, she said, "I'm jealous of Inéz because she has your love."

Before Carlos could reply, the kitchen door opened and Inéz came in. "Leandro told me..." she began. She took in the scene of Mara, wrapped in a blanket, embracing Carlos from behind, and Carlos looking up at her. "It seems I'm intruding," she said icily, turned, and went back out the door, slamming it behind her.

"Damnation!" Carlos swore. He threw aside the blankets, raised his feet out of the tub and, without toweling them off or worrying about Mara seeing him naked, he pulled on Leandro's pants, which were lying on the nearby table, and his sodden boots from the floor in front of the hearth. He grabbed the shirt and struggled to get it on as he sprinted into the hallway and out the front door.

By the time he reached the veranda, Inéz, who was walking rapidly, had a good lead. "Inéz! Inéz!" he shouted, but she didn't turn around.

Inéz strode by Carlos's house without stopping. Gordo, who had apparently heard Carlos calling to her, came out of his doggy door and looked puzzled when Inéz passed him by without speaking or reaching down to pat him on the head. Carlos finally caught up with her at the edge of the plaza. "Inéz," he appealed to her. "Please stop and let me explain."

"What's there to explain? It didn't take you long to wrap yourself in a blanket with Mara's arms around you."

"Nothing was happening," he protested.

"Nothing? Mara was embracing you and you were loving it!"

"I was wet and cold and she was helping to warm me."

Inéz gave him a steely look. "I'll bet she was."

"Didn't Leandro tell you? I fell in the irrigation ditch on the way home and got soaked. Look, I'm wearing Leandro's clothes...."

"You mean you were naked under that blanket?" she said in rising tones.

"I had to take my clothes off. They were wet. I was shivering, and Mara and Selena brought blankets to wrap me in."

"To wrap you in with Mara! You are so dazzled by that violet-eyed vixen that you fail to show any common sense whatsoever where she's concerned. You love falling in love, and she's casting a spell over you. Have you no recollection whatsoever of how your previous mistress with violet eyes led you to your death?"

Carlos wanted to keep protesting his innocence, but he felt that nothing he could say would make the situation any better.

While he gathered his thoughts, Inéz unloaded more of her own. "I feel betrayed," she cried angrily, "and I feel I can't trust you. I thought we had agreed that we'd be friendly with them but not too friendly, and we would be careful not to do anything that would suggest that you have

232 _____

brujo powers. Not only were you being much too friendly with Mara, but when Leandro came over to let me know about your accident, he said that you did something extraordinary when a coyote attacked you. You *showed* him your brujo powers! Have you lost your mind? You've gone over to them completely!"

"I was trying to protect Eagle," he began, but she stopped him.

"Wait!" she insisted. "I have more to say. I'm also trying to protect Elena, who, despite my best efforts, is still very taken with Leandro. Since I can't seem to do a thing for you, I can at least save Elena. You're on your own."

Carlos's heart was pounding from exertion and emotion. For a moment he saw Inéz, in her anger, as a murderous enemy, and himself as helpless to fight back. She was Violeta, he was paralyzed, and Malvolio was waiting to strike. Then his head cleared a bit. "I hope," he said, "you'll see this less drastically once you've had a chance to calm down."

"Don't be too sure of that," she declared. "If you love me," she continued, "and right now that seems like a big if, you will under no conditions try to see me for a couple of days. I won't walk to Mass with you tomorrow, and I won't speak with you if you come to the Beltráns' kitchen door or the front door either." Turning on her heel and walking away, she said to the empty air in front of her, "This conversation is over."

Carlos made his way back to his house and went in. Gordo had curled up on a kitchen chair. Addressing his dog, Carlos said, "What a mess! Inéz will never forgive me." Gordo responded as he usually did, by wagging his tail enthusiastically. "At least you still love me, old boy," Carlos told him, reaching down to pat his four-legged friend.

21

Duende

Carlos spent what was left of Saturday in a state of abject misery. The right side of his torso ached from hitting rocks when he'd fallen into the irrigation ditch. His mental state was even worse. Inéz had ordered him to keep his distance until Monday at the earliest. Much as he wanted to see her and straighten things out, he didn't dare risk offending her further. When José came home in the evening, he sensed Carlos's mood and didn't try to draw him out about it. After a light meal of chili and cornbread, they went to bed early without speaking about the coyote incident or Carlos's trip with Leandro to visit Old Man Xenome.

Carlos had a bad night. Ordinarily, he fell asleep the moment his head hit the pillow, but tonight he stayed awake for hours and hours. Thoughts about recent events churned through his mind. An image came to him of a long rope strung between two trees with pulleys at each end. Someone had tied scraps of paper to the rope, and each scrap had a different word scrawled on it in large print: "Inéz, Leandro, danger, wolf, Mara, masquerade, coyote, kiss, Inéz, betrayed…." The rope, drawn by an invisible hand, presented each of the scraps of paper in an endlessly changing sequence. As he watched, an unwilling observer, he concluded that the least of his worries was Leandro. Whatever else he'd learned in the past few weeks, he had become certain that his own brujo powers far exceeded Leandro's. Leandro's method of transformation was inferior to his, and Leandro apparently didn't know how to hurl bursts of invisible energy at an opponent. Leandro was only a danger if he learned that the man he knew as Alfonso was the brujo named Carlos Buenaventura. And even that was not a serious danger unless Leandro was in the service of Don Malvolio, a topic on which the evidence was still inconclusive.

He was upset about Inéz being angry with him and hurt that she wouldn't accept his word that he hadn't betrayed her. That put him in a stubborn mood, and he resolved not to grovel in order to get back in her good graces. She needed to meet him at least halfway.

Finally he fell asleep, only to have several disturbing dreams. In the most vivid of them, he found himself caught in a gigantic spider's web. It was bedecked with jewels — diamonds, emeralds, and rubies — that flashed in the sunlight. He tried to move and discovered that his legs and one arm were caught in the web. Every effort to break free only led to more of his body being stuck to the web. The sight of a large spider lurking off to his left made him frighteningly aware that he was naked. On closer examination, he could see the spider's face was Mara's. She was smacking her lips in anticipation of biting him and, once her venom had paralyzed him, making a meal of his lifeblood. He still had one arm free with which to try to fend her off, but he had a fatalistic sense that it was only a matter of time until that arm would also be caught in her web, leaving him totally at her mercy.

He awoke with a start to find Gordo pawing his arm and whining anxiously.

It was almost the early morning hour at which he usually arose to meditate. Not wanting to go back to sleep and have another unpleasant dream, Carlos got up, made a small fire in the fireplace, and assumed his sitting meditation posture.

Little good seemed to come of his efforts. Usually, even when he started with unsettled thoughts, he soon achieved some calm. This morning he was almost as restless while meditating as he'd been while trying to go to sleep. His body, particularly his right side, was still very sore from his fall. He eventually gave up on meditating and resolved to face his troubles in an active way.

He went to the kitchen and made breakfast for Gordo, himself, and José, who was waiting there to ask how Don Carlos's trip with Leandro to Tesuque Pueblo had gone. Carlos mentally pulled himself together and answered José's inquiry by reporting that the trip had gone very well. "Xenome," he said, "was much more forthcoming with us than I had expected. He wouldn't tell us about a shaman's technique of achieving transformations, but he described what he'd learned about how witches do so. His story was based on his battles with a bruja who created mischief in Tesuque and another pueblo."

"That was probably Nambe," José said. "Nambe Pueblo has a history of troubles with witches. Did Grandfather Xenome share any details with you?"

"Yes," Don Carlos replied. "From what your teacher told us, this bruja used several methods to prepare herself for transformations. These included ingesting vision-inducing plants, chanting for long periods, and calling on spirit allies to aid her. Once she'd achieved a trance state, she was able to project herself into natural phenomena—the wind or animals, her favorite being coyotes. I gather that her success was greatest when her witchcraft was driven by strong emotions like hate and anger. Hers was not a transformation in a physical sense; she did not change her bodily form. She mentally projected her bruja energies with such force that she took possession of and manipulated whatever she made into her host."

José nodded. "And once her victims believed in her magic, they were likely to credit the smallest event—a gust of wind, a tree falling, an animal's glare—as the product of her witchcraft. She may have had power of her own, but her victims' fears served to empower her further."

"I believe you're right," Carlos agreed. "Old Man Xenome didn't say so, but I can see how the same techniques could be used to do good. What if the shaman's magic was rooted in positive emotions—empathy for a suffering person or a wish that the person he's treating be able to let go of feelings of anger? Might not that work toward the desired result, especially if the sick or suffering person was given hope by his or her belief in the shaman's good intentions?"

"If you're asking me what Grandfather Xenome is teaching me," José replied, "you know I'm not permitted to reveal those secrets, but your description of how a medicine man might heal someone sounds reasonable. In fact, I believe you used an approach like that to help Inéz heal from the wounds that Dr. Tiburcio inflicted on her spirit."

Mention of Inéz's name caused Carlos to flinch inwardly. Some healing definitely was needed between the two of them. On reflection he also felt that his earlier resolve to insist that she meet him halfway wasn't a skillful approach. Gentle patience had worked once, and it had a better chance of healing the rift between them than demanding concessions from her.

The sound of bells ringing across the plaza led him to excuse himself to get dressed and leave for Mass. He hurried, but even so he was late. He scanned the small chapel and saw that the only unoccupied space was a place halfway up on the right side. He hesitated, aware that at least half of those in attendance would notice his late arrival, but when he saw that the person next to the empty space was Elena Beltrán, he walked forward and stood beside her. She glanced at him and smiled. He hoped that was a good sign.

After Mass, he and Elena walked out together without speaking until they reached the edge of the plaza. "Papa wasn't feeling well this morning," Elena announced, "and Mother stayed home with him, which is why neither of them attended Mass today. And you're well aware, I suppose, why Inéz didn't come."

"All too aware."

"She was in a very bad mood this morning," Elena reported. "She practically bit my head off when I asked why she wasn't dressed for Mass and why you hadn't come by for her. Then she apologized and said she wasn't angry with me, she was furious with that.... Well, she called you a bad name."

"What was that?"

Elena looked embarrassed. "Me and my big mouth. It was nothing, really."

"Then what was it?"

"She said she was furious with that skunk, Alfonso."

For some strange reason, perhaps simply knowing that Inéz liked

Elvira, the only skunk she knew, he felt relieved. "That gives me some hope; she could have called me much worse things."

"Are you and Inéz having a lover's quarrel?"

"I hope that's all it is," Carlos replied. "As long as we're lovers quarrelling and not enemies, we'll work things out eventually. Let's go over and talk with the Cabreras or the Archuletas."

He reached out to take her arm, but a worried look had come on her face. "What's the matter?" he asked.

"They might not be too eager to speak with us."

"Us or me? I wasn't especially late to Mass."

"That's not it," she said, biting her lip in dismay. "Oh my! I should keep my mouth shut."

He looked at her with concern. "Elena, I regard you as a friend. Also, I expect you have a better sense of what's going on in town than I do. Please tell me why the Cabreras and the Archuletas might want to avoid speaking with me."

As soon as the words were out of his mouth, he realized what the problem was, but he wanted to hear it from Elena first.

She wasn't fooled. "I think you know," she observed. "It's pretty obvious. Marco Cabrera and Nicholas Archuleta both serve at the governor's pleasure."

"Yes," he said, "and the governor's wife is determined to make it clear to all that I have dropped a full notch, if not more, in social standing. So be it. All the more reason to appreciate the friendship of you and your family."

In a seemingly heartfelt gesture, she placed her hand on his arm and replied, "You are always welcome, most welcome, in our home."

He laughed. "Perhaps not now. Inéz made it plain that I was not to come to either the kitchen door or the front door today. If she saw me approaching, she would probably run out and brain me with a skillet. I'm afraid you'll have to walk yourself home."

She smiled and assured him, "I can find my way. Don't worry."

Instead of returning to his house, he went to visit Pedro and María at the stable they managed for Raul Trigales. Pedro answered Carlos's knock on the door to their rooms. "You've created quite a stir in local circles," Pedro announced. "First you fall off your horse and next you run through the streets and have an argument with Inéz."

"Gossip spreads like wildfire in this town," Carlos complained. "May I at least get in the door before you pounce on me? As for the argument with

Inéz, I admit that I was being too friendly with one of the female entertainers and that angered her. I only hope this is like a summer storm — lots of thunder and lightning — that blows over quickly."

"You didn't mention the possible consequences of thunderstorms," Pedro observed, "the heavy rains and flash floods that cause lots of damage."

"I'm remaining optimistic that no permanent damage will result from our quarrel. What should worry you more is that I fell off Eagle when he and I were attacked by a rabid coyote. This was as we were fording the north irrigation ditch."

Pedro dropped his teasing tone and grew solemn. "A rabid coyote on the outskirts of town," he said, "is bad news. I'll talk with Captain Posada. He should organize a hunt for this creature. If it has attacked a horse and rider, it's even more likely to attack a riderless horse or a sheep. That's a dangerous situation."

"I agree, Pedro." The conversation seemed to end there. Carlos glanced around the room, noticing that it was well-scrubbed and that Pedro had made some improvements to it. Carlos turned to Pedro and asked, "How are you and María settling in?"

"Everything's fine. I've got the routine down. Of course, our lives will change when the baby arrives."

"He seems to be thriving in the womb," Carlos observed.

"I know you believe the baby is a he, and knowing that your brujo vision enables you to see into people, I'm happy to hear you say he's healthy."

"It's not quite correct," Carlos said, "to say that I can see into people. I can't, but I can see the auras generated by all living things, and whenever I see María, I see two auras — hers surrounding her whole body and a tiny one coming from her belly — both of them bright. As to whether I'm right that the tiny one is a baby boy, let's wait and see. Speaking of María, where is she?"

"Resting."

"Then I'll be on my way. Give her my warm regards."

"Try to stay on Eagle from now on," Pedro called after him.

Carlos answered in an equally light-hearted vein. "Thanks for the advice. I never would have thought of that on my own."

He took a short detour to the west of the stable to see how Orfeo's work was coming along on Dr. Velarde's future home. Two doors down he could see several members of the Díaz clan, the grandparents and their four grandchildren who were living in Segunda, the house they were renting from him. The only Díaz he couldn't spot was the eldest granddaughter, Marisol.

He wondered idly whether Marisol might be a good choice as a cook and housekeeper for him now that Pedro and María had moved out. When Pedro and María had moved into Barbon's old place, María had been upset to find the kitchen filthy from Barbon's careless housekeeping. Marisol, who heard about the problem, had come over and offered to help. "I'm just sitting around playing cards with my brothers and sister," she said. "I'd rather be useful." Marisol, it seemed, was a hard worker who saw what needed to be done and did it. But he knew immediately that it would be unwise to broach the possibility of employing her. Given Inéz's present mood of mistrust of him regarding other women, she would strongly disapprove.

Resolving not to pursue that thought, Carlos returned to his house and had lunch. Only he and Gordo were home. Sunday was José's day off from his work, and he'd taken the opportunity to ride to Tesuque Pueblo and visit Old Man Xenome.

With no other obligations, Carlos resumed his project of setting white stones around the base of his house. He was nearly done and wondering how to spend the rest of the afternoon when he heard the footsteps coming up the lane. It was Leandro, carrying a shirt and trousers that Carlos recognized as his. "I want to return these," Leandro said. "The girls hung them near a fireplace to dry."

Carlos stood up. This was an interesting situation. He wondered what Leandro had thought about having witnessed Carlos's use of his brujo powers against the coyote yesterday. But the harm, if there was any, had already been done, so he greeted Leandro cordially. "I have your clothes too," he said. "Come inside and we'll exchange outfits."

The exchange completed, Carlos and Leandro sat down at the kitchen table. With what struck Carlos as genuine concern, Leandro said, "The three of us are very sorry if we caused trouble between you and Inéz yesterday. That certainly wasn't our intention. The girls wanted to come over and tell you in person, but I told them to stay away. If Inéz learned that they'd been here, it might do more harm than good."

"You're probably right," Carlos agreed. "Thank you for being discreet."

"That's not in my nature," Leandro declared. "Part of the trouble we've caused is the result of the way we live. Our morality is looser than conventional peoples' and scandalous to straight-laced individuals like your governor's wife. But didn't you once say that actors and entertainers rank very low in Spanish society, with only Natives ranked below them?"

"I don't recall saying that," Carlos replied. "But your description is accurate."

"Frankly," Leandro said, "I'm puzzled. You don't avoid our company. Don't you risk losing your status as a result?"

"Yes," Carlos agreed. "But I like my life as I'm living it, and if I ever decide to return to Mexico City, I can reestablish myself as an upper-class gentleman. So you see, I'm not risking much by behaving as I do in this distant outpost of Spanish control."

Leandro nodded absently. After a moment he acknowledged that he had something else on his mind. "I've been wondering," he asked, "precisely what your relationship is with the world of shamans and sorcerers. I couldn't help but be impressed by how respectfully Old Man Xenome treated you, and your display of power yesterday in dealing with the coyote was remarkable magic — or sorcery, by another name."

This turn of the conversation required a careful response. "I never thought," Carlos said, "of that burst of invisible power as sorcery. My teacher, Sánchez, the ex-sailor I told you about yesterday, never used that word for it. I had the impression that he'd learned it as something to be used in warfare. That seemed borne out by his statement to me that the technique wouldn't work unless accompanied by a strong emotion — fear, hatred, or anger — precisely the feelings that would arise in battle."

"That sounds a good deal like Xenome's description of how the Apache witch he fought used powerful emotions to give force to her magic."

"That's an excellent observation," Carlos said. "I'd not seen that before."

"So are you saying that your instruction in throwing a force at an enemy came from someone who was self-taught?"

"No," Carlos replied. "But the only time Sánchez said anything about how he'd learned the technique was one day when he was frustrated with me because I was making no progress. 'You have too sunny a disposition for this activity,' he said, and added that he thought it was due to my having been born in June on the longest day of the year. 'You would be better off,' he told me, 'if you were like my father. You may think I'm tough, but my father was mean to the point of being vicious. When I didn't quickly learn how to hurl invisible energy, he hit me on the side of the head so hard that he knocked me down. And that,' Sánchez said, 'was on one of his good days. When the full moon was out, he went off by himself and came back the next morning with blood on his clothing.' But perhaps," Carlos added in a dismissive way, "he was just trying to impress me."

Leandro followed Carlos's description of Sánchez and his father, which was a total fabrication, with intense interest, and his eyes narrowed at Carlos's attribution of his sunny disposition to his connection with the sun and his description of the savage effect of the moon on Sánchez's father. Carlos realized, too late, that he might seem to be suggesting that Sánchez's father had been aligned with the Moon Moiety of sorcerers.

"I think," Leandro declared, "your Sánchez was probably a sorcerer and, from what you say, his father certainly was."

"If so, I wasn't aware of it," Carlos replied, "although you're making me realize how unusual his abilities were. I'd always assumed that such power bursts were an ordinary enough phenomenon that most men could learn if they had proper training. But now it's my turn to let my curiosity lead me to a question. You clearly have an interest in sorcery. Does your practice of magic ever draw on sorcery?"

Leandro shrugged. "About all I can say is that there's no firm line between magic and sorcery and alchemy. They are all occult arts."

"I see," Carlos replied. "Then perhaps you can enlighten me on a quite different point. The other night when Selena went into a trance during the séance, she contacted a spirit who asked for someone named Carlos. What was that all about? Do you know who this Carlos is?"

To Carlos's surprise, Leandro didn't seem reluctant to talk. "I've told you," he began, "that I have a mentor in magic and alchemy I call Master. I was orphaned at a very young age, and he saw something in me that made him adopt me as his apprentice. At that time he was over sixty, and he told me, in bits and pieces, about a sorcerer named Carlos, who long ago had prevented him from obtaining a jewel, Montezuma's Emerald, which was said to give the person who possessed it incredible power and wisdom. It was a bitter loss, and he blames this Carlos for it."

So, Carlos thought, with a mixture of dread and relief at the ending of his uncertainty about the identity of Leandro's mentor, he *is* Malvolio. Carlos carefully considered his next words. "Are you saying, then," he asked, "that the magician you call Master is obsessed with taking revenge on this Carlos?"

"Obsessed is too strong a word," Leandro replied. "His greatest commitment has always been to searching for knowledge. He is a purist and an idealist. He pursued his work in alchemical transformations in hopes of ultimately finding a means of raising man to a higher level of being, transforming him, if you like, into an angel, with all the powers angels possess. Regrettably, he is now an old man, and he has fallen short of that goal. The potion that I described to Old Man Xenome, which gives me superhuman strength for a brief time but has unfortunate bestializing effects, is the farthest my teacher has gotten toward the ideal of an angelic transformation."

Leandro paused. "And so, you see, he is searching now for Carlos because he believes Carlos possesses the secret of a higher form of transformation."

This information, if anything, bothered Carlos more than the confirmation of his suspicions that Leandro was Malvolio's apprentice. "How—?" Carlos began.

Leandro, no longer evasive and secretive, seemed eager to unburden himself. "The story goes back a long way," he said. "As I understand it, when my teacher was only fifteen, the Great Magus discovered him in a monastery, recognized his potential, and took him as one of his apprentices to be instructed in all three of the ancient occult arts: astrology, alchemy, and magic. Some years later, as the Great Magus was nearing death, he set up a contest between my master and his other best student, the object being to determine which of them would be his successor. Unhappily for my master, the other student was chosen. Not content to be second best, my master went his own way. He delved more deeply into the study of alchemy, wanting to be known in his own right as the greatest alchemist who had ever lived. He created a coat of arms to bear witness to who he was—not the apprentice of the Great Magus, but the proudly illegitimate son of a nobleman from an ancient Aragonese family, the de Lunas."

Leandro laughed. "There," he said, "I have told you his secret surname, which is the one he gave me at the time he adopted me."

Leandro waited, as if expecting Carlos to join in his laughter. It occurred to Carlos that Leandro was a little giddy, as though he might be coming down with a fever.

"Now," Leandro went on at last, "what is really incredible is that these important events in my teacher's life—failing to get possession of the emerald and failing to achieve the highest method of transformation—have come together like two arrows in a bull's-eye, and at the center of the bull's-eye is—Carlos. For my master recently told me that he believes that his youthful rival, whom the Great Magus preferred, had learned a superior method of transformation, and passed it on to his student, who is none other than Carlos!"

Leandro, almost hysterical now, it seemed to Carlos, laughed again and continued, with difficulty, to speak through his laughter. "And though my teacher sent me to find Carlos (ha, ha, ha!), I am not sure what he wants to happen once I do, whether he intends to kill Carlos (ha, ha, ha!) or to seek to learn about Carlos's method of transformation."

Carlos tried his best to join in the hilarity. He pulled out his handkerchief and noisily blew his nose as if to stifle his laughter and dabbed at his eyes as if to wipe away tears. "But why are you telling me all this?" Carlos asked when he had sufficiently recovered from his ersatz laughter. "From the time we first spoke until now you have offered almost no information about your mentor, and Selena and Mara were equally close-mouthed about their connection to him."

"The Master wanted it so," Leandro replied. "He did not want anyone, least of all this Carlos, to know that he has been seeking to locate his old rival's apprentice. So I have had to be very discreet in my inquiries. Originally, I had wanted to meet my teacher's best student, Don Mateo Pizarro, simply to learn what he knew about transformations. But when I heard that Don Mateo had died mysteriously, it seemed to me that only a sorcerer with equal or greater powers, someone like this Carlos, could have defeated him in battle, and I thought that in locating the sorcerer who killed Don Mateo, I might also find Carlos."

"You still haven't answered my question," Carlos pointed out, "as to why you're telling me so much more today than you were willing to earlier."

"To be candid," Leandro replied, "for a time I thought you might be this Carlos, because you had passed through Nombre de Dios at almost the same time that Don Mateo died. And the ease with which you entered into *duende* also indicated that you were attuned not just to ordinary reality, but to magical reality also. Then Friday you demonstrated powers that stem from what seems to be a sorcerer's technique. Even your extraordinary skill at fencing strikes me as drawing on abilities beyond those of an ordinary man."

Leandro paused, as if expecting an answer. "On one of the first occasions that we talked," Carlos said, carefully, "I told you that I was raised in an orthodox Catholic and upper-class household and educated, my private exercises with Sánchez aside, by Jesuit tutors, scarcely the environment or the education one would expect of a sorcerer."

"Nevertheless," Leandro replied, adding with a smile, "I've entertained some hopes that you might be Carlos and that you would become my ally in the pursuit of occult learning."

"I would be flattered," Carlos said, "by your assigning extraordinary capacities to me and by your implicit invitation to join you in occult study and practice, except that within the Catholic society of New Spain and New

Mexico such affinities are not welcomed and often punished severely. Please don't suggest to anyone in Santa Fe that you suspect me of harboring such interests. That would endanger me."

Leandro looked distressed. "I have no intention of spreading such rumors," he explained. "Mara, Selena, and I from the first felt a bond with you and your Inéz and have wanted to draw you into our circle. When we leave Santa Fe, we'll do so with nothing but the warmest feelings for the two of you."

"I'm glad to hear that," Carlos said. "But I hope you won't leave us too soon."

"Before dawn tomorrow morning, I'm going to start with the Trigales children on a trip to Trujillo's hacienda. After they've performed there, we'll probably go another day's travel to the south to a second ranch whose owner has invited me to entertain his household and their neighbors. Once the Trigales children and I return to Santa Fe, I expect that the three of us—Mara, Selena, and I—will head south soon thereafter."

"We'll have to give a party in your honor before you leave," Carlos suggested.

"We would enjoy that," Leandro declared. "But, speaking of parties, what are you doing after dinner tonight? Having no performance scheduled, the three of us were going to dance at home. If you join us, it would be a chance for you to do the *Duende* dance, not simply be an observer. That way you can experience its full effects."

Carlos knew doing so would be unwise on several accounts, not the least of which was that Inéz would disapprove. But he was just enough annoyed with her to be in no mood to let her dictate his activities. Also, now that Leandro's relation to Malvolio had been clarified, that knowledge gave Carlos a feeling of power. Besides, he was extremely curious to experience *duende* as a participant. "Yes," he told Leandro, "I would like to come."

"Excellent," Leandro replied. "Wear dark clothes, preferably black." Then he rose, put on his coat, and left.

About an hour later José arrived home from his visit to Tesuque Pueblo. "How was your trip?" Carlos asked.

"I'm learning a lot, although, as you know, I can't say anything more. However, Grandfather Xenome told me about a dream he had last night that he wanted me to share with you. He said that in the dream he saw dark storm clouds, heavy rain, and thunder and lighting. At the center of the storm the air was strangely clear and calm. Inside this dead space, he saw five figures.

One was an old man, thin, gaunt, and menacing. He was dressed in black and riding a black horse. The other four figures were monsters, seven or eight feet tall, with no hair on their heads, grotesque faces, and long, powerful arms and legs."

José paused, seeming to expect some response from Don Carlos. When none was forthcoming, José asked, "Do you know what that might be about?"

"I have a good idea," Carlos replied. "But it's complicated. Are you going to have dinner with me?"

"No, thank you," José said. "I promised to have dinner with my mother tonight."

"Very well. I'll tell you what I think the dream means in the morning. Say hello to your mother for me. I've been invited to the Trio's place and probably won't get home until late." José looked surprised at the mention of the Trio, but he simply nodded and left.

Carlos ate a light meal, dressed in an all-black outfit, and went off to join the Trio's party. As he walked toward their house he played Leandro's conversation over in his memory. It had not escaped his notice that Leandro had referred to something Malvolio had recently told him. But how recently, and where? He was aware that Leandro had taken two trips of several days' duration in the past few weeks. Could those have been to meet with Don Malvolio somewhere south of Santa Fe, the direction from which Carlos had felt darkness was approaching? Then there was José's report of Old Man Xenome's dream—surely the black-clad figure was Don Malvolio.

Don Carlos berated himself for not having fitted the seemingly mismatched pieces together earlier. But it was indeed difficult to square the evil, cruel Malvolio of his imagination with the scholarly idealist of whom Leandro had spoken with such respect and admiration. Carlos temporarily shelved the problem by keeping Malvolio in the back of his mind as a distant threat, and letting the forefront of his consciousness be pleasantly occupied with the thought of the evening's approaching entertainment.

He knocked on the entertainers' door, and a woman answered. She was wearing a black dress and a full-face black mask, and had it not been for her violet eyes he might not have been certain that the woman who greeted him was Mara. In a whispery, conspiratorial voice, she said, "Be very careful. *Duende* is dangerous."

Selena, also in a black dress and a black mask, had approached and heard the last part of Mara's warning. "Yes," she said in normal tones. "*Duende* is powerful, but Mara is being overly dramatic."

As Mara closed the door, Selena took Carlos's arm and led him to the *sala*.

All the furniture except for a bench had been removed. The only light in the otherwise dark room came from the fire in the fireplace and three candles in wall sconces. "Darkness," Selena explained, "intensifies the *duende* mood, which is, after all, an exploration of unfamiliar places within our souls."

Picking up a mug of steaming liquid and holding it out to him, she said, "This is a special tea Mara and I drink before dancing. See what you think."

He took the mug from her, sniffed the steam, and recognized the contents. "Brandy in tea made with a mind-altering desert herb is a powerful concoction," he remarked.

Selena laughed, apparently not displeased that he'd identified the mug's contents on his own. "At least," she commented, "you have some idea of what you're getting into. Doing the *Duende* dance is intended to carry us beyond our ordinary state of mind." She picked up two more mugs, handed one to Mara and kept the other herself. The three of them touched the mugs and Selena offered a solemn toast, "To the journey."

"Let's sit together on the bench," she suggested. "We can drink our tea and give its effects time to take hold. Leandro is getting ready. He'll be along shortly. While we're waiting, Alfonso, tell us what you remember of the *Duende* dance you saw at the Beltráns' party."

Once they were seated, Selena on his left, Mara on his right, Don Carlos described what he'd observed. "As the *seco* pole strikes a regular beat, the dancers stamp their heels in a one-two-*three*, one-two-*three*, one-*two*, one-*two*, one-*two* pattern. The tempo gets faster and the dancers keep pace and, turning counterclockwise, they lift their arms above their heads. Then they open their mouths and make a high-pitched trilling sound. Finally, on the twelfth beat of a sequence, the dancers come to a dead stop."

"Your memory is excellent!" Selena exclaimed. "And tonight we can dance with greater freedom than in a performance, since the only audience is ourselves. We will be constrained by keeping the rhythm, but strangely that will free us to allow creative inspiration. You may want to stop, even though we continue. Or you may improvise as the spirit moves you, but always" — she pronounced the word 'always' with great emphasis — "abandon yourself to the *duende* spirit, plunging into the realm of emotion and enthusiasm — the realm of your soul. Let go. Don't hold back. If what you're feeling seems ordinary or normal, that's not *duende*."

Selena fell silent and Carlos said nothing in reply, since the phrases that came to mind seemed flat and conventional. Also, he was beginning to feel the effects of the damiana tea. All his senses had become sharper. He smelled the natural incense of the piñon, juniper, and mesquite wood burning in the fireplace. The flames of the candles seemed to grow brighter and double or triple in size. The burning aftertaste of brandy lingered in his mouth, and he felt the soft warmth of Mara's arm pressing against him.

In the silence, he heard footsteps approaching down the hall. Leandro strode into the room dressed in black from head to toe. A scarf covered all of his face except his eyes. He looked much as he had the first time he and Carlos had met, except that tonight his eyes seemed darker, like the eyes of Leandro after he had done his phenomenal pirouettes at the Trigales's party, like the menacing Leandro who had danced with Inéz in such a threatening, bestial way.

Leandro struck the *seco* pole he was holding sharply on the floor. Selena stood up and told Carlos and Mara, "Time to begin."

The three dancers took up positions about five feet from each other in the middle of the room, facing the fireplace and with their backs to Leandro, who immediately struck the floor again with the *seco* pole. On the third strike of the pole, Carlos joined Mara and Selena in stamping his heel hard on the floor. At first Leandro set a slow pace, and Don Carlos found that by concentrating and counting he did not miss a beat. As the tempo accelerated, the rhythm seemed to be less in his mind and more in his body. He let go of counting and found that he could maintain the rhythm effortlessly.

He gave himself up to sensations—the vibrations of his heel striking the floor and the visual panoply of the dancers' auras—golden, violet, and deep orange-red—against the increasing darkness of the room, which he took to be the darkness of the *duende* spell. When he began to turn in place and raise his arms above his head he seemed to be a flame in the darkness, and when Mara and Selena began to vocalize he joined their voices in a kind of ecstasy. He was volitionless, possessed by the dance.

Then, with jarring suddenness, the beat of the *seco* pole stopped. Instantly, Carlos's feet also stopped, as did Selena's and Mara's. In the ensuing silence the air seemed to vibrate.

"Now we are prepared," Selena said in a clear voice. "We are at the threshold. Leandro and I will enter first. Alfonso and Mara will sit and be our witnesses, and then enter in their turn."

In an entranced state, Carlos and Mara sat down. Selena and Leandro, facing each other, took each other's hands and began to sing a melody whose slow notes, ascending in half-tones and then in unexpected intervals, was like nothing Carlos had ever heard. Leandro paused and Selena repeated the phrase alone. After a few notes Leandro joined her, singing his own line from the beginning so that the notes and words intertwined in harmonies so strange and beautiful that Carlos found tears sliding down his cheeks. Though they were singing in a language he did not know, he could hear that the ends of the lines rhymed. After a while it seemed to him that they were singing about *magic, love, death,* and — possibly — *endless life.*

The song went on and time did not seem to exist. Carlos followed the strange harmonies into some place deep and dark. When they stopped and he looked up he saw Leandro and Selena still facing each other, Leandro holding a glass of dark wine. He drank from it and passed it to Selena. When she had drunk she turned to Mara and Carlos and said softly, "Now it is your turn."

Mara and Carlos stood up and moved toward the other couple. "First you must sing," Selena said. Mara sang the first phrase of the song twice. "Now, Alfonso, you must repeat it," Selena said. Carlos opened his mouth and from some unknown part of his brain he repeated the difficult phrase perfectly, both the notes and the words he did not understand.

Selena smiled, "That was very good," she said. "Alfonso, hold Mara's hands and keep singing that phrase over and over. She will weave her part through yours."

Though they were standing two feet apart and only their hands were touching, Carlos felt as if both his voice and his hands were caressing Mara's body, and he was being caressed in turn. The musical phrase he was singing seemed to him to be saying *endless night* or perhaps *endless life.* He was sunk in rapture so deep that when Mara stepped toward him, dropped his hands, and slipped her arms around him, his arms went around her without a thought, and he bent to kiss her as she lifted her face toward his. The kiss was soft, lingering, and so intense that his very soul opened itself to her. When it ended Selena was standing beside him, offering Carlos a glass of dark wine, which he took from her.

In the distance a door opened and closed noisily. There was the sound of pounding feet and Pedro burst into the room. "Don Alfonso," Pedro shouted, "what are you doing here?" Pedro grabbed him by the arm, spilling the wine Carlos was holding. "We've been waiting for you at home for an hour! Have you forgotten that you promised to come to our place to celebrate María's birthday? She's in tears, thinking you forgot about her!"

Leandro, Selena, and Mara had backed away from Carlos and from

Pedro's ferocious energy. Carlos, who had only partly regained his ordinary consciousness, had no memory of having promised to visit Pedro and María. Pedro took the wine glass from him and put it down on the bench, and Carlos allowed Pedro to drag him to the door and out into the crisp, chill night. Once they were outside, Carlos collected his wits sufficiently to ask, "What's this about a promise to come to your place? It's not María's birthday."

"I know," Pedro growled. "But I had to give some reason for bursting in like that. I'd stopped by your house, and when José said you'd gone to the Trio's, I knew that probably meant trouble. Then I find you in some sort of trance, completely unaware of the danger you were in."

"Danger?"

"Yes! I can't believe how careless you've become with those three! You were in a trance, holding a glass of wine and about to drink it, and who knows what drug or poison might have been in it? At the very least, you were putting yourself in their power!"

Carlos had recovered sufficiently to be annoyed. "Pedro" he said gruffly. "I appreciate your concern for my welfare, and I admit that I went there wanting to experience more of an altered state they call *duende*. But there was dancing and singing, nothing more. Oh, some damiana tea and brandy at the beginning; that was all!"

"Maybe so," Pedro replied, "but things are rarely that simple with you."

They had reached Carlos's house. Pedro opened the door and nudged Carlos to go in. As he did so, Pedro said, "I heard from Ana that Leandro is leaving Santa Fe early tomorrow morning with the Trigales children. If there's any apologizing I need to do for breaking up his party, I'll do it when he gets back. Meanwhile, I hope Inéz doesn't hear about this."

22

Hay Soup

For a man who'd been warned several times in the past twenty-four hours that he might be in grave danger, Don Carlos slept a deep and peaceful sleep. He dreamed of sitting with Inéz beside their Sacred Pool and watching as animals with brilliant auras in diverse colors came to drink. Elvira, who seemed to be in a very good mood, practically pranced past, prancing being a rare and wonderful accomplishment for a skunk. The sun was on his face, magical animals everywhere, and his beloved Inéz was at his side.

He awoke before dawn, got up, and began his meditation practice. He sensed danger, but of late that was nothing new. He resisted the impulse to stop meditating and go to investigate because it was his practice to sit still and allow every thought, worry, fear, and impulse to arise and, eventually, fade away. Watching, not acting, was the essence of his meditation practice.

José's desperate cry, "Fire! Fire! Help!" broke his calm silence. He jumped up and charged into the kitchen. Gordo was barking to sound the alarm. Carlos dashed out the kitchen door. To his right, smoke was pouring from the part of the stable where the hay was piled. As he and Gordo ran around the corner to the horses' stalls, José continued to cry for help and the horses were neighing frantically.

Don Carlos took in the scene at a glance. The situation was dire. Fire had spread through the whole area where the hay was stored. To his left, flames were close to Eagle's stall and Eagle was kicking at the stall door in an effort to escape. In the loft Carlos could see José's stricken face through the flames. "I can't get past the fire," José shouted. "I'm trapped and I don't see how you can get me out before I choke on the smoke. Save the horses. Open their stall doors and lead them to safety!"

Don Carlos sized up the situation and feared that José was right. The ladder to the loft and the hay rake were both missing. Even if he immediately started pulling burning hay out of the stack with his hands, he might not reach José in time and the horses would perish. But if he took the time to save the horses, José would die.

The thought flashed through his mind that in his confidence that his brujo powers were sufficient to protect himself, he had never suspected that his friends and property might be attacked by his enemies.

Don Carlos quickly considered all the options for a transformation that might bring the situation under control and finally chose the best one that came to mind, despite the danger it entailed. Never before, in all his lives as a brujo, had he transformed himself into an inanimate substance, and he could not be confident that he would be able to reverse the process and return to his human form. But he couldn't think of a better option and was determined to save his friends, even if it meant sacrificing his own life.

This decision made, he stripped off his clothes and ran toward the fire, intending to form himself into a wall of water that he hoped would be broad and high enough to smother the flames raging through the hay. Mustering his brujo powers to make the total volume of water as large as possible, he had just the barest moment to observe that becoming a wall of water was much more challenging than becoming a hawk or owl or even, as he had in battling Mateo Pizarro and his henchmen, a giant monster. During those transformations he had changed into solid objects. A wall of water required an extra expenditure of energy to keep the water from running off in all directions before he could use it to douse the fire.

It took every bit of Don Carlos's strength to throw himself forward in water form without losing control of his now-liquid body, literally pouring himself onto the flames. As he did so, he was beset by many questions. Am I spreading myself too thin? Will this be enough to put out every bit of the fire? What will be the effect on me when I hit the burning area and begin to run off in every direction in liquid form?

A partial answer to the last of these questions came quickly. He felt as though some force was pulling him apart, as indeed it was. His awareness of himself began to fade, lacking as he now did any physical center of his consciousness. Perhaps, he thought, I'm dying, and he knew all too well that if he died in an unconscious state he would be reborn as an ordinary man with no knowledge of his past lives and his deep nature as a brujo. If that occurred as a consequence of his saving José and the horses, he could accept it, although he knew he would miss his life in Santa Fe, especially his camaraderie with his two-legged and four-legged friends. Above all he would miss his Inéz.

These thoughts flashed through Don Carlos's mind in an instant. He made a feeble effort to collect himself, to draw his water form that was already running off in every direction together again into his human form. He grew weaker and weaker, more and more dispersed physically and disoriented mentally. Then everything went blank.

José slid down the wet, smoldering haystack from his sleeping place in the loft to Don Carlos's side. Carlos didn't look good at all, a shadow of his normal self. He was lying naked in the hay, cold and not breathing regularly. He seemed smaller and lacked body tone altogether. Every twenty seconds or so a spasm ran through his body and he gasped for air. Otherwise, he lay totally still. José was terrified.

Gordo stood nearby whining anxiously. José turned to him and said, "Bring Pedro." The little dog gave José a puzzled look. José spoke more forcefully: "Go get Pedro." Gordo seemed to understand. He dashed off in the direction of Pedro's house.

Seeing that he couldn't do much, José told Carlos, "Don't die while I'm away. I'm going to get Inéz." After covering Carlos's naked body with a tarp, José ran as fast as he could to the Beltráns' house. He was in luck. Inéz was in the kitchen, starting breakfast preparations. José banged on the kitchen door, which was still locked. "Come quick! Alfonso has had an accident!"

A look of sheer horror came on Inéz's face. She put down her knife, threw aside her apron, and ran to the door. "Where is he? What happened?"

"He's at our stable in back of the house. The hay piles were on fire. He put the fire out, but he collapsed in the hay."

Inéz pushed past José and broke into a run. José couldn't keep up, she was going so fast. What he saw ahead was Inéz, running faster than he would have thought humanly possible, the skirt of her smock pulled up so as to not impede her movement.

Inéz, shocked at José's announcement, deeply fearful for Carlos, suddenly had a vivid flash of a memory from the distant past. She was wearing a short leather tunic with a bronze breastplate and helmet and was carrying an iron-tipped spear and a small, round shield. She and seven other men, similarly outfitted, were running across a field. Ahead, beyond a low hill, they could see smoke rising, which told them that in their absence their village had been attacked. Inéz, the Inéz that had almost reached the southern edge of Santa Fe's plaza, realized that this ancient self was a male, a Basque village leader named Iñigo, and like virtually all rural Basques of that era, he was also a brujo. What that ancient self found on the other side of the hill, Inéz dimly knew, was loss. Well, she thought, there's another battle to be fought this morning, a battle to save Carlos, and I'm not going to lose it.

Pedro was already with Carlos when Inéz and José arrived. "Is he alive?" Inéz asked.

"Barely," Pedro replied. At that moment, Carlos gasped, and Pedro and Inéz looked at each other hopefully.

Inéz threw herself down beside Carlos. "Carlos," she said forcefully, "you are not going to die on us; stay with me; come back to me and us, Carlos."

Each time Inéz spoke his name, Carlos's body gave a shudder. "He can hear me in some distant part of his brain," Inéz asserted, "but he's not getting enough air." With that, she leaned over him, inhaled deeply, and then placed her mouth over his and exhaled. "Carlos," she said on pulling away, "I'll breathe for you, but I need you to start breathing on your own as soon as possible." She immediately returned to inhaling and then exhaling into Carlos's mouth.

A minute or two passed, although it seemed more like hours, and Inéz paused for one breath to ask José, "What happened?"

"I was sound asleep when the horses woke me up with terrified whinnies. I saw flames leaping up from the haystack. The fire had already reached the loft, and there was no way out. The ladder was nowhere in sight. I didn't see how I could get away without getting burned, although I knew I'd have to jump out of the loft soon if I was going to have any chance to escape alive. The smoke was choking me.

"I screamed for help, and Alfonso came dashing around the corner of the house. By then the fire had spread across the hay storage area over to the wall of Eagle's stall. The poor horse was in a panic. I could hear him kicking frantically at the stall door.

"Alfonso looked at what was happening for a few seconds. Then he stripped off his clothes, threw himself at the haystack, and disappeared. In his place was a huge wall of water. It was as broad as the hay storage area and tall enough to reach the loft where I was crouched. The wall of water crashed into the burning hay and smothered the flames. He was lost in the smoke that rose from the smoldering hay. Finally, I saw him lying naked in the middle of the remaining hay."

Inéz got to her knees and lifted Carlos's torso off the hay. His body was completely limp. "He weighs hardly anything," Inéz cried, suddenly understanding. "All this water—the puddle over there, the soggy hay—it's all part of his body. He spread himself around in water form to stop the fire; we've got to collect as much as we can and, God willing that he regains consciousness, make him drink it to restore his weight."

She turned to the two men and told them what to do. "Pedro, carry Carlos into his bedroom and pile blankets on him. He's deathly cold. José, collect as much water as you can in buckets and basins. Use a cup to get the water from that puddle. Squeeze all the moisture you can out of the hay."

Pedro picked Carlos up and was shocked at how little he weighed. Inéz lifted his head, which had fallen limply downward, and held it gently in her hands as she and Pedro hurried Carlos into his house and laid him on his bed. "Pedro, are there any more blankets here? I see only two on the bed."

"Yes, there are two or three more in the part of the house where María and I used to live. I'll be right back." In the very short time it took for Pedro to return with three extra blankets, Inéz had climbed into the bed and was lying next to Carlos, intending to try to warm him by holding him close to her body.

Pedro covered the two of them with all the available blankets. "I'll go help José collect water," he said.

"Wait a moment, Pedro. I think something deep inside Carlos responds to our voices. Carlos, dear Carlos, stay with us," she whispered fervently in his ear. Then she said to Pedro, "Tell me how you came to know that Carlos is a brujo."

"It was on our first trip together," Pedro began. "We were traveling north to settle in Santa Fe. Once we reached the high desert, Carlos kept disappearing for long periods at night. When I asked him about it, he said he'd never needed much sleep and found it stimulating to walk through the desert at night. But twice I saw an owl flying around the area. It was a type that shouldn't have been in that region at that time of year. Not long after that he admitted that he was a brujo who had a particular skill at transformations. I told him that didn't bother me at all. I had an ancestor, my mother's father, who was a brujo, although not with anywhere near the powers that Carlos has."

Inéz spoke with her customary irreverence to Carlos, "You big lug. Don't you dare leave us. Dig deep down and use those powers to return to consciousness and full health."

José had come in the room with Carlos's mountain lion bracelet in his hand. "Here's something that might help," he said.

Inéz took the bracelet and slipped it on Carlos's wrist. "Oh, Carlos," she said with a sob, "you're so diminished in size; the bracelet won't stay on you, your wrist is so much smaller. I'll hold it in place for you," and she wrapped her hand around the bracelet and lay back, embracing him. Pedro pulled the blankets over the two of them.

"Why do you keep calling Alfonso Carlos?" José asked.

"You've surely suspected," Inéz replied, "that Alfonso is a brujo of some sort. Carlos is his secret name, a name known only to Pedro and me and now to you. It's the name he's carried through many lives, five before this one, I believe. He is a brujo of incredible power, possibly the most skilled practitioner of sorcery in our time. Can you imagine what skill it took to form himself into a wall of water and, what was even more challenging, to hold water in place without any container except his own personal power? All that was in the service of his friends, you and our horses."

"He's remarkably generous and joyful," José said pensively.

"I had the same thought," Pedro said. "Gordo had come, barking his head off, to the stable door. Then he dashed off toward Carlos's house, and I followed him. When I saw smoke ahead, I was pretty sure Carlos was in trouble, and it came to me what a kind person he is. He's always been so ready to take in strays—the halt and the lame like Gordo and me—and he's treated us as equals, our infirmities be damned."

"I'm one of those strays too," Inéz said. "Carlos saved me from a life of hellish suffering and then gave me love without demanding that I marry him. He loved me—loves me, damn it, he's still an 'is,'—and gave me freedom. Another stray he took in."

"Me too," José declared, "and Diego."

"Maybe you and I," Pedro said to José, "ought to get out back and see how much more we can collect of Carlos in water form." They hurried out of the room.

Inéz snuggled up against Carlos. He was still very cold, but his breath was coming a bit more regularly, almost in a normal way.

"I thought they'd never leave," said a shadowy figure standing in the room's darkest corner. "Your healing sorcery is helping Carlos, but I've come to lend a hand."

Although Inéz could barely see the figure who'd addressed her, she could tell it was a man. When he walked toward the bed, she could discern his shape and attire more clearly. What an odd way he was dressed, she thought. On his head was a black wig that had eagle feathers mounted on it, and he wore an earth-colored mask with turquoise and black circles drawn around its eyes. The face of the mask had a broad snout, the mouth of which opened to reveal sharp teeth. His clothing was equally strange—a throat piece, armbands, an apron over his belly, and leggings, all decorated with white spots on a gray background. His only ordinary apparel was a turquoise-colored belt and brown moccasins.

"I am Toho," the man said, "the mountain lion kachina, a friend of this man Carlos. You must be the woman he loves so much."

Inéz's eyes filled with tears. "Thank you for coming, Toho," she said, "I'm afraid I might lose him. Can you help?"

"I'm here to do what I can. I was impatient to join you but held back because the others were here, and I'm glad I heard what they had to say. Your Carlos is a fine person. What I'm going to do, with your permission, is to merge myself with him, sharing my strength with him. In so doing, I'll be putting myself in his place, and I hope you won't mind hugging a mountain lion."

"Please merge with Carlos in my arms," Inéz urged him.

Toho merged himself with Carlos's body with a tenderness that surprised Inéz. She told herself she would have to revise her image of mountain lions as aggressive and dangerous.

It wasn't long before Inéz felt Carlos's body growing warmer and his breath coming more freely and strongly. The mountain lion bracelet grew so hot that Inéz worried she would have to let go of it, but to her relief that didn't prove necessary.

Toho spoke, though it wasn't so much an audible form of speech as it was words that came silently into Inéz's consciousness. "I'm rather enjoying myself," Toho told her. "I've always favored four-legged females with long tails and nice thick pelts. I never considered that it might be so pleasant to lie in the embrace of a hairless two-legged. I assume human males prefer females with little fur on their bodies. Is that true of Carlos?"

"I'd say that Carlos finds women appealing whether they have lots of body hair or are furless."

Toho seemed to find this highly amusing and laughed so hard that Carlos's body rocked in place. "I don't suppose I'll ever understand humans, but I share Carlos's enthusiasm for females."

Inéz and Toho lay embracing Carlos for some time, she from outside his body, Toho from within, he now and then making a soothing hum that Inéz realized was a purr. He didn't stir until he heard the back door of the house open. "I think I'll leave," he said, "before your other friends return and see me. I don't go around showing myself to strangers, and in case that puzzles you because we've been so intimate, the reason I showed myself to you was because you're a bruja who loves our friend Carlos."

"Bruja? What makes you say that?"

"It's obvious, isn't it? But I've got to go."

"Wait, Toho. Is Carlos going to live?"

"I believe he will, although he'll be weak for a while. Have him drink as much as he can of that water the men are collecting. It will help him a lot." Pedro was opening the door to enter the room, so Toho departed, passing through the wall next to the bed in a great rush.

It was late Monday afternoon, ten or more hours after he'd put out the fire, before Don Carlos became conscious of anything around him. The first things to filter through to him were snippets of conversation in his bedroom. Even these fragments, phrases and whole sentences, came to him in a muffled way, as though he was submerged under water with waves washing over him. No wonder he didn't catch much of what was being said.

The first long fragment he heard may not have been from a conversation at all. It sounded more like something Inéz whispered in his ear. "Don't you dare leave me alone," she'd said. "I wouldn't say this to your face, but I don't think I could go on living without you."

Some time later, he thought he heard a voice that sounded like Elena Beltrán's. "Don't worry, Inéz," she said. "Mother wants you to know that Diego will come over and cook for us, or we'll all go to the Trigales place and eat with them."

Other bits and pieces he overheard didn't collect themselves into intelligible statements until he heard José exclaim, "Inéz! Wake up! I think his eyelids fluttered."

Sure enough, he had opened his eyes the tiniest bit. What he saw was curious. Looking upward at what he decided was the ceiling of his bedroom, all he saw was water. Was a stream running through the room? If he was at the bottom of a streambed, why didn't someone pull him out into the air?

Inéz's face appeared above his. Those entrancing gray eyes looked at him with hope, or that's how he interpreted her expression. How could she breathe under water, he wondered? He'd always suspected that she was a bruja and this seemed to prove him right.

"Are you back with us?" the Inéz face asked.

"Still under water," he mumbled.

It took Inéz a moment to sort out what he'd said. "Do you feel able to sit up?" she asked.

He nodded, though the act of moving reminded him of having been seasick while crossing the Atlantic in a previous life. The room swam around in a dizzying way. Nevertheless, he was glad when Inéz and José gently helped him sit up in bed.

"Dizzy," was all he could manage.

"Take your time," Inéz told him. "Can you tell us how you feel?"

"Strange. I'm not all here and what's here is in liquid form. I feel like a column of water that's going to collapse on itself any moment."

Inéz looked extremely pleased. "That was a nice long two sentences.

Pedro!" she called. "Bring some of the soup that's heating in the kitchen. Carlos might be able to drink a little."

"Shhh," he replied, looking over at José. "That's my secret name. No one's supposed to know it."

"Too late," she told him. "Everyone in the room is in on your secret."

Pedro arrived with a large cup of lukewarm soup. Carlos didn't seem to have the strength to hold the cup to his lips, so Inéz held it for him, and when it proved difficult to figure out how much he could swallow at once, she had Pedro get a spoon and gave it to Carlos one spoonful at a time. He was very, very thirsty and drank every last drop.

"Strange taste," he said. "Chicken, charcoal, and hay."

"Don Carlos the brujo is gathering his wits most successfully." Inéz's statement was accompanied by a brilliant smile and Carlos was rewarded with a kiss on the cheek.

"Not bad," Carlos said, eyeing her admiringly. "I should get sick more often."

"Don't you dare!" Inéz exclaimed.

"Was that really a hay-flavored chicken soup?"

"Yes, dearest. We figured out that parts of you were spread through the hay, so we've been collecting as much water as we can and want you to drink it to restore yourself to yourself."

"Isn't that," Carlos asked, half in mock protest, "like drinking one's own blood, spit, or urine?"

"Ugh!" Inéz said in reply. "You're getting silly, and you've sat up long enough." With a gentle push she shoved Carlos down on the bed, and he fell asleep the moment his head hit the pillow.

Carlos didn't wake up again until the next morning. Sunlight was streaming in a window. Inéz was curled up against his back and Gordo was propped up against his chest. He felt much better than he had the last time he'd been awake and tried to shift to a sitting position without disturbing his bedmates. It didn't work. Inéz awoke instantly, and Gordo stood up, wagged his tail happily, and tried to lick Carlos's ear.

"Take it easy; this is Dr. Recalde speaking. If you must sit up, at least let me help you."

"What day is it?" Carlos asked, as she helped him sit up. The room whirled about.

"It's Tuesday morning, more than twenty-four hours since you decided to play one-man fire brigade. You still look terrible, but that's a big improvement over yesterday's I'm-a-corpse performance."

"Dear Inéz, I'm so glad my status has returned to that of a person always good as an object of merriment. Did you spend the night here in bed with me?"

Inéz smiled. "I'm feeling merry because I'm convinced you're going to live, and yes, I spent the night cuddled up next to you."

"Some men will do anything to get the woman in bed with them. I should have thought of this tactic long ago."

"Please don't make jokes about almost dying. Let me get you some more of your favorite hay-flavored chicken broth." She slipped off the bed, left the room, and soon returned carrying a tray with a large bowl of soup and a slice of bread.

As she carried these items toward him, Don Carlos couldn't resist the impulse to say, "Isn't it the Moslems who believe men go to heaven and are surrounded by beautiful women? Is it possible that I've died and gone, probably by mistake, to Moslem Paradise?"

"You are not," Inéz pointed out, "surrounded by many women but only one, and you're still in the land of the living and have been told not to make jokes about dying."

"I am feeling better; what was the turning point at which you thought I would recover?"

"Toho came and merged with you, and we lay together doing our best to heal you."

"You lay around with Toho? That sneak! He waits until I can't defend my interests and then steals a hug from you."

"He was very nice, Carlos, although he did say that he preferred females with thick fur pelts and I fell drastically short in that category. He also said that I was a bruja, which I hardly believe, but he said it with great conviction."

"All joking aside, Inéz, I'm glad you met him. I probably owe my life to the two of you."

Carlos finished the soup and ate half of the piece of bread, tossing the rest to Gordo, who gulped it down greedily before Inéz could intervene. No sooner had Carlos finished his meal than he lay down and immediately fell asleep.

It was the middle of the next morning, Wednesday, before Don Carlos woke again. Inéz was sitting in the room's only chair with a board on her lap, cutting up some vegetables.

"My status as a patient must have been upgraded while I slept," Carlos observed.

"Good morning, sweetie," she replied. "What's this about your status as a patient?"

"Apparently, I'm no longer in such critical condition that I require the company of an angelic woman in bed with me to give me a reason to keep living, and you seem to be preparing something more solid than hay soup for my lunch."

Worry showed on Inéz's face. "All you've eaten for forty-eight hours is a couple of bowls of hay soup and half a slice of bread. You need more solid food to rebuild your strength."

José knocked and entered the room, greeting Carlos with a huge smile. "You'll be glad to know that the horses are all right. I rode Alegría this morning, and I'll take Eagle out tomorrow. I've also cleaned up the hay storage area and laid in a wagonload of fresh hay."

Don Carlos sat up on the edge of his bed and ate breakfast. His appetite was much improved, and he didn't have any trouble eating everything Inéz had brought him. "Do you suppose," he asked, "I could try standing, perhaps with one of you on either side in case I faint?"

Inéz wasn't keen on the idea, but finally agreed to give it a try. To everyone's surprise, Carlos managed to rise without help. The room swayed in a threatening way for a minute, then stabilized, and he took several tentative steps over to the chair Inéz had been using. "That felt good," he declared. "Not good in the sense of normal, but managing to get up improves my morale enormously. I have a question that just occurred to me."

"What is it?" Inéz asked.

"I've lost track of time. When are the Trigales kids supposed to get back to Santa Fe?"

"Tomorrow or the day after tomorrow," José replied. "They were to perform at Francisco Trujillo's hacienda last night and then entertain people tonight at another ranch farther south on the Camino Real. It will take them all day tomorrow, and maybe part of Friday too, to get back to town. I talked with Diego earlier this morning, and he said the Trigaleses are planning a welcome-home feast for them to be given Thursday or Friday."

"I may not have said so to you," Carlos said with a nod in Inéz's direction, "but I never felt good about Leandro going out of town with the Trigales kids. José, would you do me a favor?"

José didn't hesitate. "You've saved my life twice now," he declared. "I owe you more than one favor."

"Here's what I'd like you to do. When you go out with Eagle tomorrow, take the road to Bernalillo and beyond, if necessary. Keep going, even if it takes hours and hours, until you meet Leandro and the Trigales children on their return trip. Laugh if you want about the claims I make for my brujo's intuition, but I have a bad feeling that you won't meet them on the way."

"I could leave right away," José said.

"Tomorrow morning should be soon enough. From what you said, they won't even start back until tomorrow. If all's well, you'll meet them at about the halfway point of their return journey. I'll rest easier if I'm sure they're all right. Now back to bed for me."

Inéz jumped up from the bed where she'd been sitting and moved to help him. "You needn't fuss, sweetie," he told her. "I'm feeling much better." She regarded him with obvious skepticism, but she let him walk the few steps it took for him to reach the bed unaided. He looked over at her and could tell something else was on her mind. "Why the frown?" he asked. "I made it easily."

"It's nothing much," she replied.

"But it's something. What?"

"You're alternately suspicious of Leandro and overly friendly with him. I don't understand what's going on with you. The kids will be fine. They love him and have been excited beyond belief to have him teaching them magic tricks."

"I don't doubt that they're very fond of him. He's a charming fellow, and I've become fond of him too. But clearly you're not familiar with the folk tale *The Pied Piper of Hamelin*."

"I've never heard of it; what's your point?"

Carlos filled her in. "It's a very old story, dating back at least three centuries and found in many versions. One of my tutors had a particular interest in charitable societies that aided children, and he told me about it.

"According to my tutor's version, Hamelin was a town in Europe that was suffering from an infestation of rats. One day a piper dressed in a pied outfit not unlike the multi-colored clothes Leandro wears at his performances came to town. He offered to rid the town of rats, if they would pay the price he set. They agreed.

"The piper commenced to pipe on his long pipe, the rats ran after him, and he walked into a nearby river. The rats all drowned, and the piper came back to collect his fee. The townspeople were a stingy bunch and didn't want to give a total stranger such a big sum of their hard-earned money, so they reneged on their agreement.

"A little while later, one festival day when all the town's adults were in church, the piper came back and played his pipe on the street. All the children came out of their houses and followed him out of town to a secret location, sometimes said to be a cave. None of them was ever seen again."

"That's a terribly sad story," Inéz said, "but Leandro's not a total stranger, and Raul Trigales is not going to renege on what he's promised Leandro for entertaining the children. Go back to sleep. Everything, even you, will be okay."

"I hope you're right," Carlos replied, and immediately fell asleep.

Evening came, and Carlos again got out of bed unassisted. With Inéz hovering at his elbow, he walked slowly to the kitchen, where he ate a hearty meal of eggs, potatoes, and hay soup. "You'll be glad to know this is the last of the hay soup," Inéz told him.

"I'm not sorry to hear that," he replied, "although it wasn't all that bad, except for the slightly smoky flavor underneath the other seasonings."

"Next time try not to burn the hay I need for soup," she said. It was a joy to be teasing again.

"You've spent two nights here in bed with me. How is your employer, Cristina, taking that—not to speak of the town gossips? Is it going to get you fired?"

Inéz answered with a smile on her face. "No, I'm authorized to be here. Cristina was so frightened by you being on the edge of dying that she threw the rulebook out the window."

An hour later, after a brief visit from Pedro, who'd come by to check on him, Carlos was feeling at least half himself. "Since I've rarely been sick, I never felt I could say anything for certain about my powers of recuperation, but I feel I'm bouncing back quite quickly."

"Don't overdo it," Inéz replied. "You're such an optimist that I can't trust you to have the good sense to give your recovery adequate time."

Grinning happily at the thought, Carlos said, "I could have a slight relapse, if it will keep you around for a few more nights."

"Comments of that sort are more likely to convince me that you're imagining you're so much better that you'll soon be getting into trouble again."

"Me, trouble?" he replied.

"I suspect that trouble is your middle name," Inéz said. "But I love you nonetheless."

Pleased to hear Inéz loved him—it seemed all was well despite the problem he'd caused between them by snuggling up to a violet-eyed dancer — Carlos lay back and closed his eyes to sleep, less because he felt particularly tired than because an inner voice was telling him he needed to be well rested to meet what loomed ahead.

23

Kidnapped

Carlos's conviction that trouble was close at hand was soon confirmed. Shortly after midnight José, who had been dozing in a chair in the kitchen, burst into Carlos's bedroom, scaring Gordo, who was curled up next to Carlos, and startling Inéz, who had been asleep on the bed beside them. "Someone's pounding on the back door. Should I open it? I wouldn't bother asking, except for the strange event of the fire."

"Let's see what's going on," Inéz said, and she and José hurried to answer the door. Carlos, reminding himself to move slowly, followed them.

Mara was standing at the door and allowed Inéz to pull her inside. She was wearing a long woolen nightshirt. She was in great distress, out of breath, and weeping. "Selena's dead, I think," was all she managed to get out between gasps for breath. "Please come and help, if she can still be helped!"

Without waiting for a response, Mara turned and ran out the door and down the lane toward the house she shared with Selena. Inéz and José followed on her heels, and Carlos trailed along more slowly. He noticed that he was feeling stronger than he'd expected. Getting outdoors seemed to revive his physical strength.

By the time he got to Mara and Selena's house the other three had gone in, leaving the door open behind them. He pushed inside and turned down the corridor leading to the bedroom wing. The door to the two dancers' bedroom was open and light was showing. He went to the door and looked in. Selena didn't look alive. Her skin was pallid, and her jaw had fallen slack. She looked very, very bad.

Inéz picked up Selena's arm and then touched her neck. "She's cold," Inéz declared. "No pulse either. No sign of life."

Don Carlos wasn't so sure. He gently nudged Mara and Inéz aside and looked at Selena from close up. Her aura was extremely faint, but she did have an aura, proof that she wasn't dead. He put his ear to her chest and listened, motioning for everyone else to be silent. There it was; a single heartbeat; and, after a long pause, another faint beat.

Turning to Mara, he asked, "Is there any water in a tub?"

"Yes," she replied, puzzled. "There's some in the wash tub. We were going to wash some clothes Monday morning after Leandro left. By now the water's probably stone cold."

"Cold is good. José, pick her up and follow me to the big tub in the kitchen." José hesitated, not used to touching women's bodies. More sharply than he expected, Carlos said, "Inéz, help José. Get on the other side of Selena. Mara, hold her head up."

The three organized themselves and picked Selena up as Don Carlos had suggested and carried her to the kitchen. He tested the water in the wash tub, and it was, as Mara had predicted, cold. The bath tub stood empty nearby with two buckets of water next to it. Don Carlos didn't know if what he had in mind would work, but he didn't hesitate to try it. He told the other three, "José and I are going to empty the water from the two buckets and the wash tub into the bath tub." This accomplished, he continued, "Keep holding her just the way you are; I'll grab her feet. What we're going to do is to maneuver around the tub until we're holding her over it. When we're in position, we'll plunge her body in. She's in a coma probably caused by a sedative or poison of some sort. The jolt of being plunged into cold water may bring her back to consciousness. Mara, be careful to keep her nose and mouth above water."

No one challenged Don Carlos's instructions, so he nodded and they went to work.

Once they had Selena above the water, Don Carlos told them, "I'll count to three; on three we'll plunge her into the water and pull her out immediately. Here goes: one, two, three."

There was a lot of splashing, but no response from Selena. Her body remained limp and inert. "Again," Carlos said. "One, two, three." Still no response.

"Don't give up," Carlos told them. "This time," he added, "I want Mara to slap Selena's face, not gently either. This is a life-and-death situation and we have to be strong."

To everyone's amazement, a coordinated dunk and some hard slaps from Mara brought Selena around. Her eyes fluttered half open and she feebly tried to kick her legs. "Pull her out, strip off her nightclothes, dry her, and wrap her in towels and blankets to get warm. Her strength, and a little help from her friends, has brought her back."

Inéz and Mara undressed Selena. José averted his eyes. Carlos heaved a sigh of relief that his intervention had worked. The two women dried Selena off and wrapped her in towels. Then the four of them carried her to the bedroom. After they'd given her half a glass of brandy, some glow returned to her skin. As they all began to relax, Mara explained what had happened. "The last thing I remember is Monday morning. We got up very early to see Leandro off on his trip with the Trigales children. He made us a pot of very rich, very sweet hot chocolate. It was a special treat, he said, and just for us. I think he had coffee. An hour or so later, both of us felt unaccountably tired and decided to go back to bed. I didn't wake up until a half hour ago, and you say it's now Thursday morning. I tried to wake Selena, and couldn't...and she was so cold! I thought she was dead. So I ran to you, Alfonso," she said, looking at him, "to get help."

Selena began to stir and finally spoke. Her voice was whispery. "He was two people, you know—Leandro, our protector, and another person that came out when he used his transformation elixir. Then he became a monster." She closed her eyes tightly, and then opened them again. "His appearance changed, and so did his inner being. We were afraid of this being, whom we called Damián."

She was silent for a few moments, as if gathering her strength. She turned her face to Carlos and went on. "Alfonso, though Leandro liked you, Damián envied you, and he talked about either destroying you or enticing you to join him and serve him."

She paused again. "He planned it. Damián planned the evening of dancing *Duende* in hopes of recruiting you, and he was furious when Pedro's arrival upset everything. He was so angry! Mara and I tiptoed around and escaped to our room as soon as we could. But on Monday morning he seemed to be Leandro again, as if the night before hadn't happened. And that is what is most horrible—it was Leandro, not Damián, who tried to get rid of us!" She and Mara looked at each other for a long moment. Then she added, "I think he has taken the Trigales children for his own purposes. They must be in grave danger."

Carlos, Inéz, and José exchanged a glance. Carlos broke the silence. "I hope you're wrong, Selena, but the situation may be very bad. At least you and Mara are all right. Inéz, José, and I will go home and talk about what's to be done next." Leaving Mara to help Selena, the three friends walked slowly back to Carlos's place, Gordo trailing along behind.

Once they'd reached the house José stayed in the kitchen while Carlos and Inéz went off alone to the bedroom. "I'm glad you decided to discuss what we should do," she said. "I was afraid you were going to fly off tonight to check the Camino Real south of here."

"I was considering it," Carlos admitted, sitting down heavily.

Inéz frowned. "That would be foolish, and you know it. Just the way you sagged down in that chair tells me that you're still much too weak for any heroics." He started to speak, but she cut him off. "There's a perfectly reasonable way of proceeding. You should go back to bed. At dawn José can start south. If Leandro's party is headed back, José ought to meet them somewhere north of Trujillo's ranch, about midway between Santa Fe and the ranch where they performed last might. He can return here as soon as he has some news."

Carlos didn't like it, but he conceded that another day of rest would put him in better shape for the challenges he was sure were ahead. The only point he added to Inéz's plan was a practical one. "Tell José," he said, "to borrow a horse from Pedro. That will leave Eagle, Alegría, and Pepper fresh if there's any long-distance riding to be done on Friday."

Inéz went to the kitchen and gave José Carlos's instructions. José agreed immediately, and once that was settled, Carlos went to bed.

Church bells, the early call to daily Mass, woke him the next morning, much later than his usual hour for rising. He got out of bed and dressed. Sounds and smells from the kitchen drew him in that direction. Inéz glanced up from her work, looked him up and down, and commented, "I probably shouldn't encourage you with a positive appraisal, but you look much better today."

Carlos could tell that she was apprehensive, worried that he would try to do too much, and he did his best to reassure her. "My plan," he told her, "while we wait for José to return with news, is to sleep a lot, eat a lot, and perhaps, if my ever-vigilant friend permits, take gentle strolls to get my legs under me."

Inéz eyed him suspiciously. "You're being awfully reasonable about your condition. What are you plotting?"

"I can be reasonable when it's called for. Prudence is my watchword."

"Careful with that line," she warned him. "I'm growing more skeptical all the time."

"Set your worries aside," he assured her. "Let's eat, drink, sleep, and, above all, be merry." Sitting down at the kitchen table, he added, "Whatever you're cooking smells wonderful. May I have some?"

Inéz set out a variety of dishes for him, and he helped himself enthusiastically. "You're a fabulous cook," he remarked as he stuffed his mouth.

"Don't try to talk with your mouth full," she replied.

"Yes, Mother," he said with a smile and went back to eating.

Pedro showed up as Carlos was at last ready to push back from the table. Going right to the point, he said, "José arrived in a hurry and asked to borrow the best-conditioned horse in my stable. What's going on?"

Carlos looked over at Inéz and let her answer. "The best possibility is nothing at all. But it worries us that Mara and Selena got very sick after drinking hot chocolate Leandro made for them Monday morning."

"Hmmm," Pedro said thoughtfully. "And Carlos's haystack fire was Monday too. Could Leandro have set it?"

"It's possible," Inéz replied. "It's also possible that Leandro has kidnapped the Trigales children for some as-yet-unknown purpose."

"Not good at all," Pedro observed, shaking his head.

Speaking up at last, Carlos raised a question that had been bothering him. "Do either of you have advice about what we should say if Raul Trigales stops by? We don't know anything for certain, and I don't want to upset him and Bianca with conjectures."

"You'd better come up with something," Pedro replied. "I met him on the plaza, and he told me he might drop in on you this afternoon."

They mulled over the options for a while until Carlos decided they shouldn't keep Raul and Bianca in the dark about their worries. "Pedro, could you track Raul down and ask him to be certain to stop by to see me this afternoon? Tell him I would visit him, but I need to stay here and rest."

Early in the afternoon, about the time he thought Raul might come by, Carlos got up and invited Inéz to join him on the front veranda. "I can wrap up in my overcoat and add some blankets, if needed. Being outdoors, even in town, does me a world of good," he added persuasively, and she agreed that he ought to try it.

After sitting quietly for a while, he smiled at her and said, "I'm feeling much better."

"Don't try to distract me with your feeble attempt to claim good health."

He was saved from coming up with a clever reply — he earnestly wanted to engage in spirited wordplay — by Raul Trigales's arrival.

After an exchange of pleasantries and Raul's sincere expressions of concern about Carlos's health, Raul asked a question that was obviously bothering him. "Some strange events have taken place—your near-death in a fire and the stories that the two women entertainers were discovered to be very sick. What's going on?"

Carlos replied, "We're not sure, but we must acknowledge that we're worried about the fact that your children went off with Leandro the Magician on Monday, about the time the fire broke out in my barn and Mara and Selena became ill."

A look of concern came over Raul's face. "What do you mean? The children aren't expected back until tomorrow. Are you saying that Leandro had something to do with your fire and the women's illness? That he has run off with my children?"

"We don't know anything for certain," Carlos said. "That's why I've asked our young friend José to ride south from here. The hope is that he'll meet Leandro's party and return to tell us that our worries were unfounded."

"I hope you're right," Raul replied, but he looked very uneasy. "Let me know the minute you have any news." Carlos assured him that was their intention, and after a little more talk, Raul left and Carlos went back to bed. He slept the rest of the afternoon and into the early evening before getting up to have another meal Inéz had prepared.

Looking across the table into her gray eyes, he said, "I like having you around."

"You know very well that I can't stay much longer," she replied. "I have a job that I'm neglecting, and as you know I need to keep it." Apparently feeling that her tone had been too severe, she added, "I wouldn't have wanted to be anywhere else than here these past four days."

Three hours after sunset José burst into the room. Carlos was propped up in bed with Gordo snoozing in his lap. Inéz was sewing, repairing a torn seam in one of his shirts. Carlos had been contentedly admiring this domestic scene.

Suddenly everything changed. Out of breath and obviously tired, José announced, "I have news and it's not good. I'd ridden beyond Bernalillo, almost to Trujillo's, when I met an itinerant trader headed for Santa Fe. We pulled up and exchanged greetings. I asked him if he knew anything about Leandro and the Trigales kids. He said he'd seen their show last night at Mauricio Olmedo's ranch next to the big meadow rest stop on the Camino Real.

"I asked him if he knew whether they'd started back this way, and he said no, that he had met them as he was starting north for Santa Fe at dawn, and that they were heading south. They were all in the carriage, except the magician, who was on horseback."

José went on, "I said I was surprised that they weren't headed north to Santa Fe. The trader said he'd asked the magician where they were going, and Leandro told him he was taking the children on a side trip to a spot where his magic was particularly powerful."

Upon hearing José's report, Don Carlos knew what he needed to do and that Inéz would be angry and violently opposed, and he disliked the idea of having her angry with him again so soon after the Mara incident. How to break the news to her? He could sneak off, but that was a coward's choice, and besides, he could use her help. Turning to José, he said, "I know you're exhausted, but I need you to go to Raul Trigales and tell him what you've learned and that we may have a dangerous situation on our hands."

Once José had hurried off, Carlos addressed Inéz. "A search party, a posse in fact if not in name, will need to start south at daybreak tomorrow."

"But you're not going to wait until then, are you?" she asked, anger already rising in her eyes.

"Sweetheart," he said as soothingly as he could.

"Don't sweetheart me," she replied. "You're going to ask me to let you play hero again, even though you're in a weakened condition and may have to confront a monster, Leandro in Damián form. Let Raul Trigales offer to pay a ransom, he's rich enough. He can get his children back without you risking your neck."

It's a good thing, Carlos thought, that I haven't yet told her about Xenome's vision of Don Malvolio and his ogre allies. They're surely involved. I'll have to skirt that issue. He chose his words carefully. "Inéz, here are the options my conscience allows. I could sneak off and try to do this on my own, or you could help me and monitor my activities to be sure I don't try anything too crazy."

"Your doing anything in your present condition is crazy," she said angrily.

"Here's what I hope you'll be willing to do. It's dark, so I'll take the form of a barn owl. They have terrific wingspans and can travel great distances, especially if the wind's blowing in the right direction—toward the south—as I believe it is.

"I have no intention of confronting Leandro-Damián, only of seeing what I can learn about what he intends to do with the children. What I propose is to fly along the road looking for their horses and carriage. I'd like you, José, and Raul to meet me on the Camino Real at the rest stop just south of the small settlement soon to be officially named Albuquerque. The Olmedo ranch is right there and we should be able to get a meal and rooms for the night at the ranch. Bring Eagle, some food for me, and my clothes and boots."

"Why do you need a set of clothes?"

"Can you imagine an owl wearing a shirt, pants, and boots? I have to leave them behind. And you'll also need a long, supple piece of leather to wrap around your arm."

"Why a leather wrapping for my arm?"

"The next time I see you it will be daylight, and I'll probably be a red-tailed hawk."

"I don't approve of any of this. I'll follow you south as you ask, but be forewarned that I'm furious with you. You have no right to put my love for you to this kind of test."

"Inéz, I don't want us to part on such a bad note. Please try to trust me to be careful. There's a good chance that my flying south will speed my recovery. I promise that if I grow tired, I'll stop wherever I am on the road and wait for you and José to come along."

"Go on your way before I say something more I'll regret, especially if I never see you again. You know I wouldn't be angry if I didn't love you, but I'm not feeling any sort of positive emotion at the moment."

Carlos got up off the bed and went to the door to the kitchen. "All right," he said, "I guess that's the best I can expect." Blowing a kiss to Inéz, he closed the bedroom door behind him, took off his clothes, and peered out the kitchen door to be sure that no one was around. Stepping outside into the night, he changed himself into a barn owl and took off. Inéz had come out of the house by the front door and was standing in the street. He flew over her head and made a tight circle as a gesture of parting. He knew she saw him and understood, but she didn't wave back.

The flight went more smoothly than Don Carlos had expected, and he was also pleased to note that it was serving to restore his energy. A favorable wind enabled him to coast for many miles without too much effort and to quickly cover the distance from Santa Fe to Bernalillo and then on to the rest stop area where he'd told Inéz to meet him. He kept going a bit longer until he reached the southern edge of the rest stop, which was the farthest point Leandro had told Raul and Bianca Trigales that he was going to take their children. Don Carlos didn't see any sign of the Trigales party along the Camino Real. Turning around, he retraced his flight in a northward direction for ten miles, carefully scanning the area to the east of the road where the Trigales carriage might have ended up if it had strayed off that side of the road. Nothing. Reversing direction and heading south again, he checked the landscape west of the road. Again, he didn't find the Trigales party; however, he noticed many small nocturnal animals foraging and registered the fact that they would have made excellent meals for an owl. He decided he was getting hungry, which was a good sign, except that he was also getting very tired. He landed in a tree with a good view of the big meadow at the rest stop and the main buildings of the Olmedo ranch on its far edge. He locked his talons on the tree branch and settled down to sleep contentedly until dawn.

As the sky lightened he woke up, feeling refreshed. Time for a change. He transformed himself from his nighttime form as an owl into a red-tailed hawk and took flight from his roost with vigorous beats of his wings. His plan was to explore the Camino Real south of the Olmedo ranch for signs of Leandro and the Trigales contingent: four children, a governess, and a carriage driver. His worst fears were soon realized. Six miles to the south he saw a large flock of turkey vultures circling and then diving to a site below them. Certain that something on the ground was dead or dying, Don Carlos flew in the direction of the scavengers. He took a high-angle approach above the nearly three dozen vultures either circling or on the ground. What had attracted them was two bodies—a man and a woman—lying near an empty carriage a little distance west of the road. The carriage horses were nowhere to be seen.

Plummeting from the sky in a straight-line dive, he landed between the two dead bodies. Turkey vultures leaped away, startled. Don Carlos's arrival was not welcome, and there were loud protests from the vultures about his intrusion on their breakfast. Although he was vastly outnumbered, he didn't feel threatened, nor did he intend to stay long because the meaning of the scene he'd come upon wasn't difficult to interpret. The throats of the governess and carriage driver had been slit. It appeared to Don Carlos that their bodies had also been mutilated, although he couldn't be sure because vultures had been tearing at their flesh for at least a full day, assuming the two victims had been killed early Thursday morning. The only other item of importance was a folded note addressed to Raul Trigales and nailed to the door of the carriage. In his hawk form Don Carlos couldn't open it, but he assumed it would contain a demand for ransom.

Repelled by what he'd seen, Don Carlos saw no reason to linger. He took off, sent on his way by a chorus of contemptuous commentary from the turkey vultures, and flew directly back to the agreed-upon rendezvous site with Inéz and José. Perched on a high branch of a cottonwood tree, he had to admit that he was weary. He relaxed and dozed off.

When he awoke it was mid-afternoon. He saw his friends approaching, Inéz on Alegría, José on Pepper, and Eagle trotting along on a lead rope.

His heart soared at seeing his friends. To arrive so soon, they must have left Santa Fe not long after his own departure and made excellent time. He fervently hoped that Inéz's anger at him had diminished.

Don Carlos the red-tailed hawk lifted off from his tree branch and made a low approach, coasting in front of his two friends to draw their attention, then rising fifty feet into the air and displaying his virtuosity by wheeling in a tight turn and circling back toward Inéz and José. They reined in their horses. Carlos was pleased to see that Inéz had followed his instructions and had brought a long piece of leather that she wrapped several times around her right wrist, holding it out to one side to facilitate his landing.

With great skill Don Carlos made a soft landing on Inéz's wrist. He rather hoped she would give him a welcoming kiss, but either she didn't feel like kissing a hawk or she was still angry with him—a little of both, as it turned out.

"Did you have a good ride?" he asked, but from their blank looks, it appeared that neither Inéz nor José got his message. Puzzled as to why the mental projection of his words wasn't working—perhaps his fatigue was the problem—he waited for Inéz to make the first move at communication.

"Did you find the children?" she asked. He shook his head side to side to indicate that he hadn't.

"Any clues about what happened?" He nodded yes.

"Where did you find these clues?" He tried to gesture with one wing toward the south.

"Here in the rest stop area?" Another side-to-side negative.

"Beyond?" An affirmative nod. This was getting tedious, so he took off, circled them once and then flew a hundred yards across the rest stop meadow to a barn on the ranch belonging to Mauricio Olmedo. He changed into his human form and grabbed a tarp to hide his nakedness. Moments later Inéz and José reached the barn. He called to José to bring him his clothes, dressed, and hurried out to join his friends. Once he'd mounted Eagle, he said, "Good to see the two of you."

"I'm sorry," Inéz replied, "I didn't wave to you when you flew off last night. I was angry, and I'm still annoyed at you, but if something had happened to either of us, I wouldn't have wanted us to part in anger."

Carlos nodded. "I'm glad to hear that." After a brief pause he went on to say, "Right now I'm tired and hungry. I saw plenty of mice and other small nocturnal creatures out and about, but my human dietary preferences won out over my owl-form, and I didn't eat a thing. Can we go to the main house of the ranch and see if they'll offer us some food and a room where I can rest? Once we're settled in, I can tell you what I've learned."

As they rode the short distance from the barn to the ranch's main house, Carlos asked, "By the way, where's Raul?"

José explained. "Señor Trigales has organized a party consisting of himself, two hired hands, and spare horses so they'll have fresh mounts if they're needed in a manhunt. They're a couple of hours behind us."

Upon arriving at the main house, they dismounted and tied their horses to the hitching rail outside. The ranch's owner, Mauricio Olmedo, came out to greet them with his wife, and both expressed great concern when they heard that the Trigales children, whose performance they and their own children had enjoyed two nights earlier, were missing.

"The children were very good," Señora Olmedo observed, "but I thought the magician was a bit" — she hesitated, groping for a word — "overexcited, perhaps. Like a skittish horse, showing the whites of its eyes. Though he gave a very flashy performance."

"There's something else," Mauricio volunteered. "This is the third time the magician has been here in the past three weeks. The other two times he was accompanied by a Franciscan — a short, bald man with black eyes that looked right through you. The Franciscan's name was Gustavo de Illueca. They both stayed overnight and left, heading in opposite directions, right after breakfast the next morning. I was glad the Franciscan didn't stay around. Something about him gave me the chills."

"When was the last time the magician met with the Franciscan?" Don Carlos asked.

A frown came on Mauricio's face. "I'm not sure exactly — about eleven or twelve days ago, I think." Turning to his wife, he said, "Do you remember?"

"Sunday before last, the last Sunday in January," she answered without hesitation.

Don Carlos wasn't certain what to make of this information, but he thought it might be important and thanked the Olmedos for providing it.

The Olmedos showed them the way to the dining room and then went off to get their cook to prepare something for them to eat. While waiting for their meal, Carlos filled Inéz and José in on what he'd found. "The news is very bad," he began. "About six miles south of here, a short distance west of the road, I found the bodies of the governess and the coachman. Their throats had been cut, and vultures had been working them over for nearly two days. The children were nowhere to be seen. Neither were the carriage horses. I didn't stick around any longer than it took to see that there's a note nailed to the door of the carriage. Why don't you wait for Raul Trigales to show up, have him collect the note, and return here to discuss our next move? Meanwhile, I want to rest. Even three hours will be good."

"While you're resting" Inéz asked, "wouldn't it make sense to have José and me go to the killing site and pick up the note to have it here when Raul arrives? I assume it'll be easy to locate."

"Yes, that makes sense, and you'll have no trouble finding the place. As I said, it's west of the Camino Real south of here. The circling vultures will pinpoint it for you."

Inéz and José went off to retrieve the ransom note, leaving Carlos to sleep for three hours. The sun was setting when he woke up, looked out the window, and saw that Raul Trigales and his two hired hands had arrived and, still mounted, were talking with Inéz and José in front of the hacienda.

Carlos hurried out to join his friends. Raul greeted him, "Alfonso, I can't thank you and these two enough for everything you've done so far. You found my poor servants' bodies and Inéz and José brought back this note, which indicates that my children are still alive. Listen," he said, and unfolding the ransom note, he read from it.

Trigales, Follow the enclosed instructions in every detail or you'll never see your children again.

1) *Fill the canvas bags you'll find in the carriage with a total of a thousand pesos.*

2) *Bring the pesos to me by noon Wednesday. Any later and one or more of your children will die.*

3) *The delivery point is just beyond the front edge of the Chupadera Mesa on the Old Apache Trail. Leave the four bags by the stone cairn in the middle of the trail.*

4) *Come by yourself, and don't try to follow me. Don't wait around. Instructions for how to find your children will be delivered later.*

If you fail to follow these instructions in every detail, the children will die. Failure to raise the full sum will also have consequences. If even one bag doesn't contain a full two hundred and fifty pesos, one child dies. Two not-full bags and two die. Three not completely full bags – the third dies. I'll let the fates decide who dies. Remember that card deck they used for their performance? They'll get to draw one of three cards that weren't used that night. Whoever draws 'Death' will have his or her throat slit on the spot. Whoever ends up with 'The Tower of Destruction' goes next. Whoever draws 'The Moon' will be the third to die. I reserve the right to keep the fourth child in bondage as my slave.

Inéz drew in her breath, horrified.

"The note is unsigned," Raul said.

Carlos asked, half to himself, "Leandro-Damián? Leandro under the influence of his bestial potion?" Raul looked at Carlos uncomprehendingly. "Never mind," Carlos told him. "The purpose of the ransom note is to ensure that you will move heaven and earth to come up with enough silver pesos to fill all four bags. Can you do that, Raul?"

"Two hundred and fifty pesos in each bag? I don't keep anything close to that much coin around, and there's hardly any time to raise the rest. Even if I leave for Santa Fe right now, which isn't really practical given that it's an overcast and moonless night, I'll have barely five days to raise the money and get to the drop-off point on the Old Apache Trail."

Carlos spoke up. "I'll get you started with a hundred and fifty pesos I have hidden at my place from my recent real estate dealings. That will fill more than half a bag. I'll tell you where to find them before you start back, but I agree that it's not practical to head off now. You need to stay here tonight and start at dawn tomorrow."

"I can contribute thirty pesos," Inéz announced, "and Elena can show you where I keep my little horde."

Don Carlos was astonished. "I thought you were a peso-less widow," he said.

"A woman has to have some money on hand if she needs to make a run for it, as I once thought I'd have to, and I've saved every peso I could since you drove my tormenter out of town."

"You're splendid friends," Raul said, "but you realize that you're not likely to get your money back. I can't ask you to make that great a sacrifice."

"Money's replaceable," Carlos told him. "Your children are not. Once word spreads about the situation, I'm sure you'll raise the full sum very quickly." Raul dismounted, thanked them profusely, and went to talk with the Olmedos about arranging for himself, his two men, and their horses to spend the night. As soon as those arrangements were made, José and Raul's men went off with the horses.

Inéz, Carlos, and Raul moved into the ranch's dining room to warm themselves by the fireplace. They briefly discussed what would come next, agreeing that Raul would ride back to Santa Fe alone, leaving his men and extra horses behind to rest. As soon as possible he would rejoin them at the Olmedos' and continue south approximately seventy more miles to rendezvous with Carlos and Inéz at another ranch that offered rooms and meals to travelers on the Camino Real. This was the Chavez hacienda, which was located east of the Rio Grande near a ford that was used to cross to Socorro, a largely abandoned town on the river's west bank. These details settled, Raul excused himself to rest up for an early start and another hard ride the next day.

Once they were alone again, Inéz, eyeing Don Carlos warily, said, "I notice you didn't volunteer to go back to Santa Fe. What scheme are you hatching for how we'll spend our time until Raul returns?"

"I have," Carlos began, "several things I'd like to accomplish. I want to go to the murder site to see what I can learn about who did this. I doubt that Leandro acted alone, and I'd like to know how many other killers are involved. Then I want to go south to the start of the Old Apache Trail and talk with some local hawks and owls regarding what, if anything, they know about the killers. Finally, I want to scout the delivery site — by air as a hawk or owl."

"And you're going to slay these monsters all on your own while Inéz waits, wringing her hands, for Carlos the White Knight to return here."

"You don't have to be sarcastic, Inéz. I don't see what direct role you can play in a process that requires me to disguise myself as this or that wild creature."

"I'll tell you exactly what you can do. You're the master of transformations, right?" He nodded. "Once we get to the Socorro area, you're going to transform me into an owl, a hawk, or whatever other animal form you're taking at that moment, and I'm coming along to keep you out of trouble."

"I don't like it on two grounds," Don Carlos objected. "For one thing, I don't have any experience transforming someone else into a spirit animal. I could do you harm."

"Stop right there! You once told me a very funny story about transforming your little sister into a mouse, and you brought her back to her human form without bad results."

"True. But I didn't know what I was doing, and I don't have enough experience with the process to be confident it'll always go well. And even if it does, I might to need to make a quick exit, and it would endanger both of us if I had to take the time to transform you as well as myself."

"I'm not ignoring your concerns, Carlos, but we'll never know how well or badly my proposal will work unless we try it. The first step, investigating the site of the murders, will be safe enough. Then we'll ride south together in order to have our horses and clothes along. Even the second step ought to go well, assuming I can communicate with hawks and owls once I'm in their form. That was really frustrating this morning when all I could do was ask you yes or no questions."

"I'm pretty sure you'll be able to talk with them once you're a hawk or owl. All right, I'm not going to argue. This will either work or it won't, and if it works, flying around with my best friend could be a lot of fun, as well as useful."

"You're on probation, so don't push your luck on the 'best-friend' front. How do we get started?"

"Our first need is to get some rest," Carlos replied, "and this is a good place to do so. Mauricio told me that he has plenty of room for us, so let's settle in, have a big meal and a good night's sleep, and start off fresh at dawn tomorrow."

José, who had found them in the dining room and joined them next to the fireplace, had been listening intently to the exchange between Carlos and Inéz. "If I'm following you correctly," he began, "as a brujo Don Alfonso, or Carlos if you prefer, can transform himself and others into birds of prey and fly long distances."

"Yes," Inéz said.

"Then I'll make one last check to see how the horses are settling in and join you later for dinner."

As José went off toward the stable, Carlos turned to Inéz and said, "Notice that José accepted our plan without raising a lot of questions."

Inéz got his point immediately. "Yes," she replied with a nod. "An apprentice medicine man doesn't find it strange that a brujo can transform himself into an owl or a hawk and fly around."

Some two hours later, after an ample meal in the company of José,

Raul Trigales, and his two hired hands, Carlos and Inéz excused themselves in order to rest and make an early start the next day. Somewhat tentatively Carlos asked Inéz if it was all right with her if they shared a room. She replied firmly, "That's exactly what we'll do, because I have no intention of letting you out of my sight." With that detail settled, they went to their room, took off their boots, and climbed fully clothed into bed.

Once they were settled, Carlos raised a topic that had been on his mind for some time. "I've been thinking," he said, "about your experience with Toho. Can you tell me what led him to say that you're a bruja?"

"I don't know," Inéz replied. "He didn't give any explanation. My best guess is that he thought I had some talent as a healer."

"Didn't you say that, when you were running to my burning stable, you had a fleeting memory of being a Basque man named Iñigo running toward your burning village?"

"My impression is that I was a village leader with that name in some past life, and that all rural Basque men in that era were brujos."

"But Toho," Carlos pointed out, "said you were a bruja here and now, and I'm living proof that you're a healer in the present. I feel as though I owe my life, this life, to you."

"I thank God that you survived, but I think Toho had more to do with it than I did. I just wanted, with all my heart, for you to live." She was silent for a long moment, "It's strange," she continued. "When I go back in my mind to that time with you and Toho, I feel such tenderness for you. But when you are clearly well—like now, your old self again—I find I'm still irritated with you for having betrayed me with your closeness to Mara."

"I guess there's no way," Carlos complained, "that I can convince you that my being wrapped up in a blanket with Mara with my feet in a tub was innocent."

"Hmpf!" Inéz snorted. "You have a history of romancing women in tubs!"

"The only part of me that was in a tub was my feet! Besides, those stories are out of my past, not my present."

Inéz shrugged. "Men are no more monogamous than a stallion in a herd of mares. You're a virile man with a strong erotic drive. I shouldn't have expected anything different from you."

"I can see that my protests of innocence aren't much use. I hope where words don't suffice my future actions will. I've always been a man of action anyway."

"Yes," Inéz agreed. "For as long as I've known you, you've always been impulsive rather than reflective. That's a major difference between us. You've had the power to gain what you wanted through actions and never needed to be introspective. Lacking power for most of my life, I've had to do a lot of soul-searching."

"Allow me," Carlos replied, "to say in my defense that for nearly a year now I've been trying to do the same, even though I'm not inclined toward introspection. But I'm not unaware of my emotions, and I've also experienced what it's like to be betrayed. The night before the fire, I had a very revealing talk with Leandro in which he told me many intimate details about the life of his master, Don Malvolio. It gave me, if not sympathy for Malvolio, some understanding of the reasons for his resentment and bitterness. And Leandro's openness, and my feeling of understanding, created a bond between us, or so it seemed to me. Then came the fire, which Leandro almost certainly set, followed by news of his having attempted to kill Mara and Selena, and finally the revelation that he has betrayed the Trigales's trust in him. The more I've thought about these multiple betrayals, the angrier I've become."

Inéz was quiet for a few moments, and Carlos sensed her mood had changed. "I can see," she said at last, "that my harboring anger and resentment toward you is not a good thing. As for Leandro, what he's done is done, and you, Mara, and Selena are all still alive. What's important now is to save the children. And toward that end we need to be well rested. Let's get as much sleep as we can tonight."

Carlos was surprised at this sudden about-face in her attitude. "Yes," he agreed. "You're right about needing to rest. The only problem is I'm rather stirred up."

"So you, too, have emotions," she observed with a smile. "But I'm sure you'll go to sleep the minute your head hits the pillow, and I'm the one who will lie awake for hours."

"Sorry," he said. "I've always been able to fall asleep easily."

"You're very fortunate. And now you really must go to sleep."

As Inéz had predicted, Carlos fell asleep almost as soon as he closed his eyes. She tossed and turned until midnight.

24

Monsters

*S*hortly after dawn, Carlos, Inéz, and José shared a light meal of leftovers they'd saved from the previous night's dinner and then slipped out the side door of the main ranch house and walked to the stable. They retrieved their horses and loaded a few supplies—blankets, food, and water—that they'd bought from Mauricio Olmedo for their journey south on the Camino Real to the Chavez hacienda. They had with them an extra horse Raul's ranch hands had loaned them to serve as a pack animal.

After a little more than an hour's ride they reached their first destination, the site of the abandoned carriage and the bodies of the servants. Circling vultures marked the place. The smell of death grew heavy in the air as they left the road and approached the killing site, and their horses tossed their heads nervously. Don Carlos drew to a halt near a small clump of pines. "We'll tether the horses here," he said, "and walk the rest of the way to the carriage. Keep your eyes open as we go—I don't know what we're looking for. Footprints, certainly. But also something that might tell us more about what happened."

Their horses safely tethered, they walked carefully toward the carriage. The marks of the carriage wheels and the horses' hoofprints were plainly visible in the mashed-down dry grass. When they reached the carriage they walked around it, studying the ground. Each of them scouted in ever-widening circles as the vultures, disturbed from their feeding by the arrival of the humans, circled warily overhead. Flattened and scuffed places in the grass indicated that several people had done a good deal of moving around, but beyond that told no story. Don Carlos's brujo vision could not pick up, three days after the fact, any readable personal auras, only the indistinct vibration of terror. It was not a pleasant place to be.

Finally Carlos decided that if there were personal auras strong enough to remain anywhere it would be right next to the servants' bodies. Taking out his large handkerchief, he tied it over his nose to reduce the smell and strode purposefully over to the place where the two bodies lay. Their clothing was torn and there was not a lot left of them. Moreover, Carlos thought, the bodies looked as if they had been moved around somewhat. He didn't think the vultures were strong enough to have moved an entire body, so it had to have been the killers. Studying the dark areas of the bloodstained grass and dirt, Carlos saw what was clearly a footprint—a very big footprint—and then, a little distance away, two more big footprints that suggested a large man standing with his feet spread wide apart. Carlos's suspicions were confirmed: Ogres, he said to himself.

Carlos called Inéz and José. They came toward him, Inéz eyeing the bodies and walking rather tentatively, Carlos thought. "Look here," he said, pointing at the ground. "Look at the size of these prints!" He glanced up and saw that, having made a connection with the footprints, he could make out a faint bloodstained trail between where he stood and the road. He followed the trail fifty yards to the point at which the footprints joined the road, perhaps a hundred yards south of the place where the carriage had been left. Inéz and José, wordless, came along behind him.

"Ogres," he announced. "Two for certain, possibly three or four. Do you know anything about ogres?"

"No," said José.

"Monsters by another name. Large and powerful, grotesquely ugly, and violent—said to specialize in killing and eating people. I suspected ogres the moment I saw that the servants' bodies had been moved around and mutilated. More so than the vultures could have done."

Inéz shuddered. "That's more than I need to know. But how did they carry off the children? What role did Leandro play? The itinerant trader José met said Leandro was on horseback—are we dealing with Leandro on horseback or a monster Leandro-Damián?"

"I can't tell," Carlos replied. "But from what Xenome told José, I suspect there are four ogres plus Leandro-Damián."

"How did Xenome know?"

"He had a vision of four monsters headed in this direction, accompanied by a dark figure I suspect may be Don Malvolio."

Inéz digested this in silence. Finally she said, "So we are headed off in pursuit of four monsters, each of whom may or may not be carrying, in broad daylight, a terrified child tucked under one arm, and led by Leandro-Damián, possibly riding a horse. I'm sorry, but this is too much even for my credulity."

Carlos took Inéz by the arm and began to steer her back toward where they had left their horses. "Dear Inéz," he said gently. "All we know for certain is that the servants were murdered, the children are gone, Leandro is gone too, and there is a ransom note telling Raul to deliver four bags filled with pesos to Chupadera Mesa, more than a hundred miles south of here. We also know that Leandro has some way to increase his size and strength and that he is capable of horrible things. He and the other monsters may indeed be able to carry a child under one arm and to move at a fast pace for very long distances."

They had reached their tethered horses, and he stopped. "I want to get to Chupadera Mesa before Raul does and scout the situation. Although it's a very long ride to the Chavez hacienda, if we push the pace we ought to be able to reach it by nightfall. And if we can get there before dark, I'd like to continue on another three miles to spend at least one night with a rancher, Hernán Alvaros, who lives near the Camino Real south of the Chavez place. Hernán owes me a favor and will put us up. Unlike the Chavez hacienda, which rents rooms to travelers, his ranch is a private place, and for what we're going to be doing, the more privacy the better. After resting there tonight, we can pursue the part of my plan that involves talking with hawks and owls along the Old Apache Trail tomorrow. And if you're worried about us catching up with Leandro and the ogres, that's not going to happen. They have a full two-day lead on us, and we don't want to catch up with them even if we could. We wouldn't want to alert them to how quickly we've gotten on their trail."

"You're being uncharacteristically prudent," Inéz observed. He sensed she doubted that he was being entirely truthful.

"I'm not worried about us," Carlos told her. "The crucial thing is to avoid doing anything that puts the Trigales children in danger."

Carlos, Inéz, and José rode along in silence, each lost in thought. For Don Carlos, simply being in open country near the Rio Grande nourished him. He drank in the sight of the river, the valley, and the mountains visible both to the east and the west. Even in winter some birds moved through the brush and deer grazed on the stubbly grass in an occasional meadow. Life was everywhere, and he responded to the countryside through the restorative effect it had on his body.

Shortly before noon they reached Las Nutrias, one of the *paradas* (rest stops) used by travelers on the Camino Real. Don Carlos signaled that it was time to take a break and have something to eat. Although there were many signs that the site had been used recently by other individuals and parties, on this day Carlos, Inéz, and José had it to themselves. After watering their horses they sat down behind several large rocks, using them as shelter against the cold wind. José passed out bread, cheese, and dried apricots from their supplies. Clearly something was on his mind. "What can you tell us about ogres?" he asked Carlos. "I've never heard of such creatures before."

"I don't know much," Carlos admitted. "I've never seen one, in case you're wondering."

"Are they natural creatures, or black entities from the spirit world?"

"I wouldn't call them natural," Carlos replied. "This is only a guess, but I would speculate that they are the result of a crude transformation somewhat like the one that Leandro uses to change himself into Damián. A normal human being ingests a drink that causes radical shifts in his or her body. The concoction Damián drinks produces only temporary changes. He soon returns to his ordinary form. Perhaps a highly skilled sorcerer, a magician like Don Malvolio, has discovered a more potent formula that can change humans permanently into monsters who become larger, stronger, and, to our eyes, grotesque and ugly."

"These ogres," José ventured, "seem to be very violent."

"Yes," Carlos said. "Leandro admitted that even the mild concoction he drank had a side effect of stimulating violent urges. Xenome suggested — I'm using some of the same words he did — that doing violence to one's body prompts an angry response, a willingness, even a desire, to do violence. If a sorcerer could first create such creatures and then direct them to do his will, ogres would be a powerful weapon to use for whatever ends he wished."

"Carlos," Inéz announced, "this talk is making me extremely nervous. You have great powers at your command, and you're inclined to use them. Despite what you said earlier, I'm afraid you're planning to attack these gigantic monsters. That prospect scares me."

"I can't see how my fighting them would achieve our principal goal, which is to rescue the Trigales children."

"That's one of your Jesuitical answers. I've learned to spot them. You suggest that it wouldn't be helpful for you to fight these monsters, but you don't say that you won't."

"Inéz!" he protested. "I have many brujo powers, but foreknowledge isn't one of them. I don't know what will be necessary to rescue the Trigales children. Hopefully, Raul pays the ransom, the children are returned safely, and that ends this terrible situation."

Inéz eyed him skeptically, but she didn't pursue the matter further. "Shouldn't we get going again?" she asked, and the three of them mounted their horses and rode on.

Carlos was glad that Inéz hadn't pushed him on certain details of their plan. He had been completely truthful with her in saying his only goal at present was the safe return of the Trigales children to their parents. Battling a sorcerer or ogres was of no importance to him. But he had been concerned by the fourth point of the ransom note, which ended with words: *"Don't wait around. Instructions for how to find your children will be delivered later."* Carlos feared that no such instructions would be forthcoming. If that fear proved true, it might mean that the children were no longer alive.

It was past sunset when Carlos, Inéz, and José, weary from a very long day in the saddle, arrived at the main house of the Alvaros ranch. Carlos dismounted and knocked. A female servant came to the door, and Carlos told her he hoped to speak with the master of the house. She showed them to a dining room where Hernán was eating dinner alone. He looked up in surprise and asked, "Don Alfonso, what brings you here?" and immediately added, "That didn't sound as friendly as it should. I'm glad to see you. Will you and your friends join me for dinner? I hope so. I live alone since my wife died and have plenty of bedrooms, if you want to stay overnight."

Happy to accept the old rancher's hospitality, Carlos introduced Inéz and José, and they sat down to dinner with him. By way of explaining why they'd shown up on his doorstep in need of a place to stay for the night, they told Hernán about the kidnapping and their pursuit of Leandro and his confederates.

"When would the kidnappers have passed through here?" he inquired.

"We don't know for sure," Carlos admitted. "It could have been any time from late Thursday night to early this morning, depending on how fast they were moving."

"Come to think of it," Hernán said, "an odd thing happened night before last, an hour or two after sunset. All the horses in the barn became very nervous. My vaqueros and I thought a predator, a cougar or a wolf, might be prowling around. But in the morning we didn't find any tracks." Although Don Carlos said nothing, he was sure that ogres passing near the ranch on the Camino Real had frightened the horses.

After dinner, Carlos and Inéz went to their room and got in bed. Inéz again kept her clothes on, but just before he fell asleep, Carlos put his arm around her waist and she didn't push him away. An hour later, he was roused from sleep by Inéz shaking his shoulder and saying, "Carlos, please wake up."

She was sitting up in bed, leaning toward him on one arm, shaking him with the other. Instantly alert and concerned, he asked, "What's the matter?"

"Every time I start to fall asleep, I keep seeing that poor man and woman, Raul's servants, their throats slit—."

Carlos sat up and put his arm around her shoulders. He said, "It was a gruesome scene."

"Yes, they were three days dead and that was horrible to look at, but what I'm seeing is worse. My mind is showing me them alive and terrified and someone holding them and slitting their throats to kill them. Carlos," she cried. "How can a human being do such a thing? You said these ogres were human once. They didn't have to kill the servants; they could have held them all for ransom. You said they are ugly and desire to do violence. It's more like they're cursed. And Malvolio? Is he the one who laid a curse on them? And turned poor Leandro into at least half a monster? Oh, Carlos. I don't know where these questions are taking me. You know I'm not a good Catholic. I'm angry at God for the mess the world is—for the cruelty and suffering that people inflict on each other. How can God allow children to be kidnapped and terrified and probably killed?"

"Sweetheart, sweetheart," Carlos replied. "I don't have an answer to your question, and I can't think of anything my Jesuit tutors taught me that would help. But then I'm more a story-teller than a philosopher, so let me tell you a story about myself.

"Even before I became Don Serafino's apprentice, I had it pretty easy in life. I was a Chibcha high priest's only son, raised in privilege by loving women, a mother and an aunt. Then Don Serafino took me under his wing and instructed me in brujo techniques. I acquired knowledge and power that protected me against many of the ills that afflict most men, including fear of death. I was born in all my lives on the summer solstice, and I always had a sunny disposition and a life filled with light.

"What I'm going to say next may seem off the topic at first, but bear with me. Late in my fourth life as a brujo, I had everything I wanted, but I was beset by a nagging dissatisfaction with things and couldn't identity why that was so. A Gypsy fortune teller came to the port city where I was living, and I decided to consult her. I didn't have great expectations regarding what might come of talking with her, and for that reason I suppose I wasn't taking our session too seriously. But she sensed that I was distancing myself from her. 'I can see,' she said, 'that you're special in some way. If you want the clearest reading of your situation, you must tell me how you're different. If you don't do so, we're wasting time.'

"Her words gave me a jolt, and I told her, as I'd never told anyone else, that I had the capacity to maintain consciousness of my deep self through death into a subsequent life. To my surprise, she didn't scoff.

"What she told me was this. 'You are a very fortunate man. Everything, including the preservation of your consciousness through death, comes easily for you. But your greatest gift is your ability to see the beauty and goodness of the world. Since this is so clear to you, you can't comprehend why almost no one else shares your perspective, why most people, most of the time, are seemingly unaware of how magnificent the world is and cause misery for themselves and others by pursuing wealth and power. This is a source of great distress to you. Your response, one could even call it your deepest flaw, is to retreat into your own world, the pleasures of which are readily available to you because of your special gifts and training.'"

"Didn't she tell you what to do?" Inéz asked with great seriousness.

"I asked, but she didn't offer any advice. All she said was that any answers would have to come from within me. I confess that afterward I essentially returned to my usual way of living, distancing myself from most of the world's troubles by using my brujo powers to pursue pleasure. But my encounter with Zoila led me to see that my penchant for pleasure-seeking caused me to squander my greatest gift, seeing the unity and wonder of all creation.

"Dearest Inéz, you've recently talked about how different our lives have been. You've been repeatedly betrayed and unable to protect yourself against cruel treatment. I've had an easy life, with a lot of pleasant experiences and very little pain. Yet I'm struck by the fact that although you and I come at the problem of human cruelty and human misery from very different directions—you from experiencing suffering, me from distress at seeing how people callously inflict suffering on others—we nevertheless end up having to face the same question: how to live in a world where these things exist and are realities we have to deal with."

Inéz sighed. They both lay down again. "Thank you for listening to me and responding so frankly," she said, snuggling into his arms. She soon fell asleep. She didn't wake up until it was time to put their boots on and go to breakfast.

During breakfast, Carlos asked Hernán if he and his friends could use a small shed that he remembered seeing on the property the last time he'd stayed with him. Hernán shot a questioning look at Carlos, but agreed immediately. "When I was here last year," Carlos explained, "I noticed several red-tailed hawks in the trees beyond the shed. My friends and I would like to see if we can attract them to the shed. It's tricky work and requires us not to show ourselves for hours at a time. We'll need you to warn your vaqueros to give the shed a wide berth until we're done. If that's too disruptive to your usual ranch routines, we can pursue our project elsewhere."

Hernán declared that he didn't mind at all. During winter, he and his hands rarely went near the shed. He had one request that reflected a characteristic Carlos had often observed among many country people— curiosity about the details of even the smallest unusual events in their surroundings. "Will it be all right," Hernán asked, "if I keep an eye on the shed from the back windows of my house? I'd like to see if you can lure those hawks to you." Carlos told him that would be no problem.

Carlos, with Inéz and José following behind him, walked through the field to the shed and entered. It was just as Carlos remembered it. There was a wide door on the side of the shed toward Hernán's house and a small window in the shed's opposite wall that faced the trees and the river beyond. "What are you up to?" Inéz asked.

"I've been thinking," Carlos replied, "about the problem of clothing and transformations. José, you didn't know this, but if I don't take off all my clothes beforehand, I end up as a hawk struggling to get free of a man's shirt, pants, and boots.

"Leaving my clothes behind isn't a problem if I'm returning to my starting point. But if I'm going from one place as a hawk and returning to human form at another, I'll end up arriving at the second place stark naked. So what to do? Long ago, my teacher Don Serafino told me that it was possible to transform a large object into a smaller one. You probably wondered why I brought an extra shirt and pants along with me this morning. What I want to do is to try to change the extra shirt and pants into something small, preferably a piece of cloth or rope that Carlos the hawk could carry in his beak or his talons. Or someone could tie it around his leg before he took off. Once I arrived at my destination in hawk form, I could loosen the band with my beak. That still leaves a small problem of how to reverse the process for a return trip. I don't think hawks are very good at tying something around their legs. The return trip would require me to carry my clothes in my beak or talons. What I propose to do, with you two helping, is to spend the morning experimenting with what, if anything, works well."

Don Carlos first put his extra clothes on the shed's floor. He had never learned the technique for transforming inanimate objects, and he wasn't sure he could come up with a way to do so now. His worries seemed borne out when for the next half hour he tried without success to effect the transformation of his clothes into a compact cord or a single small piece of cloth. Frustrated, he picked up the extra clothes and threw them down, exclaiming, "Moses in the Old Testament was able to change his staff into a snake, but look at that—no rope and no snake either."

"Moses had God on his side," Inéz observed with a wry grin.

"You're a big help," Carlos laughed, and his mood lifted.

"Couldn't you," José suggested, "do as brujas and witches do, and change objects using spells and incantations?"

"My mentor, Don Serafino, always scorned that as an inferior type of magic."

"Carlos," Inéz said, "this is no time to let pride get in your way. If you know anything about spells and incantations, why not give them a try?"

She was right, of course, Carlos thought to himself. In fact, he observed, there was something in Inéz that led her to insights that he, for all his brujo powers, missed. But it wasn't a time to explore that perception; there was work that needed doing.

From one of his earlier lives, Don Carlos pulled up a memory of confronting a witch, a bruja whose specialty was laying spells and curses on neighbors who had annoyed her. He recalled that this bruja had taken revenge on a neighbor's daughter by changing the girl's treasured necklace into a pile of cow dung. The magic this involved—transforming one inanimate object into another inanimate object—was basically what he needed. He had been a witness to the incident and had overheard the incantation that she'd used. It took him fully ten minutes to come up with the words of the spell, but he finally succeeded. Staring at his clothes on the ground, he held in his mind the image of the string he hoped they would become and, with a decisive movement of his arm toward the clothes, he pronounced the bruja's incantation. To his surprise, it worked. There, instead of a shirt and pants, lay a short, thin piece of rope.

José's eyes widened and his face broke into a smile. Inéz exclaimed, "You did it! You're amazing!" Immediately, she added, "But don't let that go to your head."

"Time for part two of our adventures in Hernán's shed," he said. "Inéz, are you ready to let me try to transform you into a red-tailed hawk?" She nodded her assent. "Then José and I will turn our backs while you take off your clothes."

"I am not taking off my clothes," she objected. "I don't fancy standing around naked in an ice-cold shed while you try to transform me. If you succeed in changing me into a hawk, the two of you can disentangle me from my clothes, which, as you say, will be piled all around me."

Don Carlos sighed. "You're right, Inéz, as always, or at least almost always." She raised an eyebrow at 'almost always,' so he hastened to get started. "It might help," he suggested, "if all three of us listened to the cries being made by the hawks flying over the field. Inéz, let them penetrate deeply into your bones and sinews. Once you're a hawk, simply do as I do."

The three of them fell silent. Don Carlos didn't see any reason to rush. He looked out the back window of the shed at the nearby field and the trees beyond. He called to mind everything he knew about red-tailed hawks, both from having watched them closely and from having been one. Several times he heard the hunting calls of hawks that were circling above the field. Each call sent a jolt of subtle energy through his mind and body. His brujo awareness reached such a high level of attunement that he thought he could feel the air rushing past the wings of the circling hawks. The moment, he knew, was right. He envisioned Inéz in hawk form. He turned and was thrilled to see a handsome female red-tailed hawk peeping out of the pile of clothes that had fallen around her. She was, as was true of female hawks, larger than Carlos would be when he transformed himself into a male hawk.

José stepped forward and pulled away the clothes that were draped around Inéz's hawk form. Don Carlos then turned his back to José and Inéz and quickly undressed. Perhaps he didn't need to be so discreet about being naked in their presence, but he didn't want to embarrass anyone. Once he was naked, he again fell silent and stood motionless looking out the shed's back window. On hearing a hawk's cry in the distance, he effected an easy transition to hawk form. As always, he experienced a fleeting disorientation by virtue of having lost a full five feet of stature.

He walked toward the window, lifted his wings, and easily flew up to the windowsill and perched there. He looked back into the shed and saw that Inéz had started after him. She began to beat her wings in an attempt to join him on his perch, but she fell short and tumbled back into the shed. José stepped forward to help and picked her up and placed her next to Don Carlos.

It was time to fly. Don Carlos launched himself with several strong strokes of his wings. He went only a short distance before turning back to see how Inéz was doing. Pretty well for a beginner, he thought. Her flight was wobbly, and initially she didn't attempt anything except to fly in a straight line. Soon, however, she began to fly in wide circles and gained altitude. She seemed to be enjoying herself. He caught up with her and called, "Can you hear me?"

She replied, "Yes, this is absolutely thrilling."

"Let's continue to circle the field until you're entirely secure in flight. When you're ready, set a course to the west over the trees and the river. Once we're on the west side of the river, let's fly to that cliff we can see in the distance. If we're lucky, we'll be able to ride the updrafts, allowing rising air currents rather than our own efforts to lift us."

For the next hour, the two hawks played exuberantly in the realm of flight. He enjoyed every moment of it. The cottonwood trees' winter-bare limbs, the wide river a bright gray mirror of the overcast sky, the imposing front of the mountain's east-facing slope—it was all splendid. But nothing could be compared to the exhilarating feeling of riding updrafts above the highest nearby cliff. With great reluctance he finally called to Inéz that they'd better start back before they grew too tired. Her reply, "I hope we can come again," told him all he needed to know.

Having attained a fairly high altitude above the top of the cliff, they were able to coast most of the way back to the shed, scarcely needing to use their wings. Their initial approach was so rapid that Don Carlos feared it was too fast, and he called to Inéz to make a broad circle to slow her flight. She followed his directions, but when she dove in the shed's window she made a crash landing that pitched her over onto her beak. We need to practice landing, Don Carlos observed.

He turned his back to José and the hawk Inéz, changed back into his human form, and dressed quickly. At the very last minute a problem had occurred to him that left him in a state of near panic. Would he be able to return Inéz to human form? Imagining a hawk had helped to transform her into a hawk form, but she'd been helping by listening to hawk calls in the distance. Would an image of the Inéz he loved be sufficient to reverse the process? He set out to try.

"Oh, no!" she gasped from behind him. "Only half way!"

He turned and saw that 'half way' described her condition. She was still a hawk in size, but in a magnificent confusion of woman and hawk, her head and arms were those of his beloved Inéz, while her torso and legs were those of a fully feathered hawk. A vision of a mythical beast embodied stood before him, glorious in an exotic way, but her eyes pleaded with him not to leave her in that state.

He turned his back, closed his eyes, and concentrated again on Inéz.

After what seemed like a frighteningly long interval, though it was probably no more than a minute, Inéz spoke. "Keep your back turned while I get dressed. Don't you dare peek." Soon she announced that he could look. He did so and was relieved to see that she looked unharmed, and possibly had a special glow in her eyes.

"Why did you have trouble reversing the transformation?" Inéz asked.

"Nothing special," he replied. "I simply don't have any experience along those lines."

"What aren't you telling me?" she said. "I can always tell when you're leaving out some important detail."

"If you must know," he told her, not believing she would approve — this honesty business could be messy — "I was wondering if, in order to restore your body to its exact human form, I needed to have a clear image of what you look like unclothed, and I've never had that privilege."

"Oh," she said, and changed the subject to how wonderful flying had been, repeating what she had said before: "I hope we can do that again soon."

"Tonight we'll rest, but tomorrow I suggest that we fly down the Camino Real to where the Old Apache Trail cuts off to the east toward the Chupadera Mesa. We'll follow the trail a few miles and then ask some of our red-tailed hawk brothers and sisters whether they saw the ogres pass through earlier this week carrying the Trigales kids."

Carlos, Inéz, and José spent the early evening talking with Hernán Alvaros. The old rancher reported excitedly that he'd seen two red-tailed hawks fly into his back pasture shed. "How did you manage to get them to do that?" he asked.

Carlos, having foreseen that this question might arise, had asked José whether his training to be a medicine man included imitating the calls of various animals. José had replied by demonstrating a variety of animal calls, one of which was the red-tailed hawk's. In answer to Hernán's inquiry, Carlos said, "José called them to us," whereupon José smiled and gave a very convincing example of the red-tail's rasping 'kkeeerrrr.'

Before going to bed, Carlos, Inéz, and José agreed on a plan for the next day. "I don't think Raul Trigales will reach our rendezvous site at the Chavez hacienda tomorrow. It will only be Monday, and he'll have had to return to Santa Fe, gather the ransom money, and ride here as fast as he can. Nevertheless, we want at least one of us to be waiting for him at the Chavez hacienda. José can ride over there tomorrow morning, rent rooms for us, and keep an eye on the road for Raul. Meanwhile, Inéz and I will conduct our reconnaissance of the Old Apache Trail."

Monday morning José left early for the Chavez hacienda and Carlos and Inéz walked to the shed in the rear pasture of Hernán's ranch. Without wasting any time on trying to condense their clothing—unnecessary because they were making a round trip from the shed and back to it—Don Carlos changed Inéz into a hawk. The transformation went easily, and Carlos helped the hawk step out of Inéz's clothes. He wondered whether he was getting better at it, or whether her human form was looser from having assumed a hawk form the previous day. He then stripped, changed himself into a hawk, and led the way out the shed's window.

They coasted south above the Camino Real until they turned southeast above the Old Apache Trail. It wasn't long before they located a male hawk, whose name they later learned was Salvino. Salvino was taking an after-breakfast nap on a tree branch. Don Carlos and Inéz landed as lightly as they could on the branch, and Carlos struck up a conversation.

"Good morning, sir," Don Carlos offered.

"It was a good morning—good breakfast, good sunny day, and a good roost—until you two came along. I was enjoying a nice nap, as you surely could see."

"We're sorry to intrude," Don Carlos replied, "but several very large and ugly wingless two-leggeds have killed two human friends of ours and stolen their young. We believe the killers came this way two or three days ago. Did you, perhaps, see anything that might fit this description?"

"I did. I'd just caught a juicy rabbit right next to the trail and was about to eat it when the ground began to tremble. I thought it might be an earthquake, but I soon learned otherwise. Coming down the trail were five two-leggeds. Four of them were huge; they were dressed like mestizos and they had large, ugly faces and extremely long arms and legs, and they were loping along at a pace faster than a wild horse's gallop. The fifth, who was a Spaniard dressed in black and not as big and ugly, kept up with their pace. I didn't like the looks of them, so I flew off, and one of them scooped up my fat rabbit and gulped it down without chewing. Made me mad!"

"Were they carrying anything?"

"The four bigger ones all had heavy black sacks slung across their backs."

"Could those sacks have contained a human child?"

"I suppose so. Now I've told you a lot. Is this pretty female your mate or a short-term hunting companion?" Addressing Inéz, he said, "It's too early in the year for mating, but why don't you come back a month from now? Ask for Salvino."

It looked to Don Carlos as though Inéz had a hard time not letting on how funny she thought it was to be propositioned by a hawk, but she politely replied, "Although I live far north of here, I'll certainly keep you in mind when mating season rolls around."

After a little small talk about the weather, Don Carlos and Inéz took off. She asked, "What next? I hope you're not going to pursue these monsters."

"Definitely not. I think we should go back to Hernán's place, thank our host for his hospitality, and ride over to the Chavez hacienda to get a lot of nourishment and sleep. Part three of my plan, checking out the ransom delivery site, ought to be done at night in owl form. That will eliminate the possibility that we'll be spotted as anything other than a couple of owls out hunting."

Inéz agreed readily. "I didn't even notice that I was hungry until Salvino started talking about that rabbit, and suddenly I was overcome with a desire to have some fresh rabbit."

"I think," Don Carlos said, "you're taking your hawk-form a step too far." They shared a laugh about hawk diets. Once again, there was a "halfway" moment when Don Carlos attempted to return Inéz to human form. Eventually, he managed to do so, and the rest of the day went smoothly.

25

Evil

*N*ight came, and Carlos, Inéz, and José dined at a conventional hour, well after eight o'clock. As they were finishing their meal, Inéz gave Carlos a searching look and asked, "I've never known you to be so relaxed when there's a potentially dangerous task ahead. Are you feeling all right?"

"I'm in excellent spirits," he replied. "My brujo powers have been greatly strengthened by our flights, and I was particularly pleased," he added with a smile, "when you brushed aside Salvino's attempt to proposition you. As for our relatively leisurely pace, there's nothing much we can accomplish right away. Tonight, leaving around midnight, we'll make an aerial reconnaissance along the Old Apache Trail. Tomorrow's Tuesday and I'm assuming that Raul will arrive. By Wednesday, the ransom-delivery day, we'll have a better idea where things stand and, I hope, a good plan for rescuing the Trigales children."

"You used the word rescue," Inéz observed. "Do you think we'll have to fight with the ogres to free the children?"

"I doubt it," Carlos said. "They'll have no reason to keep them captive once Raul pays the ransom."

"What do you make of what Salvino said, that the ogres were accompanied by a Spaniard in black?"

"It must have been Leandro-Damián in an advanced form of transformation that's given him the capacity to keep up with the ogres," Carlos replied. "We'll see if we can learn anything more tonight by following the Old Apache Trail to the ransom drop-off point."

Members of the Chavez family who owned the hacienda and inn had gone out of their way to show sympathy once they heard about the kidnapping of the Trigales children, and they were entirely supportive when Carlos told Renaldo Chavez, the hacienda's owner, that he and Inéz were going out at midnight and might not be back until close to sunrise. Carlos sensed that Chavez wanted to know more. But he was too polite to pry and Carlos didn't volunteer anything else.

Carlos and Inéz rested until midnight and then crept out to the hacienda's little-used barn. "Night is the time to enter the owl's world," Don Carlos whispered.

Inéz nodded her assent and simply said, "I'm ready."

He chose to transform her into a barn owl, a largish owl with white undersides and an oval face that had a ghostly appearance. He helped the owl step out of Inéz's clothes, then undressed quickly and transformed himself. The open barn doors made their exit easy, and they flew off together. Inéz seemed to be in good control of flight from the very first.

They took a southward course above the Camino Real until they reached the cutoff for the Old Apache Trail. Their destination, the Chupadera Mesa, was slightly more than thirty miles to the east, and its mass soon began to loom into view ahead. The trail continued beneath it, skirting its western edge. Don Carlos had told Inéz that he believed some or all of the kidnappers would be watching the drop-off point and would react violently if they thought they were under surveillance. "Once we draw near the mesa," he told Inéz, "our best bet is to fly a little distance from the side of the trail, maintaining total silence between us. The moment we see the drop-off spot, we'll land where we can see the cairn but, hopefully, not be seen. Possibly the watchers will be asleep, but I can't be sure because I have no knowledge of the nocturnal habits of ogres."

The drop-off location proved easy to find. It was barely a quarter of a mile past the beginning of the mesa, at a point where the trail went up and down over the mesa's fingerlike edges. The cairn was at the bottom of one of the trail's downhill sections. There were many hiding places from which watchers could view the scene. Don Carlos and Inéz landed in a patch of brush on the slope above the trail, a vantage point from which they could see a cairn below — a pile of stones in the middle of the trail — and Leandro resting nearby.

Don Carlos used his sorcerer's vision to scan the area. No ogres were in sight; no Trigales children either. Carlos concluded that the ogres had taken the children farther south on the trail. To check his theory, he motioned with his head — he didn't want to risk any spoken message, even in owl form — that he wanted to follow the Old Apache Trail a bit farther. They lifted off from their hiding spot almost simultaneously. A half hour later, Carlos dropped to the ground in the middle of the trail, followed closely by Inéz. "Is it safe to speak?" she asked.

"I don't see why not," he replied. "There's no sign of ogres in the vicinity, though you can see here" — pointing to some huge footprints in the middle of the trail — "that they've passed this way."

"With the Trigales kids?" she inquired, clearly apprehensive.

"I can't tell, though the ogres were carrying them earlier, according to what your hawk friend told us."

Ignoring Don Carlos's reference to Salvino, Inéz declared, "I don't like this one bit. Why take the children so far from the drop-off point?"

"Who knows?" Don Carlos replied. "But one reason might be that by hiding the children a long way from the drop-off point, the kidnappers will be able to put a lot of distance between themselves and Raul while he is trying to find the place where his children are hidden."

Inéz still sounded worried. "And I suppose you'll try to follow the ogres and recover the ransom money?"

"I don't believe we'll be able to follow the ogres or recover the ransom money," he said. "Our highest priority is rescuing the children, and the ogres will almost certainly be long gone by the time we manage that. Right now I think we've learned all we can. Let's head back to the Chavez hacienda and get some sleep while we wait for Raul to arrive."

They reached their destination shortly before daybreak. Don Carlos had been puzzled by his previous failures to change Inéz from a bird form back to a human on the first try. Pondering the problem, he realized that he'd always achieved the same type of transformation on himself without needing to analyze how he did it. It just seemed to come naturally. The key, he concluded, might be simultaneously having a clear sense of who Inéz was, both her interior and her exterior being. He decided he might achieve that by concentrating on his own wordless inner sense of who she was, on his deepest knowledge of her.

Immediately, he heard rustling sounds behind him; then Inéz announced, "I'm dressed. Whatever you did this time, you got me back to my human form without a hitch."

He turned and was relieved to see her as herself. He took her arm. They walked to the main house and shared breakfast with three ranch hands who were about to start their daily chores. Their plates clean—apparently flying around all night in owl form stimulated one's appetite—they excused themselves, explaining that they needed some sleep because they'd been up practically all night. This comment elicited inquisitive looks from the vaqueros, but they refrained from asking what Carlos and Inéz had been up to. As he and Inéz settled back in bed to sleep—he in a shirt and trousers, she in a woolen nightshirt she'd borrowed from Señora Chavez—Don Carlos remarked, "Our irregular hours are certainly giving the locals plenty of cause for speculation."

Carlos slept deeply until noon. When he woke up, he glanced at Inéz, who was still asleep, and reflected on how enjoyable it was to have a mate, even a mate with whom he wasn't mating, join him on his flights in hawk and owl form. Being a brujo who didn't marry made less sense to him all the time. At that very moment she opened an eye. "Time for lunch?" she asked.

"Good idea," he replied. "But before we go down to the dining room, I have a question for you. Have you had any more memories of your long-ago life as a Basque man named Iñigo?"

"Why do you ask?" she said, sitting up. "Was I talking in my sleep?"

"You let out some sort of strangled cry," he replied. "I didn't know whether or not to wake you."

"Yes, I did have a dream about my life as a man named Iñigo." She was silent for a moment. "It was a terrible dream," she said finally. "There was something like clan warfare going on—not a real war, against foreigners or invaders, but between rival families in our region, and it had been going on for a long time. Even if you didn't belong to one of the feuding clans, you were likely to get caught in the cross fire.

"I was the leader of a local brotherhood, or militia, that we formed to protect ourselves from the clan violence that spilled over into our villages and towns. That fragment of a memory I had when I was running to help you after the fire—that memory was about me running to try to rescue my family from my burning house. My comrades and I were returning from some sort of expedition—I think we'd gone to help relatives in a neighboring village. Anyway, we were coming back up the hill toward our village—in the dream I was running, because I saw smoke.

"My house was just beyond the hill, on the outskirts of the village, and when I reached it I saw that it had been burned to the ground. I ran to it and called out to my wife and children and began searching in the ruins. Nothing—I couldn't find them. They might be dead and buried under the smoldering timbers and parts of the roof, or maybe alive and hiding somewhere in the hills. I think that was when I cried out. 'Gone, all gone!' I cried. I must have partly awakened, because the dream ended there." Inez's face quivered. "I don't know what happened to them."

Carlos took her in his arms. He couldn't think of anything soothing to say. Though it was a dream from a past life, he wondered whether it might also be an image of what they might find in the next few days. Dead children, or children forever lost.

Eventually, Inéz regained her composure. Without speaking, they left their room and went to the dining room. During lunch Carlos felt restless. José came in to say that the horses had been fed and that there was still no sign of Raul Trigales. Carlos examined his mood and realized that he was more on edge than he'd admitted. He wanted to do something, anything. Inéz noticed—it's getting as though she can read my mind, he thought—and said, "Carlos, you're so fidgety it's driving me crazy."

"I think I'll go for a ride on Eagle," he announced.

Inéz was not pleased. "If you're planning," she said, "to sneak off by yourself and get in trouble, you can forget about it."

"Nothing of the sort," he replied. "I just want to take a ride. You and José are welcome to come along."

A half hour later the three of them were riding north on the Camino

Real, a direction that ensured they wouldn't miss Raul Trigales if he arrived while they were on the road. Whatever Carlos might have intended to do on a solitary ride, since he had companions he decided to use the occasion as a teaching opportunity. Two miles into their ride he announced, "There's a flat spot off to our left next to a dry stream bed that's strewn with boulders." He turned Eagle in the direction he'd indicated and led the way to the place. They all dismounted, tethered their horses, and, at Carlos's suggestion, stood facing the boulders.

"My master in sorcery, Don Serafino," he began, "taught me a variety of brujo techniques, but the skill I want to demonstrate today, and perhaps even help you master, wasn't one I learned from him, and I'm not sure how to teach it. Let me show you a technique I call energy bursts."

He walked toward a medium-sized boulder that must have weighed nearly a hundred pounds and stopped about ten feet from it. As he approached the boulder he concentrated on his right arm, gathering an energy charge in it. With a quick arm movement, barely more than a flick of his forearm, he directed a blast of invisible energy at the boulder, which rolled two or three feet away from him. Instantly gathering more energy in his arm, he sent a stronger energy blast at the boulder, splitting it into three pieces.

He turned back to his friends. José had a look of astonishment on his face. Inéz, though, didn't look happy. "I knew you were up to something," she said, "and now I can see that you're testing your skills preparatory to fighting these brutes."

"All I wanted to do," he replied, "was to demonstrate this technique."

Inéz didn't believe him. "I don't want you fighting with these monsters," she insisted.

Growing a little exasperated, Don Carlos said, "I've told you that I'm just going to watch what happens at the drop-off, not attack anyone or anything. But what if they spot us and attack? Energy bursts are an excellent defensive technique. Please see whether you can learn to do them."

Inéz acquiesced, though without any enthusiasm. For the next half hour she and José tried to follow Don Carlos's instructions. Initially they attempted to move fist-sized rocks that were located no more than five feet away. Frustration began to build when nothing at all happened despite their best efforts. Don Carlos varied his instructions: "Imagine that you're blowing a gust of air at them, except it's coming from your hand. Focus on believing, rather than doubting, that this will work. Instead of thinking of stones as heavy, think of them as weightless objects."

Nothing worked. Eventually, Don Carlos drew himself up and said forcefully, "To send out a bolt of energy you must concentrate the energy at the core of your being. Don't be discouraged. Keep working on learning to concentrate your energy deep within."

At that very moment, José scowled, waved his hand at a mid-sized boulder, and shouted "Scat!" so loudly that his voice came back as an echo from a nearby cliff. The stone rolled two feet away from him.

Inéz clapped her hands together. "Hey!" she exclaimed. "You did it!"

Don Carlos laughed good-naturedly. "Inéz, if you look more closely, you'll see that José had help."

By squinting her eyes and using her peripheral vision, as Don Carlos had taught her to do, she could see a shadowy figure crouched down behind José's boulder. It was José's spirit ally, the horse kachina.

"Wait a second," Don Carlos murmured in a barely audible voice. "Inéz, why don't you call on a totem spirit to aid you? Toho took quite a fancy to you despite your body being furless, and here he comes now. Look across the stone field to that cluster of trees."

A large cougar had emerged from the trees on the other side of the boulder-strewn clearing. Don Carlos gave Inéz instructions. "Focus on that cabbage-sized round stone he's standing next to. Concentrate your energy at your core and thrust it forcefully at the stone."

Inéz gave him a skeptical look, then furrowed her brow and tensed her hand in a fist as she made a strong effort to enter a concentrated state. With great force and a loud grunt she thrust her fist at the stone, and the cougar immediately began rolling it into the woods, continuing until both he and the stone disappeared from sight.

Inéz was incredulous. "That was remarkable," she said, "except that was a real cougar, not Toho in human form as I saw him in Santa Fe."

"That was not an ordinary cougar," Don Carlos said with great solemnity. "Have you ever heard of an ordinary cougar rolling a stone around? That was a spirit animal."

"Do you require a spirit ally, Toho or another one, to accomplish energy bursts?" she asked Don Carlos.

"No," he replied, "but perhaps you and José need a spirit ally's help."

At that moment they heard hoofbeats and, turning toward the road, saw Raul Trigales approaching with two of his ranch hands, each of whom was leading a heavily laden pack horse. Carlos hailed Raul's party, and he, Inéz, and José mounted up and joined them. As they rode toward the Chavez hacienda, Raul reported that he'd managed to borrow the total sum the kidnappers had demanded. "I'll be in the poorhouse for years, and in debt to people like you, but I have to rescue my children. I intend to leave early in the morning to make the delivery. I don't know how we can guarantee that they'll tell me where to find my children, and that worries me."

It worried Carlos too, but he didn't say so. Instead he remarked, "We can't be involved in the ransom delivery, but after it takes place we'll do all we can to help."

Another thing he didn't say was that he and Inéz planned to rise long before daybreak the next morning, change into owl forms, and wing their way to the drop-off point. When that time came Carlos and Inéz quietly left the hacienda's main house and walked to the barn. As they did so he took Inéz's hand and said thoughtfully, "Everything that's happened in the past two months has forced me to look at my habitual way of dealing with challenging situations through action and depending mainly on myself and my brujo powers. I've come around to feeling that Don Serafino's approach of training apprentices and then setting them on solitary paths won't work for me. When things quiet down, I want to build a circle of allies who don't need to be brujos. I'm thinking first of you, but also of Pedro, María, and José, who know my secret identity and therefore are naturals for this circle. I'm not asking you to react one way or another to this idea now. I simply wanted to tell you what I'm thinking."

Inéz squeezed his hand without saying anything. They entered the barn preparatory to changing into owls. After some debate, Inéz agreed that they should leave their clothes behind. There was a chance, she conceded, that they might need to make an emergency change of form and even the momentary delay occasioned by the process of transforming their clothes as well as their bodies might put them in danger.

After a long flight Don Carlos and Inéz landed half a mile from the drop-off point, a precaution they had agreed would keep them out of sight of watching eyes. Next, Don Carlos transformed himself and Inéz—the process was faster every time he did it—into coyotes, and in that form they trotted toward the top of one of the eroded fingers of the mesa that overlooked the drop-off site. He then led the way into a vertical ravine, thirty yards from the boulder-strewn overlook he'd chosen, where they disappeared from view of anyone in every direction. There he made one final transformation, changing himself and Inéz into ground squirrels, creatures with low profiles and the same coloration as the mesa itself.

The two squirrels ran back to the overlook. The sun had risen, and they crouched down in a deep shadow next to a large rock, a perfect hiding place with an excellent view to both the north and the south on the Old Apache Trail. When they scanned the area below them, they spotted four ogres and Leandro, no longer in Damián form, crouched behind boulders a few yards away from the cairn that stood in the middle of the trail.

The ground squirrels remained alert and motionless for hours. A few minutes before noon they saw Raul Trigales approaching, mounted and leading a pack horse. Don Carlos worried that Raul was exposing himself to the danger of being captured and joining his children in captivity, but given the terms the kidnappers had imposed, there had seemed to be no alternative. Raul halted next to the stone cairn that marked the drop-off point. He dismounted and unloaded four bags that contained the ransom from the pack horse. He shouted, "Here's your money. Now tell me where to find my children." Carlos could hear the anguish in his voice. Not receiving an answer, after only a short pause he mounted his horse again, turned around, and rode off, the pack horse following behind.

After Raul had been out of sight for nearly half an hour, the four ogres emerged from their hiding places. Leandro came into the open also. He went directly to the money bags, opened them one at a time, and, under the watchful eyes of the ogres, examined the silver coins, testing them randomly for authenticity by nicking them with a knife blade. He then slowly counted the pesos in one bag to be sure it contained the requisite number of coins. Apparently satisfied, he tied all the bags shut, put them in four backpacks, one for each ogre, and they all started off on foot southeast down the trail.

Don Carlos waited until Leandro and the monsters were out of sight before transforming himself and Inéz into crows, a type of bird he thought was less likely to draw attention than two red-tailed hawks. Even so, the two crows took great care in following the kidnappers, staying far behind them and gliding along the rims of ridges and hills to keep as low a profile as possible. It probably wasn't necessary to be so cautious. Leandro and the monsters never looked back.

Up ahead the sky was dark, as if a storm were approaching directly over the road. Swinging off to the west, he and Inéz took a circuitous route completely out of sight of the road until they were on the edge of the darkness overhead. It was not a natural storm cloud. There was no wind and no rain, simply a dense blackness that cast a dark shadow over the ground beneath.

The two crows flew back toward the road and into the edge of the shadow, soon landing on a sheer outcrop overlooking the trail. Don Carlos transformed the two of them into weasels, and they crept forward until they could see a figure in black seated on a black horse beneath them.

The man in black was unmistakably Don Malvolio, the sorcerer who had cut Don Carlos's throat in his previous life. The very sight of him made Carlos shudder at the memory. Then Malvolio had been a slender man with a narrow face and chiseled features, a handsome face even though its eyes were hard. The Don Malvolio he'd seen that fateful night in Violeta's bedroom had been in his mid-fifties, which would make the man he saw on the road below close to eighty.

Leandro and the ogres arrived and approached Don Malvolio. Leandro made a low bow and said, "Master, here are the four bags of silver pesos. I have examined them and each bag is filled with genuine pesos."

"Open the bags for me to see," Don Malvolio commanded. Leandro obeyed. Malvolio dismounted, stepped forward, and slowly scrutinized the contents of the bags. After selecting a few coins from each bag and weighing them in his hand, he seemed satisfied, backed up two steps, and spoke again. "The full ransom appears to be here. Unfortunately you have failed me in the more important task I assigned you, which was to locate Carlos Buenaventura. When I brought you and the two women together I gave you three years to find him. The time is up.

"As you can see, I'm not well. I believe that some of the alchemical preparations I ingested in my youth—potions which seemed largely ineffective at the time—have been at work in me for many years and have slowly brought about transformations, but in the direction of age and illness, not power or—yes—elevation to a higher level of being. As long as I am alive, I believe that transformation is still possible to me, to repair the wreck I have become. And I believe that the Great Magus taught this particular power of transformation to his student Don Serafino, and that Serafino in turn taught it to his student Carlos Buenaventura, who is perhaps the only living man who possesses this knowledge. So, while this money is useful"—he gestured in the direction of the sacks of pesos sitting on the ground—"it is even more important for me to find Carlos and to persuade him, either through force or sympathy, to help me.

"Finding Carlos was the task that I sent you on three years ago, giving you nothing more than bare instructions and two girls—my daughters—to help you, knowing that they, in their own ways, have powerful skills, and because I know, from one of my encounters with him, that Carlos has a fatal weakness for violet-eyed women. But after three years, and traveling to the northernmost hinterlands of New Spain, you have nothing to show for your efforts.

"You may wonder why Brother Gustavo is not with me today. I left him in El Paso del Norte, doing the work of the Inquisition in which he's assisted me for more than a decade. But in the past six weeks, I twice sent him to meet with you south of Santa Fe to tell you that time was growing short and to impress on you my need for a large sum of money. I must remind you that this kidnapping scheme was your idea for meeting that need.

"What you don't know is that Gustavo visited Santa Fe itself on several occasions, doing so in the form of animal allies — wolves and vultures — that he manipulates with great skill. On one of these occasions he confronted Don Alfonso Cabeza de Vaca, the *hidalgo* that you suggested might be Carlos. Although Gustavo's wolf ally approached Cabeza de Vaca in a menacing way, nothing in that *hidalgo's* response indicated brujo powers. From what Gustavo reported back to me it was clear that you had not located Carlos Buenaventura, who to my certain knowledge is an Indian, which is why I told you to look for him among Indians and medicine men."

"Old Man Xenome!" Leandro exclaimed. "Could he...?"

"He has some power," Malvolio said. "He sensed me when I watched him from a distance. But he does not have the power I seek. And yes, I am aware that your friend Don Alfonso also has some powers, but he is an upper-class Spaniard. I must say that I am disappointed in you, Leandro. I had great hopes for you."

Carlos, listening intently, was relieved to have his intuitions validated on learning that Don Malvolio and his assistant Gustavo had been behind the dark entities that had so disturbed him since New Year's. What he hadn't known was that Leandro had been in contact with Malvolio through this Gustavo, leading him to plan and set in motion the kidnapping scheme. But what truly astonished Don Carlos was that Malvolio apparently believed that Carlos's mastery of transformations extended into quite another realm, one Carlos had never even imagined. Transforming himself into a spiritual being? That such a thing was possible had never even occurred to him.

Moreover, Carlos knew that if Malvolio died in full possession of his brujo consciousness he would be reborn, something that Leandro, to judge from the present conversation and other things Leandro had said, was evidently ignorant of. Carlos felt he was missing something. Why had Malvolio not instructed Leandro in the process of being reborn?

Carlos had no chance to pursue these questions because events suddenly moved forward with great momentum. Leandro, standing before Malvolio on the road below, seemed to wilt under his master's strong expression of disappointment in him, and for several moments he stood, head downward, at a loss for words. Finally he lifted his head and looked at Malvolio. "I hope I may continue to serve you, and serve you better, Master," he said at last. "There is nothing I would not do for you."

"Hmmm," replied Malvolio. "We will see. What have you done with the children?"

"The children?" Leandro asked, as if mystified by the question. "I did nothing with them. When the ogres showed up, the carriage horses bolted and dragged the carriage off the road. The coachman was struggling to calm them, so I got off my horse and freed the carriage horses from their traces. They immediately bolted again, and my horse charged off after them. But we didn't need them. Two of the ogres took care of the servants, and then we all ran off with the children. Fortunately, the transformation elixir enabled me to keep pace with the ogres to the ransom site. Once at the site, I gave the children to the ogres to hide and stayed at the cairn to wait for Trigales to come there."

"And what did the ogres do with them?"

"I don't know," Leandro said helplessly. Turning to the ogres, he asked, "What did you do with them?"

The ogres actually looked sheepish. "We played a game with them," one growled. "We told them we would hide them in a safe place, a cave we knew about in Los Organos, and their father would come to find them. It would be a game for him too. That way they were cooperative, and less afraid."

"You are indeed idiots," Malvolio sighed. "Well, no matter. Leandro will be blamed."

"Take me with you, Master!" Leandro cried. "I'm known to be the kidnapper. I'm a dead man if I'm found!"

"Yes, indeed," replied Malvolio. "And what about the girls? What do they know?"

"About the kidnapping, nothing for sure. Besides…" Leandro hesitated. "Besides, they are dead. I couldn't think of any way of raising a lot of money, as you ordered me to do, other than kidnapping the children. It was easy, as both the children and their parents trusted me. But at the last moment I realized that the girls know too much about me—and also about you," he added cravenly, "and I had to dispose of them. I couldn't take them with me and the ogres, and I couldn't leave them behind. Once the kidnapping became public knowledge, Mara and Selena would have been seen as my accomplices and would be tortured for information and subjected to horrible punishments. As their protector, I couldn't leave them to such a fate."

Malvolio looked coldly at Leandro. "Yes, I see. You killed my daughters, thinking that was the best way to carry out my charge to you to protect them. Well, I suppose I shouldn't be surprised. The question remains, what am I to do with you now?"

Leandro waited in silence.

"Since you let the Fates — in the form of these ogres — decide in the case of the children," Malvolio declared, "I suppose we should let the Fates decide about you too." He turned to the ogres. "Bring me a coin," he said. An ogre came forward with a peso from the ransom bags. Malvolio took the coin in his hand, looked at Leandro, and told him, "Call. If it comes up with your call, you live. If not, you die."

Leandro blanched. "Heads," he said weakly.

Malvolio flipped the coin, caught it between his hands, and lifted his top hand. "Tails," he announced.

Malvolio nodded to the ogres, and they leaped on Leandro as one. In a moment he was invisible under their bodies. His screams, even muffled, were horrible, and they echoed off the walls of the narrow defile through which the road passed. Inéz, above, in weasel form, shut her eyes and flattened her body to the ground, inadvertently dislodging a small rock that tumbled down the steep slope. Don Malvolio, instantly alert, looked up and threw a blast of invisible energy toward the weasels' hiding spot, dislodging even more stones.

Don Carlos, although he'd reacted with lightning speed, barely had time to withdraw from the edge of the overlook and drag Inéz with him before Malvolio's energy blast arrived. With great urgency, he told Inéz, "Run!" Together they dashed almost a hundred feet across the top of the ridge until he found a burrow and dived into it, followed immediately by Inéz.

Ten feet into the burrow Don Carlos bumped into a sleepy black-tailed jackrabbit who awoke with a start and snarled a warning. "I may not stand much of a chance with you, but I'll try to do serious damage before you kill me. Why not back off so we can both stay in one piece?"

Don Carlos apologized and explained why they'd intruded on the jackrabbit's lair. "We're in danger," he told his fellow beast, "and want to lie low until the danger is over. If we have to make a run for it, I assume you have a second exit that we can use."

Although the jackrabbit wasn't happy with this prospect, it was better than certain death in a fight with a weasel. "What danger?" he asked suspiciously.

"It's a long story," Carlos replied. "Sorry to involve you. By the way, my name is Carlos. What's yours?"

"Enos."

"Well, Enos, for now we need to sit tight."

For a very long time Don Carlos didn't make a move. Before exposing himself and Inéz he wanted to be certain that Don Malvolio and the monsters had left the vicinity.

Don Carlos had just begun to believe it was safe to leave the burrow when he felt a heavy tread on the ground above where he, Inéz, and the jackrabbit were hiding. Then he heard a loud, guttural voice that he was sure was an ogre's. "Lots of animal burrows in this area," the voice said. After a pause the same voice said, "Nothing else. Nobody watching. You can all go on. I want to catch me a little creature. Tasty snack."

"Move quietly to the second exit," Don Carlos told Enos and Inéz. "Wait for me there, but don't leave the burrow until I tell you to."

"What the hell do you think you're doing?" Inéz asked. "I demand that you tell me!"

"I'll wait here until the monster puts his arm in the hole. When he does, I'll let you know. Hurry, he's making his move."

Even as he said this, the rank scent of the ogre wafted into the burrow, and Don Carlos knew that the ogre was putting his arm down the jackrabbit's hole. When the ogre's hand was only inches from his nose, Don Carlos attacked with all the formidable weapons a weasel has at its disposal. He shredded the ogre's hand with his claws and tore one finger nearly off with his teeth. He instantly released the hand to avoid being dragged out of the burrow when the ogre, howling in pain and rage, yanked it back.

Time to run for it, Don Carlos told himself, hurrying twenty feet along a winding tunnel until he found Enos and Inéz waiting at the exit. "Inéz, stay here," he told her. To the jackrabbit he said, "Move stealthily so as not to catch the ogre's attention." They slipped into the open. Don Carlos glanced back and saw the ogre focused on the burrow entrance, ripping up huge clods of dirt as he followed its route into the ground.

Once over a slight rise, Don Carlos spoke reassuringly to the frightened jackrabbit. "Close your eyes, and don't be afraid. I'm going to change my appearance into hawk form. I know hawks are no friends of yours, but I'll pick you up as gently as I can, fly low to the ground to the next hill over there, and let you down. The more distance we can put between you and that monster, the safer you'll be."

Enos was trembling in fear, trying to decide which danger was greatest, the one posed by the monster that was tearing up his burrow or the threat raised by going for a ride in a hawk's talons. He eventually chose Don Carlos the hawk, hunkered down, and allowed himself to be picked up and carried across a small gully to a patch of tall grass on the next rise.

Enos immediately found the opening of an old burrow and began to clear it for occupancy. The dirt flew, and the little creature soon disappeared from view.

Don Carlos flew back toward the exit end of the burrow, just inside of which Inéz was crouching. His plan had been to call to her to step out of the burrow so he could pick her up and carry her off in his talons as he had carried Enos. But his cry alerted the ogre, who looked up and saw Inéz's weasel head pop out of the burrow, and he made a dive for her himself.

Something had to be done instantly. Still in mid-air, Don Carlos, with a ferocious effort of concentration, changed Inéz into her Iñigo form. Inéz-Iñigo ran a few steps and seized a stout fallen branch with a jagged point at one end. Meanwhile Don Carlos, calling on his spirit totem, Toho the mountain lion kachina, changed himself into a giant cougar almost equal in size to the ogre. The ogre, momentarily startled by two opponents who suddenly loomed up in front of him, growled and went for Inéz-Iñigo. She didn't flinch. Standing her ground, she thrust the pointed end of the branch into the monster's open mouth. Blood spurted in every direction, but the ogre's momentum and strength kept him moving forward, and he bowled Inéz-Iñigo over and was about to fall on her. The transformed Don Carlos was equally fast and strong. He leaped forward, seized the back of the ogre's neck between his teeth, and gave a powerful jerk that broke the monster's spine.

Inéz-Iñigo scrambled to her feet and said, "That was too close for comfort." With one thought the two strange beings, Inéz in the form of her ancient Basque Iñigo self and the giant Carlos-Toho, reached for each other and embraced. Both were trembling. "I didn't think knights who saved maidens in distress ever trembled out of fear," Inéz whispered into Carlos's chest.

"In situations like this," he murmured, "if you're not afraid, you're crazy."

After having been momentarily distracted by his concern for Inéz,

Carlos remembered their situation and forced himself to think about the threats they might still face. "Careful!" he said. "We may not be out of danger yet. Let's go back to being little creatures, preferably weasels." He quickly effected the transformations.

Once he was in weasel form Don Carlos turned his attention to the site of Enos's former burrow, now torn up along half its length. Glancing over at the dead ogre lying nearby, Carlos saw that in death the ogre's body had collapsed in size to reveal a mestizo man of medium height, an ordinary poor peasant who had been changed by Don Malvolio into a huge monster.

Don Carlos and Inéz crept cautiously to the cliff edge and looked down. The scene of Leandro's death was a terrible sight. The ogres had torn Leandro limb from limb and devoured his entrails. But despite the indignities done to his body, Leandro's handsome face had somehow survived. Don Carlos scrambled down the steep slope with Inéz not far behind. He transformed himself back to human form and Inéz, at her request, into Iñigo—both of them naked and unconcerned about it. Moved by compassion, the two men collected Leandro's body parts, piled them in a small depression at the side of the trail, and covered them with stones. Poor Leandro! Carlos thought. Malvolio's potions, though briefly giving him superhuman strength, had drawn his mind into inhuman darkness.

These melancholy thoughts did not prevent Don Carlos from noticing that, although vultures were already circling overhead, the dark clouds that had previously loomed over the area were now only faintly visible to the south and were retreating farther every minute. Don Malvolio, doubtless accompanied by the three surviving ogres, was moving away at a great pace. The sun came out brilliantly. A few creatures emerged from hiding. It was almost as though the departure of Don Malvolio's presence allowed the natural beauty and goodness of the mesa to flourish again.

Don Carlos told Inéz-Iñigo that he wanted to say goodbye to Enos and to thank him for his help. He changed their forms to red-tailed hawks and they lifted off and flew to see Enos.

Enos was peeking out of his new burrow and was momentarily alarmed by the arrival of two hawks nearby. Don Carlos assured Enos he was safe and asked him how he was doing. Enos relaxed a little and replied, "Everything's fine. I think this old burrow once belonged to my grandfather. The renovations went quickly, and what a day! After sharing my former burrow with two weasels, I was attacked by a monster, and carried here by a red-tailed hawk. I can't wait to tell my girlfriend. But what was that all about?"

Carlos gave Enos a quick summary. "Those dreadful creatures kidnapped four children of a friend of ours. Their father came and paid the ransom, but the villains had no intention of returning the kids. The only clue we have to their whereabouts is that they're hidden in a cave in Los Organos. I've passed near the Organos Mountains on several occasions. They cover a very large area. The likelihood that we can locate the cave in which the children are trapped seems slim, and the thought that they'll starve to death is terrible."

"If it's anything to do with caves," Enos replied, "ask a bat."

26

Angels

Applying Enos's advice was easier in theory than it proved in practice. Their jackrabbit friend directed them to a nearby cave, and after Don Carlos changed himself and Inéz into bat form, they entered the cave and saw several hundred bats sound asleep. Choosing one at random from those on the edge of the cluster, Don Carlos woke the bat. Though thoroughly annoyed at being disturbed, the bat—it was a male named Benito—expressed sympathy once Don Carlos told him about the plight of the kidnapped children.

"I've had no contact with bats from a cave so close to the big river," Benito told them. "I have a distant cousin who liked to roam and he described a gigantic cave a long way from here in the direction of the rising sun. If you hurry, you might be able to get there by sundown and see bats by the tens of thousands emerging from the cave, a mighty horde so great that they darken the sky. I've always wanted to see that for myself, but I'm a stay-at-home."

Don Carlos realized that Benito's information was of no help, since the cave he described was far to the east of Los Organos. He thanked Benito and flew out of the cave. "You could have talked with other bats," Inéz said, a bit accusingly.

"I don't think it would do any good," Don Carlos replied. "Our exchange with Benito convinced me that we'll do better if we talk to a bat or bats in the Los Organos area."

"Where is Los Organos?" she asked. "I've never heard of it."

"The Organos Mountains are a long way from here, east of the Camino Real in an uninhabited area north of El Paso del Norte." Having said this, Don Carlos turned himself and Inéz back into hawk form, preparatory to commencing a flight to Los Organos.

"How do you know so much about this place?" Inéz inquired.

"I've passed it three times, once going south and twice going north. Even so, I might not remember Los Organos so vividly except it was the site of a botched attempt at transformation."

"Really?" Inéz said. "What happened?"

"You saw the difficulty I had trying to change my shirt into a string. Last July when I was returning to Santa Fe from Mexico City, my brujo powers were very strong, and I decided to try transforming an inanimate object into an animate being. I'd always wondered whether I could do it, and if I could, whether I could reverse the process.

"My intention was to transform a small dead tree branch into a brown snake—an animal roughly the same shape and color as the branch. I brought the image of a brown snake into my consciousness, but the tree branch changed into a squirrel, and not just any squirrel, but an albino squirrel. Before I could try to reverse the process it gave me an alarmed look and ran away. That warned me off working with inanimate objects until recently."

"Actually," Inéz said, "an albino squirrel strikes me as marvelous—some sort of magical creature."

"Perhaps," Don Carlos said, "But the result upset me."

"What upset you?" Inéz asked.

"For one thing, the outcome was so different from my intention. If my transformations don't match my intentions, it's a bad sign. In addition, I felt sympathy for the squirrel I'd created. Squirrels have protective coloring to disguise themselves from predators like hawks. Can you imagine how easy it would be for a hawk to spot a white squirrel?"

"You have a point," Inéz admitted.

"Yes. But right now we need to fly south and hope to reach Los Organos tonight and talk with some bats. We can switch to owl form at sundown. We'd better hurry. The Organos Mountains cover a large area, and I worry that we won't find the cave in question in time."

Inéz agreed, and they lifted off and flew rapidly southward.

Hours later, after the sun had set and they had assumed owl form, they reached the west front of the Organos range. In the moonlight Inéz immediately understood how the mountains had acquired their name. The range consisted of row upon vertical row of upthrust spires that resembled the pipes of a huge organ. Her spirits sank. "How," she asked, "can we find a single cave here?"

Don Carlos had an idea. "I think you might be correct in suggesting that the albino squirrel I created from a tree branch was a magical spirit being. I remember where I attempted that transformation. It was in a dry ravine on the west side of the range. Follow me, and I'll take you there."

After a short flight, the two owls reached their destination and dropped to the ground in a dry streambed. "I think we should change back into human form," Don Carlos suggested.

Inéz objected vigorously. "If we change into human form," she pointed out, "we'll be stark naked. I'm not keen on roaming around in the dark with no clothes to protect me against the chill."

"Even if we'd started out with clothes in condensed form," he replied, trying to defend his earlier argument to leave their clothes behind, "we would have lost them long ago in the midst of all the sudden shifts of form we've had to make. Let me change into human form and sit here quietly to see whether there's anything about this place that might explain why my effort a year ago turned out the way it did."

Inéz in owl form obligingly turned her back on him. Carlos, naked, assumed a meditative position. He concentrated first on generating sufficient internal heat to keep himself comfortably warm, which involved raising energy in his chakras, especially the lower three. Once he had accomplished that, he began to pay attention to the auras of nearby plants and rocks, which were surprisingly strong. The place was very still, and he soon felt a deep calm. He also became aware that Inéz, in owl form, had dozed off.

Ten minutes after Inéz had fallen asleep, he heard a small voice say, "I hoped you would return some day, but I didn't want to come out until the owl fell asleep." "Heard," he realized, didn't accurately describe the way he received this message. What he heard was more like an inner voice than a sound.

In the dim light of the moon, which was nearing its first quarter, he could just make out an albino squirrel sitting beneath a large bush. On the assumption that the squirrel could read his thoughts, he replied mentally rather than verbally, "I'm glad to see you again. I've been worrying that your white pelt would make you an easy prey for predators."

"Thank you for your concern," the bell-like voice of the squirrel said.

"But you needn't worry. I'm quite capable of defending myself against predators. But I sense that you're troubled and have something on your mind other than my well-being."

Don Carlos acknowledged that the squirrel's assumption was correct and quickly summarized the story of the Trigales children's kidnapping. "Any idea," he asked, "where the cave in which they're said to be hidden might be located?"

"You're in luck," the albino spirit being replied. "It's not too far away. If you follow this ravine to its end, you'll soon come to the base of a steep cliff. The cave you're seeking is halfway up the slope. I know because I sensed a great disturbance in the area two days ago and went looking for its source. Three ogres—yes, I know an ogre when I see one—were digging a pit inside the cave and carrying out great chunks of rock. Another ogre guarded four children, who were wrapped up to their necks in bags and sitting against the wall of the cliff. After the excavators had created a big pile of debris at the cave's mouth, the ogres carried the children inside. They returned without them only a few minutes later."

"I wish I could stay and talk more with you about your life in this ravine," Carlos said. "But it's urgent that I rescue the children right now. I'm sure you understand."

"I do. But before you go, please tell me your name. I've always wondered what it is."

"Carlos Buenaventura. And yours?"

"I go by the name Albina Ardilla. I'm sure it was something else before I became a squirrel, but I have no idea what I used to call myself."

"Thank you for helping us, Albina."

"Think nothing of it," she replied. "Truth to tell, I owe you a deep debt of gratitude. Had you not transformed me, I might have spent the rest of my days as a dead tree branch subject to being carried along by flash floods or consumed by fire. Your intervention gave me a new life."

Don Carlos couldn't resist asking one more question. "How did you happen to inhabit a dead tree branch?"

"Unfortunately," Albina said, "I'm vague about nearly everything that happened to me before you came along. All I remember is a confrontation with a black entity. By the barest chance I managed to save something of my old self, a soul, you might call it, which survived inside that tree branch."

"So," Don Carlos replied, very interested in the topic, "even though the tree branch looked dead on the outside, a conscious being was locked inside it. That would explain why I was able to transform a dead branch into a squirrel. It surprised me because that wasn't my intention."

Albina nodded thoughtfully and said, "Please come again after I've had time to see what more I can remember." With that she melted back into the dark underbrush.

Don Carlos changed himself into owl form again, woke Inéz up, and told her he'd learned the location of the cave. He then instructed her to follow him to the ravine's end and on to the mouth of the cave in the cliffs above.

Albina's directions brought them to the ledge where the mouth of the cave was located. They settled down on what proved to be a broad flat place. The cave's mouth loomed straight ahead and was surprisingly large, high enough for an ogre to enter without having to bend over. To the right of the cave's entrance was a big pile of rock and other debris, evidently the result of the ogres' recent excavation of a pit inside the cave. To the left a clump of thick brush partly obscured a trail that Don Carlos had noticed during their approach flight. By a long winding route the trail led down to the ravine where Albina lived.

The two owls stood at the entrance to the cave. On realizing that to complete the rescue one or both of them would need to change to human form, Inéz voiced objections. "If we return to human form," she pointed out, "I'll be stark naked again. I wish you would find a solution to this problem. Do something with your brujo powers."

Don Carlos was momentarily stumped. After some thought, he had an idea. "Wait here," he said. He flew a short distance to a clump of brush, landed on the top of the tallest bush, and dipped his wings in among the branches. He flew back, trailing spiderwebs. "You can be an angel with wings to lift the kids out of the cave," he told her. "I'll give you a robe made from these spiderwebs, and you'll have an aura of angelic light around you to help you find your way in the cave." Even as he spoke, the robe materialized, with Inéz in her human form within it.

"I don't like it," she complained.

"Why not?" he asked, though he had foreseen that she might object to being clothed in spiderwebs.

"You've dressed me in a robe that leaves my arms bare. I'll freeze."

"It's not that cold, and you have lovely arms."

"Sleeves! I want sleeves, and right now!" Her jaw was set in that don't-mess-with-me way she sometimes had.

"All right. Done, but I think you looked more angelic without sleeves."

Pulling a lock of pale hair forward where she could see it, Inéz said, "And this is wrong too."

"What now?" he asked, feeling a little exasperated.

"You've made me a blonde. I look too much like your old inamorata, Camila, probably due to another slip into your unconscious. I want my hair to be mine, curly and black."

He started to protest, "A black-haired angel? I never heard of such a thing." A warning glare from Inéz made him give in immediately. "Oh, all right. Have it your way. Done. Would you please get going on your rescue mission?"

A slightly sullen angel went into the cave, but when she called, "Hello, anybody here?" her voice had a sweetness to it that expressed pure love.

A weak answer came from inside. It was Cristofer. "We're here in a pit. I can see your light. Over here to your left."

After only a brief pause, Inéz the angel flew out with the littlest Trigales child, Anton, in her arms. Inéz put him down next to Don Carlos and told him, "Stay here with the owl."

"He looks scary," Anton protested.

"Don't worry, Anton. He's my friend and a cuddly fellow. I call him Hooter and you can too."

Working quickly, the angel brought all four children to the cave entrance, where they clustered around her. The children, Don Carlos noted, were holding little satchels as well as the bunched-up drawstring sacks that the ogres had used to transport them. Addressing Carlos, the angel-Inéz said, "We'll be all right now, Hooter. They found water running down the cave wall into the pit, and they had a little food. Their mother had sent them off with these purses—she indicated the small bags each child was clutching—containing their nightshirts and hairbrushes and some bread, nuts, and dried apples in case they got hungry. Evidently the kidnappers didn't want anything belonging to the children to be found, so they stuffed the purses into the large sacks they used to carry off the kids. They finished the food yesterday and are hungry now. Go to El Paso del Norte and get Rafael and some of his soldiers. Hurry! We'll wait for you inside the cave where it'll be a little warmer."

Don Carlos the owl took off and swung onto a course that would take him by the most direct route to El Paso del Norte. He soon fell into an easy rhythm that quieted his mind and drew him deeply into himself. His primary feeling was relief, great relief at the successful rescue of the children. Bodily tension of which he'd been unaware while concentrating on the task at hand now dropped away. Its departure, combined with the pure joy of flight, was exhilarating.

A new level of awareness arose. Reflecting on the events of the past month, he saw them as it were with the depth and clarity of his owl eyes. What the owl saw told him much about his relationships with both friends and enemies.

He now saw Malvolio in an entirely new light. Putting together what he'd learned about Malvolio from Leandro and what he'd heard from Malvolio himself, Don Carlos realized that his previous conviction that Don Malvolio was an incarnation of pure malice had been based on two past-life encounters in which Malvolio had been bent on killing him. But Carlos now saw that Malvolio was a man of much greater complexity than he had previously believed. Despite Malvolio's claim of poor health, his personal presence was commanding, even awe-inspiring. Carlos could understand Leandro's subservience to him. Also, from what Leandro had said, Malvolio was dedicated to the pursuit of learning in order to deepen his understanding of the material and spiritual worlds. Both intelligence and ambition evidently fueled Malvolio's desire to transform himself into a higher order of being— not in itself, in Carlos's view, an unworthy aspiration. But what was most effective in altering Carlos's attitude toward him was that Malvolio was now seeking him in hopes that Carlos would help heal him. Though Carlos remained uncertain as to how he ought to respond to this information, the knowledge changed him.

Don Carlos's owl-eyes also looked at his relationship with Mara. He saw that he had allowed himself to be drawn into an enchantment that he'd found all too desirable, excusing himself on the grounds that he was a voyager in the realms of consciousness, and that in her capacity for achieving *duende* Mara seemed to be guiding him to realms previously beyond him. But here, flying over the night landscape of southern New Mexico, he could see that he'd also been perpetuating his habit of thoughtless sexual adventures. In some cases—Mariana and Daniela—his affairs had been lightly undertaken and without consequences, but his reckless passion for Violeta had led to his death. Allowing himself to be enchanted by Mara had exposed him to great danger and had been a betrayal of Inéz.

His evolving relationship with Inéz, he saw, offered a way out of the pattern of his pursuit of women. He knew that was true without immediately seeing how it would play out. Unlike Zoila, Inéz did not have the knowledge to be his guide in a path toward spiritual illumination. But he now saw that a relationship with her offered a way of learning to know another human being on a deep level and to fully enter the world of ordinary human life from which his great brujo powers had kept him separate—rather proudly so, he realized.

Don Carlos had always known that the practice of his brujo powers was an integral part of remaining in touch with his true nature, but he now saw that, like the expansion of his vision that owl eyes gave him, an expansion of consciousness was what the practice of his brujo powers was really all about. It was this expansion of consciousness that enabled him to literally inhabit other forms of life through transformations, and to concentrate and direct his mental energy and send it out in a burst like a lightning bolt. But the ability to use these techniques was not in itself the ultimate objective of the Brujo's Way. And now it occurred to him that a more expansive understanding of the Brujo's Way, like the expansiveness of the owl's vision, might mean that his consciousness would include more, not less, of the experience of the human condition in the world, and that Inéz, because he loved her, and because of her experience of suffering, could be his guide in that.

Don Carlos the owl made good time to El Paso del Norte. Arriving after midnight, he was once again confronted with the no-clothes problem. Fortunately, no one was on guard in the courtyard outside the outpost's barracks, so he dropped down on the steps of the commandant's residence, changed to his naked human form, and entered by a side door that was luckily unlocked.

He knew his way around the house from having twice been a guest of the previous commandant. He tiptoed upstairs to the master bedroom. It was dark inside, but his sorcerer's vision enabled him to see Rafael and Camila in bed, sound asleep. Rafael had left some of his uniform, a shirt and trousers, hanging on the back of a chair. Carlos put them on and leaned over Rafael and whispered softly, "Rafael, it's Alfonso. Meet me in the hall. It's urgent."

Don Carlos backed out the door, followed soon by Rafael, who'd put on a robe and whose exit gait was more a sleepy stumble than a normal walk. Still groggy, he asked, "When did you arrive? What brought you here?"

Don Carlos explained about the children and where they were. "Have you heard of a cave in the Los Organos range about forty miles north of here?" Rafael shook his head. "No matter," Carlos added, "Get some of your men ready to leave at dawn or even earlier, if you feel the moon's light is bright enough for you to follow the Camino Real safely. You'll need to bring three or four extra horses for the children.

"When you reach Estero Largo, the place some people call Las Cruces, you'll see a red-tailed hawk sitting in a large oak tree. Every morning he flies up the ravine to the east to hunt. Follow him. Although the route is unmarked and rough, horses and riders find it passable. At the end of the ravine you'll have to dismount and climb a trail that leads about halfway up the cliff to the cave."

"Where will you be? Why can't you lead the way?"

"I can't, and I don't have time for explanations now. This is an ask-me-no-questions-and-I'll-tell-you-no-lies type of situation. In fact, please forget that you ever saw me; for reasons I can't reveal, my name must not be connected with this rescue. If anyone asks, tell them that an old Indian who wouldn't give you his name came by, said he'd been hunting in the Organos Mountains when he heard the kids calling out, and gave you precise directions for finding the cave."

Rafael responded with alacrity. "We'll leave as soon as I can organize my men," he told Carlos and immediately ducked back into his bedroom to get dressed. Don Carlos took off Rafael's clothes, slipped out of the commandant's residence, and returned to owl form. He lifted off and circled overhead until he saw Rafael with four soldiers and four extra horses leaving the barracks courtyard and turning onto the road. Then he flew north to the rendezvous site, where he landed in the tree at Estero Largo, changed into a red-tailed hawk, slept for a few hours, and waited for Rafael and his men.

It was almost noon when Don Carlos, having slept for a few hours, awoke and saw Rafael and his soldiers barely a hundred yards from his perch. He launched himself into the air and veered off in the direction of Los Organos. An hour and a half later, the soldiers reached the end of the ravine and dismounted to start up the cliff trail to the cave. Don Carlos the hawk caught an updraft and effortlessly rose to the level of the cave, landing on the ledge. Peering into the cave, he saw Inéz in angel form, still giving off a dim glow of heavenly light, sitting up and evidently telling a story. The Trigales children, covered by their large sacks, were snuggled up to her.

Cristofer looked up and shook the angel's arm. "A hawk just landed only ten feet from us."

"That's all right," she told him. "That's Hooter's friend Redsy. He won't hurt us."

Don Carlos immediately took off and flew downward from ledge, disappearing from sight just as the angel and the four children came to the cave's entrance. His maneuver had precisely the effect he'd hoped it would. Inéz stepped to the edge and looked down. Upon seeing Rafael and three of his soldiers starting up the trail—the fourth soldier had stayed with the horses—she turned back to the Trigales children and pulled them into an embrace. Don Carlos, riding another updraft, reached the cave's level in time to see the angel give each of the youngsters a tender kiss. "You're going to be fine," she said. "Some soldiers will arrive at any moment to take you home. I have to leave before they get here because I don't show myself to grownups— only to owls, hawks, and children."

After giving the children a parting hug, she added, "Start down the trail and meet them partway. There's no need for them to climb all the way up here." Anton began to cry and clung to the angel's skirt—quite transparent in the bright sunlight, a design flaw for which Don Carlos was certain he would be reprimanded. The angel detached Anton from her skirt and gave him a gentle shove toward the beginning of the trail. "Shoo," she said. Speaking to Carmela, the Trigales twin who was nearest, Inéz added, "Please take Anton by the hand and guide him down the trail."

With tears in their eyes, Carmela and the other three children did as they'd been told, calling back to the angel, "Thank you for rescuing us."

Turning to Don Carlos, Inéz gave him a sour look and announced, "As for you, Redsy, you're in trouble again. Change me into a hawk so we can start our trip back to the Chavez hacienda."

It turned out that Inéz had lots of complaints about clothes, or the lack of same, though to his surprise she didn't mention the diaphanous nature of her angel's outfit. She unburdened herself of several issues she had with Don Carlos as they flew north. "That angel robe was thoroughly unsatisfactory. It was so thin that I practically froze to death last night. You could at least have left us a blanket or two."

"I didn't think of that and neither did you. I'm not even sure I could make blankets out of rocks and bushes or whatever. And the kids got some protection from those large sacks."

Inéz ignored his point about the sacks. "A fat lot of good it is," she grumbled, "to be traveling with a brujo who can't even provide blankets. And I must say I'm not keen on long-distance flights. Swooping and soaring in a small area can be exhilarating, but this multi-hour cross-country flying is no fun, and I'm tired to the bone from being airborne for most of the past two days, when, that is, we weren't running around as weasels or whatever and battling ogres. Of course," she added hastily, "I'm happy beyond belief that we were able to rescue the children."

He didn't know what to say, so he didn't reply.

After a long silence, Inéz started up again. "Flying into the wind makes it all the harder. Can't you do something about the wind, turn it into a tail wind or something useful?"

"We benefited from a wind blowing south on our trip to the cave," he reminded her. "Now we have to pay the price when we retrace our route."

"Didn't you hear me? I asked you to turn the wind around. What good are your powers of sorcery if you can't provide simple conveniences like a nice tail wind?"

"Although I might be able to do that over a small area, this wind is spread across the whole region. That's more than I can control."

"Haven't you heard," Inéz asked, "that the only way to get out of a hole is to stop digging? You need to apply that rule. You're digging yourself in deeper every time you give me one of your supposedly reasonable answers."

Another long silence, a merciful silence from Don Carlos's point of view, followed. However, Inéz had more to say. "I'm hungry, and no, I don't want to dive down and catch a mouse. I'm miserable and you've done nothing whatsoever to help."

"I'm sorry, Inéz. We could stop and rest for a while if you like, or we can keep going and get back to the inn a little earlier. It's up to you."

"I have to make all the tough decisions?" she grumbled. "Let's keep going. I want to get some dinner; even a snack will do."

The sun was setting when two very tired red-tailed hawks flew into the barn behind the Chavez hacienda. They changed to their human forms, dressed, and walked to the house. Upon inquiring where they might find Raul Trigales, they were sent to the hacienda's patio. Raul was sitting there with José, staring off into space.

Inéz slid onto the bench next to Raul, took his hand, and said, "We have good news! Your children are safe. They're tired and hungry, but they're fine. They're on their way back from El Paso del Norte with soldiers under the command of Captain Rafael Villela."

Raul turned to her, his expression a mixture of disbelief and joy. "It can't be! Is it true?" He began asking questions about where, when, and how had they been found. "Why are they coming all the way from El Paso del Norte?"

When he'd slowed down a bit, Carlos said, "Before we answer some of your questions, we need you to promise us something."

"Anything! Anything, of course."

"Raul, we need you to keep our names out of this story as much as possible. In particular, people would wonder how we managed to get to El Paso del Norte and back in the short time it's taken us. The explanation would reveal information that must remain secret. Please agree to ask us no questions. The less you know the better."

"Of course I'll do as you ask, but what can I tell people?"

"Rafael will say that an old Indian man who wouldn't give his name came to him yesterday and reported that he'd heard some children crying in a cave in Los Organos, less than a day's travel north of El Paso del Norte. With the directions he was given, Rafael and four soldiers went to the cave and found the children. For all I know, they may be on the road north to here right now, though most likely they'll not start back until tomorrow, by which time the children should be well fed and rested."

"I'll head south to meet them as soon as possible. Is there anything else you can tell me?"

"Nothing much. I'm sorry the ransom money couldn't be recovered. The kidnappers got away, and we have no idea where they've gone."

Inéz cleared her throat. "There's the small matter of the angel who rescued the children and spent the night shivering in the cave with them, waiting for the cavalry to come."

"An angel? A real angel?" Raul didn't know quite what to make of this news.

"That's what they'll tell you," Carlos said. "You have to realize that they were cold, hungry, frightened, and underslept. You could consider it a hallucination, a figment of their imaginations, but they definitely saw something."

"Don't you dare dismiss it as a hallucination!" Inéz said heatedly. "Encourage them to believe in angels. Tell them they are special and loved. That's why an angel came to help them."

"I gather you're not going to explain this either," Raul observed.

"There's nothing to explain," Inéz replied. "Listen to what they tell you and don't dispute their perceptions. They are lovely children. If I were ever to have children, an unlikely prospect I assure you, I would feel blessed if I had children like your four, Raul."

Turning to Carlos, she said, "I am bone tired and starved. Alfonso, buy me a huge meal and carry me off to bed."

"I'm at your service," he replied. He asked Raul to excuse him and Inéz and led her toward the dining room.

"Don't get any funny ideas about the being carried to bed part," Inéz told him as they walked away. "We'll keep our clothes on in order to help you maintain some semblance of self-control. You have broken so many of Inéz's rules of order in the past few days that your account with the Treasury of Merit is badly overdrawn. You need to be very, very good to rebuild your balance."

"I promise to be good," he said, and he did try. He bought the starving Inéz a big meal, and after they'd said good night to José and wished Raul well on his journey at dawn to El Paso del Norte, he gathered her in his arms and carried her upstairs, which, to his surprise, she allowed him to do. They took off their boots and crawled into bed, otherwise fully clothed, and she fell asleep five seconds later.

Don Carlos continued to be well-behaved—well, mostly. When his beloved showed signs of being deeply asleep, he carefully put his arm around her waist and snuggled up to her. Four hours later she half woke up, and instead of pushing his arm away, as he feared she might, she put her hand over his, giving him the feeling of being embraced in return. He decided that he must have rebuilt at least a small balance in his account at the Treasury of Merit.

27

Beginnings

*D*on Carlos woke up and sleepily turned over, expecting to find Inéz in bed with him. No Inéz. Surprised, he woke up more fully. Then he noticed that daylight was streaming in the window and realized that it was much later than his usual time for waking up. He swung his feet over the side of the bed, pulled on his boots, and stood up. He went to the door and stepped out into the hallway. He heard voices coming from the dining room, which was just down the hall. As he entered the hacienda's small dining room, he saw Inéz and José seated at a table. The room was otherwise empty. José noticed his arrival and gestured for him to join them. Inéz looked up and flashed a brilliant welcoming smile. Carlos felt better immediately.

He went over to their table, and before he could say anything, Inéz grinned and said, "That's a first."

"What sort of first?" he asked.

"Your sleeping later than me."

He sat down on a bench next to the table and replied, "I guess I was pretty tired. We had a very active day yesterday, but you seem as bright as can be."

"We rescued the children! I'm euphoric! Probably I'll calm down soon and feel absolutely exhausted. I'm surprised that you needed to sleep so late. I thought your brujo powers were inexhaustible" — then, stopping herself, she studied him with concern. "Of course! I'm forgetting that you nearly died a little more than two weeks ago. I can't believe I forgot that, especially since I've done little else the past two weeks other than urge you to take it easy."

"You engaged in some very strenuous activities too," Carlos pointed out. "If you fade out soon, it wouldn't be a surprise. You fought with an ogre and spent a long, cold night comforting the Trigales children, not to speak of flying hundreds of miles and going through what seemed like countless transformations. You've been nothing short of heroic!"

José had been looking uncomfortable, and from what he said next, Carlos gathered that he felt as though he was eavesdropping on a private conversation. Standing up, he said, "I think I should check on the horses and leave the two of you alone to talk."

"You don't have to rush off," Inéz said. "You're the third person in a threesome that pulled off this rescue. We don't have secrets from you."

"Thanks, but I should check the horses to be sure they're ready in case you decide to leave for Santa Fe later today. That's my job. So excuse me, please." And he hurried off before either Inéz or Carlos could try to talk him out of it.

"I know I've been a nuisance," Inéz said, "mother-henning you since your battle with the fire. But I want it clearly understood that I've been amazed by the powers you've demonstrated. We wouldn't have had the slightest chance of saving the children if you weren't an extraordinary brujo."

"Those are generous words, Inéz, but the fact is that a lot of luck was involved. To cite a major example, had I not met Albina last year, and had she not still been living, and what's more, living near the cave where the kids were hidden, we probably wouldn't have found them. The Organos are simply too large an area to search successfully in a short time."

"Somehow I think you would have figured it out."

"We'll never know, and you mustn't exaggerate my brujo powers. I'm very good at some sorcerer's techniques—most obviously, transformations, talking with non-human beings, and releasing blasts of invisible energy. But there are other skills that some sorcerers have that I don't. I've never learned to travel across great distances in a disembodied way. I don't have foreknowledge, and I've encountered certain phenomena in the past two months that forcefully reminded me of other limitations in my powers. Even my brief confrontation with that wolf threw my physical and energy bodies badly out of balance. In his last conversation with Leandro Don Malvolio said that his assistant, Brother Gustavo, was the force behind the wolf's power. Fortunately, he misread me and, seeing me as no threat, he withdrew. But what if he had stayed and had brought the full force of his power to bear?"

"The good news is that you won't have to contend with Don Malvolio again," Inéz observed.

"I'm not so sure," Carlos said musingly. "You heard Malvolio say that he believes I have a power that he needs for himself—some sort of transformative healing power. He will go on looking for the Carlos who has that power."

"So," Inéz said, looking away. "Nothing has really changed."

"What do you mean? Everything has changed."

"Has it?" She turned to him. "Don Malvolio is not after you for revenge, but he's still after you. A considerable part of you is still focused on him. What about what you called the Unknown Way, the union with the Divine that Zoila showed you? What about whatever role I might play in that, if that's not too presumptuous a question?"

"You know I want you to play a role in my life," he said seriously.

"I *don't* know that," she said, equally seriously. "I think I'm a bad match for you."

"On the contrary, dearest Inéz," he replied. "I'm learning what a perfect match you are for me."

"Nonsense!" she said. "I fuss a lot, while you tend to see the bright side of things. I keep failing to follow Elvira's advice to let you be free, which I quite agree you need to be. I resist marriage for a variety of reasons, primarily right now because I need to first find out who I am separate from you. And, perhaps worst of all, I keep wanting you to share your innermost self, while you would prefer not to do that."

He let out a long breath, uncertain how to respond. "To do them justice," he said at last, "each of those sentences would require a long answer. Instead, let me start by saying that you have many, many qualities that I love. You often surprise me, and I enjoy surprises. You make me think about myself in new ways. You're a splendid fencer, the most challenging of any I've met in this life. You're a creative cook and lovely to look at."

"Beauty fades," she shot back. "That's hardly a basis for anything lasting."

He sighed. "Maybe what I need to admit first is that I don't have any experience with a lasting relationship."

"True enough. You've courted many women, enjoyed them for a time, and then moved on."

"That certainly was true in the past," he replied. "But I'm changing. I'm no longer convinced that a brujo should avoid attachments. I believe Don Serafino got that wrong, and you're the one who's helping me see things differently."

"You didn't find it difficult to leave those women. Who's to say you won't leave me too?"

"Inéz, you always tell me not to make promises I can't keep, but I don't intend to leave you. And don't forget that you don't have any experience of a healthy relationship with a man. You might leave me too."

"Perhaps I should," she said softly, her eyes tearing up.

Shocked, he replied, "I hope you're not serious when you suggest that."

"I simply mean that I'm already too dependent on you. How can I get back to the bedrock of my soul, my self before I was fourteen, if so much of what defines me is my need for your companionship and protection?"

"I will do my best, am doing my best," he said, "to honor your need for independence." Inéz started to speak, but he held up his hand to stop her from doing so and continued. "You're emphasizing the difficulties in our relationship, most of which arise from our different personalities and personal histories. A union of opposites is not easy. Indeed, it's certain to have ups and downs, rough spots as well as joyful moments. But I'm more and more convinced that working through the rough spots is well worth the pain because the end result is something deeper, more fulfilling for both parties. And give me credit for being a seeker, for all that I'm less inclined to explore my inner life than you are."

Inéz didn't say anything, looking down at her hands folded on the table in front of her. Carlos was silent too, waiting for her to respond. Finally, she spoke. "What do you want our relationship to be, now and in the foreseeable future?" she asked.

"I want us to be best friends, as I believe we are now, partners in learning how to deepen our relationship. I want you to feel free to challenge me, even as you explore who you are, now that you're not controlled by a man who essentially owned you. And what do you want?"

"I'm not as clear about that as I'd like to be," she admitted. "You're a good man, the best I've ever met, and, as you could tell from my reaction when your life was in danger, I would be terrified to lose you. Yet I'm conflicted, too, because I don't feel I'm a full person and am still learning who this woman Inéz is. Your suggestion of best friends as a label for our relationship is as good as I can do."

José came in the dining room door, stopped, and said, "Excuse me for interrupting. I've checked the horses and they're ready to go whenever you want to leave. Also, the weekly market is opening for business and there are crafts for sale that I'd like to look at. I hope to get jewelry as gifts for my mother and sister, and I could use Inéz's eye to help me make good choices — when you're free to come out, that is. I particularly like some items a Spanish woman named Esperanza Peña has for sale."

Without waiting for an answer, José ducked out the door.

José's mention of Esperanza brought a smile to Carlos's face. "Why the smile?" Inéz asked.

"Did I ever tell you about what happened on my last trip through here — the boy I met who was gambling his saddle and the cardsharp who was all too eager to clean the kid out?"

"No, I don't recall you doing so."

"This Esperanza is the boy's mother. I'd like to go with José to the market and ask her how her son is doing."

Inéz didn't comment, but when he stood up she did so too, indicating that she would accompany them.

They left the hacienda and walked to the nearby market area. José was hurrying ahead. Esperanza was easy for Carlos to spot. José had already reached her side and was looking over the goods she had spread out on a blanket. As he and Inéz approached, Carlos saw Esperanza's daughter, Yolanda, sitting cross-legged a few feet behind her mother and holding her child in her lap, no longer a baby.

Esperanza looked up and her face broke into a welcoming smile. "Señor Cabeza de Vaca! How happy I am to see you again."

"I'm glad to see you too," he replied. "Let me introduce my friend, Señora Inéz de Recalde. I believe you're already dealing with our friend José, who has asked for Inéz's help in choosing gifts for his mother and sister."

For a moment Carlos was worried that Esperanza might ask whether Inéz was the woman for whom he'd been shopping for a gift the last time he'd passed through. That might have been awkward, since on the previous occasion he'd been looking for something for Camila, to whom he'd proposed, and had decided that a gift for Inéz might be open to misinterpretation. But before Esperanza had time to ask any questions, José drew Inéz closer to the jewelry display, picked up two items, and said, "I very much like this necklace for my mother and this bracelet for Ana."

Inéz examined the two items closely. "Both are beautiful, but José, you should not reveal your interest too early. That will make it difficult to get the best price. Perhaps we should shop around before buying these."

Esperanza intervened immediately. "You needn't worry about the price, Señora. Don Alfonso did me and my family a very great favor when he was last here. You can be certain of receiving a friendship price."

"And how is Jorge?" Carlos asked, referring to Esperanza's son.

"So far he is totally reformed and hasn't gambled at all since you warned him against his habit so forcefully. Once or twice he's been tempted to gamble, but he carries that cardsharp's marked card in his pocket and, just as you advised him, he takes it out to remind him not to start down that path again."

Turning to Esperanza's daughter, Carlos inquired, "How is your son, Yolanda? He seems to have grown a lot since I last saw him."

"He's very healthy," she replied, smiling broadly and revealing a perfect set of white teeth. She was an unusually attractive young woman, Carlos noted.

"The boy's father is a no-good," Esperanza put in acidly. "He never married her and never supported her and the baby."

Yolanda looked down, embarrassed. "Yes, he has abandoned us," she said, "but I am getting better at weaving and will soon be able to support myself."

"Yolanda made this fine wool blanket and that saddle blanket," Esperanza announced with obvious pride.

"The saddle blanket has an interesting geometric design. It's very handsome," Inéz said. "Would you consider selling it to me as a gift for our friend José?"

"Of course."

"José," Inéz said, "why don't you go over and pick up the blanket to see if it suits you?"

Carlos wasn't sure why Inéz was directing the conversation away from what he saw as their main purpose, helping José select gifts for his mother and sister. But, as often seemed the case, she had noticed something that he might otherwise have missed. When José went over and examined the saddle blanket, he found himself standing near Yolanda and her baby, and Carlos observed that he looked at both, but particularly at Yolanda, with more than idle interest.

Soon Inéz took charge and began bargaining with Esperanza about prices for the saddle blanket, necklace, and bracelet. José, meanwhile, had struck up a conversation with Yolanda, and she rewarded something he said with a melodious laugh. Carlos remained a spectator only. Eventually, he heard Inéz say to Esperanza, "Those are very low prices. Are you sure we aren't impoverishing you, taking advantage of your good will to pay you less than the cost of the materials?"

"As you suggest," Esperanza replied, "I am giving you a favorable price, but I would be much poorer if Don Alfonso had not succeeded in convincing my son to refrain from gambling, and, in any case, as you surely realize, the prices craftspeople usually ask for items are well above the cost for materials, so we are not taking a loss on any of the three pieces."

"I'm glad to hear that," Inéz said, and soon the sales were completed.

Very tentatively, Carlos proposed something that he'd had in mind ever since he had heard that the market was open, and he had spotted an item of jewelry that fit his plan perfectly. He leaned over and whispered in Inéz's ear, "Would you let me buy you a gift? I would like you to have a friendship ring to wear on your right hand." Worried that she might reject the idea out of hand, he hastened to add, "It wouldn't obligate you to anything more than what we've already agreed to do, which is to explore the meaning of our friendship."

To his surprise, Inéz, after only a moment's hesitation, with a solemn look, agreed. "All right," she said.

Carlos turned to Esperanza, pointed to a ring near the back of the blanket, and said, "I would like to buy that ring for my friend Inéz. What is its price?"

"First we need to be certain it fits," Esperanza replied. She picked the ring up and handed it to Inéz, who tried it on and found that it was a perfect fit. Esperanza turned to Carlos and said, "For a man you are unusually observant about the size of your friend's hand."

"Thank you, Esperanza, but you haven't named a price."

"The ring is a gift to the two of you from me."

"I can't let you do that," he protested.

"Yes, you can," she insisted, and that seemed to close the matter. Warm farewells were exchanged all around, and Carlos, Inéz, and José walked back toward the hacienda.

Carlos was beginning to worry about the time. "If we don't start back immediately," he pointed out, "we're not going to get very far today."

"I want to get back to Santa Fe no later than tomorrow," Inéz announced. "I've been away from my job much too long, weeks, in fact, counting the time I spent nursing a brujo back to health."

"We can't cover that much ground in less than two days," Carlos told her. "Besides, I'm sure your job is safe. You've earned the eternal gratitude of everyone in the Trigales-Beltrán family."

"That's not the point," Inéz replied, her jaw firmly set. "I want to get back to Santa Fe right away, the sooner the better."

"I have a suggestion," José said. "Why don't you change yourselves into hawks and fly to the Olmedo ranch near Albuquerque, where Señor Trigales left several horses? You can reclaim them and ride on to Santa Fe, and you might even get there as early as sundown tonight, or noon tomorrow at the latest. I'll follow along with Eagle and Alegría at a normal pace."

This was an excellent idea, Carlos thought, though not without some problems. What explanation could they give the Olmedos when they showed up without horses? How would they transport their clothing during the flight? And wouldn't it look strange for José to take nearly two days longer than Carlos and Inéz to get home to Santa Fe?

As it turned out these problems were easily resolved. Carlos knew he could use his brujo powers to handle the issue of their clothing, and José asserted that he simply would refuse to explain his tardy return. José also came up with an ingenious solution for what to tell the Olmedos. "Tell them," he suggested, "that on your return trip you stopped and dismounted at the site where the servants had been killed because you wanted to pile stones over their remains. Something spooked your horses and they ran off and you had to walk the rest of the way to the Olmedo ranch. It's only six miles. You can also tell the Olmedos that not long after you reached the Socorro area you heard that the children had been found, so you turned around and came back. Then the next day I'll show up with Eagle and Alegría, the two supposed runaways, and say that I found them grazing by the road, still under saddle. That ought to tie up all the loose ends."

Carlos, Inéz, and José gathered up the few belongings they had at the hacienda and went to its stable for their horses. They mounted them and rode northward on the Camino Real to the boulder field where they had practiced casting bolts of invisible energy. Carlos and Inéz crouched down behind two particularly large boulders and undressed. Don Carlos applied his skill at transformations to change their clothing into two leather thongs and himself and Inéz into red-tailed hawks. José came over and tied the thongs around Don Carlos's legs, and the two hawks launched into flight.

Don Carlos steered them on a course above the river. He took special delight in the varied landscape of that route — mountains to the west, the river below, and a mix of trees, fields, and low hills along the river's eastern banks. After an hour's flight, he turned to Inéz and said, "I am so happy. I hope you are, too."

"Yes," she replied, "and we're making good time. A tailwind helps a lot," she added.

Don Carlos felt that she smiled as she mentioned the tailwind, even though her hawk's face was not designed for smiling.

"Is it too much to hope," he asked, "that we'll remain best friends and that our love will grow deeper?"

"Mmmm," she replied noncommittally. "What will be, will be. Don't assume too much because I accepted that ring from you. I liked it and had been considering buying it for myself. But it's much better to receive the ring as a gift from you than to buy it myself."

Inéz saying that it was much better to acquire the ring as a gift from him made Carlos glow inwardly; it struck him as a positive commitment to their friendship. There was probably something, he thought, that he should have said in response. But he couldn't come up with anything quite right and observed, not for the first time, that his brujo powers seldom revealed what he should do in relation to the mystery that Inéz still was to him. He was, however, certain about one thing. There was even more joy in flying around in hawk form with his beloved friend than there was in flying around alone. And it was also nice to have a tailwind.

Glossary of Names

Alaniz, Emiliano: Don Carlos's brother-in-law
Alaniz, Fortunata: Don Carlos's sister, Emiliano's wife
Alvaros, Hernán: owns ranch near Socorro
Alvarez, Joaquin: Don Carlos's stepbrother
Alvarez, Francesca: "Francie," Joaquin's wife
Alvarez, Rodrigo: Don Carlos's stepfather
Archuleta, Nicholas: New Mexico's attorney general
Archuleta, Lucila: Nicholas's wife
Archuleta, Gerardo: their son

Barbon, Arturo: Santa Fe stable owner
Barbon, Roberto: Arturo's brother, owns inn
Barrera, Gilberto: Don Carlos's next-door neighbor
Beltrán, Javier: Santa Fe merchant
Beltrán, Cristina: Javier's wife
Beltrán, Elena: their daughter

Cabeza de Vaca, Alfonso: Don Carlos's public name
Cabrera, Salvador: New Mexico's vice governor
Cabrera, Regina: Salvador's wife
Cabrera, Marco: governor's secretary
Campos, Diego: Don Carlos's Indian servant
Castro, Teodora: Indian bride
Ceballos, Emilia: Bernalillo ranch owner
Chavez, Renaldo: owns inn near Socorro

Damián: Leandro's bestial self
de Illueca: *See* Illueca, Gustavo de
de Luna: *See* Luna, Leandro de
de Recalde: *See* Recalde, Hernando de
de Recalde: *See* Recalde, Inéz de
de Sena: *See* Sena, Bernadino de
de Silva: *See* Silva, Ricardo de
de Tortuga: *See* Tortuga, Ignacio de
de Vargas: *See* Vargas, Diego de
Díaz, Atilio and Caterina: Don Carlos's tenants

Gallegos, Pedro: Don Carlos's manservant
Gallegos, María: Pedro's wife
Gómez, Felipe: Indian stable hand

Herrera, Zoila: Don Carlos's meditation teacher

Illueca, Gustavo de: Malvolio's apprentice

Jiranza, Orfeo: Don Carlos's carpenter

Lobo, Camila: *See* Villela, Camila
Lugo, Ana: José Lugo's sister
Lugo, José: Don Carlos's Pueblo Indian servant
Lugo, Lázaro: Ana and José's cousin
Lugo, Rubén: Ana and José's cousin
Luna, Leandro de: magician

Malvolio: sorcerer
Mata, Mara: dancer
Murillo, Amado: government courier

Olmedo, Mauricio: rancher and inn owner
Ortega, Elias and Ernesto: Don Carlos's tenants
Ortiz, Juan: Chapel of San Miguel's sexton
Ortiz, Ramona: Juan Ortiz's wife

Peña, Esperanza: street merchant
Peña, Jorge: Esperanza's son
Peña, Yolanda: Esperanza's daughter
Peralta, Ignacio: governor of New Mexico
Peralta, Pilar: Ignacio's wife
Peralta, Juliana: Ignacio and Pilar's daughter
Peralta, Victoria: Ignacio and Pilar's daughter
Pizarro, Mateo: Malvolio's apprentice
Posada, Tito: Presidio commandant
Posada, Margarita: Tito's wife
Recalde, Hernando de: Inéz's husband
Recalde, Inéz de: Don Carlos's love interest
Romero, Serafino: Don Carlos's master brujo

Sánchez: Serafino's assistant
Sena, Bernadino de: Santa Fe blacksmith
Serafino: *See* Romero, Serafino

Readers Guide

1. In *What the Owl Saw*, Don Carlos Buenaventura, a brujo with great powers, is a man in his sixth life who remembers many details of his previous lives. If it were possible for you to do so, would you want to live multiple lives that you remembered?

2. The novel begins on the last day of December 1705. The recent past, particularly the Pueblo Revolt of 1680 and the Spanish *Reconquista* of New Mexico in the 1690s, provide an important, though unstressed, backdrop to the story. If that backdrop were absent, what difference would it make in the story?

3. Inéz asks Carlos, "Why do you attend Mass, really?" What does his answer—actually, his answers—reveal about his religious convictions? Do you find them surprisingly Christian, given that he is a brujo and, as such, a pagan?

4. Don Carlos uses the word sorcery to define his practice of the Brujo's Way. Inéz observes, and he agrees, that much of what he calls sorcery involves a highly refined form of close attention or focused concentration. Is that aspect of his powers in some sense natural, simply the product of special training? Which of his powers are better described as paranormal?

5. Inéz also has ties with non-Christian religion, including the folk religion of her Basque ancestors. Assume for a moment that Don Carlos is right that she is or was a bruja, vague though her bruja abilities remain compared with his. What personal power, womanly or bruja in its source, does she display?

6. Don Carlos has a very negative view of his old enemy, Don Malvolio. Early in the book about all he can say is that Malvolio is evil through and through. But Inéz suggests, "Surely, there's more to it." As more is learned about him later, does he become a more complex character? How so, or not so?

7. The arrival of the Trio—Leandro the Magician and two dancers, Mara and Selena—first introduces the term *duende*. What best defines *duende*? Is it a dark state, as the most important modern description of it argues? (See Federico García Lorca's "In Search of Duende," edited by Christopher Mauer, 1998.) Or, as Don Carlos would like to believe, is it something more benign? But doesn't the dark mystery of *duende* have great attraction for him?

8. In Don Carlos's time the study of occult phenomena—magic, alchemy, astrology—was believed to be a way of knowing the world and gaining power over it in much the same way that, in our times, science is believed to be a way of knowing and gaining power over the world. Many modern readers see the practice of magic and alchemy as simply the product of fantastic beliefs and superstitions. Is it possible for you to imagine yourself in a world where occult phenomena were taken for granted as real?

9. Pueblo Indians lived in close contact with New Mexicans of Spanish descent, which made Santa Fe a bilingual, multicultural society. Is there any evidence in the novel of strains or conflicts between Native peoples and the Spanish colonizers?

10. Pedro de Urdemalas (see chapter 7) is a popular figure in Hispanic folklore, the subject of hundreds of stories from the 1600s onward. Note that although the victims of Pedro's ingenious scams are mostly upper-class people, he is no Robin Hood, stealing from the rich to give to the poor. How can such a self-centered scoundrel enjoy such popularity? Are there comparable figures in recent books, movies, and television dramas? For a more elaborate version of Carlos's story, see "Pedro de Urdemalas" in Genevieve Barlow and William N. Stivers, eds., *Stories from Spain* (2nd ed., NY: McGraw Hill, 2010).

11. In several chapters, four-line poems/songs known as *versos* or *coplas* appear. These are part of a New Mexican folklore tradition with deep roots in Spain. Based on the examples quoted in the novel, how would you describe the prevailing spirit of these verses? Readers wishing to read more such verses should consult the writings of Aurelio M. Espinosa, a leading folklorist who collected hundreds of such items, including the

specific *versos* quoted in the novel, which are from an article by Espinosa published in the April 1926 issue of the *New Mexico Historical Review*.

12. Don Carlos asserts that self-doubt is the mental state most destructive of individual happiness. True?

13. Don Carlos is ready to do battle with evil — and is convinced that his brujo powers will enable him to overcome an evil adversary — but he doesn't seem to experience the horror of evil the way Inéz does on seeing the mutilated bodies of the Trigales's servants. Is Don Carlos, in a way, immune to suffering? Is Inéz too sensitive to it?

14. By the end of the novel, has Don Carlos made any progress in his pursuit of the Unknown Way? Is it a mystical path of transcendent bliss achieved through intensive meditation, or is it a way of learning to live in the world?

15. Does Carlos and Inéz's relationship change in the course of the book? How so, or not so?

www.ingramcontent.com/pod-product-compliance
Lightning Source LLC
Chambersburg PA
CBHW020426030726
47495CB00006B/1680